T0304829

Kay Brellend is the bestselling author of *The Campbell Road* series, *The Bittersweet Legacy* trilogy, and *The Workhouse to War* trilogy. Kay never imagined she would become a writer, certainly not a writer of novels inspired by her own family. *'Writing has been an absorbing journey for me. I have learned much about my ancestors and their toughness and resilience and I feel pride in my roots in the worst street in north London.'*

Please visit her website http://www.kaybrellend.com for news, upcoming titles and more.

By Kay Brellend

Women's War series

A Daughter's Heartbreak
East End Orphan

The Bittersweet Legacy series

A Sister's Bond
A Lonely Heart
The Way Home

The Workhouse to War series

A Workhouse Christmas
Stray Angel
The Workhouse Sisters

EAST END ORPHAN

Kay Brellend

PIATKUS

PIATKUS

First published in Great Britain in 2024 by Piatkus

1 3 5 7 9 10 8 6 4 2

A CIP catalogue record for this book
is available from the British Library.

ISBN 978-0-349-43554-1

Typeset in Palatino by M Rules

Printed and bound in Great Britain by
Clays Ltd, Elcograf S.p.A.

Papers used by Piatkus are from well-managed forests
and other responsible sources.

Piatkus
An imprint of
Little, Brown Book Group
Carmelite House
50 Victoria Embankment
London EC4Y 0DZ

An Hachette UK Company
www.hachette.co.uk

www.littlebrown.co.uk

For Mum and Dad, with much love.

Prologue

1923, Mayfair, London

She'd never loved him as her husband had. In her opinion the boy was rather too clever for a seven-year-old orphan gifted advantages in life. By birth he would have had nothing but his angelic looks to recommend him. As a baby he had charmed her with his pale hair and brown eyes that had shaded into green. His colouring mirrored hers ... a good omen, she'd thought, when bringing him home. But from his developing character she knew they would never have anything else in common. Praise from kith and kin for her handsome son were scant compensation for the challenge he'd present as he grew. She was unwilling to rear the mischievous brat. Others would judge her though so she kept this to herself. Everybody understood a mother on her own faced problems. Educating one child was costly; two were beyond her means if she were to keep this house. She'd made her choices and one of the adopted East End waifs had to go. She knew which one.

'Is it wise to tell the boy the truth, Mrs Harding?'

'Wiser than it is to lie to him I think, Sergeant Drover,'

she responded tartly. Having poured the tea, she handed a cup to the policeman. 'Jake is sharp and has been taught to be honest. I would be a hypocrite if I didn't practise what I preach.' She glanced dispassionately at the child standing silently by the door. 'I hope his new guardians will continue to discipline him so our efforts with him are not wasted.'

The sergeant turned ruddy at the put down. His top lip took on a faint curl. Madam High and Mighty pointed out the boy's talents but didn't want him. Such was the way of people determined to be posh. They believed themselves superior but could be incapable of showing kindness. Not that Sergeant Drover didn't pity her for being widowed in such a wicked way.

'Has there been any progress on finding the villain who robbed and murdered my husband?' She had read the turn of his thoughts.

The sergeant took a gulp of his tea then put down his cup and saucer. He swivelled his eyes to the child. He hadn't reacted but still Drover didn't think it was right to talk about this in front of him. He appeared a stoic little chap – no wobbly lips in evidence – even so it seemed unfeeling to imagine he wasn't moved by recent events. He'd lost his father and soon would lose his mother due to her cruelty rather than crime. 'I'm afraid our enquiries haven't turned up any new leads, Mrs Harding. But of course we haven't concluded our investigations.'

'Oh, investigations!' She gestured dismissively. 'Admit it; there's little prospect of recovering what was stolen.' The loss of ten pounds and a gold timepiece wasn't the crux of Violet Harding's problems, though she could do with the cash and with pawning the watch to raise funds. Without her husband's regular salary from his position in Whitehall,

2

she found herself reduced to living on his pension. At the reading of Rupert's will she'd discovered that was not the crux of it either.

The ignominy of being told by a stranger that her husband's mistress had given him a child of his own had topped everything; unbelievably, worse was in store. Rupert had left instructions that his assets must be divided. The only respect he'd shown his legal wife was allowing her the marital home and banning his paramour from the will reading. Weeks on, Violet's guts continued to squirm at the idea that she might have found herself sitting a yard away from Molly Deane while the smirking solicitor acted as their referee.

On the cab ride home from the galling episode, Violet had understood something else, equally hurtful: she was barren. She'd believed her husband to be at fault when she'd not conceived in eighteen years of marriage. Both her sisters had children but no, he had had a natural daughter, named Rebecca. By her calculations the child had already been born when they adopted their babies from the orphanage.

Had Rupert not been set upon when leaving his club on a stormy evening a month ago she'd still be ignorant of any of this. In a way, she was glad about that. She might have stabbed him herself, had she known.

Violet had little recourse to revenge now he'd gone, though she dearly wanted to hurt him back. But Rupert had had a favourite son even if the boy wasn't his flesh and blood. Cutting ties with Jake would be little hardship for her but her dead husband would be grinding his teeth to dust in his grave. The child she had come to adore would miss his brother, but Toby would be occupied with a good education and forget Jake in time.

'You should go to Lambeth and ask the lady who lives there about my father. She might know what happened to him.'

Violet swung around to stare at Jake, who'd unexpectedly reminded her of his presence with his shocking outburst. 'Be quiet and speak when you're spoken to,' she hissed. After the sergeant had gone she'd interrogate him about how he knew where Molly Deane lived. She felt enraged that Rupert might have taken Jake with him when visiting his paramour.

'What lady might that be Master Jake?' Basil Drover bent his knees, lowering himself to gaze into a small face that was earnest and undeniably handsome.

'I saw them walking together in Andover Street,' explained Jake. 'There was a girl with them as well . . . smaller than I. She had brown hair like the lady.' He was sure he was being helpful but though the policeman seemed interested, his mother was angry.

'Stop that nonsense,' she snapped. 'Go to your room, Jake.'

'Let the lad have his say.' The sergeant sounded blithe but there was a curious gleam in his eyes.

'I told you he is a clever boy,' said Violet. 'It doesn't do to encourage him, Sergeant. He likes being the centre of attention.'

'I'll hear him out. He might have a point . . . about the lady . . .'

'I doubt he saw anything. He has a vivid imagination,' Violet fumed. 'He entertains his brother with his made-up tales. Don't you?'

Jake nodded.

'A Charles Dickens reader, eh?' chortled Drover.

'Certainly not,' she snorted. 'The boys are instructed in the classics.'

She jabbed her head and Jake obediently left the room, although he knew the policeman wanted him to stay. Outside, he hesitated to listen to what happened next but he saw Dora Knox hovering some yards away. Being the clever child he was, Jake realised the maid had brought in the tea tray then loitered to find out what the policeman wanted. His mother had sent her outside saying she'd pour herself.

They stared at one another and the girl gave him a sympathetic smile before disappearing downstairs to the servants' quarters. She was the only one left now. The proper cook had left soon after the day of the funeral. Now Dora did everything and the meals were horrible because she was only sixteen and untrained. Jake could hear a muffled conversation through the door panels but gave up trying to make out what was being said. He guessed it was about him misbehaving. He heard a scuffling noise and saw his younger brother peeping from between the banisters. Jake bounded up the treads to sit beside him.

'You're not really going away are you?' asked a mournful Toby.

'I am, but you won't have to go,' Jake said and put a reassuring arm about his shoulders.

'Don't want to be here on my own without you.'

'You'll be all right; Mother likes you.'

'You'll come back though, won't you when you've learned to be good?'

Jake nodded, although he knew he wouldn't. His mother didn't want him any more. He felt upset but also invigorated at the idea of a new beginning and another place to explore. He'd liked his father but he was gone, and now it was his turn to be released from a home he'd never fitted into. Jake wondered if his late father had felt uncomfortable too and that's why he'd stayed out a lot and become friends with another lady. He'd miss his brother, although he truly believed Toby would be all right without him. Their mother was different with Toby. She called him her poppet, whereas he himself was referred to as 'the boy', or 'the orphan'.

The brothers understood they were adopted children: when of an age to comprehend their beginnings, their father had sat them down and explained that the Great War had made it impossible for their real mothers to keep them. He'd said that even though they looked alike, they weren't blood brothers but a different sort of brothers. From the moment they'd been chosen by him and his wife, they'd no longer been orphans, he'd said, but their sons and they would always be loved and cared for in a nice home. Their father had lived up to his promise but their mother had stopped halfway.

'Come on, let's go and play in the bedroom with the train set.' Jake grabbed his brother's elbow and urged him to run up the stairs.

'Where is the school you're going to?' Toby looked up from removing items from the Hornby box.

Jake shrugged and leaned forward on his knees to put a locomotive down on a length of track. 'Somewhere in London, I think. Sergeant Drover's coming back later in the week to take me there. Mother doesn't want to go with me.'

'London ... so it's not far then.' Toby sounded relieved. 'You'll come back at the weekends I expect.'

'Perhaps ...' Jake doubted he'd be allowed back and knew he'd miss Toby. 'I heard them say it's Dr Barnardo's home so I suppose he's the headmaster.'

'Doctors are nice,' said Toby, remembering when he'd had chicken pox and a kindly old gentleman had given him medicine to soothe his skin. 'I bet you'll have lots of friends,' he said wistfully. 'You won't forget me, will you?'

'Never ...' Jake solemnly promised and sat back on his heels to gaze at his younger brother.

In the parlour, Sergeant Drover sucked his teeth in sympathy while being regaled with the shocking costs of funerals these days and school fees shooting ever upwards. Inwardly, he was wondering why Mrs Harding didn't move to a less fashionable address to keep the family together. She couldn't really prefer her big house to her little son, could she? He allowed her the benefit of the doubt; the woman would still be in shock over her husband's murder and in a panic over the prospect of coping without him. She might right the wrong she'd done young Master Jake by fetching him home in the New Year when she was more herself. Whatever excuses he found for her it seemed a mean thing to do to any child just a month before Christmas. He was a bright kid, no doubt about it. Thanks to him there was another lead to follow in this murder case.

The upstanding husband had been walking with a dark-haired woman in Lambeth's Andover Street. No prizes for guessing the nature of that relationship. Parts of Lambeth were renowned as popular with rich gentlemen who wanted to house a mistress. Not flash enough to draw attention, but not too shabby either. An ambitious young woman, living on her looks, would find the area most acceptable.

'Does your late husband have kith or kin Lambeth way?'

'I told you the boy was fantasising, Sergeant Drover.'

'So ... nobody for Mr Harding to have visited over there that you are aware of? Female cousins or nieces of any sort?'

Violet resisted calling him insolent. Later in the week he was to do her a great favour; she wouldn't antagonise him. 'I know my husband's family, Sergeant. We were betrothed for two years and married for eighteen more.'

'Yes ... of course.' He put away his notebook and pencil. 'Well, I'll be off for now then.'

'You won't forget to come back, will you?' She picked up a letter from the Barnardo's home in Stepney. 'They have confirmed arrangements and expect Jake at ten o'clock on Friday.' She should thank him for having offered earlier to escort the boy for her when she said she was loath to ask the solicitor to do it for an exorbitant fee.

'I will, unless you change your mind and wish to accompany him yourself.' He hesitated in taking the letter.

'It would be too upsetting for me to go there.' And indeed it would be, she thought. Offloading a child at an orphanage was what the lower orders did. 'Thank you for assisting in this, Sergeant.' Drover was treated to the first smile of his visit. 'I appreciate your help. I won't change my mind, you see.'

After he'd gone, she went upstairs and called Jake from the bedroom where he and Toby were mimicking the sounds of steam trains. He closed the door obediently behind him and she gave him a stern look. He held her gaze steadily without flinching. She found him far too sure of himself and those green eyes of his were quite unsettling at times. 'This woman you spoke of,' she said. 'When did you see her with your father, Jake?'

'Last Christmas. Carol singers were in the street—'

'Last Christmas?' she interrupted, in surprise. She had

imagined it had been a recent sighting, not almost a year ago. 'Were you with your father?'

'No ... with Mr Nash. He was taking me to a Christmas concert in Lambeth. Toby didn't come. He was in bed with a cold.'

So not only did Jake know about this woman and Rupert; the boys' tutor did as well. Nash would be dispensed with soon in any case. Arranging a boarding school for Toby was next on her list of things to do. She'd miss his company, but if he were to fly high, a good education was essential.

'I think you are mistaken; it was a long time ago and you might have forgotten exactly what you saw. No more of it, to me or to Sergeant Drover. Do you understand?'

He nodded solemnly. As his mother turned away he said, 'I remember it, though. I don't forget anything.'

Well, the deceased Lothario had a wide-ranging taste in women, thought Basil Drover as he entered the house in Andover Street and followed Mrs Deane along the hallway. Harding's widow was a slender blonde, in her late thirties; his mistress had a buxom figure and dark hair and was easily fifteen years younger.

Once in the back parlour he glanced around but there was no sign of the child Master Jake had spoken about. He knew there was one; when making enquiries in the street to discover at which house he might find a dark-haired woman with a young daughter, the neighbour had confirmed with a sniff that he was looking for Mrs Deane who lived at number two.

'So what can I do for you, Sergeant?' asked Molly Deane with admirable insouciance considering her fists were clenched behind her back. She feared she knew what he wanted, and after a night of carousing had left her with a thumping head, she could do without this trouble.

'Well, as I said, madam, I'm investigating a crime and I believe you might have known the unfortunate victim.'

'A crime?'

'A murder.'

'Oh, Mr Harding, you mean.' She'd been mistaken in what had brought him here and had allowed a note of relief to creep into her voice. Rupert Harding's comings and goings had been regular and over time neighbours had cottoned on to their relationship. An account of his murder and his photograph had been in the newspaper as he was a bigwig in the City. She imagined somebody had ratted on her and brought the coppers sniffing around.

'Did you think I'd another crime in mind?' Drover's ears had pricked up at the inflexion in her tone.

'No . . . although I have to say the area is going downhill. Three times this week I've been tormented by little blighters playing knock down ginger. If it happens again, I'll summon you myself.'

'I see . . . well, as to Mr Harding, you did know him then. Might I ask the nature of your relationship?'

'You might, though I imagine you are able to guess at it. We are both adults, Sergeant Drover, so no need for either of us to act coy.' She gave him a cheeky smile. He wasn't bad looking and probably only a few years older than she was. Having the name of the local rozzer in her little black book could be a smart move.

His sardonic smile let her know he'd regretfully decline. 'You have a daughter I believe, Mrs Deane. Is she Harding's child?'

'Who told yer that?' Molly barked, forgetting to act refined.

'I can't disclose my sources. Is she his offspring?' Drover sensed he'd touched a nerve.

'Yes,' she said and turned away. 'Out of respect for all concerned I'd like that to remain between us.'

Basil nodded his agreement although it seemed bit late to consider the feelings of the betrayed wife. He began to sympathise with Violet Harding and to understand why she was a sourpuss. Maybe she'd known about her husband's mistress and had been protecting her pride by keeping schtum about her rival.

'Where is your daughter?

'Staying with a friend. Now if that is all ... '

'Had you seen Mr Harding on the night he was murdered?'

'I was expecting him to call but he didn't turn up. I assumed he'd gone straight home. He did that sometimes if he came out of his club the worse for wear.'

Drover knew from the coroner's report that the deceased had been intoxicated on the night in question. 'Will you be leaving here now your circumstances have changed?'

'What concern is that of yours?' she asked spikily.

'I might need to speak to you again and wouldn't want to find you gone.'

'I'll be here; Mr Harding wasn't my only gentleman friend. I don't think I need to say more than that. Now, if you'll excuse me ... '

He allowed her to lead him back along the hall and once outside set off into the early dusk of the November afternoon. He put away his notebook and buttoned the pocket flap over it. There was no point in stirring up a hornets' nest because the dead man couldn't keep his trousers buttoned. Sergeant Drover decided to close his line of enquiry with Mrs Deane. Pursuing it unnecessarily would only unearth sordid details to upset the victim's family and spoil the children's memory of their father when they were older.

From behind a screen of curtain Molly Deane watched his back until he was out of sight around the corner. Before she dropped the net into place, she spotted someone along the street, emerging from the shadows.

George Payne had been the love of Molly's life for years and she believed she held the same place in his affections despite his roving eye. He was holding a young girl by the hand and hurrying her in the direction of the house. When she stumbled, he picked her up and carried her.

'What was that all about?' George Payne had burst out with a question before the door was shut. He put the girl down and the bag containing the bottles of brandy and port was carried into the kitchen and dumped on the table.

'Nothing I can't deal with,' Molly retorted. 'What did the doctor say about Rebecca?' She bent to soothe the six-year-old, who'd trudged up to her mother and started to grizzle.

'Tonsillitis he reckons.' A medicine bottle appeared from a pocket. 'He said to dose her with this twice a day.'

Molly kissed Rebecca's pale cheek. 'Let's get you into bed then I'll bring you up some warm milk.'

The little girl nodded her dark head.

George followed mother and daughter up the stairs. 'I've got a delivery turning up later; I don't need coppers sniffing around. I recognised him and he would've known me if he'd caught a look at me. Drover's his name and he's a bloodhound from the other side of the water. Must be my lucky day: clocking him first and getting under cover.'

Molly soon had her daughter tucked up in bed in her nightclothes. Then she turned to answer George. 'It was Sergeant Drover. He's investigating Rupert's murder. I suppose I should've guessed I'd get a visit about that.' Molly sat down on the edge of the bed and smoothed the child's hair until she put her thumb in her mouth and started to doze.

The couple tiptoed outside the room and shut the door then Molly lit two cigarettes and handed one to him. 'No need to fret, Georgie.' She patted his cheek. 'Your pals can come with the stuff this evening. Now I think about it, I reckon his wife's got a bee in her bonnet after the will reading. The cow sent Drover here.' She smirked. 'Can't blame her, I suppose. The copper's not a fool though; he knows she's a jealous woman with her claws out. Drover won't be back.' She blew smoke from the corner of her mouth. 'So, it's business as usual.'

Chapter One

The Christmas shoppers were out in force which was the way he liked it. A crowd of people was useful to somebody who never knew when he might need to hide.

At just sixteen years old, Jake Harding had already attained the build of an average grown man. His precocious maturity meant he could browse merchandise without appearing out of place. In other ways his looks were a drawback. His artfully tilted Homburg didn't adequately disguise his pale blond hair or the memorable colour of his eyes. At this time of the year, staff were extra vigilant and he could already sense the weight of a suspicious stare. He was an old hand at it now, but never blasé. He paid the sales assistant for the gentleman's vanity case he'd been examining, earning himself an apologetic smile. A scent of leather wafted from his fingers; a redolence of childhood and his father's brush and comb set encased in calfskin. He'd not thought about any of his family for a while and wanted to bury the memory. He couldn't afford sentimentality distracting him into having to pay for goods. The woman took

15

his cash to ring into the till and while she was occupied with her business, he did his.

With his wrapped purchase in one hand, the other remained in his pocket while he wove through the throng. He cursed beneath his breath at his accomplice's ill-timed grab on brushing past. Jake resisted turning around to see if the clumsy idiot had dropped the five leather wallets on the floor. He changed direction and headed towards the haberdashery department. He'd seen something in there that would make Old Peg's eyes light up. She'd asked him to look out for things that would make good Christmas presents. Pretty stuff was what everybody was after right now, she'd said. He could do without pretty; he wanted practical from Santa. A nice cash bonus to boost his savings. Old Peg wasn't known for her generosity though, at any time of year.

A loud woman was helpfully commandeering the assistant's attention while other customers tutted and grew impatient to be served. Jake turned over boxed handkerchiefs with one hand while the other helped silk scarves to slither off the display at his elbow and into his pocket. Only a necessary few remained to cover the depleted stand so he stepped away and adjusted his hat: a signal that he was heading for the exit to find pastures new. He didn't rush; store walkers were on the lookout for thieves making a dash for it, but he wasn't dawdling either while heading off through the gentlemen's hosiery department.

He almost crashed into a pillar as he spotted people up ahead he had amazingly appeared to have conjured up. Or perhaps it wasn't them; he hadn't seen them in close to a decade ... he could be mistaken.

His heart was thudding in a mixture of thrill and trepidation that outdid anything experienced on a shoplifting expedition. The risk of loitering with the stolen scarves on him was momentarily forgotten. He changed direction to circle the square counter set in the centre of the aisle. Two assistants were serving, one each end. Jake stationed himself on the opposite side to the youth and the woman, keeping his face lowered. He glanced up from beneath the brim of his hat and a twinge of dormant emotion stirred in his chest. His mother barely got a look in; he couldn't stop staring at his brother, and did so a second too long. A pair of quizzical eyes on him startled Jake awake. He melted away into the crowd and a woman behind soon filled his space, shaking the socks she wanted to buy to gain the assistant's attention.

He might be adept at making himself invisible but Jake couldn't blot his family from his mind. His mother was as slim and elegant as he remembered but appeared older now her hair was speckled with grey. His younger brother had some catching up to do to match his height, although he was already stockier. Toby's hair had lost its bright blondness and turned mousy but his eyes were still vivid blue. Jake recalled where he was, forcing himself to stay alert. Using subtle glances, he located his accomplice, relieved to find him close to the exit. But he couldn't resist taking a last look. Toby had forgotten seeing him already, probably having settled on mistaken identity.

Being a thief, Jake knew straight away why the girl was crowding too close to his family. She was behind Toby and her lively eyes were directed over his shoulder at the merchandise. Her fingers were descending towards his pocket. Jake noticed they were slender and white before they disappeared. Then she was off, too hastily in his professional opinion. She'd trodden on toes, drawing attention to herself. But her victim remained unaware of what had happened.

Jake upset her getaway by bumping into her and casually touched his hat brim in apology. He kept going. So did she, clueless as to what he'd done. He'd been right thinking her an amateur.

'You dropped something.' Having made another tour of the sock counter, he'd nudged and spoken to his brother without losing step, trusting Toby would retrieve the wallet that had fallen at his feet.

Once outside Jake glanced around and spotted his pal pacing by the kerb. Before he'd taken two steps in that direction he felt his elbow yanked. He struggled but couldn't break free of his captor.

'Now, what've you been up to, eh?' asked the fellow with a thin moustache and thick eyebrows arched over a pair of dark eyes. But what really drew Jake's attention was the white scar that ran along his jaw and disappeared beneath his chin. It looked as though at some time in the past his throat had had a lucky escape.

Despite the man's piratical appearance Jake relaxed. This wasn't a plain clothes copper; and it wasn't one of the store detectives either. He knew all of those operating in the West End. He'd made it his business to. In Selfridges was a short stocky bloke with a bald head; Debenhams had a pair operating together: thin, ginger-haired men who could be twin brothers. Then Dickens & Jones had a man and a woman patrolling and she was the trickiest of the lot. He'd evaded her in the nick of time only last week.

'I asked you a question.'

'What's it to you?' Jake scowled defiantly. 'You're a customer, same as me.' He squirmed again, to no avail.

'I'm not a customer, son. I'm a crook, same as you. Just better at it.'

Over the man's shoulder, Jake could see his sidekick gawping anxiously at him. He frowned and jerked his head, instructing him to get going. They never hung around after a shopping trip. The daft sod was standing in a trance in the middle of Oxford Street with his pockets bulging with stolen goods. Herbert Brick was a year older than him but had the brains of a rocking horse. Jake knew he was the force behind this team. He rolled his eyes in exasperation and the youth finally got the message and scarpered along the street.

'That's the trouble,' said the spiv. 'Get involved with a dunce and they bring a heap of trouble down on you. I clocked him first, but didn't take me long to spot you was his mucker. He might just as well have stuck a target on yer back, the way he kept staring at you.' He began to propel his prisoner towards an opening between buildings. 'Got something to say to you ... something you might like.' He yelped as the boy turned his head and bit the fingers gripping his shoulder. 'You little bleeder!' He cuffed Jake's ear and made a woman passing by stare at him in disapproval. 'Taking the rascal home to apologise to his mother. Young people these days ... no respect ... ' He clucked his tongue and gave her a wink.

'If you think I'm letting you pinch the gear we've lifted, you can think again,' snarled Jake and kicked him. He was equally furious at himself. He liked to think he could detect a rival thief watching or operating in the same store. Although he'd spotted the girl, this fellow had outwitted him. He'd been slipshod because he'd been staring at Toby and his mother.

'I ain't interested in your bits and bobs, sonny.' The spiv shoved him away, and used the heel of his shiny shoe to rub the sore place on his shin. He took cigarettes from his pocket and stuck one in his mouth, then offered the pack.

After a brief hesitation, Jake took one, struck a match from a box taken from his own pocket, and lit up. 'So what are you interested in then?' he asked, blowing smoke.

'Proper earners. Like what's in those bags. She's my tag and she's better'n yours.' He tipped his head to a rather porky-looking young woman standing by the kerb hailing a cab. A vehicle drew up and the driver obligingly lugged the large bags inside the boot then in waddled the woman and off they went.

'Now in that cab with her are a couple of nice furs plus a heap of other good stuff. Her coat lining's got special pockets big enough to take dresses and hats and anything else you care to name.' He smirked. 'I've got some useful storage of me own. He patted his overcoat and chuckled when he saw Jake shoot a scouting look around. 'Don't worry, I'm clean now; it's all safely on its way. Not bad for an afternoon's work.' He watched the youth staring after the vehicle. 'My girlfriend's actually a skinny little thing, y'know.' He guffawed. 'Told her she can't put on an ounce or she'll never fit inside a cab fully loaded.'

Jake stifled a smile as he continued to gaze through the dusk at the red dots of the cab's taillights. He took another drag on his cigarette before dropping it and squashing it under his boot. 'Well, if you're waiting for applause, mate . . .'

'Sarcastic little sod, ain't yer?' The fellow braced an arm on the wall to block the boy in as he made to saunter off. 'Don't want nothing off you. You see, I'm the one offering something.'

'Not interested. Work for myself, always have, always

will. Won't risk getting arrested for somebody else to take the cream.' This was far from the truth; he was beholden to Old Peg and risked incarceration every day because of her. He didn't want this flash Harry to know that. 'Not my style, bowing and scraping.'

'You're a bit too arrogant, son; other than that, I do like your style. So what's your name?'

'What's yours?' Jake stuck his hands into his pockets and cocked his head.

'That's the spirit; it's important when you get nabbed to front it out. You're passing tests but there's more to learn ...'

'You heard the expression you can't teach your granny to suck eggs?' asked Jake drily.

'Nickin' odds 'n' ends won't make you rich.' The spiv didn't sound patronising, rather, philosophical as he rubbed his jaw where the scar was. 'No point to it if you don't make it big. If you're ready to make real money then pleased to meet you. Me name's Johnny Cooper.' He stuck out a hand and waited until he was on the point of giving up.

'Jake Harding.' The hard grip on his fingers was contested but Jake wasn't quite there yet and pulled free. 'Now I know who you are, I'll steer clear of you when you're working a patch 's long as you show me the same courtesy.'

'Courtesy, eh? You conduct yourself well for a kid.'

There wasn't much that upset Jake, other than a reminder of his early life and the privileges – like an education – that he had prematurely lost. 'Yeah, I do conduct myself well; gentleman in the making, me,' he said sourly.

'Tell you something else won't make you rich: looking a gift horse in the mouth. I'm intrigued: why d'you lift that wallet then give it back to the mark?'

'What's it to you?'

'You look like the lad. Relative, I'm guessing.'

Jake wasn't getting into that conversation, so turned the tables. 'If the girl's your dipper, I'd get rid of her. She'll bring a load of trouble down on you.' He mocked with a headshake. 'No finesse.'

'She's not working for me,' scoffed Johnny. 'I know who she is working for though. She's too inexperienced to do a West End run. She's part of a family concern and family's always bad news.' He wagged a warning finger. 'You took a risk getting involved; ain't people to mess with, that lot. Who is he? Your cousin? You seemed shy of him noticing what you'd done. Why help him if there's bad blood between you?'

'Nosy bugger, aren't you?' Jake pushed past and started towards the mouth of the alley. 'I'm done chinwagging; been hanging around here too long.' It was no idle concern. Enough time had passed for the thefts to be noticed. The woman who'd sold him the leather vanity case would recall her suspicions when questioned.

'Anyone else spoke to me like that I'd throw a right-hander. You're lucky you're just a kid and I've taken to you, Harding. So how old are you, anyhow?

'Old enough.'

'Good. In that case, here, have one o' these.' Johnny had followed him to hold a business card over Jake's shoulder as the swarm of shoppers made it impossible for them to walk side by side. 'Come and see me. Reckon we might do business ... though leave yer pal behind.' He slung an amused glance at the youth who'd tiptoed behind a street lamp to watch proceedings. 'Lost cause, him; but you show promise.' He flicked the card with a manicured fingernail. 'I conduct me meetings in the Bricklayer's Arms. Out the back in the snug. Ask the landlord, he'll point you in the right direction.' The card remained in his fingers so he poked it into Jake's breast pocket. When the chatter stopped, Jake glanced over his shoulder but Johnny Cooper was already lost from sight.

'Gawd's sake, what was that all about?' Herbert Brick sidled up the moment he was sure the coast was clear.

'Time we were out of here.' Jake glanced back at the brightly lit windows of the store. It all looked quiet but instinct told him the Old Bill would be circling before long, and so would his description.

'Old Peg said to hit Dickens & Jones as well.'

'Not risking it,' said Jake. 'We've got a reasonable haul so let's head back. I'll tell you about it on the way.'

As they set off, he slipped Johnny Cooper's business card from its resting place and read it. He was too young to drink in a pub, although he was no stranger to a tipple. All the same, he reckoned the Bricklayer's Arms off the Old Kent Road was worth a visit.

For now though south London could wait; he was off back to Rook Lane in Whitechapel.

Chapter Two

Although everybody referred to her as Old Peg, Jake realised his boss might only be about ten or fifteen years older
than the fellow who wanted to poach him. Late twenties,
Jake guessed Johnny Cooper to be. Whereas the spiv had
a youthful swagger about him, Old Peg could've been
born looking like a tired old crone. In the months Jake had
known her she'd not changed out of her dark overall and
mobcap. Neither did she style her string-like hair that was a
mixture of mouse and grey. Its length was always between
her chin and her shoulders, as though it had given up
growing at that point. She was a bony woman with a good
height and most of her teeth, but her eyelids were constantly
at half-mast making her appear not quite with it. She was
with it, and when new recruits eager to keep a thieved item
back for themselves, he and Herbie had discovered she was
impossible to hoodwink.

She hated alcohol and warned them she didn't tolerate
drunkenness, but snuff constantly disappeared from the
back of her hand up her nose. She never mentioned having
any family, but she did have money, from somewhere. And
she wasn't letting on about that either. Jake and Herbert

had returned early one day after being chased by an irate shopkeeper. They'd kept their lucky escape to themselves, and something else as well. Peg had forgotten to lock the gate on their departure and they'd not needed to ring the bell for entry. Before banging on the kitchen door to announce their return, they'd stopped to watch through a chink in the curtain as she counted banknotes at the table. It was an unusual mistake for a woman as canny as Old Peg to have made. They knew that the profit she got from their endeavours didn't amount to riches, so imagined she must be taking a big cut from fencing stolen goods for others.

People were always slipping in and out of the side door after dark. Peg made sure her employees were out of the way when she saw her customers. She let the boys look at the trinkets though and regularly left stuff on the table for them to see. At present the tabletop was home to music boxes and silver candlesticks, new stock delivered to Rook Lane while they'd been out dodging arrest.

'Wotcha got then?' asked Peg, clearing a space for the booty. From beneath her heavy eyelids she eagerly observed the stash from their pockets hitting the table. She stared at it. 'Turn 'em out,' she snapped.

Dutifully they pulled out their trouser pockets to show nothing was left behind. Still she wasn't satisfied and plunged her hands into the pockets of their overcoats.

'That it?' She finished rummaging and gave a tsk of disappointment. She kept them on their toes by moaning, but this time she was genuinely peeved. She picked over the assortment of leather and silk on the table. 'What about the blouses I said to get?' She found her snuff tin and sprinkled a liberal amount onto a bumpy-backed hand.

'He wouldn't carry on.' Herbert tipped his head at Jake. 'Bloke clocked him in Selfridges and give him a talking-to.'

Her hand was close to her nose when Old Peg dropped it down in alarm, scattering snuff on the floor. 'What's that?' she hollered.

Jake sent Herbert a quelling glance. As well as being a useless decoy he was without loyalty. 'Wasn't like that,' he told Peg. 'The fellow was one of us: a thief.'

'Who was it? Warned you off his patch, did he?' She rushed to the window and darted looks to and fro between the edges of stained brocade. She overlapped the curtains so not a sliver of darkness could be seen before coming back to the table. 'Are you sure he didn't follow you?'

'We're not stupid, Peg,' soothed Jake. 'We watched our backs like we always do.' The boys didn't believe in honour among thieves. Neither did Peg. They all understood it was a free-for-all and some crooks would rob rivals as well as stores. 'The fellow was boasting he'd made a killing this afternoon . . . rubbing it in about lifting furs to wind me up.'

'Don't matter. He saw you hoisting, that's the main thing, and maybe others did too,' said Peg. 'What's up with you? Losing your touch?' She gnawed at her thumbnail while thinking. 'Reckon it's time to swap things around . . . let Herbie take over.'

Jake wasn't happy with that. Even a stranger had recognised that his sidekick was a liability. 'I was just unlucky today, that's all.'

'Johnny Cooper was his name,' Herbie piped up again, making Jake regret having told him so much. He was thankful he'd kept back about the business card in his pocket.

'Cooper, eh?' Peg sat down, her thumbnail again under

attack. 'I used to fence for him then he went elsewhere. Bet he regrets that now,' she said with a smirk.

'What happened?' Jake was keen to have any information he could about the man who'd occupied his mind and helpfully blocked agitating thoughts of his mother and brother. Despite being offhand with Cooper, Jake had mulled things over and was keen for another meeting. The spiv had an oddly affable way about him that Jake liked. He sat down at the table opposite Peg and idly inspected the jumble of stolen goods while waiting for her to enlighten him.

'Cooper got too big for his boots and mixed with real bad people. I warned him that being greedy would bring him down. He's not vicious enough to mix with the Elephants.'

'Whassat? Joined the zoo, has he?' snorted Herbie.

Jake was quicker on the uptake. He'd heard of the Elephant and Castle gang that were based in south-east London. By all accounts even the police gave them a wide berth ... or took bribes to turn a blind eye to their violent shenanigans.

'I said to Cooper: there's mean so-'n'-sos Lambeth way who won't just steal from you, they'll slit yer throat,' reminisced Peg. 'Shame he never listened cos lo and behold ...' A skinny forefinger travelled over her throat, mimicking a blade.

'I saw that scar under his chin.' Jake leaned forward in interest. 'Got it for double-crossing an Elephant, did he?'

'Sort of ... they was fighting over a woman.'

The boys exchanged a look. They met up with some local girls who were Herbie's age and lodged together. They went walking or to the picture house and sometimes stayed overnight when they could afford the girls' professional services. They didn't consider Sadie and Maria more than casual friends, and certainly not worth scrapping over. The girls saw older fellows as well, and didn't bother with the walking and picture house but got straight down to business.

'You're too young,' scoffed Peg, reading their disgusted expressions. 'Give it a couple more years and you'll be finding gels to marry.'

'No fear . . .' blustered Herbie, red around the gills.

Jake didn't think the subject merited further discussion and resumed the conversation that interested him. 'So Cooper didn't come back to deal with you after that?'

Peg grimaced a negative. 'I expect pride kept him away. He lost his place in the East End crooks' league when he moved over the other side of the water. He wasn't one to eat a bit of humble pie.' She shook her head. 'Hence why he was bragging to you.' She leaned forward, thrusting her sallow face closer to them. 'Anyway, the Elephants are too rich for my blood. So don't go bringing that sort of trouble to my door otherwise you'll be needing another place to stay. Got it?'

They nodded in unison. Still Jake continued to brood on it all. In the months he'd worked for Peg he'd never seen anybody as fly as Johnny Cooper use her services. Women regularly turned up; he imagined them to be sticky-fingered housemaids who wanted to dispose of trinkets – no questions asked. They were always clutching something or other to give to Peg, but she made sure her employees didn't see what until after the deal was done and dusted. As soon as the bell clattered in the kitchen, heralding a visitor waiting at the side gate, he and Herbie would be sent to the outhouse that was their home. Their sleeping and eating took place in the brick-built building with a tin roof. Jake imagined the small-time thieves came to Peg Tiller because they didn't trust the bigger boys to give them a fair deal. Old Peg ran a low-key racket in comparison to what others got up to and it hadn't bothered him before Johnny Cooper put ideas in his head. Now he couldn't put those ideas out of his head.

'Right; there's stew on the hob,' said Peg, on rising from the table. 'Help yourself then get out from under me feet.' The brass bell fixed close to the ceiling started to clatter, announcing a visitor was waiting for Peg to unlock the gate and let them in. 'Might be almost Christmas but there's still deals to be done.' She jerked her head at the kitchen door to hurry them through it.

Before he went out, Jake turned back to ask, 'Who won the fight?'

Peg frowned in puzzlement.

'The girl ... who got her? Cooper or the Elephant?' He remembered the woman he'd seen that afternoon, squeezing into the cab loaded with swag. He wondered if she was the one who'd earned Cooper his scar. From what Jake had seen of her through the twilight she'd not looked anything special: medium height with bobbed brown hair. According to Cooper, she was a skinny little thing, not as big as she seemed. There had been something vaguely familiar about her, although Jake couldn't say what.

'Oh, I heard she went off with Cooper.' Peg shrugged and turned away, busying herself with her snuff tin.

Outside the large end-of-terrace house was a concrete yard and an expanse of lawn as well. Set against the perimeter wall of the yard was the boys' annexe, converted from a sizeable washhouse. It held a couple of bunks for the boys to use plus a few other bits of furniture and a small stove that they could boil water on to make a drink. Old Peg charged them a florin a week each out of their wages of ten shillings for board and lodging, and for that they got fuel for the stove, warm washing water and two meals a day: breakfast and supper. She was more than fair to them and at odd times seemed quite maternal. But her philosophy was that nobody got a free ride from Peg Tiller. Jake reckoned there was a method in her madness; she knew if she treated them to some comforts they'd stick around because where else would homeless youths who'd absconded from their apprenticeships receive such a good deal?

Once they'd left with their bowls of stew, Peg examined the goods again while her thoughts ducked and dived.

This unexpected talk of Johnny Cooper seemed to herald bad luck and she didn't want anything putting a spoke in the works when things were ticking over nicely. Cooper was a maverick and a shrewd businessman. He'd only bring himself to a rival's attention to benefit himself. Peg reckoned he was after poaching Jake. She could understand why if he'd watched the boy in operation; Jake had flair and charisma and would be an asset. She knew he was destined for bigger and better things and she'd not thwart him. A gleam of greed had been in his eyes when they'd been discussing Cooper's success. The waifs and strays she took in were sometimes more trouble than they were worth once their gratefulness was lost to ambition. The girls could be the worst; they caught a lad's eye and were hopeless dreamers. She didn't bother with girls now. She favoured using boys as hoisters. They could run faster for a start. The Elephant and Castle gang, though, had a very sophisticated team of female hoisters, who were as successful criminals as the men.

Peg trailed the soft silk of a scarf across her palm then

let it drop to the table. The coppers – under siege from real reprobates – deemed her a nuisance rather than a criminal, and that's how things must stay. She'd miss her handsome lad but Jake was outgrowing her.

The bell clattered again and she tutted at herself. It was unlike her to overlook a waiting customer. She hurried out into the darkness to let the woman in.

'Told you Peg would moan if we skipped Dickens & Jones,' said Herbie darkly. He slurped a spoonful of stew then pointed the utensil accusingly. 'Be your fault if we don't get no Christmas box off her, and I need mine to buy a few presents.'

'You seeing your family on Christmas Day?' asked Jake, ignoring his pal's carping. The mention of Christmas presents had reminded him of his purchase. He removed his hat and took the wrapped parcel out from under it. He'd kept it hidden in case Old Peg had commandeered it as recompense for the to-do with Johnny Cooper and the lack of blouses. He'd been lucky she'd been too agitated to think to search under it.

The boys had settled down on their respective bunks with dishes of hot mutton stew on their laps. The single grimy window in the shed had steamed up and the two burning candle stumps printed their shadows on the distempered walls.

"S'pect I'll see me mum,' said Herbie, shovelling more food into his mouth.

Jake dipped his hunk of bread into his oniony broth and chewed. Considering Old Peg never seemed to put much effort into preparing a meal she didn't knock up a bad bit of grub in his opinion. Certainly it was better than the

31

stuff he'd been served up at the Barnardo's home ... or had been given by his previous boss at the builder's yard on the banks of the Thames. He'd been apprenticed to the builder on leaving the Barnardo's home. He didn't dwell on those unhappy times. In comparison, he thought himself in clover now. He had a job – of sorts – and a roof over his head. Best of all he had a small pot of savings and was adding to it to better himself when the time was right.

'What about you?' Herbie scraped a crust about the bowl to soak up the smears of gravy. 'You visiting your family?'

'I am ...' Having finished his meal and feeling pleasantly full, Jake sank back onto the bunk, pillowing his head on his hands. He'd spent seven Christmases at the Barnardo's home. Then he'd been apprenticed and had told his boss at the building yard he was seeing his family last Christmas. He'd gone to Kensington and banged on the door, although the house was in darkness. A housekeeper had answered. A stranger, not Dora Knox. The family were away for the festive season she'd said and had looked him up and down. She'd demanded to know his name and his business. He'd not given it and had slunk away and never gone back. Neither had he returned to the builder's yard.

This year it seemed likely his mother and brother would be home for Christmas as he'd seen them in London. He'd go back to Kensington and bang on the door and wish them a Merry Christmas. And maybe he'd be invited in to spend the holiday in the warm, and sit down to a feast of roast goose and plum pudding as he had in the years before his father had died. And maybe his brother would say how pleased he was to see him and ask him to come back home for good. Their mother liked to please Toby, so perhaps she would invite him to go home.

He'd no real wish to live with her ever again after the way she'd treated him, but his chest ached with the longing for a reunion with his brother. Over the years they'd been apart there had been days … months even … when he'd barely thought of Toby. At other times he wouldn't be able to break free of memories of them as children. He'd made up stories at night to take Toby's mind off his bad dreams. The man in the moon or the creaking of the floorboards often petrified him after dark. Tales of animals living in the forest, or adventures that stranded them on warm sands, unearthing golden treasure, were fantasies that eventually sent them both to sleep. Only hours ago his brother had barely glanced at him before turning away as though they were strangers.

Jake rolled over, pulling up the blanket. He wasn't a kid now though and he'd prove to everybody – himself in-cluded – that he could make it on his own. In future he was going to concentrate on reality and getting rich. Everybody paid attention to money.

Chapter Three

'What did he look like, this damned individual?'

'I can't really remember,' she lied.

'Was he fair ... dark? How old would you say he was?' The fellow insisted while pacing to and fro.

'I didn't get a proper look at him. He wore a hat and I'd say was youngish ... maybe.'

'What?' He pivoted on his heel to glare at her in astonishment. 'Somebody your age, you mean?'

'No ... older than me ... Oh, I don't know!' The girl jumped up from the armchair, looking tearful. 'I'm sorry! But it was only a wallet for goodness' sake.'

'Only a *wallet*! Wallets is our business, gel, and don't you forget it.' He shook his head. 'Only a wallet, indeed. You won't be saying that when you want a new frock and a pinched wallet would've got you one.' He tweaked the sleeve of her smart dress.

'Might've only had a ten bob note inside,' she said defensively and sank back into the armchair.

'Why d'you bother lifting it then?' He tapped his temple. 'Haven't I drummed it in to you to avoid no-hopers?'

'Wasn't him I was after,' she interrupted with a truthful

excuse. 'The woman was done up in a fur. They had posh accents but if she was his mother she was canny. I couldn't get to her handbag. I took a chance on the son cos he was right there with his back to me ... pockets flapping. He didn't suspect a thing.'

'Neither did you when a crafty bleeder dipped in your coat,' he scorned. 'The posh lad's probably getting an ear'ole bashing for being careless, same as you are.'

'Oh, stop going on about it. I'll get another one for you tomorrow, Dad, and keep the thing in me hand all the way home.' She was back on her feet, waving an imaginary wallet in her fist.

'That's not the point,' he growled. 'Somebody's turned us over, and things like that get around in this game. You've made me a laughing stock, gel.'

'What's going on?' Molly Deane had come into the house and heard the raised voices in the parlour. She'd only popped out for a few minutes. She dumped the bag of groceries down on the table and seeing her daughter's miserable face, gave her a cuddle.

'She's had her pocket picked in Selfridges. Bit rich, eh?' said George Payne. 'Why wasn't you watching her?'

'How much you lost?' cried an alarmed Molly, ignoring George's complaint.

'Was only a wallet and didn't get a chance to open it. He had his back to me so I didn't get a look at him really; he seemed about my age ... so probably only had a few bob to spend,' Rebecca finished in a mutter.

'Not the end of the world then, is it?' Molly puffed in relief and slanted a disapproving look at George. 'We can talk about it later.' She wiped tearstains from the girl's cheeks. 'It's been an 'ectic afternoon. Go upstairs and have a rest before tea.'

35

Rebecca left the room feeling frustrated. Her father was never satisfied. She could walk out of a swanky store with a loaded cash register under her arm and still he'd have a moan about it being too light. She was angry with herself though for being foolish and bothering to pick the pocket of a youth.

Her downfall had been the other young man; he had pale blond hair and a pair of green eyes shielded beneath his hat brim. When he started to move in her direction she'd thought he'd noticed her too. He had, but not for the right reason. When she got home and found the wallet missing she'd realised he'd brushed up against her to rob her rather than to draw himself to her attention. Her vanity had suffered knowing it. If she saw him again, she'd have the last laugh though. She'd make sure of that.

Her father would track him down if she gave him a description. After a run-in with George Payne, the boy wouldn't look handsome any more.

She'd like to know his name. She'd not spotted him before in any of the stores, but so far had accompanied her mother on only a few West End trips. It was odd that Molly hadn't seen what had happened and steered her out of harm's way. She usually intervened in sticky situations. The blonde youth was a clever pickpocket. Better than her. Which wasn't difficult. Unlike her parents, Rebecca's heart wasn't in thievery.

She sat down at the dressing table and dipped a flannel in the pitcher of water. After livening herself up with a cold wash, she dragged a hairbrush through her wavy brunette hair. She coiled a thick hank of it onto her crown then turned her head to study her reflection in the mirror. She had a good pair of cheekbones and clear pale skin. She carried on fairly assessing her looks; nice long lashes curved over a pair of brown eyes that she wished were blue. She also wished her eyebrows were thinner but her mother had told her off for plucking them, warning her they'd regrow from an ugly line if she did it again. She looked glamorous with her hair up ... more eighteen than fifteen, even without the make-up she'd been banned from using. She'd asked her mother if she could get her hair fashionably bobbed but had been told she was too young for that as well. From now on she'd make sure to look more sophisticated when shoplifting. She was playing a dangerous game, indulging this infatuation and hoping to bump into him again. But she was sure they were destined for a reunion and when it occurred she wanted him to notice her for more reason than discovering what was in her pocket.

Downstairs in the parlour Molly was shrugging off her coat. She could see George was itching to blame her for the loss and decided to get her two penn'orth in first. She was a second too late.

'Why wasn't you watching out for her?' He repeated his earlier complaint, pointing an accusing finger. 'You should've nipped it in the bud, Mol.'

'Ain't my fault. Can't be a nursemaid and a hoister at the same time. You said to bring back as much as we could for Christmas profit.' She gestured at a heap of expensive finery draped on the sofa. Silks and satins and pale lace shimmered beneath the light from the gas mantles. 'And there it is.'

He'd been pleased as punch when they started unpacking their coats of treasure as soon as they got home. Molly had then gone to the corner shop to get something for tea, missing the moment the theft from her daughter's coat had been uncovered. Either their daughter had been targeted at random or they were being tested. George was right to fret over possible damage to their reputations. Once rivals scented blood they'd pile on the pressure. 'Instead of making a fuss about losing a kid's wallet you should be shifting those, toot sweet.' Molly paced the perimeter of the room, feeling on edge.

George couldn't argue with that. Usually he'd load the stolen goods into his car within minutes of the merchandise landing in their parlour. But Rebecca's mishap had side-tracked him. Scowling and muttering beneath his breath, he started stuffing the garments into a couple of large suit-cases. Routinely, he'd take booty to his aunt who fenced stuff from her house situated off the Elephant and Castle. Within hours, runners would disperse the lot around London, as far north as Muswell Hill and south as the Kent borders. On a Christmas Eve most pubs would have a minor villain ensconced in a corner, peddling merchandise. Tipsy revellers were very happy to shell out for a beautiful bargain as a last-minute Christmas gift.

Molly watched from the parlour window as the taillights of George's Humber car disappeared around a corner. Despite the smattering of snow on the ground he was mo-toring at quite a speed and she hoped he wouldn't attract a police car on his tail.

She let the curtain fall into place with a sigh. Though she'd told George differently, she did blame herself for let-ting Rebecca down. The tyke wouldn't have got away with robbing her daughter if she'd not dodged out of sight to avoid being seen by somebody. She'd not spoken of this to George as the matter was still a sore subject between them.

Years had passed, yet Molly had recognised Rupert

Harding's wife and had guessed the woman would recall her too if she turned around and caught a glimpse of her. They had been introduced once, at the theatre, when Molly was with a male friend of Rupert's and he'd been accompanying his wife. Molly had engineered the meeting to make Rupert jealous and prod him into leaving Violet. That hadn't worked; instead, Molly had triggered his wife's antennae. The woman had picked up on an undercurrent in their polite conversation and steered him away. A wife's intuition was strong and a cheated widow's fury stronger still. Violet wouldn't have forgotten that Molly Deane had deprived her of some of her rightful inheritance.

The only similarity between Queenie Darke and Peg Tiller was their love of doing a deal. In every other respect, they were chalk and cheese.

Big Queenie, as George Payne's maternal aunt was known, resembled a caricature of a kindly old granny, plump of figure and rosy of cheek with two luxuriant plaits of iron grey hair coiled atop her head. She was vicious though. George wasn't intimidated by many people but he was frit of his Aunt Queenie, and he wasn't the only one.

'You're late; didn't think you was coming,' she snapped, and before closing the door, craned her neck to take a scouting look up and down the street. 'Get the stuff straight into the cellar. Had the law sniffing around earlier. They might be back.'

George looked alarmed. 'How'd that happen? You been grassed up?'

'Nah ... got those two next door to thank for it.' She scowled and jerked a nod at the adjoining wall. 'Been at it hammer and tongs and brought the coppers down on us.

Even after they turned up the silly old sod wouldn't quieten down. He grabbed the poker and crowned her with it. Dolly got took to 'ospital. They took Tommy to the station . . . fighting 'em, he was.' Queenie's chuckle petered out and she shook her head. 'Come knockin' on me door, prying and wanting to know if anybody else was involved in the rumpus. Couldn't question 'em, see, what with Tommy frothing at the mouth and Dolly being sparko. I was doing a deal at the time. Could've turned nasty but I managed to keep me customer out of sight in the cellar and got rid of them quick as I could.'

'You done well.' He patted his aunt's arm.

George had been eleven when his parents abandoned him. He had been brought up by his aunt and late uncle for a few years before being told to bring in a wage at the age of fourteen. He remembered their neighbours, Tommy and Dolly Rudge, fighting like cat and dog even then, when he'd lived here. Nobody had any truck with coppers and it had been a rarity indeed for a neighbour to be worried enough to call them out to deal with a rumpus. One recollection though, of when they had turned up unexpectedly, had stuck in his mind and a snort of amusement burst out of him.

'What's so funny?'

'Just thinking of when I was a kid and you had me climb over the back wall so you could hide those cans of corned beef sharpish.' He had been in such a hurry he'd fallen into the alley. Almost before he'd landed, missiles began raining down. The cans arrived too thick and fast for him to catch them all. Queenie had clipped his ear for the dents.

'I do remember that.' Queenie grinned, exposing a gappy set of smoker's teeth, and feeling more relaxed, opened the parlour door rather than descending to the cellar. 'Wartime,

40

y'see, and I started taking sensible precautions. I knew rationing was bound to come in.' She thumbed at the Rudges' house. 'Promised those two a couple of buckshee cans that day if they'd put a sock in it and let the coppers clear off.'

George could understand his aunt's frustration with them. They were the worst sort of neighbours for a person who needed to keep a safe distance from the rozzers. If you met the Rudges separately in the street when they were sober, they seemed amiable enough.

Queenie had plenty of nieces and nephews with fingers in pies, bringing her merchandise to 'disappear'. Sometimes, unexpected family reunions took place in her parlour when they all converged at once and an impromptu party would get going over a few brown ales and some pounding of the piano keys.

This afternoon, her customer secreted in the cellar had been Johnny Cooper. She kept this to herself. George and Johnny didn't get on. They had similar looks: dark Brylcreemed hair and neat moustaches. They were different characters though. Cooper was the taller and the more handsome and had an easy charm. It had been no surprise to Queenie that he waltzed off with the girl after they'd fought over her. Neither of George's parents had returned to claim their only child. Even as a kid he wasn't easy to get along with. Queenie would remind George from time to time that he was lucky she'd put up with him.

'You had a bad time of it this afternoon, so I heard.' Such an incident could turn serious and thus warranted a comment.

'Said who?' George dumped the cases side by side on the settee. He had been brooding on the theft and didn't need this reminder.

'Don't go jumping down me froat. Telling you for yer own good that it's doing the rounds already about Rebecca getting stung.' Queenie poked his arm in emphasis. 'The gel's young, still learning; she should be supervised better by you and Molly.'

'Rebecca lifted this ...' George opened a case and dragged out a turquoise dress. 'Knows enough, don't she, to come away with summat like that?'

'Lovely feel to it,' said Queenie, fingering the shot silk.

He put the garment back. 'Who was it dipped her pocket? You know, don't you?'

'I do not ...' The dress had whetted Queenie's appetite and she continued sorting through the things in the case.

'Whoever told you what happened in Selfridges, stole off us and I'll have his name.'

'Calm down, George,' interrupted Queenie. 'You're not thinking straight. This won't go no further if you keep your head and act normally.' She pulled cigarettes from her apron pocket and took one then offered the packet to him, before striking a match for them to share.

In a short while George had brightened up. 'I know who it was.' He smacked his thigh. 'I just passed Johnny Cooper's Austin in the High Street. It was him. He's been here, ain't he, to do business?'

Queenie took a hefty drag on her cigarette, wishing she'd kept her mouth shut. 'Cooper has been here and he did put me in the picture. But he wouldn't've, would he, if he was the culprit?' She tapped ash into the fire grate. 'According to him, there was more shoplifters out on Oxford Street than customers this afternoon.' She finished the cigarette and dropped the stub to join the ash-spattered kindling heaped up ready for burning. In common with most people, she kept the cooking range alight in the back room during the day and only lit a front parlour fire in the evening.

'Let's get this lot out of sight.' She went into the passageway and opened the door set beneath the staircase. Despite her age and her width, she nimbly descended the narrow stone treads to an Aladdin's cave of boxes and hanging rails. The pale gas light shimmered on sequins and mother of pearl buttons.

Twenty minutes later, having haggled with his aunt for the merchandise – and been pleased enough with the outcome – George was soon back outside in the Humber. He chuckled as he struck a match to a cigarette. He always waited to see Queenie's nose start to twitch – a sure sign she wasn't getting the best of the deal – before agreeing to it. It had been the turquoise silk dress that had swung it his way. Queenie had been keen to have that, doubtless because she had a customer in mind for it.

His aunt was right; Johnny Cooper wouldn't reopen old wounds for the sake of a kid's wallet. George reckoned his old enemy had witnessed the incident, though. Or he knew somebody who had.

He wasn't going cap in hand to Johnny Cooper to ask for the ins and outs, but there was somebody else who might tell him what he wanted to know.

Chapter Four

'How's me big sis doing?'

'I'll tell you in a moment after you tell me how you came by all of that lot.' Clover Ryan raised a dubious eyebrow at her younger brother.

'Come bearing gifts to wish you a Merry Christmas, Clo ... and to pinch a couple o' those.' He jigged the bag of goodies he was carrying; his other hand stretched towards a tray of pastries taken from the oven.

Clover tapped his hand away from the mince pies. 'If you came by those clothes straight, then sit down and I'll make you a cup of tea to go with the pies. If not ... ' Her forehead was jabbed at the door. 'You know I won't have stolen stuff in this house.'

'Ain't hot, honestly, Clo.' He tutted in indignation. 'Anybody'd think I was a proper tea leaf the way you carry on.'

Clover was sharp as a tack, but he hoped his cockney rhyming slang banter would make her lighten up. She continued to frown, with just cause, but Johnny Cooper wasn't about to admit the bag was brimming with hooky gear. And splendid it was too. His visit to Big Queenie earlier

44

had been lucrative and would have paid even better if he'd let her have this stuff as well. But his sisters took priority.

'Been getting a lot of tips off punters lately,' he said quite truthfully, 'so thought I'd treat me two favourite gels.' He had a regular job as a steward in an illegal gambling club in the West End and high rollers often doled out generous gratuities after celebrating a win at a table. His job had drawn him into the company of bad men. Once tasted, the extra money was too tempting to give up. He was sensible enough to run his own enterprise now, which kept him out of the pockets of real villains.

He tried to share his ill-gotten gains with his family. Clover deserved something back after being his mainstay for the latter part of his childhood. He'd still been at school when they'd been orphaned. At seventeen, Clover had taken over looking after him and his toddler twin sisters. Losing her respect and friendship would be agony. Yet being an honest grafter like the man she'd married was impossible for Johnny; he therefore constantly teetered between being welcomed or nagged when he came here. In Johnny Cooper's opinion playing it by the book was for mugs, especially when times were as hard as they were. The queues outside the labour exchanges were growing. The end of the Great War had brought with it not the sunlit pastures promised by the politicians, but stagnation and unemployment. Before the Armistice celebrations' bunting had been put away, the spread of Spanish flu opened a new decade of hardship and grief. The working classes suffered the most, as they always did. Johnny had found a way to even things up for himself and his sisters, and often felt bewildered by Clover's attitude. He was in a position to make life easier for her, but her pride and conscience kept getting in the way.

'Oh, give him his mince pie, Clo. It is almost Christmas, after all,' said Annie who'd skipped out of her bedroom the moment she heard her big brother banging on the door. She'd let him in and given him a hug, glad to see him.

'Don't I know it's nearly Christmas,' Clover muttered, rubbing her wrist about her perspiring face.

'Lovely 'n' cosy in here,' said Johnny with a winning smile and sniffed at the warm aromatic smell of spices.

'We're making some more mince pies.' Annie pulled together some pastry remnants on the flour-dusted tabletop. 'First have to wait for the stove to heat up again.' She began to form pie bases while gazing greedily at the bag in her brother's hand. Annie wasn't bothered about his dodgy dealings and adored being treated to nice things. Working as a housemaid she'd little left in her pocket to buy pretty clothes after paying for her keep. The second-hand stall in the local market was her usual port of call for basic essentials. Johnny's crammed bag, with a froth of lace peeping from the top, was as fascinating as a treasure trove to a girl of seventeen.

'You're a dab hand with the rolling pin, Annie,' said Johnny.

'I've been working extra hours cos Mrs Galloway's arthritis is giving her gyp and she can't whisk nothing up.' She rotated her wrist in demonstration. 'I like being cook's assistant; it's better than brushing out sooty fireplaces and polishing brass. A school leaver's been taken on to do the donkey work so I can train up properly to be her understudy.' She nudged her brother. 'I helped Mrs Galloway make madeleines the other day and one went missing while her back was turned.'

'That's m' girl.' He dropped her an approving wink. 'What's a madeleine when it's at home, anyway?'

'Coconut cake with a cherry on top.'

'Snaffle one for me 'n' all next time.' He looked thoughtful. 'You'll be getting promoted soon then, will you?'

'Have to live in for that,' said Annie with a pointed look for her big sister.

'You don't need to live in.' Clover was using the poker on the fire. 'You can stop at home for now.'

'I'd sooner live in,' said Annie obstinately. 'Seems daft toing and froing. I'm going back in an hour to help Mrs Galloway prepare the vegetables for Christmas dinner tomorrow.'

'That's as maybe, but things can stay as they are for now,' said Clover with a quiet authority that sent Annie into a sulk.

It had been no surprise to Clover to discover a male colleague of Annie's had been sniffing around. Her pretty sister's dreamy-eyed look when the name of the family's chauffeur cropped up in conversation had given the game away before Clover heard about it on the grapevine. Pinching cakes would pale into insignificance if Annie were to be sent home in disgrace with a swollen belly. Unfortunately she had always been an impulsive child and had a quick temper too.

Johnny didn't want his sisters to fall out on Christmas Eve so steered the conversation away from the rocks. 'Need any coal? I can fetch some over.' He relieved Clover of the job of loading sticks onto the fire.

Clover's fingers jerked up his lowered chin. He had an appealing face with joviality permanently etched around his eyes. The ridge of skin beneath her fingers reminded her that he was no longer the cheeky scamp he'd once been. Johnny mixed with criminals and had the scars to show for it. She'd been beside herself when she first saw the damage to his beautiful face but over the years the wound had healed well. Her fury at him for being stupid had subsided. But not completely gone. 'Paid for coal, is it?' she demanded to know.

"'Course!' he indignantly replied, easing his face from her fingers. 'I'll bring a sack over on the cart later.' He winked. 'You can pay me in mince pies.'

'Deal ...' Clover wearily stood up, stretching out her back. 'In the morning the pork will need a good heat to make a nice layer of crackling.' She put the kettle on, mentally planning tomorrow's feast.

'Forget the tea, sis.' Johnny rummaged in his bag of tricks to produce a bottle of sherry. 'This'll help a mince pie slip down nicely. Start Christmas early, shall we?' He received a smile from both sisters. The atmosphere had mellowed and he felt emboldened to dump the bag on the table. 'Brought you gels your Christmas presents. Sorry, didn't wrap 'em but, you know me ...' He shrugged.

'I do know you,' Clover said drily and watched Annie delve into the bag and extract a crepe de chine blouse.

Johnny drew forth a green velvet dress and held it up by the shoulders to display. 'This one's for you; I knew it'd match your eyes, Clo.' He handed it over, pleased to see her stroke the soft pile.

'It's a beauty,' Clover said. 'Did you choose it for me yourself?'

He tapped his nose. 'I know what suits you gels.' He neatly sidestepped the question and admired the dress she held against her figure. Clover had russet hair and an unlined complexion currently quite rosy from the cooking. She looked far younger than her thirty-three years. 'Anyway, how about we all go to the pub later like we usually do. You can show off your glad rags.'

'I'm not sure about that,' said Clover.

Johnny knew money was tight at the moment, as his brother-in-law had been laid off last week. 'Neil found work yet, has he?'

'He's out looking now,' said Clover.

'I'll come to the pub with you, Johnny,' said Annie cheekily. 'I'll have to miss me work shift though.'

'You will not,' said Clover, putting the dress down carefully on the sofa and finding some glasses. 'But you can have a small sherry now with Johnny.' She gazed at the pair of them. They were not only the spit of one another in looks, with their dark brown hair and hazel eyes, but alike in character too. Their father's kids . . .

Clover put Sidney Cooper from her mind. It was the season to be cheerful, not brood on her late father. She had loved him but couldn't deny he had been a troublemaker. Other lost family members were welcomed into her thoughts, and there were a sorrowful amount of them. 'I'm going to the cemetery in the morning. Will you come along?'

'I'll meet you over there.' Johnny said the same thing every year; he never showed up.

Annie's excitement had been subdued by a mention of the sad ritual on Christmas mornings. Her parents and her grandmother she barely recalled as she had been a toddler when they passed away. But she had dearly loved her twin sister and remembered Rosie even though they'd only been four years old when her other half died of Spanish flu the year after the war ended.

The ensuing quiet was broken by the sound of the door opening. A tall man with black hair came in and rested a holly wreath against the wall. 'This is a nice surprise,' said Clover's husband, brushing snowflakes from his shoulders.

'I could've got you one of those, mate.' Johnny was looking at the cemetery wreath. He believed it was a waste to part with cash for anything that could be pilfered or bartered.

Neil Ryan's smile was rueful; he thought Johnny an incorrigible rogue. But he liked his brother-in-law; one thing nobody could fault about the man was his love for his sisters.

'Here, have a glass of this to warm the cockles.' Johnny poured out four glasses of tawny sherry.

'Absent friends,' said Neil and raised his glass. The others echoed the sentiment and the salute.

'Any luck?' asked Clover after taking a sip. She had her fingers crossed behind her back that he'd found a job.

'Got a start after Christmas,' said Neil. 'Boat builder down on Cinnamon Wharf needs a carpenter.'

'Just saying to Clo about having a drink in the Rose and Crown later. If you like.' Johnny took a mince pie as Clover handed around the plate.

'Might meet you in there, then,' said Neil, although he doubted he'd turn up and splash what little cash he did have on drinking in pubs. He knew Johnny would offer to buy the drinks, but Neil either stood his round, or stayed away.

'Smashing mince pies, Annie. Well done, gel.' Johnny put down his empty glass, having made his sister beam. 'Right, best get off. Things to do.'

'Thanks for the presents, Johnny.' Clover walked with him to the door. She handed him a bag of wrapped presents, drawn from behind the sofa. 'These are yours.'

'Didn't expect nuthin'.' He lowered his voice. 'I know things are tight right now.'

'It's not much. Just glad you like mince pies and sherry,' she added ruefully.

'Love 'em ...' He kissed his sister's flushed cheek. 'There's a little something in that bag of clobber to suit you, Neil,' he called out, making his brother-in-law raise a hand in thanks and farewell.

'Dinner's one o'clock if you fancy it.' Clover invited him every year but just like the cemetery visit, he never turned up. And as Clover rarely saw eye to eye with his girlfriend, it was probably just as well. The couple would go to a swish hotel instead and eat roast goose and drink champagne.

After Johnny had gone, Clover returned to the bag and drew out an Argyle pattern pullover. She held it against her husband's broad chest. 'Fits you perfectly.' She handed the bag to Annie. 'Have a rummage.'

Annie grinned and went off into her bedroom with the treasure.

'Are you going to wear your new dress on Christmas morning?' asked Neil.

'How d'you know it's mine?' she asked.

'The colour ...' He ran a finger over the rich emerald pile. 'Wish I could buy you things like this, Clover.'

She put her arms around him and rested her head against his chest. 'Well, I don't. There's lots of things I'd sooner have than a posh frock.'

'A baby?' he guessed and pressed his lips to her forehead.

'Maybe next year will be the year ...'

They had been married for twelve years and no children had arrived. Neil had been recovering from war injuries that kept him in hospital for months after he returned from the Western Front. But he had healed well and Clover had fretted that perhaps there was more to it than his health as the years passed by. She didn't dwell on it; she was grateful that she'd been one of the lucky ones. Her love had come

51

back to her; many men hadn't returned and their women-folk would remain spinsters, or widows, raising families on their own.

'I'll try me hardest every day to make your wish come true.' His cunning smile earned him a thumped bicep.

'Johnny didn't buy my dress anyway,' Clover added on a sigh.

'You reckon it's all stolen?' Neil's resigned amusement was evident.

'Pretty sure it is ... and it's not funny, y'know.'

'Will you give it back to him?' Neil held his wife away to gaze into her eyes.

'I should ... I would ... but don't feel up to a wrestling match with Annie.' Clover was only half joking. 'I've more on my mind where she's concerned; like this young fellow she likes.'

'He might be sensible enough for both of them.' Fond as Neil was of his sister-in-law, Annie could be a trial and act younger than her years.

Clover knew that even level-headed fellows ... like the one her mother had loved ... the man she had died for ... weren't sensible when they had an itch in their trousers. She carefully folded the dress. 'I won't wear it tomorrow and risk getting grease on it. Might have to return everything in the New Year if Johnny gets his collar felt. I expect one day it will happen.' She gazed up at Neil; at thirty-seven his black hair was silvering at the temples and his autumn-coloured eyes were warm and steady. She stretched up to kiss his cold cheek and brushed some melting snow from his shoulder. 'Another one of these will warm you up; at least we can dispose of this evidence.' She poured two more sherries and they chinked glasses. 'Bottoms up,' said Clover.

Chapter Five

A strip of yellow light leaked from an aperture between the window shutters. By holding onto the snowy stone sill and pulling himself upwards Jake could see inside the house. A Christmas tree rose up proudly in the corner of the room and his hungry eyes followed the bushy green pyramid to its apex where a silver star reflected firelight. The hearth was out of sight but by simply watching those coral sparks he could sense a blissful warmth on his shins.

His arm muscles began to shake with the effort of holding his weight and his fingers felt iced to the ledge but he didn't want to let go of the homely scene. He continued gazing at the magnificent conifer, a tang of pine needles prickling in his nostrils. Overwhelmed with longing to be invited into that magical room, he let himself fall back to crisp whiteness and immediately lunged towards a pair of oaken doors. He gave a loud rat-a-tat. A second later he was filled with an urge to creep away before he was banished. He stood his ground. It would have been too late to make a run for it in any case: a servant had opened up quickly as though on standby for guests.

The housekeeper's sombre figure merged with the

shadows but her pale complexion and white mobcap were clearly visible in the hall light. She looked surprised, having expected somebody else to arrive, he guessed. Jake recognised her, but she didn't appear to remember him, or that he'd scuttled away without giving his name last Christmas Eve.

'I'd like to speak to your mistress, please.' His voice had broken at thirteen and his clear baritone added to the illusion that he was older than his sixteen years.

'Who shall I say?' She looked him over from top to bottom.

Her son, he would have liked to boldly reply. He lacked the courage though. Neither did he want to seem brash and start off on the wrong foot. 'If you would please tell Mrs Harding it is Jake . . . ' He waited but she didn't move. A savoury aroma wafted out of the half open doorway, whetting his appetite although he'd already eaten a bowl of mutton stew.

'Mrs *Harding*?' the frowning woman queried. She started to shake her head but the door was suddenly opened wider. A gentleman – the sort of sleek fellow Jake might see alighting from a chauffeur driven limousine – posed in the opening, a hand braced on the door jamb and the other on his elegantly suited hip.

'You can go Ethel,' he told the middle-aged servant who inclined her head and did as she was told. 'So . . . who might you be?'

The fellow's question was accompanied by a smile Jake didn't like. He'd tilted his oily dark head in that way posh people had when amused at finding themselves conversing with inferiors. It suddenly occurred to Jake that his family might no longer live here. Last year he had asked to speak to the mistress and had been told the family was away.

He hadn't lingered to ask more after that. His mother and brother might still be London residents but have changed address.

'Sorry to bother you … made a mistake,' said Jake.

'Have they arrived at last?' asked a female voice, and dainty footsteps could be heard approaching over the flagged hallway floor.

'No sign of Oswald but we have a younger scallywag instead, asking for you, my dear,' said the fellow. He turned with studied puzzlement to gaze at his wife. 'Methinks you have something to tell me …'

His sarcastic tone told Jake his unexpected arrival had bad repercussions for his mother. He'd recognised her voice and knew he had the right house even before she swept into view in a floating dress – the sort of garment that was far too fine to be found in a department store he might rob. Bond Street couture – from one of the places his boss gave them strict instructions to avoid – clothed his mother's thin figure. Too rich for her blood, Peg would have said about the gown.

An excess of riches was impossible, so Jake had thought. But the phrase finally made sense and he wished he'd stayed away. Shock had frozen his mother's expression into a wide-eyed stare. Then she had reared back out of sight as though something ghastly had met her eyes.

A vehicle sailed quietly along the street and crunched to the kerb over hillocks of stained white snow. In the ensuing melee of people slamming car doors while blaming the damned weather for arriving late, Jake climbed over the low brick wall at the front of the house. He bolted away, sliding on the treacherous pavements in his haste.

'Jake!'

He'd covered a good distance but whirled around at the shout. He saw his brother waving and running in and out of glittering patches of ice beneath the street lamps.

The younger boy skidded to a halt close by, chest heaving as he snorted steam. It seemed they might embrace but the moment was lost and instead they bashfully smiled in unison. The sparkling air sandpapering their throats and the snowman in the road brought to their minds a time when they'd tobogganed with their father on Primrose Hill. The shared memory went unremarked and their smiles faded. They weren't those children now. They were almost strangers.

'It was you in the Oxford Street store, wasn't it?' Toby blurted. 'I thought I recognised you.' He paused. 'You saw my wallet on the floor.'

'You must've dropped it,' Jake said gruffly.

'I thought somebody had tried to pick my pocket.'

'Might've been a thief operating in the store.' Jake looked at his boots. He wasn't sure why he couldn't mention seeing the girl stealing it. He supposed he wasn't a grass and she'd only been doing her job that day, the same as he was. He didn't want her to get into trouble and wasn't sure he could trust his brother with the truth.

'Come back with me.' Toby jerked his head at the house. 'They've got guests but we can go upstairs to my room. I don't want to listen to them prattling about politics and I don't want any dinner either.'

'Thanks anyway but I shan't get you into trouble.' Jake couldn't forget the horror on his mother's face when she realised he'd turned up and embarrassed her. She had recognised him though after all these years, and so had Toby. He might not be wanted but he wasn't forgotten.

'I've been thinking about you, and wondering how you were liking that school you went to.'

Jake shrugged. 'I left there years ago.' He wasn't going to say he'd hated every minute of it and had felt hungry and lonely and empty inside. He'd missed his brother dreadfully at first until the memory of his home started to fade. Then the more he struggled to remember what Toby looked like, the harder it became to bring his face to mind. Now, here he was, close enough to touch. Jake felt a surge of fondness, but it passed with disappointing swiftness; the differences between them had become distinct. He had grown coarser since he was abandoned at the Barnardo's home; his brother more refined. 'Do you still have old Nash as a tutor?'

'I should say not!'

Toby's tone was scoffing, reinforcing his brother's view that they were poles apart now.

'I'm a Rugby boy.' Toby frowned. 'You're only sixteen. Aren't you at school of some sort?'

Jake shook his head. 'Been at work for ages.' Finally, something he felt rather proud of. He was a half-grown man, his brother a schoolboy still. 'Don't you want a job to earn some money?'

'I need to study first to make a good salary in the City. I'm going up to Cambridge. University ... ' he added as though realising an explanation might be required. 'I'll be reading history and geography next year. I've done well, so I'm going earlier than most boys in my class.' He tilted his chin. 'I remember they always thought you were cleverer than me when we were little.'

A hint of the arrogance the oily fellow had displayed was in Toby's expression. 'Good for you,' said Jake with a trace of bitterness.

'So what work do you do?' Toby asked, genuinely curious.

Jake shrugged. 'Whatever comes along that my boss wants doing,' he said vaguely.

'What sort of job though?'

Jake had had enough of being questioned. Telling the truth about how he earned a living might make Toby laugh ... or sneer. He no longer knew his brother well enough to accurately guess his reaction to the confessions of a petty criminal. 'You'd better go back, you'll freeze.' Toby had dashed after him without wearing a coat and was rubbing his cold arms beneath his shirtsleeves. 'And they're looking for you.' Jake jerked a nod at the house. 'Is he your stepfather?' The oily fellow had emerged onto the step to stare in their direction.

Toby nodded and after a brief pause explained, 'Ian Winters adopted me.' He looked slightly shamefaced. 'I wanted to stay a Harding. I prefer my real Pa ... our real Pa.'

'He wasn't though, was he? Neither is she our real mother.' Jake felt rather cruel for having sounded sour and triumphant. The new housekeeper hadn't recognised the name Harding and now he knew why. Rupert Harding's house had been taken over by another man. If Dora Knox had been kept on she would have recognised him, and known what he wanted. 'Winters doesn't know about me, does he? He hasn't a clue she had two adopted sons.'

'After you went, Mama said not to speak about you to anybody.' Toby looked and sounded apologetic. 'She said people would think her wicked for sending you away, but she couldn't afford to bring up two children.'

'She doesn't look on her uppers now,' remarked Jake, reflecting on her chiffon gown.

'Money wasn't tight after she married him. It was horrible

at first after Papa died and you went away. We didn't have much at all.' His mother had scrimped for his school fees and told him they must suffer going without from time to time. A short while after he started at Rugby, and during his first holiday visit, he was introduced to his future stepfather.

'What's he like?' Again, Jake's forehead indicated their watcher.

'Don't see much of him. When we are around together we tend to ignore one another. He makes it clear he finds me a pain.' He smirked. 'Two can play at that game. Luckily, I only come home a few times a year. I'll be going back to school directly after the holidays.' Toby glanced over his shoulder on hearing his name called and Ian Winters beckoned him imperiously.

'You'd better go.'

'I'll go when I'm ready,' said Toby with a show of defiance. 'He's not my real father and I don't have to do what he says. Even if Harding wasn't our real father, I miss him, do you?'

Jake nodded and hunched into his coat. He was still interested in knowing more about Toby's new family set-up. 'Ian Winters is posh, is he?'

'Sort of. He's friends with aristos. Have you heard of Oswald Mosley?'

Jake nodded. He didn't like what he had heard about the man either.

'That's who just turned up in that car. They're all chums.'

Jake now knew why he'd thought the debonair fellow in a camelhair overcoat looked familiar. Mosley was the leader of a political group and Jake had seen his photograph in the newspaper.

'Do you ever wonder about your real parents?' Since a new father had barged into his life, and one for whom he had little liking, Toby had dwelled on the fragments he knew about his birth. His mother became irritated if he questioned her and refused to discuss the matter of his adoption. 'I'd like to know about my real family, wouldn't you?'

'Yes, I would . . . ' Jake shrugged. 'Dad told us our mothers were poor women who couldn't afford to keep us, or didn't want to . . . so they probably hope we've forgotten about them.' That fact would always unify them no matter how high his brother rose in the pecking order.

A silence lengthened and Jake knew his blunt statement had niggled his brother. Perhaps Toby had been hoping they could concoct a romanticised version of their starts in life, to suit his status. Jake was sticking with what Rupert Harding had told him; he knew his brother remembered that talk very well even though they'd both been youngsters at the time. He started to shuffle his feet in readiness to say goodbye.

'Why did you come here?' Toby asked, wanting to delay him. 'Did you hope to spend Christmas with us?'

'No . . . ' Jake turned his blushing face aside. 'Just wanted to wish you Merry Christmas after I saw you in the shop. Didn't want to seem rude. But didn't like to butt in at the time, either. Mother wouldn't've liked it.' He paused, wishing he'd not called her that. She hadn't been his mother at all really and now he would think of her as Mrs Winters. He was glad his father didn't have to share his name with her any more.

'Who will you spend Christmas with?'

'A friend,' Jake said and suddenly felt confident he would do that. Not Old Peg, as she'd gone away for Christmas. She wouldn't say where she was off to just that she had family to see. Then she'd turned out her workers; he and Herbie had been wished a Merry Christmas and given a five-shilling bonus as a Christmas box. Then Peg had started locking up. Herbie had set off to his mother's house, carrying his bag of presents. The memory of his friend jauntily swinging that bag reminded Jake that he had something for his brother.

'Here ... brought you a Christmas present ... might remind you of Dad. I hope so anyway.' Jake forced himself to sound bright as he pulled a small, wrapped parcel from his coat pocket. 'Bye then ... Merry Christmas.'

'Will you come back?' Toby called as Jake started to walk away.

'No point ... if you won't be there.'

Toby looked as though he wanted to hand the gift back. He held it out awkwardly. 'Sorry ... don't have anything to give to you.'

'Doesn't matter. Keep it, it's nice.' He was glad now that he'd been forced into buying the gentleman's leather vanity set. It was classy, a fitting gift for somebody who knew aristos. 'Good luck at university with the history and geography.'

'Good luck, yourself,' shouted Toby. 'And Merry Christmas to you too.'

Johnny Cooper might not be a friend, or his boss yet, but he had invited him to the pub to meet him. Jake was determined to go there now, but he'd not beg for a place to bed down until Peg got back. He'd slept rough before when he'd absconded from the builder's yard, and would do so again as a last resort.

He'd met Herbert Brick during that miserable stint of doorway dossing. Herbie had thrown in the towel on a dead-end job in an abattoir and had been looking for shelter, having been told by his mother not to bother her until he had paid employment again. They'd joined forces and found a bomb-damaged house in Wapping. For a few days they'd squatted in there beneath half a roof. And then they'd met Peg Tiller. Or rather she'd met them, having watched them being turfed out of the wreck by the builder preparing to pull it down. She'd offered them employment and somewhere to stay and the two of them had whooped in delight like the kids they still were.

Without understanding why, Jake felt much older and wiser today.

As he walked away, he knew from the quietness that Toby hadn't yet started his dash home to a warm house that smelled of beef gravy. Jake didn't want to look back; but deep inside remained a need to comfort his younger brother and he turned to give him a wave. He received a wave back from the hand clutching the vanity set. Then they both turned away and moved swiftly in different directions.

Pretending everything was absolutely fine wasn't difficult for Violet Winters. She could assume the role of a polished hostess and devoted wife along with the best of them. This evening she was quieter than usual. She wasn't too preoccupied though to be unaware of icy glances from her husband, demanding she buck herself up.

Her second marriage had been a financial necessity rather than a romantic choice. Ian Winters was a suave oaf. Balancing his faults were good connections plus a healthy investment fund. He had been the best she could do at short notice with the bills mounting. She had no complaints to make on this occasion; no smell of tart's perfume or drunken behaviour to bring up.

The boot was on the other foot now and she was the one with some explaining to do.

The glasses continued to chink and conversation interspersed with laughter echoed about the sparkling room while staff cleared the soup plates from the table. Her husband was a genial host but his hard eyes darted constantly to her and she knew once this charade was over he'd turn nasty. On this occasion with just cause.

There had been no time to instruct Toby in what to say before he ran off to catch up with his brother. On his return, Ian had intercepted her son outside before she could get to him. She'd watched discreetly through the window as Toby, a look of rebellious pride on his face, had told his stepfather about the Barnardo's boy. Ian was now aware of her guilty secret and she could throttle Jake Harding for coming here and causing trouble.

She had an ace up her sleeve though. Or rather concealed beneath her petticoat. She was carrying her first child at the age of forty-seven. She'd not intended to tell her husband yet as she wasn't absolutely certain herself; being pregnant was all new to her. But the right signs were there, if still unnoticeable to others.

Ian was six years her junior and on his first marriage. He had been keen for a child of his own and her age had initially deterred him from proposing. Her feminine wiles had eventually persuaded him she'd make the perfect wife. They were compatible lovers but she'd believed he was seeing younger women to get a bastard to prove himself, like her first husband.

Molly Deane and her daughter hadn't been forgotten by Violet. She'd never believed Rupert had offspring and felt justified in thinking he'd been infertile, not her. She had loved him, despite the lack of a natural family putting strain between them. He'd been a decent man and would have financially protected a child he trusted to be his. The loss of part of her inheritance hadn't been forgotten either and still rankled bitterly. There would have been no need to marry again to educate Toby if she'd got everything due to her.

Her adopted son's future paled in importance now she had her own flesh and blood to protect. A miracle had turned up out of the blue and for that alone she was feeling grateful and quite affectionate towards Ian. He had given her the one thing she had always longed for.

She met his eyes and gave him a sultry smile . . . a promise to make things up to him in the way he liked once their guests had gone.

Chapter Six

Yeasty smelling smoke and harsh noise met Jake as he opened the door of the Bricklayer's Arms. The atmosphere wasn't off-putting, but inviting. When he first left the Barnardo's home, he would linger outside taverns to gaze through the windows at cheery drinkers who seemed a world away from the grim adults he'd been stuck with for years. He preferred these pub people.

They weren't always jolly, though. He'd got knocked flying on one occasion when brawling men tumbled out of the doors of the Ten Bells, bringing with them a bunch of rowdy spectators.

This lot seemed merry enough so he sidled inside, keeping his hat pulled down and hoping he wouldn't be challenged over his age. In his line of work it wasn't wise to invite scrutiny or a run-in with the law. Thankfully these didn't seem like people who'd welcome coppers snooping around either.

On this Christmas Eve night the saloon bar was packed with revellers and it was hard to make headway. Using crablike steps, he moved around the room's perimeter then stopped, having found a gap to peer through. He didn't stare at anyone in particular in case they took offence.

His brother's cultured voice would be way out of place in here. The men barked at one another about the big East End markets – Spitalfields and Billingsgate – and the fluctuating prices affecting their profits. The women moaned about the bleeding kids driving them mad. He'd met a bunch of those: frozen little gnomes perched outside on the step, waiting to be remembered and brought a drink of pop.

Jake deduced that costermongers and their wives frequented this pub. They were dressed in their Sunday best. Florid-faced men in bulging waistcoats were upending tankards, and women in trinkets glittered and gleamed beneath the chandeliers while sipping from dainty glasses. He smirked on noticing that one had wrapped around her shoulders a distinctive paisley print scarf. He recalled lifting the scrap of silk only hours ago in Selfridges. Peg Tiller hadn't hung around with shifting those little beauties.

He began to edge forward, taking care not to bump any elbows and soak a shirt front in spilled beer. He might receive a thump if he did.

He couldn't have picked a worse time to come here and look for Johnny Cooper, yet he was reluctant to leave. The warm seedy glamour of the place was appealing, as was the raucous rendition of 'God Rest Ye Merry Gentlemen' being bashed out on the piano. His roots in the East End slums had prepared him for nights like these, he supposed.

Two tipsy young women, gold dangling on their ears and winking on their fingers, tried to swing him into a jig as he passed the piano. He laughed nervously and managed to extricate himself before the bigger of the two could jam her red lips on his cheek. His hat was now askew so he took it off and held it under his arm in case it got trampled on.

He'd made it as far as the bar and peered across a row

of beefy shoulders. The landlord and barmaid were being run off their feet and he didn't want to invite accusations of pushing in by shouting out. He planned to make discreet enquiries about Johnny Cooper.

He decided to find a nook to settle into while keeping an eye out for Cooper. He stepped backwards and in the process did something he'd been at pains not to do. A woman yelped as his heel squashed her toes and he was punished with a whack on the back.

'Oi, you clumsy thing! You trod right on me bleedin' bunion.'

He squirmed around to apologise and compounded his mistake by jogging her glass of gin. It soaked her hand rather than her clothes and she sucked her fingers. Instead of another complaint he received a wide-eyed stare that transformed into a shout of laughter.

'Blimey! Johnny said to keep a lookout in case you decided to join us later. Didn't imagine it *was* you. Jake Harding's a common enough moniker, I thought to meself. But here you are and didn't have no trouble reckernising you either after all them years. You was an 'andsome kid, and you're growin' into a bloomin' 'andsome man.' She gave him a wink and pinched his scarlet cheek.

'You're Miss Knox,' spluttered Jake, still struggling to convince himself this really was the skinny housemaid he recalled from Kensington. Her squeaky voice was unchanged but all else was different. Gone was the drab uniform, scraped back bun and colourless complexion. Her brown hair was sleek and her face a rainbow of colours: red lips, pink cheeks and blue over her eyes that reached almost as far as her thin black brows. A tawny fox fur nonchalantly coated one shoulder as though she didn't care if it fell off and was lost. Plain Dora Knox in all her paint and finery could pass for a film star.

'Well, young Master Jake, you can call me Dora now. Come on, I'll take you to see Johnny. He's just through there.'

Jake had no idea where 'there' was but he let her pull him by the arm. People didn't object to her pushing past but stood aside to let her through while she held her glass above her head to protect what gin remained in it.

They entered a room off a corridor situated behind the saloon bar. Johnny Cooper was playing cards at a table with a balding fellow and didn't immediately look up as his girl-friend returned to the snug. The roaring fire and compact size made it an aptly named hideaway.

Johnny was in rolled-up shirtsleeves but wearing his hat. He used a finger to push it back on his head. With one eye on Jake and the other on his opponent, he laid down his cards face up. 'Ace flush,' he said.

The balding fellow gave a tsk of disgust and threw down his hand. 'Had that up yer sleeve did yer?' He jabbed a forefinger onto the ace.

'What sleeve?' Johnny thrust out two bare forearms.

The disgruntled chap shoved back his chair and stalked out, banging the door while Johnny scooped money from the table. 'Sore loser ...' He gave Jake a grin. 'Decided to come and talk business after all, did you, Mr Harding?'

'Just passing so I thought I'd pop in.' Jake attempted to sound breezy.

'Well, sit yerself down.' Johnny indicated the vacant chair and Jake settled into it, putting his hat on his lap.

'It is him,' said Dora, flopping down onto a small hide sofa. 'Knew him straight off. Small world, eh?'

Johnny had told Dora about the blond pickpocket who'd be an asset to them. She'd told him about the boy from years ago with the same name who'd been separated from his brother and sent away after his father was murdered. Neither of them had believed it could be the same lad. Johnny pocketed his winnings, thinking Jake Harding had had a rough old time of it in that case.

Bumping into Dora Knox had seemed like a good omen, but from his companions' sombre expressions Jake knew his wretched history had been discussed behind his back. He'd come here for business, not for pity. He decided to stay though, at least until his frozen fingers and toes thawed out.

'So you gave up being a housemaid then?' He blurted the first thing he could think of to divert attention from himself.

'More like it gave up on me,' Dora snorted. 'Glad about that 'n' all. Never took to skivvying.'

'She was sacked,' said Johnny bluntly. They had got together some years after her stint as a domestic. Back then Dora Knox had been partners in crime with somebody else. Johnny didn't like the man or the lessons he'd taught her.

'Oh, get us another gin, love.' Dora waved her half-empty glass to stop Johnny brooding on her past lover. He hated him, which was hardly surprising considering his scarred face was George Payne's handiwork.

Her request was ignored so Dora downed the dregs and put her glass on the floor. Seeing Jake had brought back memories of his adoptive mother. At sixteen, Dora had already been naturally crafty and sticky fingered. She'd stolen a silver bangle belonging to Mrs Harding that the woman rarely wore. When she'd finally noticed it was missing it was too late to prove her maid had taken it. Dora had stayed for several more months before being dismissed. By then Mr Harding was dead and his widow was penny pinching, and watching Dora like a hawk. Violet had taken over the cooking, ignored the dust, and made her last remaining servant surplus to requirements.

It hadn't bothered Dora to leave. She'd already become entangled with George Payne, who'd promised her riches and all the fine clothes she could wear if she started shop-lifting from top London stores for him. Dora had taken to it like a duck to water.

'Bloomin' disgrace how you was treated, young master Jake,' Dora said. 'Mrs Harding was a strange one in my opinion.'

'She's not Mrs Harding now; she's Mrs Winters.' Jake swivelled on his chair to hold his palms to the fire. He'd have a final warm up then make a move. Dora wasn't going to shut up about his past and he didn't want to field questions about his time at the Barnardo's home either.

'Oh ... remarried, did she? You boys looked so alike you could've been real brothers. And such little friends, too. I used to watch you looking after Toby and think it'd be a real shame if you lost touch with one another for good. You've seen your family recently then, have you?'

Dora paused for breath and gazed determinedly at Jake for some answers. This time he didn't need to distract her from being inquisitive. A stranger did it for him. The door to the snug had been swung open. A fellow with similar dark looks and some extra years to Johnny posed on the threshold. He sauntered in, pulling by the arm a girl Jake did recognise. He turned cold, despite the smouldering logs close by. He remained calm, and in his seat, while Johnny sprang from his. Dora continued to lounge against the sofa, but Jake noticed a glance that seemed significant pass between her and the older fellow.

Dora knew what George Payne wanted. He had visited her that afternoon, digging for information about the pickpocket. She'd told him nothing, and she'd not mentioned seeing him to Johnny either. It was Christmas Eve and she didn't want to spoil a nice atmosphere. Unfortunately, a ding-dong seemed imminent after all.

'This is a nice surprise. Come to wish us Merry Christmas, have you, Mr Payne?' Johnny sounded his usual jokey self. But his eyes were hard and watchful. Years had passed since their fight, but he still held a grudge despite their pretence of letting bygones be bygones. Payne had fought dirty, while Johnny, still wet behind the ears as a villain, hadn't even owned a blade back then.

'You remember me daughter, Rebecca, don't you, Johnny?' Without waiting for an invitation, George Payne settled next to Dora, budging her hip with his to make her shift up. He then patted the space next to him. His daughter obediently sat on the edge of the cracked leather cushion, and stared at the floor.

''Course I remember her; gel's the image of you, ain't she, poor kid.' The comment received a sour smile from George. 'Only larking, dear,' Johnny addressed Rebecca. 'You're like yer mum and as pretty as Molly, too.'

'So, now we've spoken of my lot ... you going to introduce me to your young pal?' George flicked a look at Jake.

'He's my friend, if you must know,' piped up Dora. 'Mrs Winters' son, Jake. I skivvied for her when I was only a kid meself. Way before I knew you that was, George.'

'That right, is it, son?'

'It is,' replied Jake, managing to sound bored. He drew

71

together the cards and started shuffling them with reasonably steady hands. He was grateful to Dora for protecting his identity off the cuff like that.

'I saw my aunt this afternoon and Queenie reckoned you told her it was getting around that Rebecca had trouble in the West End.' George spread his arms across the back of the Chesterfield, a challenging stare fixed on Johnny.

'I knew Queenie would pass it on to you.' Johnny winked at his nemesis. 'Be obliged if you'd show me the same courtesy ... let me know if anything happens I should know about. Us villains should stick together.'

Jake shuffled the cards faster, suppressing a smile. He was on thin ice though and his amusement soon faded. He wasn't the only one in trouble: Rebecca Payne was too, for losing a wallet. Her father had twigged Johnny Cooper could know more about it than he was letting on.

'Be off with you now, Jake. Got business to discuss.' Johnny jerked a nod at the door. 'Ain't for your innocent ears.' It wouldn't matter to a man like George Payne that the culprit was barely old enough to shave; he'd go for him just the same. Johnny wished he'd not mentioned any of this to Big Queenie.

Jake realised he was being given an escape route. He didn't want to be a coward and let the girl take all the flack. He was convinced she'd recognised him when she tilted her head towards the door a fraction, urging him to leave. Perhaps she didn't want him owning up and making things worse for her. He didn't have the wallet to give back, anyway. He got up and insouciantly put on his hat, adjusting its brim.

'This him?' Payne rose to his feet and blocked the exit as Jake approached it. 'Take a good look, Rebecca.' With some deliberation he removed the hat that had just been put on its owner's bright blond head. 'If it is him ...' George smiled nastily and his curled fist playfully grazed Jake's jaw. 'Well, he can stay right here and join the discussion, can't you, son?'

With a sulky sigh, she got to her feet and looked Jake over, top to toe. 'Never seen him before,' she said. 'Told you, I only got a glimpse, but I know he was shorter and had brown hair.'

'All of a sudden you remember quite a lot,' her father said and swung a suspicious glance between the two of them.

'It's not him,' she said testily. 'Can we go now? It's Christmas Eve and I've got things to do. I promised me friends I'd see them and it'll be too late soon ...'

'Mind your tongue.' George snarled at her insolence and Jake used the moment to take back his hat.

'Kids, eh?' drawled Dora, rising languidly to her feet. She found a packet of cigarettes on a side table and lit one. 'Who'd have 'em?' She blew smoke in George's direction and behind the cloud was her mean-eyed regard. She'd have a child if he hadn't made her get rid of it years ago. He'd never got rid of Molly, as he'd promised, to make Dora his number one instead of an also-ran. Dora had been shoved aside every time Molly Deane found out they'd been seeing one another again. She held out the pack of Gauloises for George to take one, letting him know she didn't give a damn about him any more.

'Got one of those for me?' asked Johnny as she returned the pack to the table. He deftly caught it one-handed as it was lobbed in his direction.

The atmosphere crackled and the adults hurled dirty looks at one another, giving Jake a chance to sidle out.

Before closing the door he gave the girl a subtle smile, thanking her for what she'd done. She returned him the same acknowledgement. He hoped she realised he was apologising to her as well.

Jake didn't care who he upset in his need to make himself scarce. Curses followed him as he barged through the drinkers but he wasn't hauled back, and made it outside un-assaulted.

A wintry chill enveloped him as he marched along the snowy pavements that were icing treacherously beneath a moonlit sky. He pulled up his collar and shoved his hands deep in his pockets, wishing he'd been offered one of those cigarettes. He'd smoked his last one after his meal earlier and had nothing to calm his nerves.

His previous intrepid idea of sleeping rough had shrivelled. He'd be stiff as a board by morning. He'd a little money with him but doubted he'd manage to find a doss-house bed on Christmas Eve. Even the tramps wanted to treat themselves to a little Yuletide comfort. He'd go back to his lodging and break in to collect his savings. He might find room at a respectable boarding house and be able to buy himself a Christmas dinner tomorrow. The idea of roast meat made his mouth water. But if that didn't come about he'd find a shop that was open and eat bread and jam. Not much of a Christmas, but he could burrow beneath the bed-covers until his colleagues returned and made him jealous with tales about the fine old times they'd had.

He broke into a slip-sliding trot to warm himself, and to get a roof over his head as soon as possible.

Chapter Seven

A scrawny figure he recognised was trudging towards him from the opposite direction as Jake turned into Rook Lane. The bag being carried wasn't swinging jauntily now; it appeared to drag on Herbie's hand like a lead weight.

They met by the gate that barred the path to Old Peg's house. It was always double-locked when she wasn't at home, which was rare; she hardly ventured further than the corner shop. Sometimes she sent the boys to fetch groceries for her rather than leave her hermit's cave, and woe betide if they attempted to short change her when divvying up pennies afterwards. Jake and Herbie had never been allowed their own keys, even to the outhouse where they slept. They made themselves secure for the night by sliding the inside bolts on the door.

'Your mum not in either?' Jake gave them both an excuse for being unwanted and returning here for shelter.

'She's gone to me married sister's I expect,' said Herbie dully. 'How about your lot?'

Jake shrugged. 'They're always busy. Should've sent word I was coming. Never mind.' He nodded at the lofty gate.

'Give us a bunk up, then I'll pull you up after me.' Herbie was older but he didn't have Jake's height or wiry strength.

With Herbie's cupped hands boosting him, Jake launched himself into the air and managed to curl his numb fingers over the gate's rusty top rail. He took a breath before pushing himself up to swing one then the other of his legs over. It was quite a drop but he jumped and landed nimbly then began dragging the dustbin, a boot wedged beneath it to muffle the scrape of metal on concrete. He positioned it by the gate and brushed snow off the lid, then steadied himself upon it. He leaned over to offer his hands to Herbie and after much heave-ho his friend eventually made it to the top. Herbie was clutching his bag rather than holding on and lost his balance as he lifted his legs over. He crashed down onto the dustbin, sending the lid flying and the two of them tumbling onto frozen ground in a jumble of limbs.

A light went on in an upstairs window next door, and their neighbour's face appeared from behind an edge of curtain. Jake helped Herbie up and they crouched behind the dustbin, giggling like kids. When the curtain fell back into place, they scampered out of sight.

'Hope she don't think we're burglars and send for the rozzers.' Herbie puffed out, breathless with exertion.

'S'all right . . . don't reckon she saw us. She'll think it's cats at the bins,' said Jake, leading the way to their outhouse.

'How we gettin' in here?' Herbie impatiently charged the door, then used his boot on it. It didn't budge.

'Keep the noise down, you idiot,' hissed Jake and pointed at the neighbour's house. Cats might clatter dustbin lids but they didn't batter down doors.

'Well, what we gonna do now? Peg'll go mad if we break the window.' Herbie hunched into his coat, rubbing the sting out of the arm he'd bashed during his fall. He wasn't finding their predicament funny any more.

'We'll have to offer to pay for the glass between us,' said Jake practically. 'She'll understand when we explain we'd nowhere to stay. We'll freeze to death out here.' He glanced up at a dark velvet sky sewn with sequins. A treacherously beautiful atmosphere that would keep the air bitterly cold. He'd warmed up during their stunt but that was already draining away. His elbow hit the top fanlight. It shattered quietly enough and he managed to wriggle his hand between the jagged shards and unhook the casement stay.

Once they'd both clambered in through the opening Jake pulled the curtain across the hole to buffer the draught then shoved the chair against the cloth to hold it in place. They tiptoed around the broken glass and perched on their bunks, staring at one another through the gloom.

'Ain't much warmer in here,' whined Herbie, dragging his blanket around his thin shoulders.

'Got anything to eat in there?' Jake nodded at the bag being cuddled.

Herbie rummaged and drew forth a box of assorted biscuits. 'Bought them for me mum for a present.'

Jake found the candle stump on top of the washstand and lit it with a match. He opened the stove, praying it contained something to burn. It had a large half-charred log inside. He grinned at Herbie then found some old newspaper to use as kindling, employing the lit candle as a spill. 'Any water in the kettle?'

'Bit ...' said Herbie, having given it a shake. He took the lid off a jar of Bovril. 'Enough for a drink each. We'll have to swill the jar out.' He found their cups. 'Some bleedin'

Christmas this is, Bovril 'n' biscuits. Was hoping for a chicken dinner, or at least a bit of boiled bacon.'

'Stop moaning and buck up. Got a New Year to look forward to,' said Jake, coddling the fire.

'Just more o' the same,' said Herbie sounding depressed.

'Not for me.' Jake gazed at the small flame licking about the log. 'I've got plans.' With the kettle on the stove top, they sank back onto their respective beds, pulling up the covers. While waiting for it to boil, he was half aware of Herbie going on about finding the girls they sometimes saw and paying them to stay the night at their place.

'You've got some savings we could use,' Herbie said. 'I've spent all mine buying presents. I'll pay you back though.'

'Not going out again,' Jake said. 'So shut up about it.'

Jake wasn't thinking of good-time girls; he was thinking of somebody else. Rebecca he now knew her name to be, and he was wondering why he'd not noticed how pretty she was when he'd brushed past her in the store. Too busy getting her into trouble, he supposed. But he didn't regret helping his brother even though Toby and Mrs Winters had faded from the forefront of his mind.

His new friends had taken their place for now; Johnny Cooper and Dora Knox ... and Rebecca Payne. He considered her a friend for not grassing him up and getting him a thrashing.

'What plans you got then?' Herbie had reared up onto an elbow to stare at his pal through the flickering candlelight.

'Getting a new job ...' Jake knew that might depend on whether he was still wanted after the close shave with George Payne. That man hadn't known he'd be at the Bricklayer's Arms but had suspected his old foe had answers to questions about the pinched wallet. Rebecca's father had simply struck lucky finding the real culprit in the pub.

And so had he struck lucky, Jake reminded himself. If the girl had dropped him in it a fight would've started ... maybe a knife would have been involved. Rebecca's father seemed a dangerous man; Johnny's scar was surely down to him and Dora Knox was the woman who'd earned him it in the love triangle Old Peg had spoken about.

'I'll come with you to a new guvnor,' Herbie piped up. 'Working for Peg is a dead-end caper. And I was expecting more'n five bob Christmas box off the old tight-fist as well.'

'It's time for us to go it alone now, Herbie.' Jake closed his eyes, rocking his scalp deeper into his cupped hands. He wasn't sure he even liked Herbie very much. They'd been companions when they'd both been lonely and in need of a friend but Jake had plans that didn't include him. Johnny Cooper had made it clear Herbie wasn't wanted in his outfit. Besides, Herbie was the oldest and it was time for him to stand on his own two feet. If they didn't go separate ways Jake knew he'd end up resenting him as a burden. 'We can still meet up from time to time, if you like ... have a lark ... see some girls ...'

There was no reply and Jake knew his pal was in a huff. The kettle whistled softly and he sat up to make the drinks of Bovril. He glanced at Herbie who had rolled over so his back was to him. Jake took a sip of scalding Bovril. He reckoned he'd no chance of being offered a biscuit to go with it now.

By Boxing Day the biscuits were all gone and they both had grumbling bellies. Jake had climbed back over the gate and gone to buy them something to eat. A weak sun was out, melting the snow to slush. He'd headed to the local pub, knowing it would be open at dinner time, and treated them both to a meat and potato pie. He'd eaten his own food while strolling back, unable to resist the savoury smell wafting up at him.

He'd dropped a milkman's crate over the gate this time so he'd have something to step upon to assist him in his clamber up and over.

He was on top of the crate, protecting Herbie's pie by putting it in his pocket when a familiar voice shouted at him.

'My giddy aunt . . . woss bin goin' on here while me back's bin turned?' Old Peg, dressed in a smart coat and floppy brimmed hat, marched up and pushed him, toppling him off the crate and setting a bunch of big iron keys jangling in her gloved hand.

Once she'd unlocked the gate, Jake followed her inside, trying to explain, but Peg wasn't listening. She'd stopped to gaze in shock at her broken kitchen window.

Jake gawped at it too. 'That wasn't like that an hour ago . . . we didn't do it,' he spluttered. 'We only did the other one . . . ' He was pointing towards the outhouse but his boss wasn't listening.

Peg hurried to let herself into the house and assess the damage. Jake stood where he was, both bewildered and frantically wondering what had gone on. He'd been out less than an hour but now wished he'd not dawdled along eating his pie. He glanced at the outhouse, wondering why Herbie hadn't come out to investigate. He shouted for him then dashed after Peg. He found her gazing forlornly at the mess scattered on the floor. Somebody had rifled the cupboards and drawers.

Still no sign of Herbie joining them, and even if he'd been snoozing he'd have heard this commotion. A dreadful idea dawned on Jake and he hared out of the kitchen. The door to the outhouse was still locked but the window was ajar. He scrambled in, cutting his hand on broken glass in his clumsy haste. He knew there was nobody beneath the bundle of bedclothes on Herbie's bunk but ripped them off just the same.

Having shown his pal how to get over the gate with the dustbin's assistance, Herbie had fled after burgling Peg's place. Jake sank down to sit on his bed, seething with anger and disbelief. It took him several seconds to notice that the mattress felt lumpier than usual. He jumped up and saw it was wrinkled and askew. He quickly lifted it. The tobacco tin that held his savings was gone. He searched under the bunk even though he knew he was wasting his time.

'Robbed you too, has he?' Peg had unlocked the door and come in to find Jake on his hands and knees. 'Serves you right for trusting him.' She turned and left without another word.

'You trusted Herbie as well.' Jake followed Peg back into the house, sucking the bleeding cut on his hand.

'Never trusted him, nor you.' She took off her hat and put it on the table. 'Never trusted nobody in me life except ... ' Her croaky voice faded away and she busied herself tidying up to conceal her watering eyes.

Jake felt a fool for leaving Herbie alone. He *had* trusted him; or rather it hadn't occurred to him that his pal was rotten enough to do something like this. 'Has much been stolen?' he asked.

"S far as I can see, just a couple of silver snuff boxes,' she mumbled. 'I didn't lock them away safe like the rest. The fellow who was interested in buying them was meant to collect on Christmas Eve. He never turned up and I went off in a rush so as not to miss me train.' Again her voice wobbled with emotion.

It occurred to Jake then that Peg had returned a day earlier than expected. She'd told them she'd travel back on the day after Boxing Day, and they shouldn't return until then. She seemed odd: quieter. A lesser upset than this usually sent her into a paddy. She'd come back to chaos and barely raised her voice but was uncharacteristically emotional. She wasn't overwhelmed by Herbert Brick's betrayal. Peg Tiller was made of cynical stuff. Rather than question her, Jake pitched in with the clearing up, picking up tea cloths and cutlery. He put it all onto the table, letting her restore it to its rightful place.

When everything was off the floor and the table was full, keeping her busy opening and closing drawers and cupboards, Jake began loading the stove with coal. The fire began flickering into life and he put the kettle on the hob to make some tea.

She didn't object to him hanging around or pouring himself a cup, and when they were sitting opposite one another, drinking, she said, 'If anybody was gonna skip off I'd've said it'd be you.'

'I'm not a thief!' His outburst put a slight smile on her face. 'Well, not like that anyway. I'd never rob pals.' He qualified his righteous indignation.

'I know you wouldn't. You was always a different class to Herbert Brick. I thought you'd disappear to work for Johnny Cooper.'

Jake didn't comment; he continued morosely sipping his tea. He was thinking of ways to apologise for what had happened. He blamed himself for having left Herbie alone. He'd been in a funny mood ever since the matter had come up of leaving Peg and going separate ways. Jake wished now he had agreed to go out and find the good-time girls. If they'd done that, Peg would still have her kitchen window and her silver snuff boxes and he'd still have his stash of savings. He'd had almost two pounds in that tin in coins and ten-shilling notes.

'Are you quitting?' Peg gazed at him from beneath her droopy eyelids.

'What?' Jake surfaced from his guilty thoughts.

'Johnny Cooper's offered you a job, hasn't he?'

Jake remained quiet for a few seconds. 'I'll be sticking around here if that's all right, Peg.' He stood up. 'Sorry about all of this. Herbie won't have got far, anyhow. I'll look for him and bring back what he's stolen.' Again a glaze of tears appeared in her eyes and water trailed onto her cheek.

'You're a good lad, but don't worry about me. Nothing wrong with being ambitious. You'll make it big one day, I know you will.'

'What's up, Peg?' Jake sat down again. 'Why're you back sooner than expected?'

'Could ask you the same thing,' she said and rubbed at her bleary eyes.

'My lot had guests and didn't want any more.' He paused, remembering his brother's invitation to go home with him. Toby had no doubt got into trouble for running after him and been told to avoid Jake Harding in future. The brightly lit house that smelled of roast meat had seemed a warm cosy place, but it had been as cold as the snow outside. He didn't want to speak about his miserable experience to anybody. 'Did you have a nice time?' He felt startled when his boss put her elbows on the table and wept quietly into her palms.

He stood up, then sat back down, unsure whether to go and comfort her or stay where he was. He reached across to clumsily pat her arm.

'Didn't have a nice time. Me husband died,' she said. 'Wasn't unexpected, but knocked me for six all the same.'

Jake gawped at her bowed head. He'd not known she had a husband or that he lived elsewhere. She was Mrs Tiller but the boys had assumed her to be widowed as she resided alone and only wore faded dark clothes. She'd never spoken of any relatives and they hadn't asked questions, knowing she'd consider it impertinent.

'Sorry ... sorry about that ...' he murmured.

Peg wiped her eyes with her curled fingers. 'Relief for him that it's over; he'd been poorly for a while.'

'How long?' Jake didn't know what else to say.

'Since he came back in 'sixteen.'

'He was injured in the Great War?' Jake had been born in the autumn of 1916 and to him it seemed ages ago. 'Was he still recovering in hospital?'

'Sort of ... but I knew he wouldn't get back to his old self. His body wasn't badly injured.' She tapped her forehead. 'Real damage was up here after what he saw at the Somme. He spent fifteen years in an asylum.' She shook her head in despair. 'So many poor lads suffered shell shock. And not enough help for them. I felt guilty not being able to cope with him meself, but found a way to pay for proper care, and ain't concerned if how I did it ain't legal. My wages and the crumbs the War Office threw his way weren't enough to properly look after him. Workhouse infirmary got mentioned but I'd never have let him rot in one of those. I found him a decent place where I was allowed to go and visit him, and the doctors did all they could.' She used her sleeve on her eyes. 'He got flu ... matron wrote to tell me. He'd had it before so I wasn't unduly worried but this time it turned to pneumonia. When I got there ...' She began to keen softly, her head bowed, and her lank hair curtaining her face.

Jake gave her arm another comforting rub. He felt

stunned. Old Peg had been ducking and diving to pay an institution's fees. He'd always thought her somebody to be reckoned with but his admiration and respect had grown from knowing about her devotion to her husband. He knew about harsh institutions from his own experience and wished he'd had a guardian angel to look after him.

'I was a probationer nurse in the London Hospital when we met.' Peg had raised her head and her tired eyes held a spark of nostalgia. 'We tied the knot just before he was posted to France, then when he come back a year later he didn't know me.' She suddenly stood up. 'He's at peace now, and so am I.' She sniffed and busied herself with the enamel bowl and the washing up. 'Go on, off you go now, and see if you can find Mr Spooner. Ask him if he'd call when he can 'cos I've got windows need fixing.'

Jake got to his feet to do as she asked. Before he left, he said, 'I will find Herbert Brick. You'll get your silver back. Promise.' The smell of meat and onion wafted from his pocket, stirring his hunger again. He carefully drew out the bag. The least he could do was let Peg have it; she'd be hungry after her train journey. 'Fresh baked today, that was, and still warm.' He put Herbie's pie on the table and went out.

He meant what he'd said about giving up his idea of working for Johnny Cooper. He'd stay here, at least until Old Peg was back to her normal self. Being ambitious was all right but there was time enough for that. It would be mean to turn his back on her after this.

He walked up the lane and stopped by the handyman's door and gave a sharp rap. He'd pay for the broken windows out of his lost savings once he had caught up with Herbert Brick. And he'd give the bastard a pasting.

Chapter Eight

'What the hell d'you think you're doing?'

Clover Ryan clattered the teapot onto the kitchen drain-ing board, slopping boiling liquid from the spout over her fingers. She'd been startled by somebody creeping up behind and snaking an arm around her waist. He was so close she could feel the bulge at his groin pressing into her lower back. He didn't need to say a word for her to identify him. Prising his hands off, she squirmed around and gave him a shove.

'I'm offering to do what your husband can't.' A dirty laugh rumbled deep in his throat. 'I only have to look at my missus and she's up the duff again.' He grabbed her chin as she turned away in disgust. 'I wanted you when you was a girl and you wanted me right back, didn't you? How about we get friendly again? You might find yourself rocking a babe of your own before too long.'

Clover jerked out of his grip and laughed in his face. 'Well, that's never going to happen so why not make your-self useful another way.' She thrust two filled cups at him and her nod indicated the people they could hear talking in his front parlour. 'Hand these round, would you, before they go cold?' She shook her stinging fingers. 'While I bathe me burned hand.'

He didn't take the crockery or apologise for having scalded her. 'Kiss it better if you like.' He chuckled as she flashed him a contemptuous look. 'I still fancy you like mad, Clover.' Slowly and deliberately, his sultry blue eyes stripped over her from her glossy auburn hair to her shapely stockinged calves. 'I know you want a kid, me wife's told me. I can give you one, and nobody needs to know Neil Ryan ain't up to the job. Better get a move on though,' he taunted. 'You're not getting any younger, love.'

'I'll stop you there before you say something too stupid even for you, Archie Fletcher,' she said. 'I'm not a kid of sixteen now, and actually, I never really liked you touching me. It didn't take me long to work out you were a waste of time. In fact, I feel ashamed I ever walked out with you or let you kiss me.' She clammed up although there was plenty more to say. The sound of light footsteps had alerted them to a woman heading for the kitchen.

Clover's younger sister came in and stood by the door, looking like a ray of sunshine in her buttercup yellow dress. 'Thought you must've gone to China for that tea,' said Annie, sliding a look between them. 'We're all parched in there.'

'Stove's not up to heat. Kettle took a while to boil but it's ready to pour out now.' Clover forced a smile. 'Archie's offered to hand these round.'

'Being helpful, is he?' said Annie impishly.

'That's me,' he said, giving her a wink. With a final look at Clover, he backed from the room holding two rattling cups and saucers.

'Was he doing what I think he was doing?' asked Annie with a scandalised smile.

'Depends what you think he was doing.' Clover's jokey tone wasn't fooling anybody. Annie had turned eighteen and was more clued up about randy men than she had been at that age.

'Archie Fletcher just made a pass at you at his daughter's christening?' Annie wrinkled her nose. 'What a swine ...'

'Right both times.' Clover wouldn't insult her sister's intelligence by pretending it hadn't happened.

'His wife is already big and still months to go before the new one arrives. Maybe he's horny cos she's not up to any of that right now.'

'Don't go playing up to any of his winks and smiles. He can be a charmer when he wants to be.' Annie was young enough to be his daughter and Archie knew it. That might not be enough to deter him though. Her sister had a precocious air of sophistication despite being quite childlike in some ways. And she was a flirt – even with her brother-in-law. Clover knew Annie meant nothing by it; she was simply blossoming into a woman and honing her feminine wiles. But other women might not see it that way.

'Archie Fletcher? You must be joking.' Annie was lounging against the door jamb but shrugged herself upright. 'He's too old for me and anyway he's married. You should tell Neil what he did. He'll clump him ...' Annie didn't receive a reply, so piped up. 'I'll do it if you like, Clo ...'

'Don't you dare say a word. There'll be a right bust-up and not for the first time.' Clover rolled her eyes to demonstrate the scale of the trouble they could expect. 'Keep it to yourself, please. I can deal with Archie Fletcher on my own.'

'They've had a fight over you before, haven't they?' Annie had picked up on a chance to discover some juicy family history.

'That was ages ago ... when I was younger than you are.' Clover made light of it. But it hadn't been inconsequential: she'd lost her job at the tobacconist's when Neil defended her against Archie, who wouldn't take no for an answer. Unfortunately, her boss had witnessed the scrap, and his shop window being broken in the process. The men pretended it was all in the past and were civil to one another as their wives were friends. In reality, they hadn't forgiven or forgotten anything. 'Promise you'll keep your lip buttoned.' Clover pointed warningly at her sister.

Annie nodded agreement; a second later, she put a finger to her lips and jerked a significant nod at the door.

'Everything all right?' Their hostess came into the kitchen swinging a quizzical look between the sisters. Henrietta Fletcher was balancing an eleven-month-old grizzling baby on her bloated hip.

'Sorry, it's taken a while. We've been having a natter.' Clover took the child from her pregnant friend and bounced the little girl on her forearm. Luckily, she did have some news to share. 'Annie's passed her probation as a cook's assistant and will be moving to live in at her employer's next month. I'm going to miss her.'

Annie rolled her eyes. 'You're not my mum, y'know, and got me tied to your apron strings.'

'I know ... it's just ... ' Clover shrugged wistfully.

Annie gave her a hug because her big sister had been her surrogate mum ever since Iris Cooper died during the war years.

'Still got your eye on that chauffeur fellow?' asked Henrietta with a knowing look.

'Him?' Annie curled her top lip. 'He got sacked for misconduct.'

'Oh?' Henrietta looked eager for some gossip.

'He knocked up one of the housemaids who worked over the road. She got dismissed and her mother came banging on my lady's door to complain. Right to-do it was. Gave all of us below stairs something to talk about for weeks.'

'I knew I didn't trust him,' said Clover.

'You never met him.' Annie chuckled.

'Didn't need to. Big sisters have a nose for these things.' She bounced the baby again. 'And what's up with you, little one?' Jennifer, dressed in her beautiful broderie anglaise christening gown, wasn't cheered up by her godmother's efforts and continued whimpering.

'She's teething,' said Henrietta, and wiped dribble from the child's blotchy chin.

'Pour yourself a cup of tea. I'll have her and give you a breather.'

'Could do with one, too.' Henrietta upended the teapot, took a sip of tea, then carried on filling the set cups and saucers for her guests. 'If I'd known I'd be in the family way again so soon I would've waited and had the christenings both together.'

'Should've cancelled this one,' said Annie bluntly.

'Archie didn't want to. He'd paid the vicar.'

'Never mind ... it's been a lovely summer's day,' said Clover. 'The church service went off well and then back here for nice food.' She stroked Jennifer's cheek. 'Now all we want is a smile off you, young lady.'

'You've got the magic touch,' said Henrietta as her daughter stopped crying. 'I'll be knocking on your door later when I can't get her to sleep.'

'That's what godmothers are for.' Clover wasn't feeling as cheery as she sounded. Damnable Archie Fletcher had known what buttons to push to upset her. She longed for her own baby; being a godmother was a lovely privilege but scant consolation.

The tray was loaded up with crockery and the women headed back to the front parlour, Clover balancing the tea tray and Annie carrying baby Jennifer. Once in the room the first thing Clover noticed was that Archie had had the brass neck to go and talk to her husband as though butter wouldn't melt in his mouth. Neil wasn't a fool, though. A smiling glance passed between them and made it clear he'd sensed an atmosphere. Even now after years married she got butterflies when she looked at him. In her opinion he was even more handsome in his late thirties than when she'd fallen for him in his army uniform all those years ago. Some men were lucky like that; maturity complemented their looks. She'd sensed they were soulmates straight away and told him things she'd never spoken of to anybody else ... even family. In return, he'd confided in her about his unhappy early years. They were bound by their love and trust and Archie Fletcher's attempt to drive a wedge between them was risible.

He had never grown up and still acted as though he were the flash Harry he'd fancied himself to be at twenty. His wife was younger than he was yet she looked older and careworn.

'Get these handed round, shall we?' Annie nudged Clover to stop her staring into space.

Having distributed the drinks to family and friends, Annie took a turn amusing the baby by bouncing her on her knee.

'It's a shame Jeannie couldn't make it,' said Henrietta. 'It's been ages since us three were all together.'

The trio were old friends who had attended the same school. Jeannie Swift had moved to Derbyshire with her schoolteacher husband but they kept in touch by letter. Clover Cooper had also married a decent man, whereas Henrietta Randall – or Nettie as she was known to her friends – had made things worse for herself by getting hitched to Archie Fletcher. The trouble was, Nettie wouldn't have a word said against him; her loyalty made his behaviour all the more despicable.

They had grown up in the Silvertown district of the East End of London. Clover and Nettie were closest in age, and in life's circumstances. They'd suffered similar bereavements when younger, and had remained in their childhood homes where the memories of lost loved ones resided.

'What's up, love?' Clover had watched her friend gazing solemnly at her little daughter.

'Since I got pregnant again, I've been thinking of him.' Nettie discreetly wiped away her tears with the back of her hand. 'He's old enough to be out at work now. I hope he's happy. D'you think he ever asks about me?'

'He might not know about his start in life,' Clover answered diplomatically, and urged Nettie to move away from the others so their conversation remained private.

They were the only people who knew about Nettie's firstborn child. Clover understood how her friend felt; a corner of her own mind was reserved for thoughts of a different baby boy. Unlike Nettie, he wasn't her guilty secret, but her mother's, and Iris Cooper had never properly recovered from his birth.

Clover had known about the family scandal from the start. Her siblings had been too young to be told they had a half-brother back then. Johnny and Annie now knew about their mother's illegitimate son. They had been shocked at first and bombarded Clover with questions. Over the years, knowledge of their half-brother's existence had been woven into the tapestry of tragedies that the Cooper family lived with. Time had passed and they rarely spoke of it any more although nobody had forgotten Gabriel, as Clover had called the angelic infant.

Clover noticed Archie glancing their way. He appeared slyly confident that she wouldn't tell his wife what he'd done. She itched to wipe the smirk off his face but was too fond of Nettie for that, and unfortunately he knew it. 'Does Archie ever ask questions about the baby?'

'He never mentions it.' Nettie's vigorous denial jigged her mousy curls. 'It's over and done with as far as he's concerned and I don't intend to tell him the truth now.' She bit her lip. 'Thank goodness he was fighting in France and didn't see me getting bigger. He was relieved when I wrote and told him I'd done it.'

'I remember you showing me his letter.' Clover also re-membered him joining up to escape a shotgun wedding rather than to fight for king and country. In that letter, he'd not enquired about Nettie's recovery or offered to pay the abortionist's fee. He'd simply been happy for Nettie to clear up the trouble he'd got her into. Then he'd forgotten all about that first child they might have reared together.

'Enough wallowing.' Nettie set her shoulders. 'Time to buck myself up and concentrate on the kids I have got.' She curved her hand over her big belly, and ruffled her daugh-ter's flaxen hair. 'I'm going to hand round some sandwiches before they start to curl.' She glanced over her shoulder as she headed to the sideboard. 'Fancy giving me a hand, Annie?'

While those two urged people to eat up, Clover nursed

the baby and gave her brother a smile. Johnny helped himself to food from the offered plates and toasted her, double-handed, with sandwiches. His girlfriend, however, was avoiding Clover's eye.

Dora Knox was in full warpaint and dressed to kill as usual, wearing her fox fur despite the warm August day. She had hardly spoken to anybody and Clover wondered why she'd bothered turning up if she was bored by it all.

'Can we get going now?' Dora asked as Johnny continued munching contentedly on egg and cress.

'What's the rush? Quite enjoying meself, actually.' He dipped his head to peck her cheek but she pushed him off.

'Gawd ... you stink of boiled egg now you've scoffed that lot.'

He chuckled. 'Might as well get me money's worth after laying out on the silver christening set.' He frowned. 'Jennifer seems a miserable nipper.'

'She's no oil painting either; maybe she'll grow into her looks,' said Dora, examining her painted nails. 'You could've bought me an engagement ring with what you spent. I saw one I liked while we was in the jeweller's buying Jennifer's present—'

'You've not eaten anything,' Johnny interrupted. 'Fancy a slap-up meal later?' They made a good team, but he considered Dora Knox a business associate and a girlfriend rather than a wife. Poaching her from George Payne and landing himself in big trouble in the process hadn't been a good start to a romance. She was starting to irritate him with her constant hints that it was time he married her. He wasn't sure he was the marrying sort.

'If we're going up West we could see a show,' said Dora, brightening up. 'There's a new cabaret at the Palladium.'

'Palladium it is then.'

Dora enviously watched Johnny's sisters over the top of her teacup. Unlike her, they were naturally attractive with little need of lipstick and powder. Annie Cooper was wearing the yellow dress she'd wanted to keep for herself. She hoisted the garments but Johnny let his sisters have first dibs on the best of it, pretending it had all been paid for to stay on the right side of Clover. Big Queenie was then offered the rest before Dora could dip in. She'd made a point of hiding her fur so she could keep it for herself. She received a generous slice of the profits, but resented playing second fiddle to the other women in his life. Until Johnny made her an equal partner as his wife, she needed to build her own nest egg.

Clover looked classy today in the emerald-green velvet dress – another plundered garment Dora had coveted. She knew Clover thought she was a bad influence on her brother. Yet of the two of them she was the one prepared to hang up her poacher's coat and settle down. Not so long ago she would've pitied these smug married people with their mewling children. Now, she wanted to join them, but although Johnny was a few years older than her, he was content to carry on as they were. Dora loved him but had begun to wonder if she should have stuck with George Payne after all. Seeing off Molly Deane might have been easier than prising Johnny away from the sisters he doted on.

'I've drunk enough bleedin' tea to sink a battleship.' Dora put her cup and saucer onto a side table. 'You can hang around here if you like, but I'm saying toodle-oo and going home to get changed for this evening.' She glanced at their hostess. 'I reckon Henrietta can't wait for everybody to clear off so she can put her feet up. Poor cow looks ready to pop, yet says she's not due until Christmas.'

Dora straightened her fur and noticed Archie Fletcher giving her a sly look. She'd seen him follow Clover out of the room. She wasn't surprised he'd flirt in front of his wife even on a day like this. Either Henrietta was blind or a besotted fool to put up with it. Dora turned her back on him; she didn't need those sort of looks while his wife was in the room and she was with Johnny. She had her standards.

'If I see that creep staring at my sister like that again I'm going to say something, even if it is really Neil's job to warn him off.'

'Perhaps they still fancy one another. You told me Clover walked out with Archie when she was younger.'

'Not her; Clover can look after herself ... anyhow, she hates him now. Fletcher's been eyeing Annie all afternoon.'

'I said that yellow dress was wrong for her. She's too young to show off her figure in tight clothes.'

Johnny didn't like her bitching. In his opinion his youngest sister looked beautiful. 'Come on, let's go home then.' He picked up his hat from the chair behind.

'Those two are an odd couple.' Dora glanced from mousy Henrietta to her tall blonde husband. 'I suppose it's true: opposites really do attract.'

Once they'd said their goodbyes and were outside, Johnny enlightened her. 'Don't you know what Archie Fletcher found attractive about Henrietta Randall?'

Dora had spent her early years in Hackney, then moved to the West End as a live-in domestic. She'd become acquainted with these Silvertown people later on and knew little of their histories. 'I know there must have been something in it for him, knowing what he's like,' she said cynically.

'There was. He got his hands on the Randall family's

property and drapery business when they tied the knot.'
Johnny steered the Austin away from the kerb.

'Crikey, I didn't know they actually owned that place.'

'Lock, stock and barrel.'

'Only child, was she, lucky thing?' Dora had a younger
brother who'd snatched the lot. Not that the Knox family
had much to shout about. Her late parents had run a market
stall and taken their son into the business. Dora, on the
other hand, had been removed from school at thirteen and
sent out skivvying to earn a living.

'Nettie's younger brother was in line to take over the
business but Spanish flu did for Paul Randall before he'd
left school. His mother used to boast he'd build the business
into a clothing empire.' Johnny shook his head in sympathy.
'They were an unlucky bunch, like us. Mrs Randall seemed
hard as nails but went downhill after losing her husband
and her son.' He paused. 'You heard about what happened
to Martha Randall, did you?' Johnny never usually gos-
siped; on this occasion he was hoping to distract Dora until
they'd passed the jeweller's shop in case she suggested
browsing the window display. He wouldn't put it past her
to choose one she liked then return another time to palm it
if he didn't buy it on Monday morning.

'Martha had an accident cleaning her windows, that's
what I heard.' Dora had been rummaging in her bag for
her powder compact. She flicked open the gold case and
touched up her make-up.

'Open verdict, they said at the inquest, but there were
whispers that she'd jumped. Everybody knew Martha never
got over losing her husband and son, one straight after the
other.' Johnny paused. 'After Henrietta's mother was laid to
rest, Archie Fletcher began showing a renewed interest in

the heiress of a drapery business. He was quite shameless about it, but she didn't seem to let it bother her.'

'Good luck to her then 'cos he'll never change ...' muttered Dora, and left it that.

'Have you caught sight of Jake Harding in any of the West End stores yet?' Johnny's mind had turned to his own business.

This was a question Dora had become used to hearing, although of late, the youth's name hadn't been mentioned so often. They'd both been disappointed that Jake hadn't joined them. Eight months had passed since they'd seen him, but Johnny had taken to the boy and not forgotten him. Unfortunately, he didn't have a clue how to track him down.

'I still say George Payne scared him off on Christmas Eve.'

Johnny shook his head. 'That lad's not a coward.'

'He must've got a better offer then,' Dora reasoned.

'I'd've matched it. If I knew who he works for I'd go and find him.'

Dora didn't reply; she continued applying her lipstick.

Johnny savoured the silence, relaxing into driving quietly now the High Street shops were a safe distance behind.

Chapter Nine

It took Jake over nine months to catch up with his treacherous pal.

During his search, he had quizzed neighbours and local shopkeepers. He'd gone further afield to Spitalfields and spoken to the young women they were friendly with. But nobody had laid eyes on Herbert Brick in ages.

That his widowed mother lodged somewhere in the East End and had a married daughter was the sum of Jake's knowledge of the Bricks. Herbie had never been any more forthcoming about his relatives than Jake had been about his lot. It was unlikely he would've tracked the thief back to the bosom of his family, in any case. Being shunned by their kin was what had thrown them together in the first place. Jake refused to believe they had anything else in common. His friend's rotten character had been exposed and he wouldn't be surprised if Herbie had swindled his way out of his mother's affections.

He had long abandoned thoughts of getting revenge on Herbert Brick when he suddenly struck lucky. He'd been walking along Poplar High Street having just delivered a canteen of silver cutlery to one of Old Peg's customers when a familiar figure weaselled across his line of vision and disappeared inside a tobacconist shop.

Jake retraced his steps to a street corner, concealed himself, and watched and waited. He knew Peg's silver snuff boxes would be long gone. It wasn't too late to give Herbert Brick the larruping he deserved for stealing them though. After that, he'd demand Herbie hand over every penny of the savings he'd stolen. Jake knew it was doubtful he'd get back all the cash, but whatever he ended up with he'd give to Peg. It might cheer her up. She'd been very low since her husband died and Herbie did the dirty on her. She'd little interest in the hoisting side of things now, but didn't refuse the housemaids who came to her, hiding their swag inside their coats. Jake guessed she saw herself in those young women: breaking the law for love, or to climb up a rung in a dog-eat-dog world. If one of them arrived at Peg's when he was present, he'd be banished to the outhouse before he got a glimpse of silver or gold. She continued to do her deals in private and mostly after dark and he took heart from the fact that some of the Old Peg had survived her heartaches ...

The shop bell's clatter interrupted his brooding. Herbie had exited the tobacconist's and begun to bowl in his direction. Jake withdrew into the shadows and let him pass by, tearing open his packet of cigarettes. He knew better than to start a ruck in a busy street; Herbie would seem the innocent victim, while he'd appear to be the villain deserving of punishment.

After following him at a distance for a few minutes, his quarry turned into a lane that led towards the canal. Jake knew if he took a short cut across some gardens he could emerge in front of him by the gasworks. He set off at a jog, and while clambering over fences, reminded himself of their Boxing Day escapade that had started as a lark before turning nasty.

A woman was hanging out washing in her backyard but he simply kept going, doing his best to dodge a sheet's clammy caress. She bawled abuse at him but there was no time to stop and apologise; he careered on, determined to get into position for an ambush. By the time he was tiptoeing towards the mouth of the alley, cuffing his damp face, he could gauge Herbie's proximity from a strengthening waft of tobacco smoke. Then came a tuneless whistling, as though he didn't have a care in the world. A second after he'd passed by, Jake stepped out behind him, his fists primed. 'Well, if it ain't the Scarlet Pimpernel ... ' he drawled. 'Been looking everywhere for you, mate.'

Herbie swivelled on his heel and the stub of his cigarette fell from his slack lips. His lapel was smouldering before he found the sense to brush it off.

'Not stopping to say hello?' Jake grabbed Herbie's arm as he would have run off. 'Got my money?' Herbie's mouth worked like that of a beached fish. 'How about Peg's snuff boxes then?' Jake snarled and tightened his grip when Herbie struggled to free himself.

'Dunno what you're on about,' squeaked Herbie, who looked on the point of blubbing. 'You nearly give me an 'eart attack, jumping out on me like that.'

In exasperation, Jake shoved him back against the wall of the alley. 'Why d'you do it?' he yelled in frustration, and violently shook Herbie until his head wobbled. He deserved a hiding but looked so pathetic Jake let his fists drop to his side.

'Why not?' Herbie's eventual, sullen reply came as he

shrugged himself out of his captor's grip. 'Nobody helps me so I help meself.' He pulled some copper and silver out of his pockets and dropped it into the outstretched palm that had been thrust beneath his nose.

'And the rest,' demanded Jake.

''S all I've got; search this if you want.' Herbie yanked his jacket off and defiantly flung it.

Jake let the garment slide off his chest to the floor. He looked at the coins he'd been given. They amounted to less than three shillings instead of the two pounds he'd saved. 'How much d'you get for the snuff boxes?'

'Gave one of them to a girl over Lambeth and got to stay a few nights with her.' Herbie started to smirk, then thought better of it. 'Months ago that was.'

'What about the other case?' Jake hoped Herbie still had it.

'Owed rent on a room. Tallyman took it.'

'You bloody idiot. They were solid silver and worth more than that.' Jake walked off, tutting in disgust then returned to swoop on Herbie's discarded coat. He pulled the new packet of Woodbines from a pocket. 'I'll have these as well. By my reckoning you still owe me two quid. And I want it.' Herbie stood shivering in his shirtsleeves despite the warmth of the low autumn sun. 'Won't hit you though; you're not worth it.' Jake hurled the jacket at its owner and set off again.

His pal's contempt crushed Herbie more than a beating would have done. He began to trail behind. 'I only met that girl 'cos I went over Lambeth looking for you. Was gonna give you back the money I hadn't spent. Couldn't find you though. Then I needed grub and a place to stay.' His shrug of apology for having run through his friend's savings remained unseen by Jake. 'We was a good team; we can still work together.' The suggestion earned him a snort of derision but he persevered. 'You can take all the profit till I've paid you back.' Herbie was being earnest. When his money started running out, he began to regret what he'd done; at about the same time, he'd realised he was useless on his own. He'd only managed to pick up casual work in markets and building yards since leaving Peg, and missed a regular wage and the home comforts she'd provided.

'Well, you shouldn't've bothered trying to find me 'cos I'm finished with you. I don't need a parasite on my back.'

Herbie continued to dog Jake's footsteps, veering between feeling resentful, and optimistic of bringing about a reunion. 'You ain't any better'n me. You was planning on scarpering 'n' all. That spiv offered you a job, didn't he?' He poked Jake's arm in an attempt to get his attention. 'You would've pissed off to the Elephant Boys' outfit in Lambeth and left Old Peg 'n' me in the lurch. I managed to get in first but I reckon you've ditched Peg by now ... ' He skittered backwards in alarm as Jake suddenly swung around and came after him.

'Well, you're wrong about that,' Jake snarled. 'Peg was good to both of us when we didn't have that.' He clicked his fingers in Herbie's face. 'I've stuck by her. But if I had taken up Johnny Cooper's offer, I wouldn't ever have missed a so-called pal like you.'

Herbie hung his head. 'Sorry ... ' he mumbled. 'I'll come back with you then and say sorry to Peg. Now you've taken all me money I could do with a place to stay.'

'Too late for that. She won't have you back. She's not got over coming home to the trouble you caused.' Jake wasn't going to tell him about Peg's husband dying, or any of the tragedy that went before. She wouldn't want it repeated. She'd not mentioned her late husband again and neither had he. It was his way of letting her know she could trust him with her secret.

There was a closeness between them now, bordering on real affection. If she wasn't busy with customers at supper time they ate together at her kitchen table, listening to the wireless, then shared the clearing up. Her cherished possession hadn't been bought, the Marconi had been acquired. It would never be fenced. Listening to the news broadcast on the National Programme, and a cookery talk, was a ritual Peg observed. As was the polishing of the walnut case with beeswax.

Jake felt intensely protective of her and no longer simply thought of her as his boss, but his family. Last year she would have been quite capable of looking after herself and would have made no bones about telling him so. Her ambition and energy had dwindled since she no longer needed to pay for her husband's care. She was a good woman ... and if Jake was presented with a choice he'd remain with Peg Tiller in the East End rather than move to Mayfair where his home and family used to be. So he wasn't letting Herbie open old wounds for Peg by turning up out of the blue, with or without an apology.

'I'll meet you here same time next week,' Jake said. 'And you'd better have my money. Don't come back to Peg's; if you do, I'll give you that pasting and that's a promise.' He wasn't moved by Herbie's mournful expression and turned away to cross the road.

Herbie refused to give up and trotted in his wake. 'At least give us a fag. Got nothing now ... not even snout, you bleedin' crook ...'

Jake chuckled at that but he'd had enough of Herbie whining and snapping at his ankles like a stray dog. He took the Woodbines from his pocket and lobbed them over his shoulder without losing pace. He didn't need to turn around to know that Herbie had dropped to his knees to forage in the gutter.

'You're just a jumped-up nobody reckons he's somebody. You can whistle for the money 'n' all. So don't bother coming back to find me 'cos you won't.' Herbie abandoned the chase. He stood up, lit a cigarette and moodily watched until the best friend he'd ever had disappeared around the corner without a backward glance.

Once he reached the High Street, Jake speeded up towards home. If he was delayed Peg fretted that something bad must have happened. She wouldn't let him stand in on a deal, but she allowed him to collect the cash. Their customers were mostly shady sorts, she warned him, and might pay with one hand and steal the money back with the other. He had her one pound ten shillings for the cutlery canteen safely in his pocket.

He would have liked a smoke and scolded himself for not having taken a cigarette from the pack. Jake believed Herbie's tale about searching for him in Lambeth. The toerag had wasted his time though; he hadn't been in south London since the night he'd sat by a blazing yule log in the Bricklayer's Arms many months ago. Even with a long absence, Johnny Cooper and Dora Knox had remained on his mind, as had his regrets that he'd not got to know them better.

His shoplifting days seemed to be behind him and he was glad of that. Hoisters operated best in pairs to evade the store walkers but Peg had no intention of recruiting a decoy to replace Herbie. Jake now earned his wages by acting as

Peg's handyman, and his partial apprenticeship with the builder had stood him in good stead in that respect.

This started when Mr Spooner had been laid up with a bad back after his jolly Christmas and couldn't immediately attend to Peg's broken windows. The weather had been so cold Jake had offered to fix them, thinking it was the least he could do in the circumstances. Although he'd made a mess of the putty, Peg had been impressed. From then on, he did the jobs and rather enjoyed it, too. During March, a gale took off some roof tiles; he'd replaced those while Old Peg footed the ladder. Then, as soon as the milder spring weather arrived, he had painted the outside of the house and creosoted all the fences.

She'd told him he could smarten up his own quarters if he liked. He now had the outhouse to himself and with fresh distemper on the walls and a new piece of lino on the floor – got for a song from the local totter – it was tidier and cosier.

At other times he would deliver the fancy china ornaments, assorted trinkets and silverware she fenced. Sometimes those customers gave him a sixpence tip. If they had a housemaid he might get a saucy smile. He knew an invitation when he saw one but hadn't yet taken any of them up on it. Occasionally, he went to a salubrious neighbourhood. It made him chuckle that those middle-class people were embarrassed to receive their stuff. Grim-faced women would snatch with one hand, thrust money at him with the other then slam the door in his face. And they were the most likely ones to try to get away with knocking off a shilling, hoping he wouldn't notice the shortfall in the jumble of coins landing in his hand. He always did though and wouldn't leave them in peace until they'd settled up. And no sixpence tip either.

He stopped reminiscing as a rhythmic sound he'd been vaguely aware of separated into the beat of a drum and a pipe being played in the distance. He racked his brains wondering if this was a special day. People were gathering at the kerb to crane their necks for a glimpse of the marching band that could be heard but not seen. From the snatches of conversation reaching him it seemed nobody else knew what was going on either.

The procession hove into view leaving Jake disappointed: it was nothing more than a political rally taking place. Members of the British Union of Fascists were bearing flags emblazoned with a design like a lightning bolt.

Jake's fellow spectators appeared divided in their reaction to the sight; some walked off muttering in disgust. Others cheered their support. He stayed where he was, but only because he was grounded by surprise.

The parade was flanked by rows of policemen, perhaps eight in total. Jake never forgot a face and Sergeant Drover's thin visage was still recognisable despite having gathered a small moustache and some extra furrows.

The policeman seemed uncertain of having correctly identified the blond child he'd escorted to the orphanage years ago. Before him was no curious-eyed boy but a tall youth with a strong-boned, handsome face.

Sergeant Drover appeared about to break away and come over to have a word but Jake was granted an unexpected reprieve. Not that he had anything against the fellow. Drover had actually been kind to him; but back then he had been a little innocent. Now he wasn't, and talking to coppers wasn't wise ... especially when he was under observation.

The man who might have been his stepfather, had things turned out differently, was at the centre of the parade, puffed up like a peacock. Behind Ian Winters marched George Payne, flanked by equally thuggish-looking characters. Payne kept Jake in his narrowed sights but Ian Winters' interest in the eldest of his wife's adopted sons was fleeting. Most astonishing of all to Jake was seeing Rebecca Payne dressed in a light-coloured skirt and black shirt amidst the other marchers. She did a double take then stopped dead, causing a young woman behind to crash into her. With his blond hair gleaming beneath an autumn sun, Jake Harding was unmissable to a girl who had often thought of him.

Within seconds, everybody had their attention diverted elsewhere. Protestors had seized an opportunity to disrupt the rally by raiding a stationary coal cart for ammunition. A fellow barged past Jake shouting 'fascist scum' and hurled the first missile at the column. Then, like an invasion of bloated bluebottles, coal was whizzing through the air from all directions. Those under attack started scattering to find cover. Rebecca was hit on the shoulder by a nugget thrown by a man close to Jake. He instinctively shoved the culprit to the ground before rushing into the melee to shield her with his body.

'Thanks ...' she said, rubbing soot from her cheek.

'Are you hurt?' He drew her away from the thick of it and found his handkerchief to give to her.

She shook her head. 'I saw it coming so managed to dodge the worst of it.' She wiped her mucky fingers, avoiding his eye. 'This sort of thing happens all the time on these marches.'

'Didn't know you supported this lot.' He inclined closer to be heard over the hubbub and the police whistles.

'No reason why you should.' She spoke against his cheek in a voice edged with defiance. 'Anyhow, I don't support them … they talk rot most of the time.' She glanced up, studying his face. She'd been this close to Jake when he'd dipped her pocket. On that occasion he'd brushed against her with an ulterior motive and she'd only glimpsed his features. There was nothing else on his mind today while their bodies lightly touched. She felt butterflies dance in her stomach as he continued looking at her. She'd been right about his green eyes. 'If I had my way I wouldn't associate with them.' She glanced down at her outfit in slight embarrassment. 'My dad is the one who likes this sort of stuff. He drags me along to make up the numbers and to get in Mosley's good books. They're always after new recruits …' She raised her dark eyebrows and gave him a cheeky smile.

'No thanks.' Jake choked a laugh, thinking those huge brown eyes of hers were the prettiest he'd ever seen. 'Not interested in politics. Is Mosley here? I didn't see him.'

She shook her head, and her thick brown hair swung in its blue enamel clips. 'He lets his willing acolytes do his dirty work.'

'Acolytes …' Jake sounded mockingly impressed. 'You've had an education.'

'So have you if you know what it means,' she shot back.

'Yeah … some …' he said drily. 'Well, I'm glad you did come along. I wanted to see you.' He paused. 'I've looked for you a few times in the West End. Never saw you up there so thought you must be a reformed character.'

Deliveries sometimes took him close to the shopping district and he'd keep an eye out for Rebecca. Once he'd spotted Dora Knox instead. Reluctant to be questioned about why he'd not been in touch, he'd kept out of sight. After he'd gone quiet on them, she and Johnny would have written him off as a kid who wasn't ready for the big time.

109

'I've been thinking about you ... wanting to say sorry about ... well, you know what about.' Jake urged Rebecca along the pavement out of range of two men grappling on the ground, rolling close to their feet.

'Mmm ... I haven't forgotten about that, Jake Winters.' She tutted, but a hint of a smile lifted a corner of her mouth. 'Thanks for rescuing me, but I'd better go before he comes over.' She sent a nervous glance her father's way, but there seemed to be little likelihood of George Payne quitting the fight. He was energetically defending himself, his daughter's welfare apparently forgotten.

'I wanted to thank you as well as say sorry.' Jake caught hold of her arm to stop her leaving. 'I would've got a clump on Christmas Eve. Probably deserved it too. Why didn't you grass me up to your father? You knew it was me took the wallet from you.'

'Bet there wasn't much money in it, was there?' she answered obliquely. 'Why d'you risk lifting it?' She sounded genuinely curious.

Jake wanted to tell her but it wasn't the right time to explain his relationship to Toby. Or that he wasn't Jake Winters, as she thought. She'd picked the pocket of a fellow fascist's stepson and he wondered how she and her father would feel about knowing that. 'Did your father punish you for losing it?'

'Mum wouldn't let him,' she said.

Jake gestured regret for having put her in danger. 'I really am sorry.'

''S all right. I didn't want you to get hit either. All's fair in love and war, after all.' She smiled and took a step away then, on impulse, darted back to briefly embrace Jake and peck his cheek. 'See ... I forgive you, Jake Winters.

Anyway, we're quits now. Are you working with Johnny Cooper?'

Jake shook his head, and would have explained more about himself.

'Damn! He's spotted us.' Rebecca interrupted on a sigh. 'Must go or he'll come over. He'll be in a mood after this, and might take it out on you. He hasn't forgotten you, y'know.'

'Neither did you,' said Jake with a smile. 'Can I see you again?' he called as she moved further away.

She glanced back with a shrug.

'I won't forget you, Rebecca.'

'I know you won't ... not after today ... '

'You'd best get going, young lady. It's safe now to join your associates. I'll convey your thanks to Mr Harding for shielding you from the worst of it.' Rebecca's arm was gripped by Sergeant Drover, who ushered her towards the marchers. The police had drawn batons and regained control of the situation by forming a cordon around the fascists, putting them beyond the reach of the angry mob. Word had got round about the rally and more protestors had arrived to throng the pavements. Those reluctant to give up the fight were being handcuffed.

Drover's colleagues began herding the marchers into a side street but he stayed behind to speak to Jake. 'What a nice surprise. I'm right, aren't I? You're Jake Harding. I've not forgotten you. Do you remember me, son?'

'I do, sir ... '

'Well, how have you been then?' Drover beamed and patted Jake's arm in a paternal way. 'You look to have done all right for yourself, lad. I'm very pleased about that.'

Jake could see Rebecca frowning in his direction. She was

wondering why he'd lied about his name . . . or maybe she could guess why he'd hide his identity from her brute of a father. George Payne turned around at that precise moment, making Jake curse beneath his breath. He knew how that man would take seeing him being friendly with a copper.

The band of musicians had defiantly struck up again and the protracted drum roll made it necessary for Jake to raise his voice. 'I've been well, sir, thank you.' He gave the sergeant his full attention.

'And your family?' Basil Drover was curious to know whether the reunion he'd hoped for had come about. He had never forgotten Jake Harding's manner when he'd been a boy. He seemed the same character now. Charismatic . . . confident . . . a clever boy.

'I believe they are well, sir.' Jake gave up trying to watch Rebecca as the procession started turning a corner. 'I have to get going, but it was nice to see you again.'

'And you, young man . . . and you.' Drover thrust out his hand to be shaken before hurrying away to organise the reinforcements gathering in response to the police whistles.

People were going back about their business now the excitement was over. A scattering of coal on the highway and a faint drumbeat were the only reminders of what had occurred. The coalman had abandoned the purloined stock and had driven off. Thrifty housewives saw an opportunity though. They emerged from premises up and down the streets, carrying baskets and scuttles to collect what they could.

Jake headed towards home with Rebecca and her father on his mind. He hoped he'd not got her another scolding for talking to him. Then he thought of Ian Winters; that fellow had made himself scarce during the brawl rather than stand shoulder to shoulder with his fellow fascists. Jake wasn't surprised. It was easy to imagine Toby's stepfather as a coward.

Ian Winters and Violet Harding were cut from the same cloth. If she had been a brave sort, she would have fought for her two adopted sons to grow up together as a family.

They didn't need her help now though. Jake knew if he and Toby were to make up for the lost years it would be up to them to arrange a reunion themselves.

Chapter Ten

On reaching home, Jake found the gate was ajar although he'd locked it on his way out. He always did now Peg had given him his own key and her rules for its use. A knot of unease was forming in his guts as he dashed along the path that wound around the house to the side door. Nobody used the front entrance apart from the postman looking for a letterbox. Peg's customers would let her know they'd arrived by yanking on the bell pull by the gate, making it clatter in the kitchen.

The side door was also open and he could hear male voices. Mr Spooner was standing in the kitchen conversing in hushed tones with a dapper little fellow. They turned to see who had burst in on them.

'This is Doctor Bates, lad.' Mr Spooner introduced the stranger, while pressing a hand down on his coarse greying hair. 'Something's happened to Old Peg, y'see, and I had to do something as you wasn't about. She wouldn't come to at first and I was that worried—'

'Where is Peg?' Jake interrupted.

The two men exchanged a sombre glance. 'Mrs Tiller's in the parlour, resting,' said Dr Bates. 'Your neighbour luckily happened upon her lying in the street and he summoned me.'

'Lying in the street? Why?' demanded Jake, anxiety gnawing at him. 'Was she attacked?' The riot was still on his mind and he immediately thought the worst. He started for the parlour, eager to speak to her, but the doctor barred his way, peering over his spectacles at him.

'You must settle down before seeing her, young man. She's quite poorly and shouldn't be agitated. There's no foul play. I believe her heart is causing the trouble. I advise hospital rest as these things can deteriorate very quickly. The nurses will keep her under observation.'

'Hospital? She won't go there!' declared Jake, who was aware of her aversion to such places.

'So she keeps saying ... ' Bates shoved his glasses up the bridge of his nose and rolled his eyes as though he'd done with attempting to persuade her. 'She's been asking for you. Perhaps you might have more success in making her see sense. I'd sooner she went from here in an ambulance than a hearse.'

Jake read from the doctor's stern expression that it was time for unvarnished truths. 'I will speak to her about it,' said Jake although his own heart was thumping erratically as he entered the room.

Peg had been put on the couch and covered up with the crocheted blanket that usually adorned its back. 'Where have you been? Did you get paid?' Peg asked, making Jake sigh in relief as he sank to his knees on the floor beside her. There was surely not that much wrong with her then.

'Of course ... ' He patted his pocket and rested back onto his heels. 'Now what have you been up to while I was out?' He took one of her bony hands in his, managing to sound mildly reproachful; more the adult than the child.

'Oh, it's a fuss about nothing. I thought I'd nip to the

115

shop for some snuff as you wasn't here to fetch it,' she said defensively. 'I had a funny turn, that's all.' She glanced at him from beneath her heavy eyelids, gauging his reaction to her making light of it.

'Sorry I was late back. There was a fascist rally passing through Poplar High Street and I got caught up in it.'

'Mosley's lot, you mean?' She sounded interested in hearing about it.

He nodded and told her a bit about what had happened, reassuring her he had only been a bystander to the fighting. 'And you'll never guess who I ran into while I was out, Peg,' he carried on talking as she seemed to like hearing him telling a tale.

'Who?'

'Herbert Brick.'

She gave a tsk of disgust and her animation faded.

'He looked ashamed of himself, and said he was sorry for what he did and to pass that on to you.' Jake had hoped hearing Herbert's apology might buck her up but it seemed to have had the opposite effect. She fidgeted and complained of feeling cold so he tucked the blanket more firmly about her. He returned to the topic that had kept her entertained, but hearing about the rabble pelting coal at the fascists didn't amuse her for long. She turned her head away from him and a quiet descended on the room, broken only by the uneven rasp of her breathing.

He knew he shouldn't stall any longer. 'Doctor Bates says you should go to hospital, Peg, and let the nurses look after you. I'll come and visit you, if you like ... and you needn't worry about business either. I'll keep things ticking over nicely until you get back. Probably only be in there a little while, won't you.' He gave her a smile. 'Need you back as soon as possible though 'cos you're the one keeps me on my toes.' He added, 'D'you remember teaching me 'n' Herbie to dip a pocket?'

"Course I do,' she said.

Old Peg had taught her apprentices using a bell attached to a garment's pocket. Her father had been a pickpocket and her mother a shoplifter and she'd admitted that was how she'd acquired her skills.

'If the bell tinkled you made us try again until the wallet came out clean.' Jake chuckled. 'As for the sales counter you set up on the table, we never saw you lift a thing from it even though we were watching you like hawks.' Jake's praise wasn't simply flattery. While strutting around the kitchen table boasting that indeed she could hoist herself if she needed to, Old Peg had astonished them by producing items from a pocket, lifted while she'd distracted them with bluster.

Peg smiled and gave a wink of a droopy eyelid. 'Wouldn't have tried to train you if I couldn't do better than you.'

Jake continued to speak to her in a normal way about this and that, but he knew this wasn't at all normal. And he wasn't fooling himself or her by pretending he thought it was. He'd never seen her like this before. Her complexion had turned a horrible colour, similar to the putty he had used on the windows. 'Please go to hospital, Peg,' he said.

Peg grimaced her refusal to be taken elsewhere and closed her eyes. 'I know I could trust you to run the show, but I ain't getting stuck in 'ospital. I've spent all the time I will in those places as a nurse and visitor.' She tightened her fingers on his. 'I won't try and pull the wool over your eyes then. I know what's wrong with me and I know what's next.' She squinted at him. 'I've had these pains in me chest for a while. I'm not scared, Jake. And neither must you be.'

117

Jake knew he was scared, and exasperated, too. 'Why didn't you say you weren't feeling well? The doctor could've come sooner if you'd said.'

'Pah! Would've got carted off in the meat wagon sooner, that's why. I've managed to stay in me own home and carry on, haven't I?' She ended on a triumphant note. 'That's all people want when approaching the end of the line ... just to be left alone to curl up their toes in their own beds.'

'I'm glad then you kept it to yourself.' He wasn't sure he was being truthful but she seemed soothed by his words, taking his hand to pat. 'I'd rather you listened to the doctor's advice, though. I want you to get better, Peg.'

She ignored his hesitant plea and began reminiscing in a dreamy tone. 'Me 'n' my husband ... Dickie, was his name ...' She turned her head to give Jake a ghost of a smile. 'Well, we had so many plans when we was young and first married. We wanted to buy a motorbike and sidecar after the war was over. Travel around the country and find a spot by the sea to live. The Smoke wasn't for us no more. We'd had enough of it after being brought up in Silvertown, y'see. The place was all factory smoke, like a fog was down, even in summer. There it was right along the river.' A weak arm meandered in the air, demonstrating the flow of the Thames. 'During the Great War when the munitions factories were pumping out fumes day 'n' night ... well it was bad.' She sucked her teeth in emphasis. 'And then there was the disaster. Told you about that, didn't I?'

He confirmed with a nod that she had. The dreadful explosion at the Brunner Mond plant had happened during the war, shortly after his birth, making him wonder where he, as a tiny infant, had been when the East End was blown to bits. He supposed his unknown birth mother might have protected him against that danger and all others until she could no longer afford to keep him.

'We'd settle down and have our family somewhere like Yarmouth, in briny air,' Peg resumed her reminiscence of her salad days with her beloved Dickie. 'Or Lowestoft ... that was a favourite place too. We'd travelled there on the train, you see, and stayed for a few days at a boarding house. We caught crabs and paddled in the sea. Dickie was going to teach me to swim ... '

She fell quiet but Jake didn't interrupt. He squeezed her fingers to let her know he liked listening to her memories.

'None of it happened down here. Maybe when we're back together up there we'll get a second chance at an adventure. Keep an eye out for us ... ' She jerked her head heavenward. 'You might see us whip over the clouds on our motorbike ... that's if I'm let through the pearly gates, o' course. What with me being a bad sort.' She gave him a wink, but a small tear leaked from the corner of her eye.

'Don't say that ... you're not bad. You're as good as they get, Peg.'

'You don't know all of me, Jake. I think you're as good as they get.' She forced brightness into her hoarse voice. 'You'll rise above being associated with me or the likes of Johnny Cooper.' She tightened her grip on his sleeve. 'He's a lovable rogue ... but a rogue all the same, and you're not. You remember it.' She relaxed back, settling her head on the cushion. 'Dickie wanted a son; a boy like you would've made us both proud.' She turned her eyes from his anxious face and stared at the ceiling. 'You've something of the gentleman about you and will make a fine husband and father when the time comes.' The room became quiet. The autumn sun dropped away from the slit in the curtains and the light in the room faded. Peg smacked her lips together as though thirsty.

Thinking she was dry from talking for a while, Jake got up and offered her the glass of water on the chest but she turned away from it.

'Don't you forget Old Peg. And remember as well, I did all those wrong things for the best reasons. I'm not ashamed; when I lost Dickie all them years ago, I never needed the sort of comfort comes with bad consequences. But don't mean I can't understand women risking it. In here ... ' She wobbled a finger to press against her forehead. 'I know I was right to do what I did for everybody concerned. I'd do it again. Dickie got the care and respect he deserved ... I made sure of it. Oh, I'd do it again for him.' She burrowed back into her bed with a serene sigh.

Jake wasn't sure what she was talking about; he imagined she referred to the light-fingered housemaids bringing her the wherewithal to pay her husband's nursing home fees. Then again he wondered if she was delirious because she'd never spoken about it in riddles before. He simply said, 'Couldn't ever forget you, Peg.' He tried to reclaim her fingers but she wriggled them free of his, raising the hand to cup his cheek.

'You're ready to be the boss, Jake. I've got such faith in you.' She paused for breath. 'That posh woman ... your adopted mother who put you in the orphanage ... she was a fool to miss out on having a boy like you. Her loss ... my gain.' A weak growl of triumph was in her voice.

On impulse, Jake dipped his head and kissed her sunken cheek. He'd answered some questions about his past when he'd first got a job with Peg. But she hadn't pried unduly and he'd been grateful. A mixture of loyalty and shame for not being wanted were to blame for his natural reticence when asked about his family.

'Ask the doctor to come in, Jake. I want to speak to him alone.'

While the doctor was with Peg, Jake and Mr Spooner remained in the kitchen, sitting opposite one another at the pine table. The middle-aged handyman had his donkey-jacketed elbows planted on the wood and his chin propped on his hands. He looked defeated and Jake guessed he was feeling guilty for having called the doctor against Peg's will.

'You did the right thing, Mr Spooner.'

The fellow sat up straight with a sigh. 'She didn't 'arf create when she come round and knew I'd sent for Bates.' He shook his head. 'Well, I told her it was him or the coppers as I could see she might keel over again. I didn't want a corpse on me hands to explain away.' He gave Jake an old-fashioned look. 'And we both know, don't we, that she wouldn't want the law nosing around in here.'

Most long-standing neighbours – of which there weren't very many as people drifted in and out of Rook Lane and its lodging houses all the time – knew that Peg Tiller ducked and dived as they'd benefited from her services. Mr Spooner was one such. His wife was a char and occasionally little odds and ends fell into her bag while she was cleaning the big houses over the other side of town. Nobody really saw it as stealing ... more perks of the job and evening up things between rich and poor. There was more to Peg Tiller though than shifting hooky gear, and few people admitted to knowing what it was in case a question followed about how they came to know such a thing.

'Groaning something chronic she was with the pain in

her chest, and still giving me earache for saving her,' Mr Spooner concluded in a martyred tone.

'I know she's stubborn,' said Jake with half a smile; it was an understatement if ever there was one.

'Cor, she is a stubborn cow!' Spooner forcefully agreed. But he understood why she didn't want to go to hospital. Neither would he in her position. Most people round here considered being sent to hospital a final step towards the cemetery. Those places were for sick infants and for old people. The others in between sorted themselves out. And Peg was his wife's age, forty-two, despite her looking ancient.

Mr Spooner had known Peg Tiller since she set up home in the corner house many years ago. He himself would have liked that end-of-terrace property but back then he couldn't afford the rent the landlord wanted. With a growing family of seven children to feed and clothe, he and his wife had made do with what they had. The biggest house on Rook Lane, with its two entrances and spacious backyard, would have been ideal for a man in his line of work, though. After Peg bought the house he'd approached her several times about renting the outhouse to him to store his tools and ladders, but she'd no interest in doing a deal. When he'd got to understand more about her and the youths she employed, he'd realised she needed the accommodation herself and no more was said about it. After this mishap Peg might decide it was time to slow down, but Spooner wasn't sure the place appealed any more. He only had one daughter still at home and she was courting; the others had all flown the coop. He was less interested in expanding his horizons now the kids were settled and he was over his half-century. It seemed an odd quirk of nature that the need to house and feed offspring came when a couple were starting out and least likely to be able to afford the blighters.

'Seems Doctor Bates might stop here for a while then,' said Mr Spooner after several minutes of sitting quietly with only the clock on the mantel shelf to listen to, and the closed parlour door to stare at. 'I'll be off now as I've work to do.' He pushed back his chair and stood up. 'If you need any help later, come along and find me, lad. I won't mind. Don't take no notice of what I said just now; I'm feeling a bit battered by it all, you know.'

'I do know, and thank you.' Jake also rose from the table and closed the side door on their neighbour's departure. He approached the parlour, straining to hear voices within, keen to know what was happening. It was eerily quiet. His fingers were stretching for the handle when he was forced back by Dr Bates exiting the room with his medical case grasped in his hand. 'How is she, Doctor?' Jake hissed. 'Has she changed her mind about the ambulance?'

The doctor closed the door behind him before answering. 'Unfortunately not.' He gave Jake a thoughtful look. 'I've given her a dose of laudanum to ease her pain. She's resting peacefully; before she dozed off she told me all about her husband and that there are no blood relatives to contact about her condition.' He paused. 'I had no idea the woman has had such troubles weighing on her.'

'She's not been herself since Christmas when her husband passed away. After that ... when her hope had gone ... she was different: downhearted most of the time.'

'Ah, hope is a marvellous thing ... grief an equally powerful force that can break hearts and spirits.' The doctor gave a sorrowful headshake and opened his case to delve inside.

Jake bit his lip to still its quivering. He didn't need to be told Peg was likely to die to know it. But he had to be an adult about this. He'd promised her he'd keep things ticking over if she went to hospital, and seeing him crying like a baby wouldn't give her confidence that he could. If he used the right tactics he might succeed in persuading her to change her mind about the hospital.

When his father had been murdered, he and Toby had been shielded from the worst of it. They hadn't been allowed to attend the funeral. Toby had been deemed too young to go, especially in the awful circumstances. Jake had been kept away as well, to prevent any favouritism, he supposed. They'd had lessons as usual with their tutor. When their mother returned she had changed out of her black clothes and told them very little of what had happened when their father had been laid to rest. After that, nothing more was said about the husband and father who'd shared their house, right up until the day Sergeant Drover turned up to take Jake away.

He regretted not being allowed to say a last goodbye at the funeral, and to taste the sharpest grief. It would have prepared him for today.

Jake's thoughts were broken by Dr Bates clinking bottles as he continued to fiddle in his case. He extracted an envelope that had slipped to the bottom and offered it to Jake. 'Mrs Tiller said you are her chosen next of kin. She said she considers you as her adopted son, and her friend. She had this locked in a drawer and asked me to give it to you. You might want to read it later on ... ' His elevated eyebrows and a paternal pat on the arm let Jake know he advised waiting to see what transpired in the next few days.

Jake took the envelope bearing his name. A steady hand had penned the bold script. She had written her goodbye to him before today, confirming she'd known she was ill for quite a time. 'Is she asleep? Can I talk to her?' Jake stuffed the letter into a pocket, hoping he might be able to leave it unread for a long while … perhaps until Peg was back to normal and asked for its return.

'You can sit with her if you like and I expect she will hear what you say to her even if she seems half-asleep.' The doctor closed his case with a click. 'I will come back at the end of my evening surgery and see how things are then.'

After Bates had left, Jake poked his head around the door and gazed at Peg. She seemed to be breathing more easily so he retreated to the kitchen table and sat down. He felt a cup of tea might soothe his jitters but hadn't the energy to get up again and make it.

So much had happened in the space of one day that he felt overwhelmed. Despite his concern for Peg, other people remained on his mind. Rebecca … Herbie too. His rotten betrayal had contributed to Peg's decline, Jake was sure of it, and he wished now he'd given Herbie the thrashing he deserved. He pulled from his pocket the cash the wretch had given him, dumping the fistful of coins on the table. He rummaged again to retrieve the one pound ten shillings he'd been paid for the canteen of cutlery. His fingers probed this way and that and found nothing. He pulled his pocket inside out. Nothing … no banknotes caught up in his handkerchief that bore soot stains from Rebecca's skin …

He slumped against the chair with a groan of denial. He blocked his suspicions about Rebecca and thought of the other people he'd seen earlier. The protestors had been too busy rioting to bother stealing from him. Herbie was a prime candidate; but he wasn't guilty of this. He had kept his distance in case he got a clump. Besides, Herbie had the skills of a hippo when dipping and had always set the bell ringing during their training sessions with Old Peg.

Rebecca's slender fingers could pick a pocket without a mark knowing. Jake had watched her do so. And she had come right up to him to hug and kiss him before they parted. He didn't want to believe her affection had been false ... a means to an end. But more memories crushed his conceit: she'd told him they were quits now and that he'd remember her all right after today.

And so he would ... with mixed feelings. A rueful smile tugged at Jake's mouth. He felt grudging admiration for Rebecca Payne getting one over on him like that. Nevertheless, had she known what he was heading home to, he hoped she wouldn't have done it.

He'd liked seeing her again and had enjoyed their sparky conversation so much he'd been blind to mischief. Perhaps she'd done it to keep her father off her back; producing a prize would give her a reason for stopping to talk to him today. He'd praise Rebecca for getting money and revenge rolled into one like that.

Jake stood up and made some tea, and from habit, filled two cups. He opened the parlour door again and called softly to Peg to discover if she was awake and would like a drink.

There was no reply, only the sound of her rattling snores.

Chapter Eleven

'Him?' The landlord of the Rose and Crown blew a derisive phew through his lips. 'Not seen him in here for months. Maybe he's on late shift. You should try the railway yard.' He continued polishing water spots off a glass. 'What you after him for? Ain't exactly a popular sort . . . not with other blokes, anyhow.' The gleaming tankard was put on a shelf and he turned around, but the fellow asking questions had gone.

Neil Ryan stepped out of the pub into freezing December air. He was cold, hungry and ready to give up the search. He'd been in and out of numerous likely drinking holes and bookies haunts, but drawn a blank. He was considering conceding defeat and calling it a night. His quarry could be anywhere; he was an individual capable of disappearing when it suited him, or of breezing up behind you without warning.

It seemed a showdown might have to wait but he was reluctant to let it; he had more than one grievance to air and a fist itching to put some impact behind his argument. He'd promised Clover no fighting and he'd bring the wretch safely back to face the music. She'd be disappointed if he let her down.

Cursing in frustration, Neil set off towards home but indecision brought him to a halt fairly quickly. He propped his back against the wall of the dairy, and took a moment to think. Having pulled up his collar, he shoved his hands deep into his pockets. His knuckles made contact with his tobacco tin and he drew it out. Beneath the gas lamp bracketed on the wall he formed a roll-up, persuading himself to give it another half an hour. It was possible he'd get his break after the pubs turned out at closing time. There were a few small establishments he'd not yet visited. Cupping a hand around a struck match, he was dragging on the cigarette when a rumble of throaty laughter drifted on the still air. He took the cigarette from his mouth and strained to listen. Next came a woman's giggle, abruptly cut off as though a hand had muffled her mouth. He peered into the gloom and glimpsed a brief glow from a match before it died.

His aching feet regained some spring as he headed noiselessly across the road to the municipal park. A few whispered words from a voice he was sure he recognised reached his ears. Lady Luck might not be such a bitch after all then, he thought, peering through the iron railings. On the other side of the barrier was a hedge, and bare branches were blocking his view. By stretching his hand through the opening to separate twigs he could make out two merged silhouettes. The couple were by a tree trunk and it didn't take long to determine which of them had fair hair. Neil reckoned he'd found his man.

After pinching out his roll-up, he wedged it behind his ear then jogged quietly along the pavement to the spot where the railings had been purposefully prised apart at some time in the dim and distant past. Kids ... and others ... used this access after the park keeper locked up at dusk. The lads might play a forbidden game of football on the bowling green; others had more illicit uses for the place after dark. Once inside, he made his stealthy approach through undergrowth, hoping they didn't hear him and scatter: he wasn't up to a game of chase. When closer, it became clear they were too occupied to have noticed an elephant crashing through the bushes. Through the gloom Neil could see Romeo was wearing his railwayman's uniform. The cap had managed to withstand the rollicking activity and remained jauntily clinging to the back of his head. Periodically a red dot appeared as he dragged on his cigarette. Ever the gentleman, Neil thought, and almost laughed until he remembered there was nothing amusing about the reason he was here.

'Reckon it's time you got home to your wife. You're about to be a father again.'

The passionate groan rolling out of Archie Fletcher's mouth was gulped back and he sprung away from the woman, leaving her to steady herself against the tree. She swore in annoyance at his rough treatment and hurriedly straightened her clothes.

She was keeping her face averted but Neil had recognised her and said sourly, 'Well, well, who'd've thought it ...' He liked his brother-in-law and for that reason alone had disregarded the rumour that Johnny's girlfriend was all fur coat and no knickers. An error of judgement, it transpired.

'There's a name for blokes like you who creep about spyin' on people.' Archie Fletcher had almost jumped out of his skin but believed in attack being the best defence. He hurled the smouldering cigarette onto the ground in a show of belligerence.

'Yeah ... and there's a name for you, 'n' all,' Neil drawled. 'Thing is, you ain't people, mate, you're Nettie's husband, God help her. And the name for me, if you're looking for one, is mug. I could be sat in front of the fire eating me supper, instead of tramping the streets after a useless article like you.' He poked Archie's puffed-out chest hard enough to knock him back a step. 'Your wife's in labour. The handywoman was with her when I got sent out to find you. That was hours ago so could be it's over with now.' His lip curled as he took in Archie's fake indignation. The bastard knew he was in the wrong but was maintaining an air of injury, as though he'd been interrupted taking a stroll instead of fornicating against a tree. 'Your wife's been worrying herself sick that something's happened to you as you're not home from work.' He paused as a vision of Nettie's contorted face came into his mind. She'd been almost delirious with pain from her contractions, yet crying for her husband. ''S all right, I won't tell her what job I found you on. And that's for her benefit, not yours.'

'I never knew ... honest ... he never said his wife was due to drop the baby.' Dora had met Archie in the pub and he'd bought her a few drinks to soften her up before suggesting they went on elsewhere. It hadn't taken much persuasion to get her to go in the park with him. If he hadn't suggested it, she might have, being as she was short on rent this week.

'You've got eyes in your head,' said Neil. 'You didn't really think she had a bun in there, did you?'

'No need to be sarky ...' Dora retorted. 'Just saying I didn't know it was her time. She's been bloody enormous for ages ...'

'Shut up ...' Archie growled at her. 'This ain't none of your business.'

130

'Thanks very much,' Dora snapped. 'Seem to remember you wanted my business minutes ago.'

Neil interrupted their bickering that was sending a fog of alcoholic fumes into the icy air. 'Get going, Fletcher.' He thumbed over his shoulder. 'You've got a family needs looking after.'

Archie licked his lips. He genuinely hadn't been expecting this; his wife had seemed fine when he left the house at seven o'clock that morning to head to the station. She'd opened up the drapery, and hadn't nagged, as she normally did, about him packing up his job to take over running the business so she could concentrate on their growing family. Being beneath his wife's gaze all day long while she was upstairs in the flat wasn't for him. It would be too claustrophobic for Archie, who liked his freedom. The till wasn't ringing as much and the dole queues were growing. He reminded his wife they'd be fools to give up his railway income the way things were nowadays. Nettie couldn't argue with that.

'False alarm,' Archie dismissed with a hand flick. 'Baby ain't due yet. She told me that this morning.'

'Seems nobody told the nipper that; now go home and don't try to slope off elsewhere.' Neil took a menacing step closer. 'I won't be so polite when I find you next time.'

Archie barged past and broke into a trot towards the gap in the railings without another word for either of them.

'Oi ... you; what about me?' Dora was piqued at being summarily abandoned, especially as he hadn't paid her yet. It wasn't their first liaison ... or even their tenth. She and Archie had known each other for years. Archie Fletcher had been a latchkey kid with no backside in his trousers before he got lucky and got an apprenticeship on the railways.

Dora knew he was no good; she wouldn't be interested in anything permanent with him, or anybody else, while Johnny remained on her mind. She still needed to pay her rent though and glared after Archie, wishing she wasn't a sucker for a promise from a man after he bought her a few gins.

Neil was also watching Fletcher's departure, reminding himself he'd done enough and should be satisfied now. But he wasn't. He let Archie get a good distance away, out of earshot of Dora, then bounded after him and hauled him back before he could escape into the street. Spinning him around by the shoulder, Neil landed a jab on his chin . . . not hard enough to slow him down or be considered a fight, but enough to make him stagger and lose his cap. 'Stay away from my wife. I find you crawling around Clover again I'll kill you.'

Archie put a hand to his cut lip. It came away sticky and he smeared the blood between his fingers. 'Whatever she's told you, she's lying.' He gave Neil a vicious smile then swiped up his hat from the ground.

'She didn't need to tell me. I've got these . . . ' Neil tapped a finger close to his eye. He hadn't forgotten Archie following Clover around at the christening months ago. He'd asked her about it afterwards and she'd admitted her friend's husband had tried to flirt with her . . . as he did with any woman under sixty, she'd pointed out. Neil reckoned there'd been more to it, and they'd almost argued, as they always seemed to lately when Fletcher's name cropped up. There had been more recent occasions when Neil had noticed Archie directing lustful glances at her when he thought nobody was watching. He knew he shouldn't be jealous, and probably wouldn't be, but for the fact his wife

132

had once been Fletcher's girlfriend. He stopped himself brooding on it when more important things were happening indoors. 'Go on, sod off.' He jerked a nod at the street. 'We'll finish this another time.'

'Yeah ... we certainly will, mate.' Archie dusted off his prized possession by bashing it against his leg before putting it on and adjusting the brim. This wasn't enough of a last word for him though. He knew Dora had witnessed him being knocked flying; he was boiling inside, bent on revenge. 'You can have me leftovers again if you like, Ryan.'

Archie jutted his chin at the woman behind making herself presentable, but Neil knew the insult was really directed at Clover. 'No thanks,' he said through set teeth. 'Reckon Dora fancies a man in uniform. What else could she see in you?' Fletcher strutted about in his railway gear even on days off to attract female attention.

'This is what women see in me ...' Archie boastfully cupped his groin. 'You're a bit lacking in that department ain't you, pal? I feel sorry for you but it's pretty obvious why your missus begs me to do your job for you when you're firing blanks.' He was prepared for retaliation, and dodged Neil's fist to duck down and squeeze his lanky frame through the railings. His running footsteps and hoots of triumphant laughter could be heard seconds later.

'Bloody bastard ... '

'Me or him?' Neil turned to see Dora marching up to him.

'Both of you,' she snapped. About to follow her lover into the street she hesitated and turned back. 'You won't ...'

'Tell Johnny?' Neil finished for her. 'Why shouldn't I?'

'I'd be obliged, that's why.' She shrugged. 'I'm fancy-free and entitled to do what I like, but I know Johnny hasn't told you lot about us breaking up yet.' This was true; they had gone their separate ways but Dora was hoping it wasn't for good. She didn't want Johnny to know how she'd been caught out or there'd be no chance of them getting back together. Her ultimatum that either he married her or they were over had backfired. Dora was a good hoister but she was useless negotiating to shift the stuff and always ended up short-changed. She needed Johnny for that. He was fairly easy-going but he despised Archie Fletcher, as a lot of men did.

'None o' my business what you and Johnny get up to.' Neil saw Johnny for what he was: a petty crook with big ambitions, who lacked the brutishness required to make the big time. And that's why Neil liked him; despite everything, Johnny Cooper had his heart in the right place. He sympathised with Clover's frustration with her younger brother, though. Johnny was in his late twenties but acted like a kid with a moustache.

'Ladies first . . . but I am in a bit of a rush,' Neil prompted ironically, jabbing a nod at the exit Dora was blocking and seemed in no hurry to use.

This rugged fellow with his sable hair and penny-coloured eyes was rather a dish in Dora's opinion. Being stranded with him in the shrubbery was arousing her almost as much as Archie had. A bit more, maybe. Archie could be a selfish lover but Dora reckoned this one would be more of a gentleman about it, with his 'ladies first' attitude. She reached out and ran a hand over his sleeve then linked their fingers. 'Clover's a lucky woman. There's something about you, Neil Ryan. Can't quite put me finger on what it is. Like to help me try, would you?' She skimmed their clasped hands over her bosom.

'You gotta be kidding me, love . . .' The Gallic lilt in his accent was heightened by incredulity as he disentangled himself from her clutch.

'I'm not.' She shrugged and cocked her head coyly. 'Nobody needs to know ...'

'Jeezus wept ...' With a sigh, he moved her out of the way and once outside on the pavement started briskly towards home.

He was close to the banks of the Thames, passing the site of what had once been the Brunner Mond munitions plant, when moving shadows caught his eye, making him slow down to investigate.

Having established it was simply déjà vu, he kept going, reluctant to be accused of being a peeping Tom for the second time in one evening. He was some yards further on from the alley when a frown creased his face. He was imagining things, he told himself, finding phantoms in courting couples.

This eerie wasteland held ghosts aplenty. He had the same thought each time he was close to it. In his mind's eye he saw the area as it had once been, when terraced cottages and the fire station had stood adjacent to the huge munitions works. Secure behind its high iron gates, the place had pumped out sulphurous smoke and bombs, day and night, during the war years. No enemy aircraft had felled Brunner Mond, it was destroyed from within; the TNT being processed had exploded, turning the vicinity into rubble and ashes. Clover had sunk for a while beneath her grief. Even now she avoided coming near this empty space ... too many heartbreaking memories, she said. Two of the people she loved had been lost on that awful night.

Neil recalled frantically searching for her, as she searched for her relatives amidst the blazing ruins. Her grandmother had been on the late shift, and had perished along with many of her colleagues. Clover had learned later that her father had been spotted outside the doomed factory before it went up. Sidney Cooper had never been seen again; one of the restless souls not laid to rest.

Which made it odd that he thought he'd just caught a glimpse of the man in the flesh and blood. In the early days of courting Clover he had met her father and exchanged a few words. Despite a fleeting acquaintanceship he clearly recalled Sidney Cooper for the simple reason the fellow looked quite like him. They had been of the same height and build with dark hair and lean features. Both of them had been Tommies in the army at that time, too. Neil calculated Clover's father would be about fifty, which would account for the gleam of silver he'd seen in the man's hair. He told himself he was being bloody daft and that he wasn't going back to check on his suspicions. Neither would he spend another second brooding on the wretched war years, usually banned from his mind.

Trenches ... the stench of death that lingered in his nostrils to this day ... the injury that had torn open his thigh and was the bitterest relic of all. Archie Fletcher might be a rotten liar but Neil feared he'd told the truth earlier: he was no longer man enough to give the woman he loved the baby they longed for.

Chapter Twelve

'What's going on? Where's my wife?' Archie marched past a gaggle of people in his hallway and started up the stairs to his flat without waiting for a response. He'd had to stop himself telling the neighbours to clear off in no uncertain terms. He knew it was a ritual women had: congregating to offer help during a labour in expectation of the favour being returned. But having his family's affairs under scrutiny irritated him. He fumbled his key into the lock, burst inside and came face to face with Clover.

'Sshh ... don't make a racket.' Clover had been perambulating up and down the corridor to try to get his toddler daughter off to sleep. She removed a hand from Jennifer to put a warning finger to her lips. It wasn't only the child at risk of being disturbed; Clover sent a cautionary look towards the bedroom where the expectant mother could be heard moaning. Nettie was already in a state and needed a calming influence, not a bull in a china shop. Clover was relieved Archie was home though. At least Nettie would stop fretting over his whereabouts.

'Has she had the baby then, or not?' he demanded, keeping his face averted. He didn't want to be questioned about the bruise on his face but conceit also played a part in his attempts to conceal it.

'A girl ... you've got another daughter, Archie.' Clover saw his profile droop in unconcealed disappointment. 'There's something else ... ' She grabbed him as he would have barged past into the bedroom. 'Slow down and listen.' She shook his arm to impress on him the importance of what she was about to say. 'Mrs Waverley thinks there might be another baby to come.'

'What?' He turned to face her, struggling to comprehend because he wasn't really concentrating. He was brooding on the evening's previous events and didn't want this unexpected drama.

'Twins ... ' Clover spelled out then walked away. The mark on his face told its own story of what had occurred when Neil caught up with him. Apart from that, Archie smelled of alcohol and a woman. She recognised Jicky scent; not that she could afford to buy it. Clover doubted Dora Knox actually bought it either although she carried a bottle of it in her handbag. 'The midwife doesn't want you going in there yet. Let her finish her job first.'

Mrs Waverley wasn't a qualified midwife but the local handywoman. She delivered babies and laid out the bodies of the deceased. She had been doing so ever since Clover could remember. The woman had delivered her twin sisters, and umpteen other babies in the eighteen years that followed. Half an hour ago Clover had taken a pan of hot water to the midwife and Mrs Waverley had edged outside the bedroom to whisper that the first child had made a healthy entry into the world but she couldn't detect a heartbeat for the second. She'd added that she wouldn't know for certain if it had survived until Nettie expelled the mite from her exhausted body. Clover had tiptoed away, shocked but also relieved that at least one baby had been safely delivered. She trusted the midwife to know what she was doing and had been praying for a miracle until Archie eventually showed up.

'Why don't you sit in here?' Clover balanced Jennifer on one arm and opened the parlour door. She decided not to tell him the worst of it when he was struggling to deal with what he'd heard so far. 'I'll make a pot of tea then see if Mrs Waverley needs any help.'

'Twins?' Archie parroted, having finally digested things. 'That can't be right. She would've said.'

'Nettie didn't know herself ...' Clover continued to be patient, although his self-pitying tone was grating on her. 'Neither did Mrs Waverley until after the labour started. Go and sit down.' She handed him his daughter who'd picked up on the atmosphere and started to grizzle.

The little girl had been in bed when her mother's waters broke and a commotion startled her awake. Luckily, the next-door neighbour had understood the nature of the emergency being signalled in bashes on the adjoining wall. She'd fetched Clover and the midwife who lived just along the road from the Ryans. Together, they'd sped over the quarter of a mile to the drapery and up the stairs to the flat. They'd found Nettie doubled over with strong contractions. Neil had been despatched to the railway to fetch Archie but had returned to report that he'd clocked off as usual at six o'clock. It was now close to eleven o'clock and from his irritation it was obvious Archie didn't feel ashamed of neglecting his wife. He was the sort that considered childbirth women's work and his job was to wet the baby's head in the pub and accept compliments on the new arrival.

A protracted groan issued from the bedroom, then quiet ensued. Clover and Archie exchanged a glance. Jennifer stopped grizzling and seemed to be listening for another noise. After a minute it came in the form of the bedroom door being opened and a woman in her early sixties stepping out.

'So, you're home at last, are you?' barked Mrs Waverley, who'd started towards them. She was holding a bowl of thick sloshing red water and elbowed past Archie. The gruesome sight, coupled with the midwife's contemptuous glance, was enough to send him into the parlour, closing the door behind him.

Clover hurriedly followed the midwife into the kitchen. 'Is it over?'

'Boy ... stillborn ... small so died a while ago, I'd say.' Mrs Waverley supplied the information Clover had dreaded to ask for.

'Does Nettie know?' croaked Clover with tears burning her eyes.

Mrs Waverley nodded. 'Hasn't sunk in yet though. Poor cow don't know what day it is.' She shook her head. 'I'll give her a clean-up then he can go in and see her ... if he cares to,' said Mrs Waverley acidly, as an afterthought.

Clover spontaneously hugged the woman. 'Thank you for doing what you could.'

'Wish I could've done more but the girl really needed hospital care sooner.' She sighed. 'Surprised she didn't twig she was carrying two, the size of her.'

Clover filled the kettle and put it on the stove. 'I told him I'd make some tea. First I'll nip in and see her, if that's all right.' Clover bucked herself up and swiped the tears away on the back of her hand.

'Yeah ... tell her the good news that the lazy good-fer-nuthin' is back home. That'll cheer her up,' said Mrs Waverley sarcastically and upended the bowl of gore into the china sink.

A mingling odour of blood and sweat met Clover as she entered Nettie's bedroom. 'Lie still and rest.' Clover eased her friend's shoulders back onto the mattress as she struggled to sit up. 'Mrs Waverley's getting some hot water to give you a nice wash and brush up.' She smoothed damp hair off Nettie's brow and forced a bright smile. 'Archie's home and will come in and see you in a minute.'

Nettie's expression of relief at hearing he'd returned soon transformed into a pinched frown. 'I look a mess; fetch me my hairbrush would you?' She tried again to struggle onto her elbows but flopped back, wailing, 'I know I've let him down. Oh, why couldn't it have been like it was last time with Jennifer?' She covered her face with her hands. 'We almost had a son, Clo ... '

'I know, love, Mrs Waverley told me.' Clover picked up a hairbrush from the dressing table. 'But you haven't let anybody down,' she soothed. 'Least of all him,' she added beneath her breath, and began to tidy Nettie's hair, pressing curls into the lank tendrils and tucking strands back behind her ears.

'Does Archie know what's happened?'

'He knows he's got another daughter. He's seeing to Jennifer. She's missing her mum but she'll settle down I expect now her dad's here.'

'She's a daddy's girl all right ... ' Nettie managed a smile, but it soon faded. 'Archie wanted a boy this time, he'll be upset.' She turned her head aside and sobbed into the pillow.

141

'He'll be happy you and your new daughter are both safe and well.' Clover sank to her knees by the bed and squeezed her friend's hand. 'Jennifer will love that you've given her a new sister to be friends with. It'll be wonderful seeing them grow up together and looking after one another.'

Nettie nodded and gazed at the crib set by the wall. 'Would you fetch her so I can hold her?'

Clover got up and brought the snuffling baby to her mother. Another swaddled bundle, lying still and silent at the foot of the mattress, drew Clover's eyes. The haunting sight sent her mind flying back through the years. Her mother's last child had been premature and barely alive. On her grandmother's orders, Clover had spirited away the little mite so her father would never know of his wife's infidelity. But nothing escaped Sidney Cooper.

All those people were dead now … apart, maybe, from Gabriel, if he'd survived his frailty and early years. She'd always think of him by that name and never forget his tiny face.

Her friend was waiting, arms outstretched, for her baby and Clover quickly handed over the warm bundle. 'She's a beauty, Nettie, and a good weight. You must be so proud of her.' Clover had moved an edge of blanket to get a view of a small pink face. 'I can see you in her, you know. Look, she's got your dimple.' Clover touched a fold of soft skin. She was doing her best to sound jolly, yet inside her heart was breaking for Nettie's two lost boys. Her friend would be thinking of the child she'd given away all those years ago when Archie had told her he'd never marry her. Now he had the cheek to look disappointed because he would've preferred a son. Clover suppressed her anger and followed Nettie's lead in avoiding speaking about the stillborn child.

There would be time enough in the weeks to come for grief and condolences. She watched Nettie stroking the baby's face. 'Have you picked a name for her yet?'

'We favoured Leonard ... or Elizabeth.' Nettie paused and gave a wistful smile. 'Maybe Archie will like Leonora, instead.'

'That's a pretty name. I'll make some tea ... bet you could do with a cup,' Clover said gruffly then left the room struggling to breathe through the lump in her throat.

In the kitchen, she found Neil had arrived and was standing with his hands propped against the draining board and his face lowered to his shoulders. He straightened up as he heard her enter. She rushed to embrace him. 'Thanks for running the swine to ground and sending him home.' She spoke quietly in the hope Mrs Waverley wouldn't hear the insult. The midwife had no time for Archie Fletcher either, and made no bones about showing it, but loyalty to his wife prevented Clover running him down in company.

'I'll second that,' said Mrs Waverley, proving there was little wrong with her ears. She continued pouring hot water from the kettle into the enamel bowl. 'Mrs Fletcher finished the job when she heard her husband in the corridor. About the only use he has been to her 'n' all.' With that, she headed off with the washing water. 'Give me five minutes then you can send him in,' was sent over her shoulder.

'Did Mrs Waverley tell you the bad news?' Clover nestled her head against her husband's chest.

'She did.' Neil paused. 'Would it have made a difference if Archie had arrived home sooner?' He was tormenting himself thinking about those few minutes he'd delayed Archie while feeling jealous and vengeful. He wished he could turn back the clock and save that grievance for another day.

'Don't blame yourself. You did everything you could. Mrs Waverley reckons the smaller twin died before today.' She detected a hint of floral perfume. 'Archie shouldn't have needed tracking down in the first place. He knew Nettie was close to her time yet he's been gallivanting, hasn't he?' She stepped back as Neil touched her face and the Jicky scent strengthened. 'Where did you find him? And who was he with?'

'Not sure you'd believe me if I told you, love.'

'Try me ... ' she invited rather tartly.

He watched her mouth tightening into a hard knot as he finished the tale. He'd kept back the part about Dora coming on to him although he'd picked up on his wife's suspicions. He better appreciated Clover's reasons for dismissing Archie's lechery as being unworthy of discussion. Neil knew he'd done nothing wrong; he knew Clover had done nothing wrong; but jealousy was a toxic emotion that could torment and madden. Archie Fletcher ... Dora Knox ... they weren't worth arguing over.

'It's none of our business, love, what any of them get up to,' he said when Clover continued to brood on it. 'Will you tell Johnny about this?'

'If he asks I won't deny knowing about it, but I think you're right: he's old enough to sort out a cheating girlfriend on his own. If they really are finished, he might not care either way.' She paused. 'Nettie is my business though. I've known her since we started infants' school together. We're as close as sisters.' Clover shook her head in despair. 'I wish she'd never married that pig. Archie Fletcher doesn't deserve her, or his children ... '

'My name being taken in vain, is it?' Archie had come unseen into the kitchen and stood, hands on hips, surveying the couple. He'd not caught much of their conversation and wished he'd eavesdropped for longer rather than bursting in on them.

Neil stopped propping himself against the wall and approached Archie, creating a dangerous crackle in the atmosphere.

'Is Jennifer in her cot?' Clover broke the heavy silence.

'She was yawning. I put her back to bed.'

'Oh, good ...' Clover could hear the child's faint whimpering and guessed her father had got fed up with her. 'Mrs Waverley should be finished about now. She said you can go in and see Nettie and the new baby.'

'I will,' Archie said. 'Lucky man, me, eh? Two children ...' He let the jibe hang in the air before turning away with a smirk. 'Some people just ain't so lucky.'

A muscle jumped in Neil's jaw but he said nothing, just watched as Archie pulled open the door.

'Another thing, Archie ...' Clover said.

He turned back with a bored expression.

'Mrs Waverley has been a real diamond,' Clover said. 'I know she can be a bit brusque, but it's only her way. She got here within minutes of being called out and did everything she could for Nettie and the babies. She never charges much. Her fee's usually—' Before she could name the amount Archie cut across her.

'She didn't save me son, did she?' he retorted. 'So what use has she been to me?'

'Just you wait a moment ...' Clover was incensed by his attitude and his lack of appreciation for what had been done for his wife in his absence. She sprang forward to remonstrate but Neil caught her arm, holding her back. 'It was too late to save the second baby—' She began to explain but was again interrupted.

'I think it's time you two were on your way.' Archie flicked a finger at the door. 'Thanks for turning out to help Nettie, but you ain't needed any more. I can take it from here.' Pursed lipped, he waited for them to leave.

The neighbours had already gone to find their beds by the time Neil and Clover descended to the street to do the same at close to midnight. They'd decided there was no point arguing with Archie; it would only upset Nettie. The man was itching for trouble so it was time to withdraw gracefully. They'd said their quick goodbyes to Nettie and Mrs Waverley. The midwife's mild remark that she'd no need of a chaperone was taken as a rejection of their offer to wait downstairs to walk home with her. So they'd set off.

Clover knew Neil's attitude to concede defeat was wise but she worried about her friend. Nettie had looked happy with her husband beside her, cooing into the cot. The new mother was deserving of praise rather than criticism. Clover knew which her friend was likely to receive once everybody had gone.

Carpentry callouses on Neil's palm rubbed his wife's fingers as he took her hand in comfort. 'Are you thinking of Rosie?' he asked gently. He had known both Clover's little sisters and had watched Annie grow up without her soulmate. The twins hadn't been identical and their characters had been chalk and cheese, but Rosie and Annie had been inseparable, toddling after one another everywhere.

'She's never far from my mind. Funny thing is, my mum didn't struggle giving birth to her twins. I remember Mrs Waverley likening it to her patient falling off a log. I was almost fifteen then and had just started work for Nettie's father, at the drapery. It was wartime and my dad was

146

fighting in France.' She dwelled on those memories for a moment before saying briskly, 'Anyway, I've always thought life was terribly unkind to Rosie and to us, taking her from us so soon. But we were lucky to have known her for those four years.' She smiled. 'She was the sweetest child . . . and funny . . . a joy to have around.' Clover dropped her head back and gazed at a twinkling sky. She picked a star, murmured a prayer for Rosie, gone before she'd had her first day at school. 'Sidney Cooper always seemed bored by his kids but even he adored having Rosie around,' she said.

That man's name had put a frown on Neil's face. He wasn't sure whether to tell Clover he'd spotted somebody the image of her late father. He decided to leave it for another time. There'd been more than enough excitement for one day.

'Now Annie's living in at her employer's I've been thinking I could swap to an evening shift at the sugar factory . . . it pays more and they're advertising at the moment.' Clover began concentrating on practicalities and their own troubles. Neil had told her at the beginning of the week that his boss was reluctantly putting him off. Work had dried up and he couldn't afford a hired hand once the job they were on finished. It hadn't come as much of a surprise to Neil; he'd witnessed his boss arguing with customers wanting to shave more and more discount off agreed prices.

'You do enough already working a day shift.' He sounded calm but firm. 'I'll go to the labour exchange before this comes to an end and try to line something up.'

'I know you will, but it doesn't hurt to be sensible . . . just in case,' she said in the same measured tone. 'I don't mind putting in a few extra hours.' Clover knew she should grab the extra money while she could. Annie had offered to keep sending her some of her pay but Clover had refused. Her sister had flown the nest and it wasn't fair to expect her to contribute to the kitty of a house she no longer lived in. 'We could look for somewhere smaller now Annie's gone. She'll only come over and stay a few times a year and can bed down on the settee. The rent's high and we don't really need an extra bedroom.' She wished they did and the noise of children playing was in there rather than silence.

'Give me a chance to put this right, Clover.' Neil turned to look at her. 'We're all right for now and no great urgency to up sticks.'

'Maybe a fresh start is what we need.' Clover wondered if she might get pregnant in a place free of the memories of lost children.

'Look, if there's no joinery work then I can try the docks.' He knew that was pie in the sky. He passed the docks every day on his way to work and saw the gangers picking out a few men from the dozens jostling for a chance to take a pay packet home to their wives.

Neil liked his job as a carpenter and he knew he was good at it too, but supply outstripped demand. People were turning against one another in desperation, fighting for what little there was. Nobody had envisaged the victory years after the Great War would turn so bitter. He wasn't a political man but knew feeling was running high about the lack of help from the government for families sliding into poverty.

'Give me until Friday, love, and if still no dice, then you speak to your supervisor about the night work.'

As they walked on, their breath froze in the air in front of them and Neil wondered aloud whether the fire in the stove had gone out; she said it didn't matter and they'd go straight to bed. She knew he was still brooding on being ridiculed for being childless. Losing his job would give Archie Fletcher something else to fling in his face. Unfortunately, spiteful people knew exactly where to find an Achilles heel, and Fletcher delighted in twisting the knife in theirs at every opportunity.

Chapter Thirteen

Sidney Cooper wasn't overjoyed to be back in the land of his birth. Even the prospect of an English Christmas didn't excite him. As yet he'd nobody to spend the holiday with, but he was working on that. He'd quite liked being in France: better weather and cakes, for a start.

Of course, the country was still a mess due to the destruction suffered during the Great War. Having spent his early years in an East End slum he'd not been too bothered by a French landscape of crumbling ruins. After Sophie died there'd not been much to keep him on foreign soil. Not even his children. Sidney Cooper wasn't a keen father, but women seemed to like having a brood around their ankles.

He'd met Sophie at a brothel when serving as a Tommy on the Western Front. Never one to happily part with his cash, he'd meet up with her outside when he was billeted close by. During the warm summer months, they'd settle down in a poppy meadow beneath an endless sky; she'd bring a modest picnic of cheese and bread to be washed down with rough red wine, and he'd supply the blanket and cigarettes. They'd both been in places they didn't want to be and he'd grown fond of her and their rendezvous. He'd got along with her better than with his first wife, which wasn't saying much.

On Iris's death, he'd been sent back to England to make arrangements for his kids and had been greeted by an unholy mess. He didn't stay long; he returned quickly to France and promised to marry his mistress now he was free. The wedding never happened; Sidney wasn't against remarrying, only about bringing himself to light to any authority, be it French or English. Now Sophie was dead too, from pneumonia, and he was never much good without a woman at his side.

His French son and daughter were living with their grandmother. He'd promised them all he'd be back after he sorted out some unfinished English business that would yield a nest egg. There was no pot of gold waiting for him in Silvertown. And nothing in France for him either. He knew he wasn't going back.

He knew something else, too: if the man who'd tried to kill him last time he was in England was still alive, he'd find him. Revenge was a good enough reason to bring Sidney Cooper back to Old Blighty, and after all this time it would certainly be eaten cold.

Memories of his childhood sweetheart had been another siren song luring him over the Channel, but he'd discovered Lucy Dare was a lost cause. She had married and moved away from London. He'd caught up on this news with a few surviving pals willing to give him the time of day. Once they'd picked themselves up off the floor after seeing Sidney Cooper's ghost drawing up a barstool beside them, they'd recounted what they knew about his children, grown into adults in his absence.

He'd chuckled on learning he was believed to have been

blown to bits in the Silvertown disaster. His desperation to vanish into thin air sixteen years ago would have seen him making use of that line at the time. It would have been difficult though, piecing himself and the story together on his return. As it was, he'd cast himself as the victim in a more heroic slight and ignored the sceptical looks that met his tale of being missing in action during the final battle of Passchendaele. Nobody could prove differently.

Now he had to build a new life in England, and needed a woman to help him lay a foundation stone.

So far, none of the old flames he'd looked up had been delighted to see him, apart from those still plying their trade as tarts. He had mellowed in his old age though and would sooner settle down with a wife. Somebody about his own age, so no more squawking babies arriving to take up his time and his money.

He had been reminiscing while moseying along the street in the icy December dusk, but slowed down on realising he'd reached his destination. He stopped on the corner of a pleasant avenue close to south-east London's Elephant and Castle and spat on his palms, slicked down his hair, and when satisfied he was presentable enough, approached a door and knocked on it. He shuffled his feet, hoping she still lived here and was up for a walk down memory lane. Sixteen years was a long time between visits. Of all his past fancies, Molly Deane had been the youngest and the sharpest.

'Is Molly Deane at home, miss?'

A girl, enough like Molly to reassure Sidney he was on the right track, had opened the door. He had a plan in place if a husband was present: he was calling to convey the sad news of a mutual acquaintance from way back when. So far the women hadn't contradicted him, but pretended they knew the deceased rather than invite their husbands' questions. They were keen for him to leave though, and often without the offer of a cup of tea for his pains.

'Oh, you mean, Mum ... ' The girl's frown lifted and she turned to call over her shoulder, 'Somebody here to see you, Mum.'

Sidney's spirits drooped. He'd picked up on the reason for the girl's confusion. Her mother had a new surname and a man with his boots already under her bed.

Molly came to the door, drying her hands on her pinafore. 'Can I help you?' She glared at the middle-aged fellow lounging against the railings with a lazy smile. He looked a mite too comfortable ... and familiar. It took her another few seconds to understand why that was. Her features became still, then her eyes widened and her chin sagged. She turned to her daughter, idly observing what was going on. 'Watch the potatoes for me, Rebecca, I've left them boiling over.' The moment her daughter disappeared she whipped back to face Sidney, hissing, 'What in Gawd's name ... you're dead, ain't yer?'

On George's instructions, she'd been learning to improve her elocution now he wanted to mix in better social circles. This fellow had set her back weeks and reminded her of the war days she'd rather forget. Sidney Cooper had caused her to swerve off the straight and narrow before she'd turned eighteen and she'd never got back on the rails. He'd been all lies and promises back then, and she reckoned he still was beneath his air of grizzled charm.

'Reports of my death was premature, love.' Sidney spread his arms to show he was very much here in the flesh. 'Nearly did meet me maker in France, but managed to survive. I was missing for ages, y'see, and badly injured.' He tapped his head. 'Concussed and lost me memory for a long time. Ended up settling over there after the war cos I couldn't even remember me name.' He rose up a step to wedge a foot in the door. 'Still ... ' He shrugged, pretending to be reluctant to boast, or to invite pity. 'Worse things happened to others. I think meself fortunate to have come through at all.'

'France?' Molly eventually squeaked, struggling to make sense of it. 'I heard you was killed in the Silvertown explosion?'

'Nah ... somebody got that wrong. After I lost me wife, Iris, God rest her, I made sure me kids was all right then headed back to do me duty.' He shook his head. 'Gossips had a field day at my expense it seems while I was bleeding in a trench.'

'If you was in a trench they'd've found you ... sent you home,' Molly pointed out.

'German trench it was, love,' he said, straight-faced. 'Left me fer dead, they did, and after that I was on me own, behind enemy lines, not knowing what day it was, or who I was.' His foot slid further over the threshold. 'Just thought I'd pop by and see you now I'm back.' He wrung his cold hands. 'Taters in the mould out here, it is.' His heavy hint to be let in didn't get him anywhere.

Molly crossed her arms, cocked her head and gave him a long considering look. In his heyday he'd been a handsome rogue ... without a pot to piss in. Nevertheless he'd collected quite a harem. Everybody knew Sidney Cooper treated his wife badly, keeping her short of money and playing around. Yet, there had been something about him – besides him being good between the sheets – that kept fools like her on the end of a piece of his string.

'You rotten liar. You're a deserter, ain't you, Sid?' She'd heard of other men who'd hidden in France and slowly crept back over the years when they judged enough time had elapsed for things to have died down.

Sidney had more yarns ready but gave up on them. She was too astute to be taken in. Unlike the others, Molly not only looked dubious but aired her views. 'I call it by a different name.' He shrugged his indifference. 'I *was* missing and there *was* a bleedin' lot of action over there.' He gave her a winning smile and a wink. 'Make us a cup o' tea, Mol, and I'll tell you all about me French adventures.' He sucked his teeth. 'Make your hair stand on end, some of it will, and I ain't kidding about that.'

'Yeah ... now that I *do* believe,' she said drily.

She was mellowing, on the point of smiling, and he pressed home his advantage. 'You ain't changed a bit, and that's the truth.' He looked her over admiringly. 'I thought that gel must be your sister when she opened the door.'

Molly's ironic look strengthened, but she was a sucker for a bit of flattery. She took care of her looks and liked compliments. He wasn't the first to say she could pass for her daughter's elder sister. Sidney Cooper was still good-looking despite the lines on his face and the grey at his temples. He'd retained his muscular build and his ability to entertain. She would enjoy hearing about his time in France, although she knew his tales would give Hans Christian Andersen a run for his money.

But ... he was trouble she didn't need. With a headstrong daughter and an ambitious man to contend with, Sidney Cooper hanging around would just add to her problems.

'Nice to see you, and glad you're alive and kicking, but you'd better get going, Sid. Me husband's due home ... ' As she glanced past Sidney, she saw George really was on his way. She jerked a nod at a hatted fellow sauntering down the road, hands in pockets. 'Here he is. I'll tell him you're an insurance salesman.' She gave his arm a push. 'If he finds out about us, you won't 'arf be for it.'

Sidney straightened up with a sniff. In his prime he'd been quite able to handle himself, but he wasn't in his prime now. The fellow he'd sneaked a glance at, bowling down the road, looked younger than he was. He could imagine this woman being involved with a thug, although he'd also known her when she was being kept in style by a high-class gent. It was how she came to be living in this nice house. Sidney was curious to know if the toff was still on the scene and paying the rent. 'Molly Deane's married, is she?' It was Sidney's turn to sound sceptical. 'Do I know the lucky feller?'

It was her turn to wink. 'I'm Molly Payne now, Sid. That's my story and I'm sticking to it.'

'His name was Harding, wasn't it ... the posh fellow who set you up here way back when ... '

'Go on, piss off.' She shoved him harder and closed the door in his face then watched him from behind the parlour's net curtain. She noticed George was staring after the fellow he'd seen standing on his doorstep.

'Who was that, Mum?'

'Oh, just somebody I used to know when I was a girl,' Molly had spun around and answered her daughter rather breathlessly. 'He was trying to soft-soap me into buying an insurance policy. Not interested; we only had a chat for old times' sake.'

'What did that bloke want?' George had come into the parlour, taking off his hat and coat.

'He's an insurance salesman,' Rebecca supplied. 'Mum told him to clear off.'

Molly gave her daughter a grateful smile, noticing Rebecca had a knowing look on her face. 'Right, better rescue the potatoes before they stick to the bottom of the pan.' Briskly, Molly headed for the kitchen. 'Sausage 'n' mash is what we're having.'

She plunged the masher up and down as though she loathed potatoes. Sidney Cooper had come out with something that had unsettled her. Nobody had mentioned Rupert Harding in years. She'd liked him and had been upset when he was murdered. Nevertheless, the years had turned and she'd practically forgotten all about him and what had happened next. Sidney Cooper knew nothing about any of that, but the fact that he remembered Harding at all was alarming.

Rebecca thought George Payne was her father and he certainly was . . . although her birth certificate said differently. In time, the girl might ask to see it, but Molly had burned the evidence of her swindle long ago.

During the bus journey that took him across Tower Bridge and into the East End of London, Sidney had been mulling over his conversation with Molly. He took heart from their lively chat and from her speaking of 'us'. He knew he might be clutching at straws, reading too much into it, but hoped he remained on her mind, as she did on his. He'd noticed her coyly touching her hair when he told her she looked good; she wasn't indifferent to him, that was for sure.

He alighted from the bus and began heading in the direction of his old address from habit, rather than from a desire to go there.

During his chinwag in the pub, he'd learned Clover had married and remained living in her childhood home. He'd also been told her husband was an all right sort of bloke. Sidney couldn't bring Neil Ryan to mind but then he'd not had much interest in his daughters or their friends.

His son had been a different matter; he'd enthusiastically asked about Johnny, and where to find him. Sidney would sooner seek him out than go, cap in hand, for board and lodging at his old marital home. It was filled with bad memories.

He'd discovered that his favourite child had moved south of the water but still visited his sisters. He didn't know, though, whether Johnny had a wife who might interfere in a father and son reunion. A few smirks had met his question about what his son did for a living. Johnny engaged in a bit of ducking and diving he'd been told, and was also a doorman at an illegal gaming establishment. Sidney's face had lit up to know it. He'd been a docker before the war put paid to all that. Ducking and diving and gaming clubs sounded like heaven in comparison; his son had made him proud.

There was jauntiness in his step as he approached his next port of call. Clover would know where her brother was, and there was still time to return to south London and pay Johnny a visit once he had his address. Sidney was confident he'd soon have a permanent place to stay. Johnny would offer his old dad a welcome home drink as well ... just the two of them.

Sidney had come abreast of a familiar landmark that caused his smile to transform into a scowl. He stopped and cupped his hands against the window glass, peering past a display of vests and cardigans into the dim interior. He glanced up, squinting at the new name over the shop.

Randall had gone from here, it seemed, and Fletcher had taken over. Sidney still intended to track down the man he blamed for killing his wife, and trying to murder him.

He'd not asked about the Randalls in the pub, unwilling to show any interest in them. When he caught up with Bruce Randall he didn't want suspicion to fall on him for what happened next.

Chapter Fourteen

'Hello, Dad, I've been expecting you.'

Clover held open the door and gestured for him to enter. Her calm demeanour might have led a person to think she was feeling philosophical about this astonishing turn of events rather than angry and bewildered. But she'd had time to prepare herself after Neil told her he'd seen her father's double. Her husband had laughed, slightly embarrassed, to come out with such a thing. Clover hadn't; she'd known the truth before the gossip she'd heard spread about Sidney Cooper rising from the dead in a pub, almost causing the barmaid to drop a tray of glasses.

His body had never been recovered from the explosion site and her doubts as to his fate had refused to wither because her father was crafty and resourceful. Had he been outside the factory he would have done his utmost to save his own skin, unlike her grandmother who had perished protecting a child. But a decade or more passed, and the hope of him turning up began fading into guilt for imagining he could be rotten and selfish enough to abandon his family.

And now here he was, back in all his rotten selfish glory.

She'd recognised him straight away, although the dazzling father she remembered was still missing. Sidney Cooper had been about her age when she saw him last, full of colour and vitality. He appeared reduced by whatever it was he'd seen and done in the interim. And no doubt his age was catching up on him. His bristled face and brown hair appeared thinner and faded. She realised he must be about fifty-one ... the age her grandmother had been when she lost her life at the Brunner Mond factory.

Sidney was deflated by her cool greeting. He'd anticipated news of his miraculous resurrection to spread; and to receive some recrimination. Even so, a more enthusiastic welcome would have been nice. His firstborn had always been her mother's child, though, not his, which was galling considering he'd lost his freedom through her. There was no smile lighting her features; nonetheless he gazed at her beauty with pride expanding his chest. She was all thick auburn hair and intense green eyes, the image of Iris when he'd first known her.

Clover had been the reason for the shotgun wedding that had never stood a chance. He and Iris had been a mismatch, and they had both regretted the single lustful episode in their youth that had stuck them together for years.

Sidney stepped inside the house and for one of the few times in his life felt unsure what to do next.

'Cup of tea?' Clover wasn't fooled by his hangdog expression. She should hate him, but couldn't. He was her father when all was said and done. It wasn't as though his disregard for those he should cherish came as a shock. Before the war took him away he'd rarely been at home, and would fritter their rent money on drink and other women.

'Why didn't you send a message? You should have let

us know where you were ... that you were all right.' On impulse she rushed to hug him, fiercely and briefly, then broke free before he could hold onto her. He still smelled the same: slightly dirty, of stale booze and cigarettes. 'We all thought you were dead.'

He shrugged. 'Settled in France for a while ... made a life there after what went on.' He couldn't kid Clover any more than he could Molly Deane. His eldest daughter had been as sharp as a tack even as a schoolgirl.

'You had a life here,' she said flatly. 'You had children here.'

'After I found out why your mother died,' he said resentfully, 'started me thinking the twins might not be mine either.'

Clover was shocked by that low blow, knowing what he'd said was untrue. She suspected he knew it was false as well. He'd never openly spoken to her about his wife's infidelity, but their relationship had changed now they were both adults. He wasn't bothered about protecting her memory of her mother, only about justifying himself.

'You and Johnny was old enough to see to yourselves and the nippers,' he continued. 'And your grandmother was keeping tabs on you all. I reckoned you'd be better off without me.'

'The twins were the image of you, so I don't know how you can say they weren't yours.' Refusing to apologise for abandoning two toddlers was as low as it got. 'Maybe you were right about the rest, though: with your attitude, we were better off without you, even though Nan's been gone a long while now.' Clover managed a measured response, although she was tempted to holler at him.

'I was sorry to hear about what happened to your

grandmother,' he said spikily. 'Only recently found out. If I had known, maybe I'd've seen things differently.'

Clover turned away in disgust. She knew it wouldn't have made any difference. He'd kept his head down so bad news wouldn't reach him, then had turned up again when it suited him.

'What happened in France to bring you back here?'

'Nothing that need concern you,' he snapped back, irritated by her shrewdness.

Tales doing the rounds of concussion and amnesia didn't wash with Clover. He'd been in hiding but something had gone wrong for him and he was looking for a fresh start. His confounded cheek was breath-taking, yet here he was expecting to pick up where he left off.

'Look, don't want to fall out with you, Clover.' He sighed. 'Wrong's been done on both our sides.'

He was staring at her in a way that made her hesitate in demanding an explanation for the accusation.

'You knew about your mother and Bruce Randall and their bastard, but covered it up, same as your grandmother did.'

She couldn't deny that and felt heat rising up into her cheeks, not from guilt – she'd protect her mother and Gabriel again – but from the shame of being found out and from anger because he'd used that horrible word to describe her half-brother.

'And what about you and Lucy Dare?' she said quietly. 'Did you think I didn't know about that?

'All water under the bridge now,' said Sidney dismissively. 'And ain't going to dwell on it.' He took off his coat and dropped it on the settee while looking around at a nicely furnished clean and tidy space. When his wife had kept house here, the place had been a mess, as though she'd no more care for where they lived than for the man she'd married. 'I won't be in your way for long, love, but I will stop for tea, if you're making it.' He settled down on the settee – it didn't sag in the middle like the previous one – and inhaled a distinctive savoury aroma wafting from the pot on the stove. He could do with a bowl of mutton stew but doubted he'd be invited to supper. As Lucy Dare had been brought into the conversation he thought he might as well dig for some answers there. Clover beat him to it in bringing the subject up.

'I suppose you heard about Lucy and Bill getting married after Nan died.' She blinked back tears. 'Nan and Bill only had a short time together as husband and wife before the accident happened. But he and Lucy showed respect and waited before marrying. They moved away about eleven years ago now. They had a son . . . a first child for them both.'

'Good fer them . . . ' said Sidney sourly. Even when he was seeing Lucy she'd had a yen for Bill Lewis. She'd finally got her man when his wife died in the factory explosion. 'And how do you all get along?' Badly, was what he hoped to hear, but finally his daughter had something to smile about.

'Very well, actually. Don't see so much of them now they're in Essex.'

A fresh start had been the best thing for the newlyweds. Lucy's racy reputation, and the family's tangled affairs, had provided lots of ammunition for spiteful tongues. By then Johnny was working on a market stall, and showing signs of being worryingly enterprising where earning money was concerned. The Coopers had a steady supply of buck-shee fruit and vegetables and Clover guessed her brother's guvnor was scratching his head over the shortfall in his stock. Annie was at junior school and dear little Rosie had already passed away, leaving the remnants of the Cooper family dug in and battling on together in Silvertown.

Bill Lewis was a decent man and Lucy Dare had made every effort to be kind and helpful to the Cooper children to make amends for past misdemeanours with their father. She would offer to babysit the twins in the early days and take and fetch Annie from school so Clover could do her sugar factory shifts. Clover was fond of both her step-grandparents, and looked forward to their visits.

Sidney contained his disappointment at knowing all was harmonious and watched Clover setting out cups, wishing he'd not bothered with tea. He wanted to find out where his son was so he could go there for a more sympathetic hearing.

'Where's Johnny living then?' he asked brightly. 'Doing all right for himself, I heard.'

'He's over Lambeth way.' Clover poured boiling water into the pot, smiling privately. Her father was angling for Johnny's address. If he'd managed to find his son without her help, he wouldn't be here.

'Hear he's doing all right for himself,' Sidney repeated, hoping for some details.

Clover turned about. 'Depends ... ' she said. 'On what you mean by all right.' It hadn't escaped her notice that he'd not asked after the twins. 'Would you like to know about your youngest kids?'

Their eyes clashed. "Course ... what they been up to then?' He guessed the girls would be old enough to be lodging elsewhere.

Clover brought two cups to the settee and sat beside him, handing one to him. 'Annie's doing nicely. She's a live-in assistant cook in the West End.'

Sidney pulled a face, showing he was impressed to hear of Annie's good prospects. But he fidgeted further away from Clover, unsettled by his daughter's quiet authority. 'And what about Rosie?' He'd barely known his twins – and he did know they were his, despite what he'd said in a fit of pique. They'd been born early in the war, while he was away fighting and he could count the times he'd been with them on one hand. But he recalled that Rosie had been the friendliest, prettiest of the two.

'Rosie died in the flu epidemic, Dad, when she was four.' Clover was tempted to add that it was his own fault for not knowing ... that if he'd had the decency to get in touch he might have attended his little daughter's funeral. Even that tragedy might not have brought him home, though, before he was good and ready.

Sidney dropped his chin and dug into his pocket for his handkerchief to dab some genuine tears from his eyes. 'Rotten horrible thing that was,' he croaked. 'We had it in France as well.'

Clover remained quiet for a long while then said, 'It was all a rotten horrible thing, Dad.'

They drank their tea in silence, brooding on their own memories. Suddenly, Sidney piped up, 'Where's your husband and where's me grandkids?' He swivelled to look about; even without the twins, the house was too peaceful. A married woman of his daughter's age was rarely free of children hanging on her skirts.

'Neil's at the allotment, he'll be back soon. And we don't have any children.'

'Better get a move on then ... ' His joke seemed to have fallen flat, so he changed tack. 'Your husband's a carpenter, I believe.' Sidney nodded his approval. 'Skills like that are sought after.' He stored away the information that there was a spare room with no kids in it.

'Everybody's finding it hard to get work. Neil's between things, at the moment.'

Another disappointment. Free board and lodging was unlikely to be offered while Neil Ryan was out of work. And so was he, Sidney reminded himself. He needed a job as well and was hoping his son might help with that. He'd brought with him a small amount of French francs and exchanged them at the bank for less than two pounds that were fast running out.

Clover fetched a plate of biscuits to put on the table. 'If I'd known you were coming I'd've got extra in for tea.' She paused. 'You're welcome to stay and share what we do have.'

'Don't want to put you to no trouble, dear,' said Sidney, diving into the biscuits and munching on a digestive. 'You didn't seem surprised to see me just now. Found out I was back from gossip, did you?'

'People are chinwagging, but my husband told me first. He spotted you close to the explosion site, with a woman.' It seemed odd to Clover that her father should reappear at the spot where he was reported last seen. 'Why didn't you come straight away to see me? That was days ago now.'

Sidney choked on his tea, remembering the good-time girl who'd led him into the alley for business. He'd chewed over some awkward subjects with his daughter, but this was different. He put down his rattling cup and saucer. 'Well ... don't want to impose, can see you're busy and I've a few things to do meself.' He stood up and shoved an arm into his coat. 'Be obliged to have Johnny's address, dear, so I can look him up.' There was some other information he was keen to have as well before leaving. 'And how's your friend Nettie Randall doing?'

'She's married and had her second daughter earlier in the week. The little love is doing very well indeed.'

So he's a grandfather, is he . . . was the grudging thought passing through Sidney's mind about his nemesis. Aloud he said, 'The family gave up the drapery, did they?' He casually fastened his buttons. 'I came that way and saw it had changed hands.'

'Nettie runs it now. Archie Fletcher is her husband. When they married he put his name over the door.' Her father was digging to find out what happened to his rival. She'd gladly tell him in the hope he'd draw a line under the whole business. 'Nettie's the only one left of that family, Dad. Bruce Randall came back from the war but died in hospital from injuries the following year. Their son passed away not long afterwards . . . another flu victim. Then a few years later, Martha had an accident . . . ' Talking about it had brought back the unbelievable sadness of those years. She closed her eyes and sighed.

This catalogue of misfortune rendered Sidney speechless for a full minute while he battled with his mixed feelings. He felt cheated out of his revenge, yet at the same time felt sorry for Nettie losing her entire family when he had only wished one of them dead. Bruce Randall had wished him dead and had believed he'd killed him and buried his body. 'And who was it, dear, who started this rumour of me going up with the factory?' A look of enlightenment lifted Sidney's frown.

'Bruce Randall told me he'd spoken to you that night. You were on your way to find Nan at the factory.' Clover had been helping the survivors at a refuge when Nettie's father arrived with blankets donated from the drapery and told her Sidney had been in the wrong place at the wrong time.

'Might've known . . .' muttered Sidney, shaking his head with an amount of grudging admiration for Randall's nerve and ingenuity in evading a murder charge. He had really believed Sidney Cooper to be dead and buried, but hadn't counted on a soldier's survival skills.

The door was opened, and Clover smiled at the man who was hesitating on the threshold. 'Dad's come to say hello . . . but he can't stop. He's lots to do.' She found her father's company emotionally draining and would be relieved to see him go.

Neil recovered quickly from his surprise; he started forward, extending a hand to be shaken. He'd read from his wife's penetrating gaze that it'd be best if she steered this awkward situation.

'He's off to catch up with Johnny,' Clover added before her father settled himself back down in the hope of acquiring a drinking pal.

'A short and sweet visit to start us off.' Sidney gave a nervous chuckle.

'Well, it'll be nice to get to know you, Mr Cooper, now you're back,' said Neil.

'Have we met?' Sidney cocked his head, thinking his son-in-law seemed familiar.

'Only briefly . . . in passing . . . long time ago.' Sidney Cooper wouldn't have remembered bumping into him in the street, having been under the influence at the time.

'Must thank you for looking after me eldest gel; she's blooming, hardly changed from when she was sixteen.' Sidney took the address Clover had written on a piece of paper. 'Well, I'll leave you in peace now. Good luck with the job hunting, son.' Sidney gripped Neil's shoulder. 'We could have a nice Christmas together. It'd be like the old days . . .'

'I'll let Annie know I've seen you then.' Clover ignored his hint that he expected to be invited to Christmas dinner. She'd need a pow-wow with her brother and sister before arranging a family get together. She wasn't sure how Annie would take a face-to-face meeting with the father she barely knew. Of them all, she might be able to wipe the slate clean and start afresh with him.

'Yes, do give the girl my regards. See you soon, then.'

'Not if I see you first . . .' muttered Clover when the door was closed. She turned to Neil and for a second they stared at one another in bemusement. He started towards her to comfort her and the expression of love and sympathy on his face made her composure crumble. She slumped against him, sobbing.

Neil tilted up her chin, tracing her jaw with his thumb. 'Hush, love . . . I know it's come as a dreadful shock but . . .' He sighed, unable to find the right words to describe the bizarre situation. 'How will Johnny take it, d'you think?'

'Badly, I reckon,' she croaked. 'He was closest to his dad and wouldn't accept what had happened.'

'He wasn't wrong about that,' Neil said drily. 'D'you think the rumours have reached Johnny?'

'Don't know; there's not been much time for news to travel over the water.'

A couple of days ago, Mrs Waverley had banged on her door to garble out that Sidney Cooper was back from France. Within half an hour, Clover had set off to warn her brother and sister, furious that her father had let them find out something as momentous as this second hand.

Annie had taken it reasonably well but had little time

to talk as Christmas preparations were under way at her employer's house.

Johnny hadn't been home, as usual, and neither had Clover managed to track him down at his place of work. In fact, she'd discovered from one of his chatty colleagues that the club might be closing up, another casualty of the economic depression affecting the country.

Clover hadn't wanted to drop this bombshell other than in person; she had returned to Johnny's flat to push a letter through his door asking him to come over as soon as he could. She wished now she had used stronger terms to convey the urgency. Clover paced the room, nibbling on her thumbnail, frustrated tears gathering in her eyes. 'Shall we try to find Johnny before my father does? He's going to get the shock of his life if he's not warned.'

'Heh ... you've done what you can, love.' Neil stopped her restless prowling by placing his hands on her shoulders and drawing her close. 'Don't drive yourself mad over this. Reckon it might be just what your father wants: all of you kids running round after him. I hope you won't mind if I say your father isn't worth any more tears.'

'I know ... you're right ... he isn't.' Clover gazed earnestly at him through her bleary vision. 'He could up and leave again on a whim.'

'And as for Johnny: he's always got his ear to the ground, anyway,' said Neil, kissing her forehead. 'He's a big lad now, Clover, and can deal with his father himself. You had to.'

Chapter Fifteen

Herbert Brick hated Christmas. It was always a disappointment, and this year it seemed more of a let-down than ever.

Slouching against the wall, listening to the refrains of 'Silent Night' mingling with the noise of traffic, he felt too lethargic to summon up the energy to cross the road and start work. He knew he must though, if he were to earn some money and get a lodging for the night. He was already a regular at Sally Army soup kitchens but had so far avoided the workhouse. Public Assistance Institutions, the wretched places were now called. Cosy names didn't fool him; he was avoiding them like the plague.

He pulled a tin of tobacco from his pocket and stared morosely through the gloom at the carol singers grouped around a Christmas tree on the opposite pavement. Oxford Street was twinkling with lights and bustling with excited shoppers. Some had stopped their dashes in and out of the big stores to take a moment to appreciate the festive atmosphere. They were all done up in their scarves, and their gloved hands grasped their purchases as they listened to the choir. The sight of others' warmth and happiness only reminded Herbie of what he'd lost since this time last year.

Weeks ago, he'd crept back to his old stamping ground of Rook Lane. He'd loitered about, hoping to bump into Jake Harding and eat a bit of humble pie to get a permanent roof over his head again. He'd had enough of roaming from place to place looking for casual work and a dosshouse. Most of all he missed his friend, and not only because without him he couldn't seem to stay out of trouble.

Mr Spooner had spotted him, though, and started to stride in his direction. The handyman was friendly with Old Peg and would be aware of the reason Herbert Brick had left her employ under a cloud. He had scuttled away, convinced all the neighbours had been warned to keep a look out for him, in case he returned and tried to rob them next. He couldn't risk being arrested again. He'd already been up in court for shoplifting from a gentlemen's outfitters, and since he'd turned eighteen, the beak wouldn't be lenient with him next time. He'd get hard labour, not a fine.

If he had money, he'd give Peg some, but he couldn't even pay his court fines. He formed a thin cigarette with his stiff fingers, hoping a smoke might warm him and buck him up. Having carefully separated the strands of tobacco – to keep a few back for another meagre roll-up later – he struck a match and jammed the doofer between his lips. Puffing on it, he observed goings-on across the street. The build-up to Christmas didn't seem as big or as glamorous as it had last year when the crowds and noise had seemed impenetrable and he'd had his friend by his side.

Herbie glanced down at his crumpled attire, brushing ash off his threadbare jacket. He looked like a tramp, not a shopper with cash in his pocket. A store detective would suss him in no time. He studied the audience around the carol singers. The small crowd, and late-afternoon dusk, would

173

give him some cover; he'd have better luck dipping pockets and bags, he reasoned. He'd never been much good at hoisting. He didn't have Jake's manly build or his panache. His friend didn't hide at the back; he would saunter smartly into position and get one hand over the counter while causing a distraction with the other. Herbert felt exposed on his own ... conspicuous, even though he was small and often overlooked. He wasn't risking the stores, he decided. He'd stay outside in the open where it was easier to make a run for it. Decision made, he straightened up, headed towards the kerb, and clumsily stepped into the path of a passer-by. The accidental jog to his elbow sent the tobacco tin flying.

'Oi ... you ... watch where yer goin' ... ' Herbie shouted, leaping to catch his solitary cigarette paper floating on the breeze. He snatched on air then lost sight of it, and the scattered tobacco was invisible on the pavement. He brandished a fist at the fellow striding on, apparently unaware of what he'd done. Herbie kicked the empty tin in frustration and it hit him on the calf making him glance over his shoulder, cigarette clamped in his lips.

'You knocked me fag outta me hand.' Herbie had seen an opportunity in a fellow smoker. 'You owe me one now.' He stomped up, beckoning with a belligerent finger. He forgot about cadging a cigarette and his hand flopped back to his side. The spiv who'd tried to poach Jake had tilted back his hat, giving Herbie a proper look at him.

Johnny Cooper did a double take as well, having recognised that surly face. It wasn't the one he would have liked to see, but the youth might prove useful. He approached him, taking a pack of Weights from his pocket and offering it. 'I remember you, and your pal.'

'Herbert Brick, that's me,' he quickly introduced himself.

'Well, Herbert ... I reckon I know what you're up to.' Johnny jerked a nod at the brightly lit department stores. 'Your oppo's taking his time in there, is he?' Herbert looked frozen; gloveless and hatless in a set of clothes that was too small and had seen better days. But Johnny was prepared to hang about with the scruff until his partner appeared. He'd not forgotten the charismatic Jake Harding and still wanted a business chat with him, more so than ever now.

'Nah ... we went separate ways. Ain't seen Jake in ages.' Herbie craftily grabbed several cigarettes and dropped them into his pocket while Cooper was looking the other way. 'You're here on business, I s'pose. I know we're in the same game.'

'Don't reckon we are,' said Johnny, giving hapless Herbert a sideways glance. 'Not quite yet, anyhow,' he added the dry aside for his own benefit. The youth looked about fifteen but he could see from the bristle on his face that he was older than that. He was obviously struggling on his own, and Johnny was coming to know how that felt. Lately, he'd been trying to keep his head above water and it was a new and unwanted experience.

He'd always done all right for himself, from regular work and some hanky-panky on the side. He'd visited Big Queenie the other day and she'd snapped at him to lower his expectations when he'd told her what he wanted for his goods. He wasn't the only one having tough times, she'd complained. Everybody was finding it harder to earn a crust, and lately, she was cutting her own throat to make a sale. Johnny knew she wasn't pulling the wool over his eyes. The working and lower-middle classes were their stock in trade, and those people had less cash these days to buy the luxuries they dealt in. She'd told him if things continued as they were she was forgetting about fencing glad rags and going back to stockpiling corned beef. And he didn't reckon she was joking either.

'Jake said you offered him a job,' Herbie piped up, aware the fellow wasn't going to hang around for long now he'd found out Jake wasn't about. 'He ain't interested ... said he's staying put. I'm ready for a change though.' Herbie couldn't quite pull off being blasé.

'And where is he *staying put* exactly, your mate, Harding?' Johnny lit himself another cigarette, looking thoughtful.

'Why d'you want to know if he ain't interested and I am?' Herbie sounded indignant.

Johnny could ill afford to give money away but decided it was worth his while to bribe the little sod for an answer. He pulled a half-crown out of his pocket and held it between thumb and forefinger close to Herbie's nose.

'Ain't exactly tempting, is it?' Herbie sounded derisive, although he hadn't had more than coppers in his pocket all week. 'Give us five bob and I'll think about it.' He'd cottoned on to the fact he possessed valuable information, and as much as it riled him that Cooper only wanted to take on Jake, he'd sell his soul for a hot meal and a light ale. 'Three bob then, and I'll tell you where he is.' He'd blurted that out as Cooper called his bluff and strolled off.

Johnny strode back and tipped silver into an outstretched palm. 'If you're trying to kid me, I'll be back and find you, Herbert Brick ... '

'Ain't kidding. Come on, follow me 'n' I'll show you.'

'Don't need an escort, son.' Johnny pulled the lad back as he started bowling off along the street. 'I'll find me own way once you give me the address.'

'You ain't from round here ... you're an Elephant Boy.'

Herbie had remembered the story Old Peg had told them about Johnny Cooper. 'Anyhow, no point you going on your own. She won't even let you in if I'm not with you.' It was a fraudulent boast. If Old Peg saw him she'd throw a chamber pot at his head. If she saw Cooper and sniffed a deal, she'd welcome him inside, no hard feelings.

Three bob was nice, but he'd give it back if Cooper banned him from tagging along to Rook Lane. Herbie wanted a reunion with Jake himself, and reckoned he now had a valid reason for showing up uninvited and trying to wangle himself back into favour.

Herbert set off at quite a pace, before Cooper changed his mind.

Johnny called out, 'Where we heading?'

'East End ... Whitechapel to be precise.' That was all Herbert was giving away. He put on a spurt so a gap opened up between them and no more questions were asked.

Johnny cursed, attempting to keep up in a pair of dress shoes that weren't fashioned for hiking. Whitechapel was a good few miles away and if he'd had the money to spare, he would have hailed a hackney cab and taken them both on a ride. There was no way he would save himself blisters and half of the cost by hanging around at a bus stop with Herbert. He had to maintain some standards he told himself.

He brooded on the recent setbacks in his life while loping across roads and around corners. And he did consider his prodigal father's return as a setback. After he'd got over the shock, and the joy of knowing he had a parent alive, regrets had crept in.

In a state of euphoria, and after a few too many cele-bratory Scotches, Johnny had invited his father to stay with him until he found his own place. A week on, it had become obvious Sidney had no intention of room-hunting. It had also become obvious that, other than looking older, he hadn't changed. He was still a parasite, scrounging for drink money and treating Johnny's home like a pigsty. At twelve years old, Johnny had hero-worshipped his handsome soldier father and had cried his eyes out when Clover had told him they must get used to the fact that he wasn't coming back.

Apart from the cost of giving his father board and lodging and money to piss off to the pub, Sidney's presence in his flat made it difficult for Johnny to have a love life. He regretted splitting up with Dora and wanted to make an effort to get them back together. He was prepared to get married. If this downturn had taught him anything it was that being part of a supportive family was more important than anything else. Clover was always there for him; she had tried to warn him about the phoenix rising in their midst, but he had foolishly put her letter aside for another day and he regretted having done that as well.

Johnny stopped and crouched down to speedily adjust his pinching shoes. He couldn't waste too much time as he had to keep his guide in sight. For a scrawny individual, Herbert had plenty of energy, but if this was a wild goose chase, he'd be sorry he started it.

Had Dora still been around he wouldn't be in such a mess, he berated himself as he sped after Herbert. She wouldn't have tolerated Sidney Cooper sponging; she would have thrown him out, something Johnny was finding awkward to do. He was still enough in awe of his dad not to want to smash the pedestal Sidney Cooper had been put upon.

His father was proud of him in return, praising him for

moving up in the world while admiring Johnny's apartment. Not only that, Sidney was dropping hints to be found a good job alongside his son. Johnny hadn't yet told him he was being put off in a few weeks, and might be joining the queue at the labour exchange, as well as giving up his flat.

He had his other business, but there was too much risk and too little profit in shoplifting lately to chance having an amateur along. Store managers were improving their security to ensure they kept as much of their stock as possible. Johnny needed a professional partner. He needed Dora. Or he needed a change of direction.

The two of them could have got through a rocky patch if they'd put their minds to it. Besides which, he missed her company more than he thought he would. He'd been out with some other old flames but those liaisons only proved to him that he preferred being with her, in business and in bed.

Chapter Sixteen

The bell clattered in the kitchen a few seconds after Jake settled down at the table for his dinner. He put the virtually untouched pie and mash back into the oven to keep warm then pulled on his coat. He didn't ignore business even when his mouth was watering for another taste of succulent beef and onion.

He strode along the dark path, already glistening with an early evening frost. The jangling bunch of keys in his hand was an alert to whoever was outside that their wait was nearly over. He added to it a shout that he was on his way. Having unlocked the gate, he pulled it open to find a woman huddled into a coat with a woollen scarf wound tight about her head and neck. From what he could see of her she didn't look to be a regular. She looked startled to see him.

'Where's Old Peg?' she asked nervously, bobbing about to peer past his lofty figure.

Jake got this a lot from people who weren't local; those that were had by now heard on the grapevine that Peg Tiller had passed away in the autumn. Business had dwindled because of it; those customers set in their ways didn't come any more. They never said so, when shuffling back out of the gate, but he could see it in their eyes: they didn't trust him to know what he was doing because of his age. He didn't consider himself young now he'd turned seventeen and was over five feet ten inches tall. Anyway, he looked nineteen and knew he had an old head on his shoulders. Peg and Mr Spooner had both told him so.

'I'm running things now; come in.' Jake gestured her through the gate and she did take a step inside but then halted.

'What d'you mean by that?' The woman sounded suspicious and scandalised.

'Have you brought something for me to look at?' He gave her a reassuring smile. 'I'll give you a fair price. I was working for Peg for a long while. She wouldn't have wanted me to take over if she thought I was no good at it.'

The woman started shaking her head, backing away. 'Must have the wrong place and the wrong information.'

'What have you brought? Show me ... you'll be pleased with the price I give you.'

She slowly withdrew a bangle that glinted in moonlight, but snatched it back before he could examine it properly.

'Come inside so I can see it in the light. It looks pretty, and I'll pay you cash.'

'Ain't after cash for it,' she whispered.

'What?' He frowned. 'What are you after?'

'Where's Peg? I'll only talk to her.'

'You can't; Peg died months ago.'

'I didn't know,' the woman cried. 'They didn't tell me that.'

'Who?' asked Jake, feeling increasingly perplexed.

'Me friend ... she knew all about what Peg got up to. Sorry ... didn't mean to bother you.' She turned and hurried away down the street and Jake, gazing after her, was sure he could hear her crying softly.

Blowing a sigh of disappointment through his teeth, he locked up again and went back inside. After rubbing his palms together to warm them, he took his dinner plate from the oven, turned on the Marconi wireless and sat down. A carol concert from Westminster Abbey was announced as the next programme. He turned up the volume as the mournful descants of 'Oh Come, All Ye Faithful' put him in mind of Christmases spent with his brother. Their parents would take them to sit on hard pews in a draughty vast church to join in with the morning service. But they didn't care about the cold, knowing that when they arrived home to an aroma of cooked goose and sage and onion, they would have a present to unwrap from their father. Their train set had been just such a gift; he could remember the excitement he'd felt when fixing together the tracks, with Toby kneeling at his side.

And now it was nearly Christmas again; a year had passed since he'd seen Toby. His brother would be home again for the holidays. Jake didn't intend to go back and bang on the door. Last year's rejection still burned too brightly. In the autumn he had seen Toby's stepfather marching with the fascists. The oily fellow had recognised him but had turned away without any acknowledgement. Jake hadn't minded being of no consequence to Ian Winters. Rebecca Payne had taken all his attention. He'd not looked for her since; he'd been tempted to, but pride had stopped him. He knew the only interest she'd had in him that day was in getting her own back on him. But he couldn't prevent thoughts of her . . .

His nostalgia and his dinner were again rudely interrupted by the clatter of the bell. With a sigh, he shoved his meal back in the oven, having managed only a forkful of gravy-soaked mashed potato this time.

'Changed your mind, have you?' He opened the gate, expecting to see the woman with the bangle outside.

Instead he gazed upon a sheepish Herbie and, behind him, Johnny Cooper, leaning on the wall and easing off one of his patent leather shoes.

'Thank Gawd you're in,' moaned Johnny, carrying the elegant brogue and hobbling past without a by-your-leave. 'Sorry, son, for me lack of manners, but I need to get off me feet. Me dogs are barking something chronic.' He glanced back at Jake, looking uncharacteristically gormless from his surprise. 'Don't worry, son. Peg knows me ... she won't mind, 'cos I've got a proposition for her.'

When they'd turned the corner into Rook Lane it had finally sunk in where Herbert was taking him. Johnny hadn't used Old Peg Tiller as his fence in a long while. He hadn't expected Jake to be part of such a small-time outfit. The useful lad would be protected by a bigshot – somebody like George Payne – so he'd believed. He was relieved not to have a fight on his hands to poach him. He'd always liked Old Peg but knew not to take liberties with her, so a deal had to be struck. Today. Johnny knew he was badly in need of an assistant until he could sweet-talk Dora into coming back.

'Mr Cooper asked me to show him where you was,' mumbled Herbie, shifting from foot to foot. 'Didn't think you'd mind. I won't come in the house if it'll send Peg up the wall.' Despite what he'd said, Herbie took the opportunity to sidle past while Jake gawped after the hopping man. 'Like to speak to you, though, if that's all right ... say sorry to Peg 'n' all for what I done.'

'Hang on a moment, you two . . . ' Jake had shaken off his daze to shout at them. 'You can't just come barging in here.' That was as far as he got in barring the interlopers. Johnny Cooper, bold as brass and still managing a swagger despite his uneven gait, had almost made the side door. Herbie slunk along in the older man's wake, sliding wary glances over his shoulder as though expecting to be hauled back at any moment.

Jake plunged his hands on his hips and stood pondering until he accepted that, actually, he was pleased he had these visitors. He rarely saw anybody other than customers and there weren't too many of those. He had little social life other than a trip to see his casual friend Sadie once in a while, or a visit to the Spooners for a cup of tea and a slice of cake, if Mrs Spooner had been baking. He hadn't forgiven Herbert for what he'd done, but enough time had elapsed for the edges to have rubbed off his anger. As for Johnny Cooper, he had a way about him that Jake found appealing, although he wasn't sure why.

'Somethin' smells bleedin' lovely.' Herbert had stopped timidly on the threshold of the kitchen to stare hungrily at the oven radiating a scent of gravy. Johnny had slumped straight down on a hard-backed chair and rested his elbows on the table with a blissful groan. He released his other tortured foot from its confinement and pulled off his socks, bloodied at the heels.

'Where's Old Peg?' asked Herbie nervously.

'Whitechapel cemetery,' said Jake, and told them what had happened.

He had their full attention throughout the story and in parts, when Herbie felt ashamed for having burdened Peg with stress she could have done without, his head drooped

184

towards his chest. By the time Jake was nearing the end, recounting that Peg's funeral had drawn every neighbour out onto the street on a blustery autumn afternoon, to pay their respects as the hearse passed, Herbie had come forward and seated himself opposite Johnny. Both men were absorbed by the tale of Old Peg Tiller's demise, and Jake Harding's rise in status to business and property owner. When he'd nothing more to add, Jake filled the kettle at the tap and started making a pot of tea while his visitors gawped at one another in disbelief.

'So ... you tellin' me that Peg actually left you everything?' demanded Johnny, struggling with his envy.

Jake nodded. 'A lawyer has to act as trustee and oversee things until I come of age, to keep it all above board.'

Herbert Brick wiped his eyes ... then did so again. The tears continued to come. He started to grizzle softly, unable to stop himself although he tried to hide his weakness from the other two. Guilt and sorrow for Old Peg's bad luck, and her death at forty-two, had affected him. Mostly, though, his pity was for himself. He knew if he hadn't stolen from the best employer he'd ever had, but had been as loyal as Jake, he might have shared in riches.

Jake could guess at Herbie's miserable thoughts; unwilling to embarrass him he pretended to be deaf to the sobs and carried on pouring boiling water into the teapot. 'Let that brew a bit then I'll pour out.' He got his dinner from the oven then sat down with the others to dig into his meal.

'Before you hit the nosebag, son, any chance of a bowl of water? I'll need to soak me feet or I'll never get these back on.' Johnny continued pulling at the patent leather uppers to stretch them.

Jake rolled his eyes, but put down his knife and fork and again employed the squeaky tap to half fill an enamel bowl.

When he carried it over to the table he noticed Herbie chewing furiously, having shovelled a forkful of food off his plate. Jake gave Johnny the bowl then pushed his dried-up dinner towards Herbie.

'Thanks, Jake . . .' he mumbled, and grabbed up the knife and fork.

Having deposited the bowl on the floor, Johnny rolled back his trouser legs and dipped his feet. He sat back in the chair and crossed his arms, cocking his head to give Peg's heir a judicial look. 'Well, Jake Harding, reckon we'll be on an even footing in our business venture now you've gone up in the world.' Johnny's opening salvo on forming a partnership didn't get the reception he hoped for.

'Won't happen; I've had enough of this hoisting and fencing lark. I'm going straight.'

This news was interesting enough to make Herbie pause in wolfing down his food, and Johnny stop paddling his feet to wash his socks in the bowl. They both paid attention.

'I want to get a proper trade so I'm finishing my apprenticeship with Mr Spooner. He had a licence once as a master builder but his brother stole it for himself. Anyway, he's an able carpenter and knows plumbing and painting and decorating as well. He's teaching me, then when I'm ready to work on my own, I'm packing in seeing Peg's customers. I'm never going back to the West End to hoist either.'

'You've got a list of Peg's regulars have you?' Johnny saw an opportunity to get hold of some useful contacts the boy didn't want.

Jake nodded.

'Bleedin' lucky sod, you are,' Herbie finally said with a grudging smile. 'What you going to call your firm then?'

Jake shrugged. 'Harding and ...' He was about to say 'sons', but he didn't know if or when that might come about.

'Harding Brothers ...' supplied Johnny. 'You've got a brother, I remember Dora said so.'

'He's not a Harding now, and anyway, he's destined for better things than manual work.' Jake poured the tea.

'I'll be your pretend brother,' said Herbie eagerly. 'Won't take me long to learn to be your labourer.'

Jake didn't reply as he handed round the teas. He didn't sit down either, but stood by the sink and again became aware of the carol concert on the wireless, reminding him it was Christmas.

He'd imagined he'd spend the festive season on his own, although Mr Spooner had kindly invited him for roast chicken and plum pudding. Jake had turned down the invitation; Mr and Mrs Spooner had been invited out themselves to their married daughter's house and he didn't want to spoil their arrangements.

It seemed he might not be on his own after all, though. Jake felt content, but for the life of him, didn't know why the scene in his kitchen of Johnny Cooper with his feet in a washing-up bowl and Herbie licking clean the dinner plate inches from his nose, was making him smile.

And then he thought of Peg Tiller, the woman who had treated him as her son. She had left him all she had, including her notebook filled with the names and addresses of those who bought her hooky gear. Beneath each name was a neat list of the sort of goods they favoured. She had also left him all her stock of silver and gold jewellery, including her own wedding and engagement rings, plus a sideboard

crammed with rag, tag and bobtail bric-a-brac she had collected over the years. And she had left him all her money.
It amounted to almost three hundred pounds. In the letter
she had written him, she had detailed her possessions, and
where to find them.

He hadn't been able to clearly comprehend any of it for
days as he couldn't stop weeping. Grief at her death had been
overtaken by shock and disbelief after he read her letter; then
came a wondrous relief that he was financially secure. Finally,
when he opened the small jewellery box that contained her
personal treasures, emotion had overcome him again. He'd
cradled the emerald and diamond ring and a gold wedding
band in his palm. Peg's gifts from her beloved Dickie had
remained hidden until the end, like the dreams she'd had of
their motorbike with its sidecar and seaside home.

Then when he felt able to begin his new life, he went
hunting. Old Peg hadn't believed in banks, it seemed. Cash
was secreted behind loose bricks in walls and under floorboards. Some of it had even been hidden in the outhouse
where he and Herbie had slept. Jake had chuckled when
pulling a roll of five-pound notes out of a cranny beneath
the tin roof. Herbie would have delighted in finding that on
the day he stole from them and scarpered. And that's why
Jake didn't feel very much sympathy for Herbie being left
out in the cold while he'd had good fortune.

Jake hadn't told a soul about the jewellery or the cash and
didn't intend to. And he had spent very little of it. It was
money to invest in his new business ... in his future. He
knew Peg would approve.

He might not have had much schooling, or gone to university to study history and geography, but he'd make his
own luck and be his brother's equal, in his own way.

Chapter Seventeen

'Bleeding hell! Didn't reckernise you. What you done to yerself, gel?'

'Just fancied a change. Think it suits me?'

'Well ... ain't saying it don't.' Queenie Darke glanced down at the bag her visitor was carrying. That interested her most. Bottle blondes were no big deal; they were everywhere these days. 'Brought something nice for me, have you?'

'You'll want the lot when I show you.' Dora Knox smoothed her sleek blonde bob with a hand, miffed by Queenie's luke-warm compliment on her glamorous new look.

She'd heard that Johnny Cooper had been spotted squiring a Jean Harlow lookalike in Wardour Street; Dora wanted to be the platinum blonde on his arm next time he went to the theatre. She'd had a peroxide do at a hairdressing salon and had been delighted with the result, if not the cost of it. 'Can I come in then, or we bartering on the step?' she prompted Queenie, when the woman continued peering around the edge of the door at her.

'S'pose you'd better; I've got company. Me niece won't mind us doing a bit of business, though, if you don't.'

Dora's eloquent shrug preceded her squeezing past Queenie's bulk into the hallway, lugging her bag of goodies.

The older woman led the way into the parlour. 'This is Miss Knox, love,' she announced before fully inside the room. 'And this is George's girl, Rebecca. You know George, of course,' said Queenie slyly, turning to Dora.

'Yeah, I do know George. I've bumped into Rebecca before as well.' Dora gave the seated girl a smile as she dumped her bag on the sideboard. She decided to ignore Queenie's jibes. She was running out of cash and needed to do a deal; she daren't let her temper get in the way of that.

Rebecca raised a hand, acknowledging she remembered that Christmas Eve in the Bricklayer's Arms. It had taken her a few seconds to cotton on to who the visitor was, though, as the woman appeared quite different, apart from the fox fur and her air of sophistication.

Over a year had passed since that meeting had taken place but she'd never forgotten it. Jake Winters ... or Jake Harding ... if that was his real name, had ceased to be a stranger to her that night. But he was still rather an enigma and Miss Knox might prove to be useful in learning more about him.

'What's in here then, Dora?' Queenie had been fencing goods for decades but never failed to get excited by the sight of an unopened treasure trove. 'Ooh, look at that, love ... ' The moment the bag was unclasped she swung around to display a length of white satin lifted from a jumble of garments. 'Wedding night nightie if ever I saw it ... ' She gave Rebecca a saucy wink.

'You're making her blush, Queenie,' said Dora, taking pity on the girl.

'You're right; Rebecca's too young to get herself tied

down; more in your line.' She draped the virginal negligee over Dora's shoulder. 'Not your colour though, is it, Dora? Got a proposal out of Johnny Cooper yet, have you?'

It was Dora's turn to blush. Queenie was aware they'd broken up and was deliberately riling her. But she was glad that name had come up as she could now enquire after him. 'Not seen Johnny in ages. Have you?' She snatched the satin off her shoulder and dropped it back in the bag.

Queenie's jowls wobbled as she shook her head. 'Heard on the grapevine he'd lost his job at the gambling club after Christmas. When it closed up, I thought that might mean I'd see more of him, not less.' She paused. 'Maybe he's using another fence.' She sniffed in indifference. 'I did hear though that he'd moved back over the other side of the water, closer to his sisters.' She gave Dora a rather sympathetic look. 'You two didn't get back together then?'

'I'm seeing somebody else,' Dora said airily, although hearing Johnny was on Clover's doorstep had deflated her.

'Anybody I'd know?' Queenie guessed Dora had several other men on the go if the rumour she'd heard about her was true. Dora wasn't alone in turning to vice to get by, though. Decent women – many of them war widows who'd lost their regular work – were paying the rent and feeding their kids in any way they could.

'Any of this any good to you, 'cos if not I'll be on me way.' Dora ignored Queenie's insolence and began gathering up her stolen merchandise.

'Hold on ... ain't had a proper look yet.' Queenie began separating the items that interested her from the rest that were dropped back into the bag.

Rebecca watched and listened as the women haggled and eventually money appeared from her great-aunt's apron

191

pocket and was handed over. She noticed Dora didn't look too happy with the outcome.

'Well, nice to see you again, Rebecca,' Dora said to the girl by way of goodbye.

'And you, Miss Knox,' Rebecca politely replied as her aunt walked her visitor to the door.

Dora was keen to get going before Queenie started prying about her love life again. Luckily, the neighbours started a commotion that allowed her to slip outside while Queenie hammered on the wall, shouting, 'Tone it down in there, you two, or I'll be round. Dolly! Tommy! You listenin' to me?'

'Better make a move myself now,' said Rebecca as Queenie came back into the parlour muttering about the Rudges being the bane of her life.

'Not staying for another cuppa?' Queenie asked in surprise. 'Don't worry about them.' She jerked her head at the wall. 'Dolly 'n' Tommy'll shut up for a while. They know I ain't joking when I say I'll sort 'em out.' She made her niece chuckle by shaking her fist.

Rebecca had arrived looking thoughtful and Queenie had known the girl had something to chew over. Rebecca was her favourite niece and often came to spill her worries or to ask for advice rather than confide in her mum and dad. Unfortunately, Dora had interrupted them before they could get down to brass tacks. 'Have another cuppa and keep me company, eh, love? Reckon I might find a Bourbon biscuit to go with it.'

'Can't stop, Auntie Queenie.' Rebecca pulled on her coat. 'Time's getting on; I'm going to the pictures later with some friends.'

'Well, take this with you, it's just right for the spring

weather.' Queenie handed over a pretty lemon cardigan that she'd just paid for. She knew it would suit the girl's dark-haired colouring. 'Look a treat in that, you will; make your friends' eyes go green.'

Rebecca kissed her aunt's plump cheek. She'd been thinking of green eyes ... but they didn't belong to her or any of her friends.

'Thanks ... it's lovely.' She folded the fine knit wool and slipped it into her bag.

Once outside she waved, then after her aunt closed the door, Rebecca started to run to catch up with Dora Knox, who was nearly at the top of the street.

'Gawd-love-us ... you frightened the life outta me. Thought you was gonna mug me.' Dora thumped her chest to calm herself. She had kept her hand on her money in her pocket, as she always did. Locals knew that people exiting Big Queenie's house were likely to have cashed in valuables.

'Sorry, didn't mean to,' said Rebecca, panting after her exertion. 'Just wanted to have a word with you, if that's all right.'

They walked on side by side for a few seconds then when Rebecca had recovered her breath, and some courage, she blurted, 'I wanted to ask you about Jake. You called him Winters that time in the pub, but since then I've heard somebody else say he's Jake Harding.' Rebecca had decided the policeman was more likely to have addressed him correctly.

Dora slanted her a knowing look. 'Ah ... you noticed, did you, that he's a handsome lad?'

Rebecca blushed. 'He stole from me, so I've got an interest in knowing a bit about him. That's all.'

Dora smiled. 'Why didn't you grass him up then if you knew he'd done it?'

'Don't grass up people, that's why.'

Dora suspected the girl had a crush on him; but she wouldn't risk Rebecca passing on information about Jake to her father. George would track him down and batter him. She'd always liked Jake from when he was little. 'I'd guess he uses aliases. Can't say I blame him for that. In this game you can't be too cautious. Could be either name is his real name . . . or maybe neither is.' She patted the girl's arm. 'What I do know for sure: he's a clever lad so don't underestimate him.'

Rebecca also saw him as cautious and clever. He would be angry with her for stealing from him under cover of a kiss. She'd wanted him to come looking for her, for round two of their game. But he hadn't . . . which told her all she needed to know. He was either frightened of her father or he thought she wasn't worth the trouble. Whichever it was, he had disappointed her.

'So what you said about working for his mother . . . that wasn't true . . . you only said it to get my dad off his back?'

'I did once skivvy for a Mrs Winters when I was a kid.' Dora didn't reveal knowing Jake as a child. She liked this girl, but she was still a thuggish Elephant Boy's daughter and Dora's loyalty, such as it was, was to Jake. He could end up as Johnny had, with a slashed face. Guilty feelings about that fight had never completely gone away. Declaring her love for Johnny had sealed his fate. George hadn't been heartbroken to lose her; his pride had been injured and he'd retaliated violently, as he always did. Dora had never spoken loosely since. And she wouldn't now. 'You're right, Rebecca, I did want your father to leave young Jake alone.'

'You know my dad well, don't you?' Rebecca was surprised when Dora's expression betrayed she had a more intimate link with George Payne than them both dabbling in criminality.

'I know him well enough,' Dora said rather sourly. A quiet ensued as they walked on.

'I bet you miss Johnny Cooper ...' Rebecca looked startled to have voiced the thought in her head. She remembered him because he had stuck up for Jake as well on that night in the Bricklayer's Arms. She'd thought him nice doing that. 'Sorry, Miss Knox, I'm being as rude as my aunt. Didn't mean to be personal.'

'Oh, it's all right, and call me Dora like everybody else or you'll make me feel like a hopeless old spinster.' She gave the blushing girl a friendly nudge. 'I do miss him. And just between you 'n' me I haven't got anybody special to replace him. Don't want him to find that out though 'cos once a man thinks he's got the upper hand with you ...' She swayed an instructive index finger, making Rebecca smile in agreement. 'Maybe some time apart isn't a bad thing. All those sayings about absence making the heart grow fonder, and not knowing what you've got till it's gone ... wise words indeed.'

'Dreamt up by regretful people,' Rebecca added.

'I reckon you'd like a reunion of your own with somebody special, wouldn't you?' Dora raised a teasing eyebrow.

Rebecca nodded shyly and changed the subject. 'Your hair looks nice; it suits you blonde.'

'Thanks,' said Dora and affectionately touched the girl's cheek.

'Oh, damn ... what does he want?' Rebecca sighed as a Humber car turned the corner. She was enjoying this cosy chat that might've produced more information about Jake.

Dora had also noticed George Payne steering to the kerb to stop by them.

'Get in, Rebecca,' he snapped, having leaned over the passenger seat to wind down the window.

'Reckon you're in for an ear'ole bashing,' Dora whispered, having seen his livid expression. 'Tell him it's my fault. If you're late home, say I delayed you.' George had a vicious streak and she didn't want the girl to be on the wrong side of him.

"S all right, I'll tell Mum if he starts on me. He wants me to attend a rally with him and his fascist chums this evening and I'm not going. Got better things to do and nicer people to see.'

'Good fer you,' said Dora who'd heard about George Payne's interest in politics. She knew him though; the only cause he believed in was himself. He was sucking up to nobs in the hope of social climbing.

'Get in the bleedin' car, now,' bawled George. He opened his door and sprang out. 'What're you doing with my daughter? You stay away from her.' He jabbed his finger at Dora over the top of the car bonnet.

'We're just talking, that's all.' Rebecca felt ashamed of him for being rude.

'She ain't fit company,' he sneered. 'She ain't respectable and I don't want you associating with the likes of her.'

Dora stormed up to the car, placed her hands on the bonnet and hissed quietly into his face, 'And who was it made me a disgrace, eh? Seem to remember you liked being my ponce back then.'

George turned a furious red and marched around the car as though to strike Dora.

Rebecca barged into his path to keep the two of them apart. Aware of a few net curtains twitching in the terrace of houses, he retreated with a poisonous look for Dora.

Having got in the car beside him, Rebecca raised a hand to the blonde woman as the vehicle pulled away.

'What were you doin' with her?' Spittle was flecking his lips in his rage. 'What was you talking about?' If Dora had been badmouthing him to his daughter he'd turn the car around and give her the slap she deserved.

'Nothing much. I remembered meeting her in the Bricklayer's Arms on that Christmas Eve. I was saying I liked her hair blonde. She turned up at Aunt Queenie's, you see, and then we both left about the same time and walked up the road together. Look ... Auntie gave me this ... I'm going to wear it later.' She pulled out the pretty cardigan to distract him but he ripped it from her grip and tossed it over his shoulder to land on the back seat.

'You'll wear your brigade uniform. And you can go without your dinner or we'll be late now you've been off gallivanting all afternoon.'

'I'm not going. I've arranged to meet some friends and I'm going to wear my new cardigan.'

'You are going, my girl. You'll do as you're damn well told.' George stared at her mutinous face. 'Mosley asked about you himself ... said he'd like more young people like my daughter joining the group. He's a wealthy important man.'

'I don't care if he is important and don't care how much money he's got. I'm not going ... '

George took a hand from the steering wheel and slapped her smartly across the face. 'Well, maybe that'll help you change your mind, and show your father some respect,' he said. 'Buck up your ideas or you'll end up on your own, like that slut back there.'

Rebecca gasped in pain and clutched her stinging cheek.

She started to cry but stopped quickly, unwilling to let him see he'd hurt her. She didn't care what insults he used, she liked the woman. Dora seemed tough and independent. If being married meant being stuck with a bully like George Payne, then Rebecca knew she'd rather be on her own as well. In fact, she was starting to think her mother must be a fool to put up with him. Yet Molly wasn't a pushover. She'd seen her mother fight and argue with George yet something kept them together. Rebecca supposed it must be her ... their only child.

She'd gone to her aunt's to ask for her advice on how to make her father accept she didn't hold his views. She wanted to train to be a typist and get a proper job. Every time she brought that up at home her father shouted her down. He couldn't see any benefit to himself in her doing that, and so wouldn't listen. But Rebecca wasn't interested in introductions to rich people. She wasn't interested in shoplifting and pickpocketing. Although her aunt was involved in crime, Queenie was fair and believed in people making their own choices. And if George Payne took notice of anybody, it was his aunt Queenie.

His glowering looks were burning the side of her face but Rebecca refused to turn towards him. He wouldn't cow her, she vowed and continued to stare out of the window for the rest of the way home.

Dora joined the queue at the bus stop. She was aware of getting a few sideways looks. Not many women with expensive hairdos, wearing fur coats, caught the bus. She didn't care what anybody thought of her, she told herself. But it wasn't actually true. She was fed up with her sordid life and understood Rebecca Payne's yearning to follow a different path to her parents. It was as well she'd not got a daughter to look at her with disgust in the way Rebecca had looked at her father. Young women wanted more from life nowadays: an education, a good job and a respectful man. When Dora had been a child during the war, just staying alive had been an achievement with German bombs dropping on London. Women of her mother's age with men fighting abroad had wanted husbands home to help with life's battles. They put up with a lot; it was all they knew.

It had taken a meeting with a girl a decade younger to make Dora realise that if she didn't change direction now she never would, and might turn into her mother, who'd remained resentful until the day she died.

Dora wanted to be respectable and happy; she wanted Johnny. As the months had passed and he hadn't swallowed his pride and come to see her, she was wishing she had swallowed hers. She'd left it too late to ambush him at his place of work, or his flat. He'd moved away and she didn't know to where.

She could bang on his sister's door and ask some questions but after she'd tried it on with Clover's husband, she was likely to get her face scratched, not Johnny's address.

Dora's insides squirmed just thinking of how Johnny would have taken hearing about that, and about her and Archie Fletcher being caught at it in a park. She boarded the bus, sat down with her bag at her feet then used her handkerchief on her watering eyes. She regretted all of it and wished she'd not had so much to drink and made a complete fool of herself that night ... or on any other night. She wished she'd never got involved with George Payne and let him edge her into vice. Easy money he called it; maybe for him ... not for her.

She sniffed and put up her chin. She'd always thought joining the queue at the labour exchange was beneath her. Getting up at midday, going up West to try her luck at hoisting or soliciting ... that had been her way before she met Johnny. And so it was again now they'd broken up. But while she'd been with him, life had been real enough. They might have been shoplifters but they'd been a proper couple, loving and faithful. She'd been his wife in all but name and wished now she'd settled for that.

Johnny had always kept his bread-and-butter work; ducking and diving was bunce for him that paid for luxuries and excitement. As for Dora, the last proper employment she'd had was at the age of seventeen, working for Jake's mother. Her hand closed around the pound note and the silver coins in her pocket. Johnny would've prised more than one pound seven shillings out of Queenie for that haul. She'd made a fuss about not wanting this and that but there was actually little left in the carpet bag at Dora's feet.

She budged up on the seat as a fellow came to plonk himself down beside her. She could feel his hip pressing into hers and his eyes on her. She turned and glared at him until the leer faded from his face and he squirmed away.

Tomorrow she'd pawn her fur coat and buy a suitable outfit to go job hunting. Properly buy it ... not hoist it.

And she'd try to find the courage to knock on Clover Ryan's door and ask after Johnny.

Chapter Eighteen

'Well, look what the cat dragged in.'

A brunette had glared over her shoulder as the shop bell clattered. Archie Fletcher ignored her muttered insult as he entered the busy tobacconist's. But he wasn't the only one to have heard the cutting remark; so had somebody who held a similar view of him. Being nosy, Dora had taken a glance then suppressed a knowing smirk. She assumed she was standing in the queue behind one of Archie Fletcher's embittered old flames. Having bought her cigarettes, the brunette left the shop with her nose in the air.

Dora was next to be served but despite her efforts to become inconspicuous, Archie had spotted her. He elbowed past those waiting patiently, making out he was with her, to push in.

'Well, ain't you the glamour puss.' He admired her blonde hair with a grin of approval. 'Not seen you over this way in a while, Dora.' He put a pally arm about her that was immediately shrugged off.

'Not been over this way in a while.' Dora paid for her cigarettes and made for the exit. She heard the shop bell clatter and knew he'd rushed out after her. He was so conceited he probably believed she was in Silvertown hoping to bump into him.

'Fancy a drink later?' He stepped into her path, trapping her against the shop window.

'No thanks.'

'Come on . . . fer old times' sake. You're not brooding about what happened when Neil Ryan butted in on us, are you?' He pushed back his railway cap and attempted to woo her with a smile and a fondling hand. 'All in the past, and forgotten, love. I'll take you up West if you like; treat you to a Chinese meal.'

Dora slapped away his hand and gazed at him in disgust. 'How's your wife and your new baby doing then?'

Archie dropped the arm blocking her in. 'Don't tell me Dora Knox's got a conscience all of a sudden,' he sneered.

'Well, if I have it's my business, not yours.'

She walked off but he didn't give up; he followed behind. As he watched the mesmerising sway of her hips it occurred to him she wasn't dressed in her usual garb of fur coat and high heels. She was wearing a belted Macintosh and her shoes looked sturdy.

'If you're done up prim 'n' proper hoping to get back with Johnny Cooper, forget it. He's fixed up. Saw him with a young blonde . . . ahh . . . ' He chuckled in enlightenment. 'Is that why you bleached your hair?' He had a feeling that might make her stop and swing around. 'Not only that, Johnny's old man's turned up to cramp his style.' Now that really had got her attention.

Dora was annoyed that he'd guessed what had prompted her to go blonde but that was soon forgotten. It was hard to believe even Archie Fletcher would joke about Sidney Cooper, who everybody knew had tragically died. She shook her head, gave him a filthy look then marched on.

'It's true,' he crowed and watched her indecision slowing down her footsteps. 'Sidney Cooper turned up just before Christmas. Been in France all this time . . . lost his memory, so he says. And if you believe that, you'll believe anything.'

Dora pivoted to face him, astonishment stretching every feature. She was prepared to talk to him about this, but he was walking backwards, looking triumphant. 'Reckon you was already dead to Johnny even before his old man turned up. He knows, y'see, about us having fun in the park.'

Dora ran after him as he crossed the road, narrowly avoiding being run over. 'Who told Johnny about that?' she demanded, grabbing his arm.

'Who d'you think? Clover's got it in for you.' He shook her hand off him and started striding away.

Dora was struggling to believe what she'd been told about Mr Cooper. Even Archie wouldn't fabricate something this serious, though. As for Clover or Neil telling Johnny about the park incident . . . she'd had to accept that was always on the cards. She was forlorn all the same, having trusted them not to rat on her.

Having continued aimlessly for a yard or two, she came abreast of a wall and rested her back against it. She took her cigarettes from her pocket, unaware of Archie's observation. He'd also dived into his tobacco and was rolling up while loitering further along the road to see where she would head next.

Dora put a match to her cigarette and smoked furiously, lighting another Embassy from the stub of the first. When she felt calmer she realised she'd nothing to lose by going and finding out about all of this from the horse's mouth. And she'd have to do so without some Dutch courage as the pubs weren't open yet.

*

'Hello there. Not seen you out and about this week.'

'Lumbago.'

The single word was enough to make Nettie Fletcher smile in sympathy. 'Feeling better now?'

'Not too bad, thanks, love.' A grimacing Mrs Waverley rubbed her achy hip. 'It's a lovely spring day out there so I came out to cheer meself up. I need some wool to make my granddaughter a school cardigan. Navy blue is her uniform colour, and I'll take a nylon mix so it don't shrink.' She flexed her fingers. 'A bit of knitting in the evening helps keep these oiled. Can do without them seizing up on me as well.'

While Nettie sorted through the dark blue skeins Mrs Waverley ambled behind the counter to peer into the pram at baby Leonora. 'She's a bonny lass. You wouldn't think she'd come early, the size of her.' She gave the pram handle a gentle jig as the baby stretched and seemed on the point of waking. She turned to Jennifer, seated on a stool behind the counter where her mother could keep an eye on her. 'You're looking after your little sister for your mum, are you?'

The toddler nodded shyly and the woman ruffled her soft hair.

'Better take some brown thread while I'm here. Got a skirt hem needs stitching. Keep catching me boots in it.'

Having paid her dues and put her purchases into her bag, Mrs Waverley looped the handles over her arm. 'Well, Nettie Fletcher, your kids are blooming, but reckon you could do with putting your feet up. You look tired.'

'She's right you know,' said Clover, who had held the door for Mrs Waverley to go out before entering. She'd heard the last of their conversation and given her friend a thorough look. Nettie appeared pale and frazzled. Considering the man she was married to, there was little wonder at it. 'Did you skip your dinner break, Nettie?'

'Wasn't hungry,' said Nettie. 'But I closed for half an hour to feed Leonora.'

'Why don't you close early and have a rest? I'll see to these two.'

'Archie doesn't like us closing before six and losing business from women on their way home from work. Anyhow, I'm fine ... it's just I didn't sleep very well last night. Jenny's cutting her back teeth and Leonora's been colicky.' Nettie pushed her untidy curls back behind her ears. 'What can I do for you then, Mrs Ryan?' she asked with jokey formality.

'Oh, nothing really. I don't start my shift at the factory for over an hour so I thought I'd pop by and see how you all were.'

Nettie was pleased that her friend had called in for a chat. Sometimes when on her own with two crying babies the noise drove her crackers.

She'd seen some customers tut and turn around and leave the shop when one or other of the girls wouldn't stop bawling. She'd never leave them in the flat on their own, though. She'd rather be up there with them but Archie still refused to become a draper. Her late father had run the business and her mother had only taken over the reins when he went off to France to fight in the war.

'I could nip upstairs and make a pot of tea if you hold the fort, Clo.'

'Righto. I'll shout up if I get a tricky customer.'

While their mother was gone, Clover lifted Jennifer to sit on the edge of the pram then wheeled it to and fro on the shop floor. She played a clumsy version of pat-a-cake with the toddler. When Jennifer got overexcited, she put her back on the chair in case the baby was woken up. Clover called in at the drapery as much to see her godchildren as her friend. It was a poignant pleasure: learning for half an hour what it would be like to have children of her own.

She was wiping teething dribble from Jennifer's chin when she heard a noise from the inner hallway. She craned her neck and caught a glimpse of Archie in the process of going up to the flat. Clover ducked out of sight hoping he wouldn't spot her but was a second too late. He came back down the stairs and into the shop.

'What're you doing here?'

'Just popped in to see Nettie and the kids.'

'Where is she?' He glanced about for his wife.

'Upstairs, making some tea.' Clover found something neutral to say before he filled a silence by being his usual contentious self. 'Finished work?'

'Did an early shift. How about you? Thrown in the towel at the sugar factory?'

She didn't rise to his mockery. 'I've been doing night work for months.'

'Don't suppose your visitor knows that,' said Archie. 'Or maybe she does; maybe it's not you she hoped to see.' A malicious smile lifted a corner of his mouth.

'I don't follow ...' Clover might have known he'd succeed in irritating her. If he had something to say, he could come straight out with it.

'I saw Dora Knox on her way round to yours.' He'd watched her turn into the lane. The only people Dora knew up there would be Neil and Clover Ryan. 'Your husband at home to deal with her, is he?'

Clover wouldn't give him the satisfaction of seeing her react with any interest. 'Neil might be in ... or he might have gone out to the allotment.' She shrugged. 'We don't keep tabs on one another.'

'If he's hanging around during the day he must still be struggling for permanent work.'

'He's got enough to keep him busy, thanks. We're getting by best we can, same as everyone else.'

'Should've stuck with me, gel.' Archie's voice was lowered to a throaty growl as he leaned closer. 'I'd've kept you in clover.'

She gave him a sickly smile, letting him know she thought it a weak joke, and began to rock the pram.

'Oh ... didn't know you were home, love.' Nettie had reappeared carrying a tea tray set for two and a plate of biscuits. 'I'll fetch another cup. There's plenty in the pot.' Nettie quickly smoothed her mousy curls and straightened her pinafore as her husband's bored eyes swept over her.

'It's all right, Nettie,' Clover said. 'I'd best push off now, anyway, and get ready for work. Only popped in to say a quick hello and see how the children are.'

Archie wasn't lying about their visitor, Clover realised, while hurrying down the lane. A slim blonde was talking to Neil by the front door. Archie had mistaken her identity, was Clover's initial thought. She believed that Johnny's current fancy had called round. Johnny – perhaps recognising something of himself in his young girlfriend's immaturity – was growing up and growing bored with her already. Or perhaps Johnny had his father to thank for being catapulted into the role of responsible adult. Sidney was clinging to his son like a needy kid, despite Johnny having moved from Lambeth in a desperate attempt to shake him off. Their father would take advantage of his family for as long as he could and put little effort into looking for work if he could sponge instead.

As Clover got closer to home a glimpse of a sharp profile proved Archie Fletcher had known what he was talking about.

'Hello, stranger.' Clover stopped by Dora and gave her a smile. 'Didn't recognise you with your hair blonde. It suits you.'

'Spur of the moment decision.' Dora self-consciously patted her finger waves. 'Not sure it was the right thing to do, actually.'

'Right ... I'll leave you two ladies to it then. Dora caught me on the way out. See you in the morning, love.' Neil pecked his wife's cheek, gave her a private smile, and made his escape up the road.

'Come in, Dora.' Clover looked for her key to open the door. 'I'm off to work in a sec; doing a night shift, you see. I've time for a quick natter though and it won't take long to boil a kettle.'

'Oh, won't put you to that trouble.' An expectant quiet followed. 'Didn't mean to bother you. I only wanted to say that I've just heard the good news about your dad. Johnny used to talk about him a lot in the early days, when we first got together. He was cut up over losing him and it seemed so unfair after Sidney had not long returned from fighting in France. Must've been such a shock for you all to see him walking around again. Most odd ... ' Dora's awkward speech came to an end.

'It was ... very odd ... and I appreciate your concern, Dora.' Clover squeezed the nervous woman's hand. It wasn't like Dora to be unsure of herself. She'd always been the brash one. 'It's a miracle to have him back and we're doing our best to return to normal. Our father's never been the easiest person to rub along with and no change there.' She rolled her eyes. 'Johnny was always his favourite so Dad lodged with him at first.'

'How is Johnny?' Dora jumped on the chance to ask after him. Before Clover could answer she continued, 'I heard he lost his job at the gambling club when it closed down. Has he managed to find something else?'

'He's working as a night watchman at the brewery. And some days he does some casual labouring for a young fellow who's starting up a building business.' Clover shrugged to show she knew little about it.

'Sorry . . . shouldn't have asked and put you on the spot.' Belatedly, it occurred to Dora that she might have jeopardised a reunion by checking up on Johnny behind his back. 'I'd speak to him about all of this myself, but haven't a clue where to find him since he moved. I don't want him to think I couldn't care less about important happenings in his life. I do, you see. If he tells me to mind me own business, I'll leave him alone in future, though.'

'I reckon he'll be pleased to know you wish him well.'

Dora smiled wistfully. 'I wouldn't want to butt in if he's got a serious girlfriend. Would I be? Butting in, that is?'

Clover recognised a woman with regrets when she listened to one. Dora wanted to get back with Johnny, and a reunion was what her brother was after as well. He hadn't seemed happy for a while and Clover knew that wasn't wholly due to him losing a good job and gaining a bad father. Clover didn't mind playing cupid. Being apart had seemed to spur them into becoming nicer people. She knew about Dora's reputation, but Clover believed in fair dos. While unattached, Dora could see who she wanted to see, just as her handsome brother had been doing by squiring a string of women.

'Johnny's in Poplar but he's thinking of finding a nicer

room. When I see him next, I'll let him know you came over. Maybe he'll pay you a return visit.'

'D'you think so?' A spark of hope brightened Dora's eyes.

'I do indeed,' Clover wryly said.

'Is it all right if I walk to work with you? I can go that way to catch my bus.' Dora paused. 'There's something I want to get off my chest.'

"Course. I'll just fetch my things. Give us a tick.' Clover disappeared inside.

Five minutes later, they were walking briskly towards the smoke rising into the air from the factories that lined the banks of the Thames. It seemed they were both waiting for the other to take the lead and pick up where they'd left off. Finally, Clover said, 'Who told you about our father returning home?'

'Archie Fletcher. I bumped into him earlier.' There was a grimace in Dora's tone.

'So did I,' said Clover ruefully.

'Tried to hide but he spotted me,' said Dora.

'So did I,' sighed Clover with increased irony.

The two women slanted glances at one another but Dora's amusement faded.

'There's something I want to say about that evening your husband came across us in the park.'

'That's all in the past and best forgotten.'

'I want to forget it, but can't. I feel such a bloody fool. Did you tell Johnny about it? I wouldn't blame you if you did. I know I was a disgrace. If I hadn't been drunk I wouldn't have gone with Archie in the first place.' Dora turned her head to hide her watering eyes, and hoped she was being truthful. Back then she'd still been smarting from Johnny's rejection.

'We didn't tell him; he knows though because Archie blabbed.' Clover shook her head. 'He boasted about it to the bookie's runner of all people. It got back to Johnny – which was probably Archie's intention. Johnny didn't rise to it.'

'The rotten horrible swine ...' Dora choked through the fingers she'd slapped to her mouth.

'He's that all right; he didn't seem bothered about the grapevine bringing it to his wife's attention either.'

'I'm rotten as well, putting Nettie through it.'

'Can't say that hadn't occurred to me,' said Clover bluntly. 'If it hadn't been you, though, it would've been somebody else.' She didn't like that Dora had been playing around with Nettie's husband but Archie Fletcher was mostly to blame for that. He was a serial adulterer, unapologetic about the way he behaved and uncaring of having a wife and family indoors.

'It won't happen again. I'm finished with all that now, swear it. I'm starting work over Bermondsey at Peek Freans.' Dora paused, aware that they were almost at the entrance to Tate & Lyle's factory. She caught Clover's arm to prevent her going through the gate. 'While I'm unburdening meself there's something I need to apologise to you about as well. I have to do it now as there might not be a next time.' Dora frowned at the ground. 'After Archie ran off home that night it was just me and your husband in the park. I was so drunk I tried to make a pass at him.'

Clover didn't immediately reply; she was recalling the Jicky perfume she'd smelled on Neil. She could detect a faint scent of it today. 'How do you mean?' she said eventually.

'I thought he couldn't have told you, 'cos if he had you wouldn't even speak to me. Not that I would blame you. But I want to get this straight between us. Neil didn't do

211

anything . . . I swear that's the truth. It was all me, acting like a bitch on heat. I wanted to say sorry to him as well just now but couldn't find the guts to do it. So I hope you'll tell him I think he's a gentleman. You're lucky, Clover. Ain't many of those around.' With that, Dora gave Clover a sudden hug then turned and hurried way.

'He didn't say . . . but thanks for telling me.' Clover muttered this to herself as she watched the blonde woman trotting across the road to the bus stop.

'You're right on time, love. Sit yourself down and I'll pour you a cup o' tea.'

'Thanks,' said Clover starting to unbutton her coat. She pegged it up then wearily sank into the chair her husband had pulled out from under the table.

Neil was half dressed in long johns and a sleeved vest that clung to biceps honed by copious use of carpentry tools. His ebony dark hair, longer than normal as he didn't visit the barber as often these days, curled over his collar. Clover watched him as he brought the teas to the table, balancing a plate of jammy toast on the top of one of them. She took a sip of the hot strong brew, murmuring her appreciation on feeling its energising effect.

'Better than mother's milk that first morning cuppa,' he said as he sat down opposite her.

Clover eased off her work boots, wriggled her cramped toes then planted an elbow on the table. She leaned her cheek against her hand and gazed into his golden eyes, thinking she was lucky to have Neil Ryan as her husband and not just because he made a decent cup of tea. They'd been together eighteen years through ups and downs that had been enough to have wizened them both. He was now

212

in his late thirties yet still as heartbreakingly handsome to her as he'd been at twenty-one. She wasn't alone in thinking him gorgeous, it seemed. 'You didn't ask Dora in yesterday when she called on us.' She brought up the subject she'd brooded on during the long hours enveloped in the sickly aroma of sugar.

Neil started on his piece of toast and jam. 'Didn't know whether to,' he said, crunching away. He opened the newspaper his wife always brought in after a night shift, turning it to the vacancies section.

'Bit rude ... talking to her on the step like that,' Clover persisted, taking a piece of toast.

'Wasn't really talking ... other than to tell her you weren't home. It was you she came to see.'

'Sure about that?'

Neil folded the paper and sat back in the chair, crossing his arms. 'Right ... what is it you're getting at?' He studied his wife; the night shift had left her green eyes heavy lidded for want of sleep, and her auburn hair drooping from its bun. She stirred his loins as no other woman ever had yet was hinting at some misconduct of his with Dora that had nothing to do with their brief conversation. 'Come on ... out with it, love.'

'Dora walked with me to work yesterday.' Clover licked jam off her fingers. 'We had a heart-to-heart.'

'About Johnny?'

'And about you. Why didn't you tell me everything that went on in the park?'

Neil tilted his face up and sighed at the ceiling. 'Because I'm not a fool, Clover. She came on to me. I told her no.' He snapped his eyes back to hers. 'Did she say something else happened?'

Clover shook her head. 'Dora more or less said the same as you. So why didn't you tell me?'

'Because I didn't want you to be jealous over nothing ... like I am every bloody time I see Fletcher hanging around you.' He pushed his chair back and stood up. 'I'm sorry ... I thought I was doing the right thing ignoring it because it wasn't worth an argument.' He paused and came back to prop his hands against the table and gaze at her. 'Better than that, I wouldn't give Fletcher the satisfaction of ever finding out that what went on that night could stir things up in our marriage as well as in his own.' He shoved himself away from the support and cleared his used crockery from the table. 'Apart from all of that, there was enough of a drama with Nettie in labour, and I didn't want to add to it.'

Clover stood up and finished her cup of tea, then put the cup and saucer down on the draining board. She turned to him. 'Tell me next time.'

He caught her wrist as she made to walk past to the bedroom. 'What next time?'

'You're a gentleman, so I hear, and ladies find that attractive.' She raised a quizzical eyebrow and pulled the pins from her bun, letting her hair fall to her shoulders.

'Including this lady?'

'I'm dog-tired and you're off to a job interview.' She'd recognised the sultry gleam in his eyes. Tired or not, she felt a pleasant ache in the pit of her belly as his lips found the crease at her shoulder. She wriggled and lightly kissed him on the mouth but that didn't satisfy him and he didn't let go of her.

'I'm not expected until midday, and if I'm late I've got another interview this afternoon. That's the job I want. Right now, you're what I want, Clover.'

Chapter Nineteen

'Who are these people? What does he do exactly?'

'Exactly? Nobody knows,' said Ian Winters with a smirk. He sauntered up behind his wife and slid his arms around her, settling them on her small protruding belly. 'He's a spiv, my dear. What is commonly known by his own breed as "a wrong 'un", I believe.' He gave an indolent shrug on moving away. 'What does it matter in any case? He pays his dues to the cause and Mosley seems rather taken with him. You know how the fellow likes a novelty ... and a steward who can fight when the need arises.' He swung around, chuckling. 'George Payne came in handy at the Olympia rally.' Ian had made sure to keep behind the bruiser and allow him to defend them both against the mob that burst into the hall. Payne had obviously done a bit of bare-knuckle fighting in his time and agitators unlucky enough to come within his range went down like skittles.

He sat down on the bed and watched his wife powdering her face until, sensing his observation, she snapped shut the compact. He really rather loved her, he thought, lounging back onto an elbow and appreciating his good fortune.

He'd married her for this house, but it had turned out to

be a good all round move. His father had refused to give him a share of the family money before he found a respectable woman with whom to settle down. His second proviso had been that a daughter-in-law should have a decent dowry ... no gold-diggers allowed. Violet's substantial property in Mayfair had received the old man's approval and opened his wallet. And now Ian Winters, youngest son of a knight of the realm, found himself quite content with every aspect of his life.

At forty-eight, Violet was an attractive woman with a nice figure. She dressed well, knowing what colours and styles suited her. Ian always soaked up the admiring glances when she was on his arm. After her first pregnancy produced a son last summer, her bosom had filled out and her skin looked plumper. She was already in the early stages of another pregnancy, and blossoming. His young mistress wasn't quite so appealing since he had become besotted with his fecund wife and the heir she'd given him.

'Don't look at me like that, Ian,' Violet grumbled. 'There's no time, my dear, and I don't want my hair ruined.' Early in their marriage, she'd been up for any acrobatics in the hope that something new might trick her womb into nurturing a man's seed. Now she worried he'd ram himself into the developing baby. After waiting so long for her own children they were all that mattered to her.

Handing him her amethyst necklace, she sat down beside him, turning her back so he could clasp it around her slender throat.

'There's always time for slap and tickle, Vi ... ' His hands dropped to her shoulders, then slid forwards to squeeze her breasts.

'Don't call me by that vulgar name.' She sounded irritated and prised his fingers off her. 'Violet, please ... '

'Very well ... Vi ...'

She stood up before he grabbed her again, or she throttled him. 'Does he have a wife ... this wrong 'un fellow we're to dine with later?' She adjusted the gemstones against her pale-as-alabaster skin, thinking he could be vexingly juvenile. Sometimes he seemed twenty years younger instead of six; an unwanted son rather than husband.

'I think he's bringing somebody along, but whether they're married or not ...' He gave an eloquent shrug and his smirk was back. 'I've never met her, but I've met his daughter. She's about your Toby's age. The girl seems nice enough, and pretty. He seems proud of Rebecca ... brings her to meetings, so I imagine it's all above board.'

Violet hadn't taken in much of what he'd said after bristling at the way he referred to her eldest son as 'your Toby'. She knew he'd never considered himself Toby's father and had only adopted him for appearance's sake, to ensure they all shared the same name. Her husband and eldest son didn't get on; Ian was the adult, though, and should make an effort rather than act like a playground bully.

'I'll get the car brought round.' Ian stood up in a smooth movement and adjusted his cuffs. 'Wrap up warm. I want my son nice and comfy.'

'It could be a girl this time, you know. A daughter would be nice now I have two sons.'

'Three, if you count the Barnardo's boy.'

Violet's stomach squirmed. This remained a bone of contention, despite the excruciating incident not being mentioned for a while. Now and then, he would let her know he hadn't forgotten about it, and remind her of how close they had come to being incurably embarrassed in front of their eminent guests. All true; but Violet resented her husband gloating over it.

'You know I spotted that young fellow last autumn,' mused Ian. 'He was there in the crowd when our march turned into Poplar High Street.'

'Oh?' said Violet. This was the first she'd heard of it. 'Was that the day trouble started?'

He nodded. 'I recognised him straight away. He's got presence . . . tall for his age. He wasn't part of the rabble; he was giving Rebecca Payne the eye.' Ian chuckled. 'A fellow after my own heart. Maybe you let go of the wrong one, Vi, and should have kept hold of him instead.'

'*What* did you say?' she demanded in a strangled voice.

He'd been prowling the room but spun about to see her complexion had an ugly mottled appearance beneath the face powder and her eyes were slightly bulging.

'Don't get in a lather, my dear,' he soothed. 'I was teasing, that's all.'

'Why say such a thing, then?' she fumed. 'Do you think it funny that I lost my husband to a murderer, and had a difficult decision to make, regarding our two adopted boys?'

'Of course, I know that. Calm yourself down,' he said. 'You kept the right one.' Ian put an arm around her and would have kissed her in apology but she jerked her head before his lips could touch.

'If you were joking, I don't think I appreciate your sense of humour,' she said icily and swung away from him.

The moment she heard him leave, muttering again about getting the car brought round, she sat down on the edge of the bed to compose herself. A few seconds later, she was taking from the wardrobe the chinchilla fur that her first husband had bought her. The orange fox stole Ian believed the height of elegance; she thought it looked like the sort

218

of thing he'd buy for his mistress, and thus it remained mouldering on its hook.

Ian Winters just didn't measure up in any way to Rupert Harding, who had been cultured and kind. Ian considered himself to be a gentleman but Violet had hired stable boys with better manners. She appreciated her first doomed marriage more and more as the days and years passed. The couplings had been barren but had fizzed with passionate affection in the beginning ... before frost set in when the children didn't come. With Ian, the marital act was barnyard style but thankfully soon over. Through the half-open door she could see him sauntering along the landing and hear him whistling, already having forgotten about upsetting her.

Before he descended the stairs, Ian tossed the silk scarf draped over his shoulders about his neck. His thoughts returned to the cuckoo in the nest. He was confident the situation would soon remedy itself. Toby had turned seventeen and would be making his own way in the world when he graduated from Cambridge. The idea of footing the bill for setting him up in his own apartment made Ian wince, but at least he'd get the brat out from under his feet.

In Ian's truthful opinion – never to be voiced again as his wife's reaction had bordered on hysteria – she'd definitely let go of the wrong boy. He'd not forgotten the striking blond youth in Poplar. Jake Harding appeared dynamic even when standing still, whereas Toby was an insipid version of his older brother. Stocky and mousy, he was also a mummy's boy since he'd sensed a rival in the nursery.

A small fire flickered in the grate opposite the empty cot. The maid had pre-empted her mistress's wish and was seated in a chair, feeding the boy his bottle of milk. Violet approached to stroke his sleepy face with a finger, and murmured a good night to him. She never got tired of gazing upon his adorable prettiness, or wishing he had been Rupert's son.

Unlike her, Rupert had ditched his hopes of legitimate children and had settled on believing his mistress had given him a daughter. Of course she hadn't, as was plain to see now. But gentleman that he'd been, he'd done what he believed to be his duty and provided for his bastard and her mother. The memory of the swindle still had the power to put Violet's teeth on edge. If she had a complaint about Rupert it was that his gullibility had cost her dear.

With hindsight, she wished she'd put more effort into her relationship with Jake; it was only recently she'd admitted to herself to being jealous of the heroic child who had captivated her husband. Jake could achieve top marks whether doing his lessons or running on a sport's field and her husband had adored him. He had striven, though, not to show favouritism and to be equal handed to their sons, as a good father would. Cherishing their adopted boys, and giving up hope of their own, as Rupert had, was never quite enough for Violet.

She swallowed the lump in her throat and chivvied herself to buck up as she made for the door. She checked her velvet clutch bag for powder compact and lipstick then snapped it shut. A united front would be necessary in company. She pinned a smile to her lips and descended to the hallway as though there had been no cross words between them. Her husband was impatiently pacing to and fro while turning the air fragrant with expensive tobacco.

'Bloody clock has stopped.' Ian banged the glass with

knuckles divided by a cheroot, scattering ash onto the marble underfoot. 'Must be overwound. Wallace will have to unwind it, bloody fool,' he said of their manservant. 'Come on; let's get moving or we'll be late.'

Violet took the elbow he'd thrust in her direction. On passing she glanced at the French ormolu on the wall. She'd been looking at that thing since Rupert carried her over the threshold of this house, a blushing virgin of twenty years old. If it was possible to unwind it, she'd have turned it back by now.

'Don't forget to mind your Ps and Qs and be refined. No swearing and don't drink too much either. The champagne will be flowing but don't act like we're trying to fill our boots because we can't afford to buy our own.'

'We can't lately with the amount of money you've been pouring into Mosley's coffers.' Molly sat back in the hackney cab and adjusted her satin cape around her shoulders. It was late summer but the evening held an autumn chill.

'Don't go bringing up any of that either.' George carried on with his instructions. 'As far as that lot know, we're sitting pretty, same as them.'

'We were before you began all this fascist nonsense ...' Molly's renewed complaint remained unfinished after a warning look hardened his mouth.

'You can be quite loud when you've been drinking.'

'Don't keep going on about it,' she interrupted in a temper. 'I get it; I'll stick to lemonade, shall I?' She noticed the driver's eyes watching them in the mirror and nudged George to mind his tongue.

'Keep yer eyes on the road.' George grabbed the back of the fellow's seat, and pointed a finger at the windscreen.

'Very refined . . .' muttered Molly sarcastically, gazing out at a night-time scene of light and shadow. 'We should have used the Humber,' she said.

'I told you it needs a repair,' he said defensively.

'And you can't afford to pay for it because of nights like this,' she muttered beneath her breath. She was fed up that his obsession with social climbing was bankrupting them. 'Who else is coming along?' She stopped sniping; they were almost at the restaurant and there was nothing for it but making the best of it.

'A few crusty old colonel sorts and their wives.' He twirled an imaginary moustache, drawing the first smile from her that evening. 'A younger fellow called Winters and his wife are also invited. Ian Winters is more my age and lives in Mayfair.'

'Very nice . . .' said Molly, examining her nails. She had told him to attend the dinner on his own but he'd insisted she accompany him. Other wives were going to be present, he'd said, and he didn't want to be the tosser turning up alone.

'This is it.' George sat forward as they approached the supper club off Wardour Street. 'Stop here,' he barked, determined not to be seen arriving in a cab. 'We'll walk the rest of the way.'

While he paid for the ride, she craned her neck and caught a glimpse of a muted glow lighting the nightspot's windows. Some elegantly dressed people were emerging from a shiny Bentley then making their way past a concierge holding the door open. Molly checked her lipstick in her compact mirror. She felt uneasy; she'd be happier at home, wrapped in her dressing gown, drinking Ovaltine with her daughter for company.

She and George had been together on and off for decades.

They'd rubbed along reasonably well until recently, sharing similar ambitions. She'd been content to carry on doing what they were doing; living comfortably was enough for her. He wanted to pull them higher and achieve bigger and better things. That blind ambition had seen him do something unforgivable in her eyes: he'd hit their daughter.

The incident had been months ago but Molly hadn't forgotten or forgiven seeing Rebecca's face bearing his handprint. The day her daughter had visited her aunt Queenie and been given a pretty cardigan, was the day Molly stopped loving George Payne. She let him help her out of the cab although she was tempted to tell the driver to wait and take her home.

'I don't fancy this, George . . . ' She felt apprehensive and irked by the prospect of toadying to strangers.

"Course you do.' He chucked her playfully under the chin. 'We'll come away from here with another invitation. One of the crusties has a manor house in Norfolk. Weekend of huntin' 'n' shootin' would be right up my street.' He huffed in irritation, having failed to make her smile this time. 'No need to be nervous, Mol.' He gave her a little encouraging shake. 'You'll knock 'em dead.' He straightened the black satin on her shoulders. 'You look a proper rich man's wife. Hard times'll be a thing of the past if we use our noddles.' He tapped her temple, disturbing her carefully arranged brunette locks. 'Contacts is all you need in this world and the Party's got the backing of earls . . . barons . . . '

' . . . Elephant Boys and their molls who hoist fer a living,' she sourly butted into his boasting. 'How d'you know they're not all chancers on the make as well?' She'd annoyed him again but he was doing his best to keep her sweet. He had to because he needed her help with this charade.

The night air was a miasma of powdery perfume and roasting meat overlaid with limousines' exhaust fumes. Molly had breathed in the Soho smell a hundred times. She would touch up her make-up in anticipation of the glamour beckoning her inside an establishment guarded by a burly, top-hatted porter. Tonight the atmosphere seemed toxic. 'This isn't for me, George, nor Rebecca. Your daughter's made it clear she doesn't want to be a part of the Blackshirts and their rallies.'

'Well, I do want her part of it,' George snarled, done with mollycoddling. 'I want me daughter mixing with class; boys in black shirts have rich fathers. I want her married to a somebody, not a nobody without a pot to piss in. And you should want it for her too.'

'Well, I'm not sure I do.'

'D'you know how long I've been trying to get to this point?' He sounded aggrieved. 'Almost two bleedin' years and now I've made it. We've been invited to the top table with the top man and you expect me to walk away when . . . ' He abruptly let go of her arm and she heard his intake of breath.

Molly's eyes swivelled sideways as though she might look over her shoulder but his grip was back, telling her not to.

'Right, look lively, gel; we're on. Here's Ian Winters and the blonde must be his wife.' He took Molly's hand and drew it through his arm like a proper gentleman. 'See . . . told you you'd outdo her.' He gave her a reassuring pat. 'You're younger and prettier than she is. Now smile, damn you,' he said, ventriloquist-style, and raised a hand as the couple strolled towards the club. Ian Winters gave George a nod of acknowledgement before disappearing inside.

*

224

It wasn't until after the main course was cleared that Molly managed to excuse herself and escape to the powder room. She went inside a cubicle, sat on the lavatory seat, and covered her face with her hands, hoping the queasiness would subside. She'd eaten very little of the fancy food, but it was shock, not rich sauce making her feel sick. She'd no intention of going back to the table ... she couldn't. She'd been lucky winging it so far. But her luck could run out.

She pulled her handkerchief from her bag and dabbed tears of exasperation from her eyes. There had been no need for any of this. They had been doing all right by themselves. She put up her chin. She was Molly Deane and feared nobody, and that included George Payne. He'd go for her after this, but so would she go for him for landing them right in the mire. She yanked on the toilet chain then came out of the cubicle and stared at her reflection in the mirror. She tidied her hair, reapplied her lipstick then took a deep breath before opening the door.

Outside, the corridor was deserted; clinking cutlery and laughing conversation could be heard coming from the supper room. Fearing somebody might emerge from it, she walked swiftly towards the reception. The maître d' turned the corner, heading towards her with a silver platter of drinks. She stopped him before he could sweep past silently on thick piled carpet.

'My husband and I are dining with Sir Oswald. Unfortunately, I feel a little under the weather. Would you be good enough to take a message to Mr Payne? If you would tell my husband I'm going home ...'

'Would you like a headache powder, madam?' The fellow was all solicitousness and put down his tray on a hallway

225

table. 'Such a shame for you to have to leave halfway through your meal. It would be no trouble to fetch one ... '

'Thanks all the same, but I'm goin' 'ome ... ' Molly's careful diction suffered in her desperation for him to clear off and do as she asked.

She glanced over a shoulder, anticipating George's pursuit. He'd sensed something was up and had given her many pointed looks, demanding she join in the conversation. Once they were alone and he'd heard what she'd got to say, he'd thank her for keeping quiet.

'I don't want to spoil the evening for the others, you see,' Molly explained to the hovering maître d'. 'Thank you, anyway.' She hastened on, aware of the stationary fellow frowning at her, perhaps expecting a tip. He'd wait in vain; she only had enough money with her to pay for a cab.

The night air cooled her hot face as she rushed out and swung a look to and fro. Fortunately, a cab was approaching, and seeing it vacant, she barged past a couple also on the lookout, dashing into the road to force it to a halt.

She yanked open the door and scrambled inside, then fell back into the seat, panting.

'Where to?' the driver barked, miffed at not having picked up his regular good tippers. This one looked like a tart having a bad night.

'Lambeth,' Molly snapped back, straightening up and pulling her cape around her. 'And don't spare the 'orses ... ' She gazed out of the back window at the club receding from view and started to giggle in relief.

It was close to one o'clock in the morning when Molly heard the door slam then George's feet hitting every other stair as he belted up to their bedroom. He wasn't drunk then, she realised. If he was moving that fast, he had taken his own advice not to guzzle too much of Mosley's champagne.

He burst in and approached her with a pointing finger threateningly raised. 'Do you know what you've done, you selfish bitch? Made me into a bleedin' laughing stock, that's what. They knew you'd bottled it ... little Molly mouse. I heard one of the old gels say—'

'Shut up,' she interrupted him with equal, if restrained, fury in her tone. 'More to the point, do you know what you've done, you bloody stupid man?' Molly stubbed out her cigarette in the ashtray on her lap. She put the brass dish carefully aside on the coverlet then stood up to face him and show she wasn't scared. He'd hit her before, and she'd hit him right back despite coming off worst every time. She'd not put on her nightclothes but had waited to have this out with him. Her temper hadn't abated one bit in that time and she was ready to go down fighting.

George sniffed and his eyes narrowed as he tried to gauge her meaning. He'd expected to find her meek and apologetic, not ready for battle. His fists, primed to strike, fell open at his sides. 'What're you talking about? All I've done is me best to improve our lot ... especially fer our daughter ...'

She punched a fist against his shoulder, making him grunt in surprise. 'All you've done is put Rebecca in jeopardy. You and your damn crawling to posh people has brought us face to face with Rupert's widow, and I don't think you wanted to do that, did you, George?'

'What?' He half laughed. 'You gone nuts?'

'You never met her, but I did. Violet Winters was then known as Mrs Harding. Poor Rupert didn't know where to put his face on the night his wife and mistress was a foot away from one another in the Aldwych Theatre.' She paused. 'And apart from putting on a bit of weight and her blonde hair fading, she's not changed that much.'

George's surly expression flattened into uncertainty. 'Nah ... you're wrong ... mistaken identity.'

'I'm not wrong.' Molly picked up the cigarettes and matches. She lit up then tossed the boxes back onto the bed.

'She couldn't have recognised you then,' said George. 'She was nice as pie.'

Molly snorted a laugh. 'No she wasn't. She was a snooty cow; she hasn't changed in that respect, either. Whether she clocked me remains to be seen. I did me best to keep looking the other way until I could get out of there.' She dragged repeatedly on the cigarette and blew smoke furiously, but subduing her temper was impossible. 'I told you I should've stayed at home,' she shouted. 'I reckon she knew me but didn't want to say anything, same as I didn't until now.'

'You're worrying over nothing, Mol ...' George helped himself to a cigarette.

'You'd better hope I am, because you'll never get the lid back on this can o' worms.' Molly extinguished her stub on the marble mantelshelf then dropped it into the empty grate. 'Now I'm going to bed and you can sleep downstairs 'cos the sight of you makes me sick.'

George wasn't ready to concede defeat on this argument. 'So what if Harding's widow did recognise you? The settlement he left for you and Rebecca was above board. Solicitors was involved—'

'It was a swindle,' she interrupted in a weary voice as though explaining to a dimwit. 'She knows Rebecca isn't his. Rupert had the problem, not her. Violet's got a kid now, and another on the way. Wasn't you listening to her husband

228

boasting? Winters thinks he's a stud.' Molly guessed family talk had passed over George's head. He'd only paid proper attention to the name dropping. Earl this and Brigadier that was what had interested him.

'Nobody can prove Rupert Harding wasn't up to it now he's dead,' said George.

'Maybe not, but she'll have a bloody good try. Violet's married well and has enough money to send top lawyers after us. I heard she was furious when the will was read. She won't have forgotten or forgiven anything.' Molly clenched a fist and in frustration beat it against the wall. 'I should never have gone with you and given her something to think about ...'

'What's going on? Has something happened?' Rebecca had been woken by the commotion and come to investigate.

'It's nothing, love, difference of opinion, that's all. Go back to bed.' Molly hurried to her daughter and ushered Rebecca from the room, closing the door after her. She waited, her eyes locked with George's and her ears straining until a bedroom door clicked shut, allowing her to relax.

'Righto, let's have this out now then.' Molly approached George. 'And I want the truth from you.' She stared into his dangerously attractive features. She'd noticed the other women – even the ancient ones – slyly glancing across the table at the ruffian in their midst. A couple of misfits was how Mr and Mrs Payne were seen by the men in silk suits and the women with jewels clanking on their bony chests. Dazed by his own ambition, George couldn't see he was already a laughing stock before tonight. Eventually his usefulness would end. Then those people wouldn't hide their disdain but turn their backs on him.

'Did you kill Rupert?'

'What?'

'That night he was murdered coming out of his club, half cut. Was it down to you?'

George choked on a laugh. 'Where the fuck did that come from? Why're you bringing up stuff ten years old?'

'Because if the Winters sue, one thing will lead to another, like Rupert's unsolved murder. It might not only be swindles unearthed in an investigation into what you 'n' me get up to. So give me a straight answer. I know you was desperate for him not to find out the truth about Rebecca after he caught you sneaking out of here.'

'I wasn't the only one worried he'd change his will and evict you,' he blustered. 'You wanted to stay in this house. You wouldn't see me fer months in case he wised up and sent a private detective to snoop around.'

'Still do want us living somewhere nice,' Molly bluntly admitted. 'But not enough to stab somebody over it.'

As the years had rolled by, so had her suspicions about George knowing more about Rupert's death than he was letting on. George had spent time in prison for GBH and affray when younger. He wasn't as villainous as some Elephant Boys, she'd told herself, and had stuck with him, determined to build a normal family life for their daughter. But she'd made sure no more children arrived, just in case at some time she had to up and run.

'Ain't listening to no more of this.' George pitched his cigarette butt into the grate and started twirling a finger by his temple. 'You've gone loopy after seeing that woman.'

Molly couldn't deny she'd been driving herself mad. While waiting for him to return home, she'd gone over and over old events. Her biggest fear was that Violet had been doing the same thing and had decided to delve deeper into it. Fraud was one thing, murder something else entirely. George wouldn't be let out of prison if convicted of something like that. He'd swing for it.

'Answer me, George.' She grabbed his arm to stop him leaving the room, but he shook her off.

'Ain't giving it another thought,' he growled. 'You must've drunk too much, to be coming out with this stuff.' He slammed out of the door and made for the stairs.

He'd been aware of Molly's feelings cooling towards him even before this evening's trouble. George had also been aware of a man loitering outside and had wondered if she'd been playing around. On one occasion George had followed him to get some answers but had been rumbled and given the slip. Molly had said it must be the insurance man doing his rounds. George knew when she was lying, just as she knew when he was. There'd be another murder if he found out something had been going on behind his back.

He started down the stairs, blinded by rage. If he hadn't been, he might have glimpsed a flash of white further along the landing before a closing door shielded his nightgowned daughter from view.

Chapter Twenty

'What in Gawd's name do you want?'

'Don't be like that, love. Gonna let me in so I can show you how much I've been missing you?' George grabbed her wrist and pulled her against him to kiss her. She wasn't having that so he slid a foot over the threshold to stop her shutting him out. He stuck his cigarette in his mouth then produced from behind his back a half-drunk bottle of Scotch, swinging it by the neck in temptation. 'I remembered you like a droppa the hard stuff ...'

'Did yer now?' spluttered Dora, astonished to see him. She knew what hard stuff he really wanted to give her. 'Clear off,' she hissed. 'It's three o'clock in the bleedin' morning.'

The night air was blowing in from the open portal and she was shivering in the draught. She regretted turning on the gas lamp when opening the door. She didn't want him seen calling on her in her flimsies in the early hours, as though it were a regular occurrence. She'd believed the rat-a-tat heralded a neighbour. The woman lived with her elderly father who went on walkabout at all hours. Dora would get knocked up and roped in to help search for him.

They'd head off in different directions with their coats belted over their nightdresses, and a torch in hand. Dora didn't mind because everybody got old and frightened. Having started his life in a workhouse, no reassurance could convince the poor old soul his daughter didn't intend he should end it there.

George Payne was the wrong side of merry. The more shots he'd downed at home, the greater had become his resentment towards Molly and the stranger he suspected was her lover. He'd thought two could play at that game, and had come to Lambeth's shabby side. He knew Dora was fancy-free and although he wasn't ... yet ... his conceit had led him to expect a warmer welcome. Belatedly, it occurred to him to wonder why she was looking nervously over her shoulder and dispersing tobacco smoke with a hand. 'Got a man in there, have yer?' He stopped lounging against the door frame and straightened up.

'Yeah ... I've got a man; he bought me this.' She thrust some curled fingers beneath George's nose, giving him a glimpse of a small diamond. 'So don't ever come back here.' She kicked his wedging foot with her slipper but he refused to budge. A hand appeared from nowhere, drawing her backwards.

'Go back to bed, love. I can sort this out,' said Johnny Cooper who'd quietly padded up behind her on bare feet.

Having closed his dropped jaw, George jibed, 'Come out here then if you think you can, big man.' The cork was pulled from the bottle with his teeth. He spat it out and took a swig of whisky. His bravado couldn't camouflage his disappointment at discovering this romance was back on. He was at a disadvantage: drunk and without a blade in his pocket, but he couldn't back down or his reputation would suffer.

233

Johnny's father had told him he needed to stand up for himself if he were to get a good paying job to keep them both. Johnny had agreed, packed his bags, and said Sidney could have the lodging to himself and the bills that went with it. He'd headed to the East End to be nearer his sisters. But being with Dora was what he really needed. Last week he'd come to Lambeth to offer an olive branch, and had never left.

Since losing things he'd taken for granted, Johnny had toughened up. Nobody got one over on him now but they might get a right-hander. On this occasion though, seeing his rival helplessly pie-eyed was enough reward in itself. Johnny crossed his arms over his naked chest and surveyed George in his crumpled penguin suit; the white shirtfront was whisky stained, and the collar points askew, threatening to stab him in the chin.

'If you're on your way to the Ritz to gatecrash a ball, George . . . it's that way.' Johnny was chuckling as he jerked a nod in no particular direction.

George laughed right back through scraping teeth. Cooper was standing in the nude, half-cocked, and had the gall to mock him . . . George Payne, a senior Elephant Boy! A red mist blurred his vision as he swung a clumsy punch. Johnny had easily seen that coming and landed a hard jab on George's chin, sending him running backwards, arms flailing. 'G'night, George,' said Johnny. He heard the bottle of Scotch smash as he closed the door.

'I didn't know he was coming,' cried Dora, flinging her arms around her fiancé. 'I've had nothing to do with him, even while we was apart, that's the honest truth.'

'I know.' He smoothed her hair. 'I know. I trust you, Dora. Something bad's gone on for Payne to get blotto and turn up out of the blue to bother you.'

'Molly's probably had enough of him and chucked him out.' Dora rubbed her cheek against his bare shoulder. 'We can't let him split us up; he'd do it just for spite.'

'No chance of that.' Johnny kissed her brow. 'Not letting you go again.'

They'd had a frank discussion about other people they'd seen during their months apart. She'd owned up about Archie Fletcher before Johnny needed to ask, and had admitted to making a drunken fool of herself with his brother-in-law. That had come as a surprise. Johnny hadn't been an angel himself, though, playing the field like a horny teenager. They'd agreed to put everything behind them and start afresh.

'If we're married he won't come back,' said Dora. 'He'll leave us alone.'

'As soon as I get a good job, we'll get a decent place to live and book the registry office.'

'I don't want to wait. I just want to be your wife, and have some kids. I won't tell my boss I'm married; I'll take off me wedding ring so I don't get the sack. Then while I'm working at Peek Freans and you're doing your night watchman shifts and a bit of labouring, we'll get by, won't we?' She showed him her set of crossed fingers.

'Yeah ... 'course we will. We'll get married soon, love, promise, if that's what you want.' Johnny rocked her in his arms. 'Might have to hold off on a family for a while, though. I'd like my kids growing up somewhere nicer than this dump.'

He'd confessed to his womanising, but Johnny hadn't yet told her he'd given his night watchman job at the brewery to his father. It had been his final offering before he abandoned Sidney Cooper to his own devices. As for Jake Harding:

235

Johnny felt uncomfortable expecting a young man, not yet turned eighteen, to provide him with employment, especially as the boot had recently been on the other foot. With Peg Tiller's help, Jake had risen above being a petty thief and had pulled Johnny up with him into a clean life. He'd not been aware he was ready for change but when it happened it seemed destined and natural.

Johnny would always get a welcome when he showed up in Rook Lane, trying not to look too needy. The decent lad would do his best to help his friends with a pay packet. To a proud man like Johnny, that somehow made it worse.

Dora had been guessing his thoughts while worry lines creased his face. Like most working-class people struggling to find regular work to pay the bills, Johnny fretted constantly about money. She appreciated his sensible attitude. She could be impetuous and allow herself to run headlong into debt, then trouble followed.

She took a deep breath and said quickly before she changed her mind, 'No arguments ... I want you to take this back. Collect your best suit ... no, I want you to, Johnny.' He'd seen her removing her ring and started to protest. He'd pawned his Savile Row suit to buy it to prove he loved her and wanted her as his wife. She didn't wear the ring to work for fear of damaging it, but it was on her finger the moment she arrived home and stayed there until she rose from bed in the morning. It was precious, but she loved him more. If he were to better himself, a smart outfit to attend job interviews was required. She closed his fingers over the diamond on his open palm. 'As for a wedding band, a brass curtain ring'll do me for now. We've time enough for fancy stuff when we're back on our feet, love.'

He opened his hand to gaze at the gem. They both knew

how they could get back on their feet, keep the ring, and get him a new suit of clothes. But it would take them backwards, not forwards to a better future.

'I'm done with hoisting.' Dora took the lead in shutting out temptation. 'Mr and Mrs Respectable, that's us.' She sighed dreamily. 'We'll have a small do, a few ales and sandwiches down the pub after the service. Will you ask Neil to be best man?' Recently, Dora had seen Clover out shopping. They hadn't said more than hellos as Clover hadn't wanted to lose her place in the butcher's queue. But her future sister-in-law had given her a private wink to let her know she approved of developments. Dora had walked on feeling elated in the knowledge that Johnny's family had accepted her back into the fold.

'Hadn't thought about it,' mused Johnny. 'But yeah ... reckon I will ask Neil.'

'Will you ask your dad?'

'I'll ask ... the rest is up to him,' said Johnny who imagined his father was still sulking about having been forced into paying his own way. Dora gave him a sympathetic hug. Oddly, she felt relieved that she'd lost touch with her brother – her only living close family – and was spared the trouble of dealing with awkward relatives. The movement of Johnny's hands against her buttocks made her wriggle sinuously against his stroking fingers.

'Now, missus,' he said. 'Enough about what that lot's doing, what was we doing before being rudely interrupted?'

On the point of kissing, they were startled into jerking apart by renewed pounding on the door. 'Right, this time I won't be polite.' Johnny growled in frustration and strode purposefully to yank open the door.

The tearful woman dragging a handkerchief across her

eyes wasn't aware of who was confronting her. 'It's me father, he's done it again, Dor. I'm at me wits' end. He just won't listen or nuthin' ...'

'Won't keep you a moment, then, love.' Dora barged in front of her stark-naked fiancé. The hand clamped to her mouth was hiding a murderous grin as she elbowed Johnny out of sight. 'I'll just get me coat and be with you.'

Chapter Twenty-One

'You taking us out to the pub on Friday?'

Jake closed his ears and carried on sawing wood, fed up with hearing the same thing over and over again. He examined the two lengths of pine he'd cut, rubbed them over with sandpaper, then hammered them together.

'Well, what d'you say, then?' Herbie chivvied for an answer. 'Having a drink-up Friday to celebrate, are we?'

'You got a bad arm, Herbie?'

'No ... why?' Herbie uncrossed his arms and held them out to examine them.

'Thought you must've done something to yourself, seeing as that window frame's still not primed. There's another two waiting for you ...' Jake pointed his hammer at the assembled casements leaning against the wall.

'Ain't had time yet,' said Herbie huffily.

'Well, if you pack up bothering me about drink-ups on Friday when it's not even Thursday yet, you will have time.' Jake dropped the hammer onto the workbench and turned around. 'Fer Chrissake, pull your finger out, will you. These have to be delivered tomorrow afternoon and the lot fixed and glazed by the weekend ...' Jake stopped yelling as he saw Mr Spooner coming out of the new workshop, no doubt wondering what the shouting was about.

'What colour? You ain't said.' Herbie found a lame excuse.

'What?' Jake glanced over his shoulder.

'Primer. What colour?'

Jake shook his head in disgust. 'Same as last time, Herbie. That'll be white 'cos that's all we've got.' He sighed. 'No, tell you what, forget it. Go and put the kettle on instead.'

'You do know he's an 'opeless case, don't you, Jake?' Mr Spooner watched the skinny fellow in paint-splattered overalls ambling into the workshop where a primus stove and kettle was set up.

'Yep ... ' Jake continued taking nails, held between his teeth, to hammer one by one into the frame he was making. But he didn't explain his loyalty to the boy who'd been his only friend before Peg Tiller helped them escape a life of scavenging.

'On the other hand, Johnny Cooper's an asset,' continued the older man. 'You 'n' him made a grand job of the workshop.'

Mr Spooner appraised the new brick building; unlike Herbie's living quarters adjacent to it, topped by corrugated metal, the workshop had a pitched and tiled roof. He'd demonstrated how to lay bricks and Jake and Johnny had picked up the rudiments quickly. Herbie hadn't the dexterity to juggle a brick and a trowel so had been given a shovel and the job of mixing up the mortar. Mr Spooner had supervised the work, knocked some courses of bricks back down when declaring they weren't plumb, and praised them when the edifice was built to his satisfaction, allowing for false starts. He'd been proud to see two of his apprentices quickly acquiring skills. Of course, he couldn't take

240

much credit for Jake: he'd had a head start having done a year's training with another builder. Jake described that man as being a mean so-and-so, but learning the hard way had done him no harm; he'd soon be proficient in building and plumbing skills. With more practice, Johnny would shape up too.

'Not seen anything of Johnny for weeks.' Jake put down the hammer, giving his arms a rest. Hoisting scarves and blouses had softened him up; he'd forgotten how physically tough building work could be.

'Shame that fellow's not come over. This lot would have been ready to go.' Mr Spooner indicated the casements awaiting finishing.

Jake had also missed seeing Johnny, who had a way of cheering the place up when he was around. Plus, another capable pair of hands was needed. 'It's another wage to find, Mr Spooner, and Johnny has got his other work. Herbie . . . well . . . he's relying on me for a job.'

Spooner grimaced to show he was aware of that. The older two made a good team but Herbie was a cack-handed shirker and destined to remain a labourer in his opinion.

'You're being sensible, watching your outgoings, but sometimes cutting out the dead wood helps pay for other things.' He didn't make it plainer than that about Herbie being a financial drain. 'Anyway, it is pretty normal for a new firm to stray into an overdraft in the first few years while it's building up a register of customers.'

'Bank manager says I'm too young and inexperienced to have an overdraft.' Jake had his own capital but was wary of using it up too quickly. He had decades of working life in front of him and some of those years would be lean, although he prayed not as hard as these past few had been.

'That man will be changing his tune in a few years' time when you're sitting pretty.' Mr Spooner admired his protégé for being determined to do things properly and make the books balance from the outset.

'The cost of the workshop was more than I expected.' Jake frowned at the building from which came the sound of Herbie's tuneless singing and some rattling crockery.

'Well, next time you'll know to shop around for prices of bricks and cement before ordering the stuff.' Mr Spooner patted his arm. 'If you don't make a few mistakes you won't learn what's right.' He had accompanied Jake to look at a second-hand van last week and left him pondering on the pros and cons of purchasing it. 'Did you make a decision about the Bedford?'

Jake nodded. 'I put a deposit down.'

Mr Spooner sucked his teeth in cautionary fashion. 'Now that is a big expense, son. Are you sure it's worthwhile?'

'It's a risk but I want to be able to travel further afield than Whitechapel to pick up more business. Not many folk round here can afford to improve their homes.' Jake rubbed away some sawdust that had flown into his face and was tickling his nose. 'I'll make this the best building firm in the East End ... in all London.' He spread his arms and grinned. 'Pushing a handcart to take stuff to a job a distance away uses the day up. And time's money ... you taught me that.'

'True ... true ...' said a thoughtful Mr Spooner, who couldn't deny the lad had a point. Jake was an enigma. He was ambitious and enterprising, wise beyond his years, but continued to employ Herbie who was neither use nor ornament. Before Peg died she had told him Herbert Brick had robbed her and Jake too, but it seemed the lad was

242

sentimental enough to give his light-fingered pal a second chance. 'I couldn't take such risks when I was starting up in the trade.' Mr Spooner shook his head regretfully. 'I didn't dare splash out on a van; I hired carts as required and found my customers in this neighbourhood.' He said rather forlornly, 'I was never as brave as you, Jake, or as lucky, you see.'

Jake knew the fellow wasn't having a dig. It was true anyway; without his benefactor he would still be hoisting and squatting in dumps with Herbie for company. He might even be in prison, his luck at evading the store detectives having run out.

'If I had my time over again I think I'd want to be more like you,' Mr Spooner said. 'Too late now to change me ways even though it is just me and Mrs Spooner rattling around indoors. The old back's been giving me gyp again. Knacker's yard'll be next for me.' He swayed his torso to ease his spine. 'You make sure to take care of your joints. Knees is the first to go in this game.'

'I will ...' Jake smiled. 'That tea must be about ready.' He'd heard the kettle whistling.

'Better move your bench and tools inside first,' said Mr Spooner, having seen Jake examining the leaden heavens. 'It's gonna pour down by the looks of it.'

When the last of the timber was being carried inside, fat raindrops started hitting the concrete and pinging off the dustbins. Three upturned tea chests were arranged in a semicircle with another one positioned in front to act as a table. Herbie came over with the steaming mugs, plonking them down on it. They sat down and gulped at hot sweet tea while listening to the rain drumming a tune outside.

'Well, at least you make a decent cuppa, son.' Mr Spooner

243

told Herbie, foraging in a tin of biscuits. 'Maybe a job in a kitchen might suit you.'

'Ain't doing women's work.' Herbie sounded indignant.

'Best cooks are men,' said Mr Spooner. ''Course, I don't tell Mrs S. that.' He glanced between his two companions who hadn't spoken to one another. 'What was the argy-bargy about?'

'Was only bein' a pal and asking about his birthday on Friday,' Herbie said in an injured tone.

'I turn eighteen,' Jake explained. 'I'm not knocking off early though; we'll go down the pub when the job's finished.'

'Eighteen, eh?' Mr Spooner smiled. 'Won't hurt to enjoy yourself on that special day. I might come along and buy you a pint myself.'

'What's this? Mothers' meeting?' Johnny Cooper had burst in out of the rain, shaking his shaggy dark hair. 'Bleedin' cats 'n' dogs out there, it is.'

Jake grinned and manoeuvred another tea chest into position for the late arrival to use.

'Turned up right on time, I see,' said Johnny. 'Could murder a brew.' He poured himself a mug of tea from the pot then came and settled down beside them.

'We were just talking about you, Johnny,' said Mr Spooner.

'All good, I hope.'

'Saying we'd not seen you in a while.' Jake put down his empty cup. 'If you've some spare time I've work for you until the weekend.'

'Will do then.' Johnny jumped at the chance, relieved not to have to angle for a shift. 'Glad to help out.'

'Got something else to ask you actually,' said Jake. 'I

bought the Bedford I went to see. Would you drive it back for me?'

Johnny had sown the seed in Jake's mind about buying a works' vehicle when he offered to teach him to drive. Unfortunately, Johnny had sold his Austin and they'd had nothing to practise on. A van cab had been mocked up with a chair and some bricks, to represent the seat and pedals. The gear stick had been a wooden spoon. Jake had soon picked up the basics of stamping on the clutch and accelerator while moving the spoon this way and that.

'Be an honour,' said Johnny. 'Wish I still had my jalopy. Miss the old gel.' He didn't dwell on it; the only way he could afford a car would be to return to crime, and he was done with that. 'Now, I've got some good news of me own.' He rubbed together his palms, preparing to make his big announcement. He rose to his feet to solemnly say, 'Me and Dora's getting married on the day after Boxing Day.'

Jake was first to jump up and clap him on the back while Herbie started whooping. Mr Spooner added more sedate congratulations.

'Me big sister's kindly offered to do us a spread at her place in Silvertown and you're all invited. And Mrs Spooner, of course.'

'I'll bring Maria,' piped up Herbie.

'Right . . .' said Johnny rather flatly.

'You should bring Sadie.' Herbie nudged Jake.

'We'll see,' Jake tactfully said; he could tell the bridegroom wasn't sure he wanted gatecrashers, especially any known as good-time girls. There was another girl he would have been proud to bring along, but Johnny and Dora might not have been happy about seeing Rebecca Payne either. The feud with her father would have made things awkward.

Jake considered himself a fool even still thinking about Rebecca after she'd robbed him and laughed while doing it. He shouldn't have let her get away with it. She'd consider him weak and cowardly ... a pushover. At first, he'd not intended to let her get away with it. So much had happened with Peg, and the bequest and the new business that he'd let things ride. Now, too much time had passed to hunt her down to bring it up. She would think him pathetic, troubling her with year-old spilled milk.

And a year had passed since he'd seen her. Besides, there were plenty more fish in the sea and he'd noticed a few swimming in his direction. Since it had got round that he was going up in the world, he was getting the eye from local girls more than he normally did. But he preferred to stay with Sadie and a casual relationship. 'We're having a drink on Friday to celebrate my eighteenth birthday,' Jake said. 'Hope you'll come along after work.'

'I certainly will.' Johnny grinned, contemplating his boss.

A youth to be exploited was how he'd seen Jake when fate brought them together on a Christmas Eve in Oxford Street. How wrong he'd been. In a short time, the boy had become a man, and one to be reckoned with. That chance meeting might have been fate smiling on him Johnny realised. There was something special about Jake Harding that made Johnny want to stay close in the hope some gold rubbed off on him.

'Right,' said Johnny, pulling up his collar to brave the elements again. 'This is only a flying visit as I've other people to tell me good news. But I'll see you lot bright 'n' early in the morning.'

Jake gave him a wave then picked up his tools to resume work.

Mr Spooner walked around the almost finished casement Jake had been working on, examining it from all angles. 'Reckon you've already been on the sherbet, haven't you, son? That mitre's bent as a nine-bob note.' He pointed to a corner of badly joined wood then held out a hand for the hammer. 'Here, give it to me and I'll put it right . . . '

'No . . . I'll do it.' Jake's annoyance was directed at himself. He could blame the mistake on Herbie's interruptions, but that wouldn't be right. He'd not seek excuses when he should've noticed it before Mr Spooner did. 'Get the paint, Herbie.' Jake winked over a shoulder while bashing apart his last hour's work. 'If we're having a knees-up Friday, this lot will need coating up before we knock off this evening.'

Through the half-open door of the workshop he could see a sliver of light. The rain had stopped and the sun on the horizon had honeyed the humid air. Jake walked outside and squinted up at the autumn sky. He stared, but it wasn't there in the pillowy pewter clouds with their silver linings: no motorbike and sidecar. He knew she was watching though.

'I'll get the lights on inside,' said Mr Spooner, coming out to join him and watch the sun disappear. 'Be dark in an hour.'

'What do you want? Come back with yer tail between yer legs, have yer?'

'Hello, Dad,' said Johnny, ignoring the sour greeting.

'Grass wasn't greener, was it?' said his father. 'S'pose she's thrown you over again.' Sidney continued fastening his belt. 'Could've told you she was no good and you was wasting your time,' he scoffed, walking away and leaving Johnny to close the door. 'Well, if you think you're having your job back, or the best bed, you can think again.'

'Don't want me job back or the bed.' Johnny followed him into the lodging they'd once shared. 'It's all yours.' He glanced about the dimly lit room. It was bigger and slightly better than the home he had with Dora. There was a proper cooking range for a start, and a table and pair of chairs shoved against one wall. Two narrow, iron-framed beds protruded from another. But his father was welcome to the lot. He'd live in a dog kennel with Dora rather than return to this.

Sidney sniffed and suppressed his disappointment. 'What you come here scrounging for then?'

Johnny could've replied that was a bit rich, considering his father was the one always on the take, but he didn't. He said, 'Me and Dora's getting married. Just came to tell you Clover's doing us a tea when we get back from the registry office, day after Boxing Day. Be nice if you'd pop over and help us celebrate.'

Sidney seemed apathetic about what he'd heard. He continued putting on his night watchman's uniform, flicking imaginary dust from his tie. In fact, he hated his job and living on his own. Johnny had done most of the chores and the cooking. And he'd paid for everything. But if his son was getting married he'd lost him for good.

Dead end capers like night watchman jobs at the brewery weren't for Sidney. He had turned fifty-two and taking it easy was what he wanted. It wasn't as though there were even any perks in it for him, like free ale. He had three kids living not far away and believed they should look after him, a veteran of the Great War. He conveniently overlooked the fact that he'd gone AWOL for the final years of the conflict.

'So, what d'you say, Dad? Shall I tell me sisters we can expect to see you?' Johnny paused to allow his father to reply. 'Be nice for you to catch up with Annie again.' He broke the silence. 'Only seen her the once, haven't you, since coming home.'

'She don't get much time off from her job,' said Sidney defensively. It was true; none of them saw much of Annie, who was in demand by her employer and lucky to get an afternoon off a month. Really though Sidney had no interest in seeing his youngest. She had no place of her own in which he could commandeer a bed. Besides, she was blunt, almost rude, as he was. Annie spoke as she found, unlike the older two who had adapted their behaviour to keep him sweet, as their mother had. 'Anyhow, can't promise yer nuthin' as I've got plans of me own Christmastime,' he said airily, and shrugged into his jacket.

'Oh?' Johnny was intrigued.

'Got a lady friend, if you must know.'

'Good ... glad you're seeing somebody,' Johnny enthused. 'You can bring her along. Who is she?'

'Never you mind,' snapped his father, doing up buttons. 'Now if you've said yer piece ... ' He jerked his head at the door, indicating his son's time was up. 'Some of us have gotta get to work.'

Old habits died hard with Johnny. He pulled a florin from his pocket. 'Buy yourself a pint on me, Dad.' He didn't receive a thank you.

Johnny went out knowing he wouldn't tell Dora. She wouldn't understand why he'd treat a selfish man like his father when they were struggling to make ends meet and to pay for a wedding. Johnny didn't understand it himself.

Sidney swiped up the coin the moment the door was closed. He put on his cap and checked his appearance in the mirror. He didn't have a lady friend yet. But he reckoned he might soon.

Molly Deane had started looking out of her window, to check if he was hanging around outside. And when she spotted him she didn't look as annoyed as before. Once, when her old man had been at home, she'd flapped a hand to shush Sidney away. But she'd given him a smile as if to say: try another time.

When he'd been loitering on a couple of occasions, Sidney had heard the noise of an argument coming from the house. It had gladdened his heart to know all was not well between Molly and her husband – if that's who he was. Molly had called herself Mrs Payne in a jokey way and so Sidney had a clue as to the identity of his rival.

He'd made some enquiries about a fellow called Payne and had discovered that George Payne was an Elephant Boy. This had been disappointing news as Sidney knew they were a bunch of thugs, not to be messed with. But it hadn't been enough to put him off his pursuit of Molly Deane.

Soon he reckoned he wouldn't be shushed away by her but beckoned forward; he'd be ready when it happened. A house like that … a woman like that … would suit him down to the ground. He wouldn't need his son's florins then. And as for George Payne … well, he'd find a way to deal with him when the time came.

Chapter Twenty-Two

'Where are you off to, miss?'

'Seeing me friends.'

George took off his hat and coat and pegged them up. He glanced along the quiet hallway. 'Where's your mother? Did she say you could go out?'

Rebecca wished she'd left a few minutes earlier and avoided him and his questions. He treated her as though she were still a schoolgirl.

'Mum won't mind me going to the pictures; I'm seventeen, not a kid.' Rebecca could barely look at her father. She was angrier with her mother, though, and it had nothing to do with wanting to go out this evening.

Earlier that day she had been taken on a train to Richmond on a shoplifting jaunt. Molly had said they were becoming too well known in the West End and needed to broaden their boundaries. The tiring journey lugging back the goods hadn't infuriated Rebecca as much as being forced to carry on doing something she hated.

While she'd quarrelled with her mother, George had simply brooded in the background. Her parents rarely spoke to one another in a meaningful way any more. Their disagreements usually started when Molly blamed him for squandering cash on Fascist Party funds. Rebecca knew money was tight, and was ready to do her bit to contribute to the household kitty. But not by thieving. She wanted a regular job ... the sort normal people did. She'd sooner be a sales assistant than carry on like this. After all, spotting a shoplifter would be a doddle for her. She was starting to prepare for the next step towards adulthood and a life independent from her parents.

'I asked you about your mother, young lady,' George barked. He didn't like being ignored.

'Mum went out.' Rebecca was blushing, glad her father was ignorant of where her musings had taken her.

Meeting Jake had been a turning point in her life, she'd been thinking. Before falling for him, she'd not questioned her parents' methods. After that secret look passed between them in the pub, she'd begun contemplating her future; first a boyfriend, then a husband and family. She didn't want her children putting their hands in other people's pockets, or stuffing their own with stolen clothes.

Even though the girlish dream of running hand in hand through a meadow with Jake had crumbled, she hadn't forgotten him. She'd accepted he'd gone from her life, though. If he'd intended to find her he would have done so; he was the sort of person who could do anything he wanted once he put his mind to it. He was good-looking and she supposed a flirt, with his pick of the girls. He'd be about eighteen or nineteen now and perhaps had somebody serious. He might be thinking of settling down with her ...

'Your mother's gone out?' George wasn't sure he believed that and proceeded along the hallway to check. 'She was dog-tired when she got back from Richmond.'

While Molly had gone upstairs to rest, George had visited his aunt Queenie with two suitcases stuffed with stolen dresses. He'd driven a hard bargain as he needed to pay for repairs to his Humber. The garage had been waiting months for settlement and had started making noises about writs.

'She has gone out, Dad.' Rebecca gestured impatiently. 'She's not in the kitchen. Mum said I should get my own tea.'

George slowly retraced his steps, looking thoughtful.

'Dad ...' Rebecca changed her tone, having decided her father would be more amenable than her mother on this. He was the one keen to move away from their old life and into business with his posh pals.

'What, love?' he asked in a distracted way. His suspicions were with the fellow who'd been hanging around. Having told Molly he might be out for a while, George had returned sooner than expected. He had bumped into a colleague and learned of an impromptu meeting at Party headquarters. George was keen to be involved in arranging another rally and was only back to change his clothes before heading to Chelsea.

'My friend is learning Pitman shorthand and typewriting, and I want to as well.' Rebecca had mustered the courage to burst out with it.

George's irritation flared but was short-lived. He turned over in his mind what she'd said. 'You'd need a typewriter for practising on. I know where to find one.' He tapped his nose. 'If I play me cards right, I might be able to get you a little try on it.'

Rebecca smiled, delighted he'd not brushed her off as he usually did. 'It's not a stolen one, is it?'

"Course not.' He nudged her in a jokey way. 'It's at

Whitelands College. I've seen them type copy for *The Blackshirt* on it.' He mentioned the name of the Party's weekly newspaper. 'I bet you'd like to be asked to write a little piece for publication, wouldn't you?' He tipped up his daughter's chin and gave her a smile. 'Not on politics ... something else, perhaps.'

'Would I be able to?' Rebecca asked, eyes widening in excitement.

'Well, can't make no promises; but them that don't ask, don't get.' Mosley had asked earlier in the week where George's charming daughter was as he'd not seen her around lately. George was always looking to find ways to gain the top man's approval.

Rebecca clung affectionately to her father's arm. Her mind was already leapfrogging away from the idea of being a secretary, to training for a career as a journalist. And at the Party's headquarters was a typewriter she could practise on. 'Can we go now, Dad?'

'Well, your mother's not in to miss us, and there's no dinner on. No time like the present, I suppose.' He chucked Rebecca under the chin. 'We can eat while we're out, if you like.'

'Where the hell have you been? I've been worried sick over Rebecca ...'

Molly had stopped pacing the hallway the moment the key sounded in the lock. She'd rushed to the door to confront George and hug Rebecca, but her daughter whipped straight past her.

Molly had guessed Rebecca had been dragooned into accompanying George to the Party's Chelsea headquarters. She had caught a cab to Whiteland's College on the King's

Road to find them. They had been there, she'd been told, but had already left. That had been over an hour ago.

'Where have *I* been?' George prevented Molly following Rebecca by swinging her around to face him. 'That's a bit rich coming from you. Where was you earlier?'

'Doctor's surgery,' said Molly succinctly and pulled free.

That took the wind from George's sails. He sniffed, shoved his hands in his pockets and gruffly enquired, 'What's up with you then?'

'I've had stomach pains.' She kept her voice low, hoping her daughter wouldn't hear and start to fret. But Rebecca was already out of earshot, halfway up the stairs with a mumbled good night.

'Grumbling appendix, he reckons it might be,' explained Molly. 'But the silly old fool didn't even properly examine me.' Molly knew it was partly her fault for that. She'd been in a rush as she had somewhere else to head before going home and she'd hoped – in vain as it transpired – to beat George indoors. 'Now, did you make Rebecca go out? Is that why she's moody again?'

'*I* didn't make her do nuthin'. She asked me if she could come along,' he said pointedly. 'She wanted a go on the typewriter in the office. You know she's always on about learning to be a secretary. The gel's called time on hoisting, same as me.'

Molly ignored the barb. 'Where else did you go?' She leaned forward and sniffed. His breath smelled of whisky and he rarely drank at meetings. 'You've been boozing. You'd better not have taken her to the pub.'

'Don't be bloody daft.' George huffed. 'You didn't give her no tea, so I did. We went somewhere and had chops. I had a drink with mine. Now I'm turning in meself.' So far everything he'd said had been the truth, but he was making himself scarce before she fired more questions. He hoped in the morning she'd have forgotten about this or he might have to resort to lies. He'd already told his daughter to keep her lips sealed or there'd be trouble with her mother. The ungrateful little cow hadn't appreciated what he'd done for her anyway, introducing her to people who could help her get on in life.

'Rebecca?' Molly called softly from the doorway. There was no reply and her daughter remained still, turned away from her with the covers pulled right up to her chin. Molly tiptoed closer and gazed down at her sleeping daughter. She hated it when they argued. If Rebecca had been awake she would have promised her that soon they'd both embark on a different life. No more stealing ... no more fascists. Just them and new beginnings away from George's harmful influence.

After leaving the surgery, Molly had walked the long way home past the brewery. She'd been pleased to see her detour had been worthwhile. She'd waved to Sidney Cooper in his cubbyhole by the gate. He'd grinned and made to come out to talk to her, but she'd hurried on, crossing the road. She'd only wanted to keep him thinking about her and let him know she was thinking of him. She'd no time to stop and talk.

Over the past months they'd snatched some chats while the coast was clear. She'd been surprised by his persistence; he kept coming back, which reassured her that he had some feelings for her. Oddly, although she knew he was no angel, he appealed to her. She wasn't quite ready for the conversation she knew he was eager to have though.

His similarity in character to George was both a blessing

and a curse. In his day, Sidney had been a rough handful and he'd retained the look of a bruiser. George was younger, but Molly hoped he might think twice about taking Sidney Cooper on.

Molly didn't want a permanent relationship. She intended her admirer provide the first stepping stone on her getaway from George Payne.

Reaching down, she tucked the blanket higher about her daughter's shoulders. She smoothed a lock of thick brown hair off her brow, feeling proud of the beautiful young woman Rebecca had become.

She'd turned seventeen, but it didn't seem so very long ago she'd been the adorable toddler Rupert Harding had believed to be his child. If only it had been true. In time, Molly would have wrested him away from the cold woman he'd married. George had taken matters into his own hands though to ensure she couldn't, and would remain with him. She had, but she'd never married him and was glad about that. It made things easier.

Molly kissed her fingers and placed them on her daughter's cheek, murmuring a good night.

Rebecca heard the door click shut behind her mother and raised her eyelids, liberating the tears that had been blocked behind them. She turned her face into the pillow to muffle the sound of her sobs.

The pub throbbed with the sound of the piano being pounded and reeked of yeast from a thousand slopped beers.

Jake was soaking up the warm atmosphere while leaning against the bar, sipping a pint of bitter. He watched Herbie swinging Maria around by the arm as they jigged and caterwauled the words to 'We're in the Money'. Ginger Rogers would be appalled, he thought, chuckling into his beer.

Johnny and Dora were waltzing sedately, gazing into one another's eyes like teenage sweethearts, despite one of the pianist's boots thumping insistently on the floorboards. Sadie hadn't come along although Jake had invited her, for old times' sake. He was rather relieved that she accepted their youthful attachment was nearing its end, and preferred to stay away.

The jolly commotion reminded him of the first time he'd ventured inside a pub. That Christmas Eve in the Bricklayer's Arms had marked the start of his friendship with Johnny and Dora. It had also seen the start of his obsession with Rebecca Payne. He wished she was here at his side . . .

'You did well to finish that job on time,' said Mr Spooner, breaking into Jake's reflectiveness.

'Thanks for helping out with it,' returned Jake. 'Hope you didn't strain your back.'

'Oh, it'll pass. Won't be offering to go back on the tools on a regular basis though,' he warned with a finger wag.

'Happy birthday to yooou . . . '

Mr Spooner was first to swivel towards the door on recognising his wife's tobacco-roughened singing voice. She'd backed into the saloon bar, and on turning around, had revealed the large cake she was carrying, a candle burning atop the icing.

Jake's friends – and the pianist, with much striking of the piano keys – joined in with belting out the birthday tune, then they were gathering around to make sure they didn't miss the cake being cut.

Jake blushed from suddenly becoming the centre of

attention, and from the pleasure of having such a delightful surprise.

'Speech . . . ' called Johnny prompting other people into similar cajoling.

'Yes . . . say a few words, son.' Mr Spooner nudged Jake and said kindly, 'It's a fine occasion all round. A big birthday and your first big contract under your belt. The practice will come in handy for when you're a town councillor.' He gave Jake an encouraging wink.

Jake put down his tankard and cleared his throat while raking fingers through his fair hair. 'Well . . . umm . . . just like to say thanks to you all for coming,' he began gruffly. 'And thanks to Harding Brothers' workers for getting the job done on time.' His blush deepened. 'Reckon you lot are like brothers, too. Don't get too comfortable though,' he ruefully added. 'You've all got to turn up sober on Monday to start again.' He waited for Herbie's good-natured jeering to die down before concluding, 'And the biggest thank you goes to Mrs Spooner for making this smashing cake.'

The woman beamed at him then planted a smacker on his cheek. 'Only wish one of me daughters was single so I could have you fer a son-in-law, love.'

'Leave off, dear. You're making him squirm,' her husband mildly admonished.

'Well, I mean it,' she stubbornly said. 'Now let's find a knife and see what this tastes like. It's a fruit cake . . . '

'Something else to do before we start tucking into that,' said Johnny solemnly.

He lunged at Jake, grabbing him under the armpits and Herbie quickly joined in, having guessed what was coming. So had the pianist, who'd roped in some of the other fellows to help lift Jake.

'Bumps ...' shouted Johnny, making the women scatter out of the way.

Jake gave up protesting and struggling to escape. He felt his limbs become weightless and closed his eyes, letting air rush at him as his stomach did somersaults. He was reminded of Toby ... of them playing as children. Of being swung around by his father until he felt giddy with excitement and joy. He wasn't completely happy as he had been then. He felt wistful: there was no Toby here helping him celebrate ... he'd had to pretend to have brothers to take his place. He yearned for Toby as though they were tied by blood. Often he believed that they were ... must be, or the sadness would go away.

'What a performance,' announced Mrs Spooner, as Jake was deposited back to earth. 'Just as well you didn't tuck in beforehand, love.' She sawed into the cake, handing around the rich brown slices. 'Might've had currants sprayed all over the shop.'

A swaying, laughing Jake was handed his slice.

Mrs Spooner patted his shoulder. 'I'd give it a minute, son, before getting that down you.'

Chapter Twenty-Three

'You look as white as a sheet. What's up, Becky?'

Queenie stood aside to let the girl enter the house. She often used the pet name Becky, which her niece seemed to like, especially when she was feeling low.

'Another falling-out with your father, is it?' Queenie gave a sympathetic tut. 'The season of goodwill does seem to bring the worst bust-ups.' The dry comment was issued as she shut the door then trudged behind in her slippers. She'd had a few too many sherries yesterday, and a late night had left her with an aching head.

Queenie hadn't been drinking alone; she'd had a houseful of visiting relatives and things had turned rather rowdy. So much so that it had been Tommy and Dolly's turn to bang on the wall, complaining about the noise. George had been invited to come as well. He'd said the family had already got other plans for Boxing Day. Queenie knew they hadn't; George simply didn't want to let his cousins witness him and Molly giving one another daggers. He liked to maintain a united front and believed himself a cut above the rest.

'We've not been arguing at home, Auntie . . .' Rebecca had sunk down onto the settee in the parlour. Unable to sit still she sprang up. If her parents discovered what had brought her here, an argument would be the least of her troubles.

'You're a regular jack-in-the-box.' Queenie failed to make her niece smile. She hugged her, rubbing her back. 'I'll put the kettle on; a strong cup of char'll help get it off your chest.' She heard Rebecca start to cry softly against her shoulder. 'Come on now, dry those tears,' she cooed. 'Nothing's that bad.' Queenie extricated herself to go to the kitchen.

'It is . . .' croaked Rebecca and held onto her aunt's arm to stop her leaving. She knew she couldn't delay for a second or her courage would vanish and she'd never make her confession.

'How about we go down in the cellar and look for a pretty dress for you?' Queenie shimmied her stout hips and patted her coiled grey plait. 'There's a beauty in mustard silk that'll make you look like a film star. You could wear it when you come over for a sing-song round the piano on New Year's Eve . . .'

'I'm late . . . and I can't tell Mum 'cos she'll go mad, and as for Dad . . . ' Rebecca burst out over her aunt's generous attempt to cheer her up. She was unable to finish describing the brewing calamity or her father's likely violent reaction to it.

'Late for what?' Comprehension crept up on Queenie, shocking the frown from her face. Rebecca wasn't that sort of girl. She was decent, unlike a couple of Queenie's other nieces who'd give a seasoned trollop a run for her money. A catfight had started yesterday when one accused another of playing around with her husband. Queenie had chucked the pair of them out, but they'd carried on pulling hair and rolling around in the street. Rebecca was different: class through and through. 'No ... you haven't let yourself get knocked up ... have you?' Queenie's disbelief emerged in a whisper.

'I think so, Auntie ...'

Queenie yanked open Rebecca's coat to study her belly. Nothing to see there. The straining blouse buttons were a dead giveaway, though, on a girl who'd never had much bust to speak of. 'How far gone?' demanded Queenie.

Rebecca miserably shook her head. 'Don't know ... about seven or eight weeks, I think.'

Queenie urged her niece to sit beside her on the settee and drew Rebecca's head against her shoulder, letting her cry it out. There was plenty to cry about, too. It wouldn't only be the fellow involved on the receiving end of George's fist when this got out. His daughter would feel his wrath as well. 'Have you been seeing somebody on the sly? Who is he? Will he marry you?'

Rebecca shook her head. 'Don't want him or the baby. I want to get rid of it.' She struggled out of her aunt's embrace. 'You won't tell on me, will you? I wouldn't have said if I thought ...'

'Hush ... quieten yerself down.' Queenie wiped tears from Rebecca's face with an edge of her pinafore. 'I won't tell. But I want you to tell me who he is.'

Rebecca covered her face with her hands and made an effort to compose herself. 'I thought, as you know lots of people, you might have an address of somebody ... somebody to get me out of trouble.' She stood up before her aunt asked again for the father's name. 'I want to leave home, and get a proper job, but not under a cloud. I'd rather not fall out with Mum and Dad if I can help it.' She gave her aunt an appealing look while she paced to and fro. 'If I hurry up there'll be no need for them to know about this and get upset.'

'It would be better if they didn't,' agreed Queenie pithily. 'Have you told them about your plans to be independent?'

'They know I'm fed up with hoisting. I spoke to Dad about it ...' She winced at that memory. If she hadn't brought up about typing lessons, she wouldn't be in this mess. But it was too late for regrets. She'd wanted to go with him, had been excited and ready to enjoy herself that night. 'I will tell them I want to leave home ... once this is over and done with. I can't stay there any more.' Rebecca shook her head. 'They treat me like I'm a kid of twelve. Do this, do that ... don't go out ...'

'They both want what's best for you, love.'

'I know what's best for me; I can't breathe. I feel as though I'm suffocating with them.'

'Your mum and dad know better'n most about all the bad sorts out there. They want to protect you, so you don't make the mistakes they've made.'

'It's too late for that,' said Rebecca harshly. 'Anyway, they *are* the bad sorts out there.'

Queenie had little argument against that. The girl had been reared in crime and Queenie knew she'd set no good example to her either. 'So, are you intending to shack up with him ... the father?'

Rebecca shook her head. 'I'll find a proper job and get my own place. I don't mind a tiny room to start with and I'll work hard to improve myself.'

'Well, nothing wrong with any of that, if you think you can manage it.'

'Will you help me, Auntie? I don't want money from you, just some advice.'

'Well, wouldn't be much of an auntie if I couldn't give you that.' Queenie sighed. 'Ain't saying I approve of any of this, Becky. For a start, I thought you had more sense than to let a randy fellow catch you out. But we all do these silly things.' She cupped Rebecca's face in her palms and brushed her tears away with her thumbs. 'Learnt yer lesson, have you?'

'Learnt it all right ...' said Rebecca bitterly.

'Put the kettle on then, shall I?' Queenie paused before quitting the room. 'Are you sure you won't at least tell your mum?' At Rebecca's age, Molly was already a good-time girl. Queenie knew that in her early twenties pretty Molly Deane had cashed in on her looks and hooked a rich gentleman protector who'd set her up for life. Queenie didn't hold that against her. But she would find it hard to swallow if Molly disowned her daughter for this slip-up, all things considered.

'I can't tell Mum; she's been under the weather and I don't want to worry her.' Rebecca vigorously shook her head. She had caught her mother rubbing her belly earlier, and not for the first time. She'd been told not to fret over it because the doctor had said it might settle down. But Rebecca was fretting. She might not want to live with her parents because they drove her mad, but she did love them. She started to cry again.

'No more waterworks. We'll sort it out then ... just me 'n' you.' Queenie approached her niece to comfort her. After a few moments she let her go and said, 'Now, are you going to tell me who he is, Becky?' She adopted an innocent look. 'I won't go after him.' Big Queenie was quite capable of giving a fellow a kicking and had done so in the past. This time it was very personal but she wouldn't do it herself now she'd

265

promised not to. She'd plenty of associates who owed her favours.

'I can't say … promised I wouldn't, after he gave me this to pay to get rid of it.' Rebecca drew from her pocket a brooch. It was made of delicate gold filigree and blue, white and red stones that trembled as she displayed it on her palm.

Queenie goggled at the jewel sparking fiery light, then lifted her astonished eyes to her niece. 'He gave you that?'

Rebecca nodded.

'Stolen, I take it?' Queenie recovered her wits enough to say.

Again Rebecca nodded.

'Well I never. Ain't seen nothing as good as that in a long while. French made, maybe.' Queenie blew a whistle through her teeth. 'Too hot for me to handle, something like that,' she said, awe trembling in her voice.

Rebecca frowned in disappointment at the brooch. 'Somebody will buy it, though, won't they?'

'They will. And I think I know who, and how we'll get two birds with one stone out of it. But first, are you sure this is what you want to do, Rebecca?' The gravity of the situation called for a formal tone. She held her niece's hands and gave them a squeeze. 'Ain't trying to frighten you, love, but have to tell you that a visit to an abortionist ain't a nice experience for any gel.' In truth, Queenie knew Rebecca had little choice in the matter. This had to be dealt with quickly and quietly before George got wind that something was wrong. Because if he did, there'd be murders.

Rebecca nodded then sank down onto the settee and waited for her aunt to return with the tea.

*

'Bleeding hell ... I've been getting more calls today than a new prossie in town.' Queenie was putting on a cheery act; in fact, she was on edge. She had a feeling she knew what her second visitor in the space of an hour wanted.

'Oh, who's been over then?'

'Usual lot of scapegraces. Christmas time they all come around.' Queenie had led the way into the parlour that barely an hour previously had seen this woman's daughter crying her eyes out, and producing a valuable gem from her pocket. 'Shame you didn't make it Boxing Day; so how've you been then, Mol?' Queenie gave the younger woman a thorough look, recalling Rebecca saying her mother hadn't been well.

'I'm all right ... could be better. Maybe you can help with that. Was one of them scapegraces who's been bothering you my daughter?' Molly turned around to give the woman a piercing look. 'If so, I'd like to know what she wanted.'

'Yeah ... I've seen Rebecca,' said Queenie. 'Did you follow her here?'

'No ... was shopping over this way and spotted her coming out of this road. Didn't need Sherlock Holmes to tell me where she'd been.' Molly took off her hat. 'She's been different lately ... upset. She's my daughter and I've a right to know what's going on. She won't tell me but I think you know what's eating at her. What did you talk about?'

'I said I'd give her a dress for New Year.' Queenie was feeling her way into this conversation to find out how much the other woman knew. Reading between the lines, she guessed Molly was suspicious but hadn't yet confronted Rebecca, unwilling to create needless strife when they'd enough of that already.

'Ain't a new dress I'm worried about,' said Molly. 'She

267

didn't use no pads last month and ain't sure she did the month before that either. Being her mother I keep a check on such things.'

Queenie didn't blame Molly for her vigilance; she'd be the same if she had a beautiful daughter of Rebecca's age.

'So, I'll ask you again, Queenie. What's going on with my daughter? Has she asked for cash to put something right?' Molly bit her lower lip to stop it quivering.

'Sit down, Molly . . . ' Queenie sighed, knowing the game was well and truly up. Despite her loyalty to her niece she was relieved to be able to get this off her chest. In her heart, she knew Rebecca's mother should be dealing with such a matter. She'd been reminding herself of that ever since waving the girl off earlier. Molly loved her daughter and would do anything to keep her safe and happy. As for George: he'd be more concerned with his own reputation than Rebecca's.

Molly slumped back into the chair, praying Queenie wasn't about to deliver news she was dreading to hear. 'Thanks, Queenie . . . ' She rubbed a hand about her anxious face. 'Will I need a cuppa tea to take this down?'

'Gonna need something stronger than that, love,' said Queenie opening her sideboard and getting out the whisky bottle and two glasses.

Chapter Twenty-Four

'You go ahead, I'll catch up with you later, after I finish this,' said Jake. He put down his pen on the open ledger and sat back in his chair. Herbie was framed in the kitchen doorway, kitted out in his best togs, and had the air of a fellow who feels uncomfortably neat. Jake chuckled and nodded his approval.

'We supposed to take a wedding present or somethin'?' asked Herbie, squeaking up to the mirror in his new shoes. He checked his Brylcreemed hair then returned the comb to his pocket.

'Don't reckon Johnny and Dora will be too bothered about that.'

'Could get her a rolling pin, I suppose.' Herbie grinned.

'Reckon she must already have one if she's marrying Johnny Cooper,' Jake said dryly and picked up his pen.

'See you later then,' Herbie called and closed the door.

He used to complain about being denied accommodation in the main house, but now accepted he'd remain in the staff quarters. He was back in the fold, but things would never be back as they were. Nevertheless, Herbie knew he was luckier than he'd any right to be, having friends and a regular pay packet. He didn't take Jake's withdrawal to heart, or his generosity for granted; his boss maintained a fair distance between himself and all his employees. He let himself out of the side gate and set off, whistling, to collect Maria.

Having finished calculating the column of takings, Jake checked the total then copied the pencilled figures on his working-out paper into the book before blotting and clos-ing it. He stood up and stretched, then put the kettle on for some warm water to wash and shave before leaving for the wedding reception. He ran his fingers over his stubbly chin then through his fair hair, checking its shagginess in the mirror. He wished he'd had time to visit the barber's but the run-up to Christmas had been too busy.

The bell rattled over his head. It wouldn't be Herbie back again; he had his own key to the gate. It could be Mr and Mrs Spooner, offering to get a cab with him over to Johnny's sister's place. Or it might be somebody looking for work. Jobless men turned up on a regular basis at all hours of the day and night to plead for shifts as casual labourers. Jake wished he was able to employ all of them but he'd bankrupt himself if he tried. What he needed were skilled tradesmen. He took the spluttering kettle off the hob and went outside.

'I've come to see Peg Tiller, please ...' Rebecca had heard heavy approaching footsteps and inwardly cursed her luck to have to speak to a man. She almost collapsed in shock on raising her eyes and seeing who he was.

Jake was no less astonished to be confronted by the girl he often thought of but had almost given up on.

After a lengthy pulsing silence, they started talking together, Rebecca saying she'd made a mistake and Jake asking what she meant by that. Women had stopped turn-ing up to do business with Peg many months' ago. He'd

270

assumed word had spread and all Peg's old customers knew she'd gone, and a builder now occupied the premises.

'No, you don't ...' Jake caught hold of Rebecca as she would have fled. He dragged her through the gate and slammed it, trapping her against it. 'Right ... first you can tell me what you want with Peg. After that, I'll have back my thirty bob you stole.'

'You'd better let me out, Jake Harding, or whatever your name is.' She pushed at him but he didn't budge.

'Got it in one,' he said and looked her over. Her eyes were shining with defiance but she seemed nervous as hell. 'What d'you want with Peg? Brought her something to fence, I reckon. What is it?' He kept hold of her with one hand and showed her the palm of his other. 'Come on, let's have it. We'll do a deal ... less my thirty-bob discount, of course.'

Rebecca gazed up boldly into his face. 'Is she your mum?' She could see a glow in the window of the house behind him. 'How many names do you use? Are you really Jake Tiller?'

'No ... I'm really Jake Harding; Peg was like a mum to me, though, before she died.'

'She's dead?' Rebecca cried in dismay.

'Died over a year ago. I worked for her, hoisting stuff for her to fence.' He paused, recalling that the woman with the bangle who'd run off had been similarly distressed to hear Peg wasn't available. 'Who told you about Peg? And why d'you want her anyway? I heard you Paynes used a family fence.' Jake started propelling Rebecca towards the house. 'We can't talk out here ...'

He sent a significant glance at next door's upstairs windows. Rebecca's eyes had followed in time to see a

271

curtain falling back into place. She stopped struggling. She certainly didn't want to draw attention to herself, but there was more to it than that. Not so long ago she would have gone out of her way to see him. Now the meeting felt bittersweet.

'If you're not using your relative, you're doing some business on your own account. You don't want your father wise to what you're up to, do you?' He opened the kitchen door and ushered her inside, remaining by the exit to prevent her bolting. He was no longer bothered about the money she'd stolen but he did want answers to some questions.

They stared at one another by the light of the flickering gas mantles until he noticed her eyes glistening. 'What's wrong?' he said, approaching her. 'If you're stuck for money I'll buy whatever it is you've got. I don't usually do these sorts of deals 'cos I'm finished with thieving.'

'So am I,' she said and turned away so he wouldn't see her use the heel of her hand on her tears. What a cruel game fate was playing. She had longed to discover if he still liked her as much as she liked him. He did. Despite his sham anger their bond remained. It had been there from the first time he brushed against her body to steal from her pocket. 'If Peg's not here I won't bother you further,' she said hoarsely. 'Got things to do.'

He grabbed her fingers before they could reach the door handle and pulled her round to face him. 'Show me what you've got.' He let go of her and beckoned. 'Whatever it is, I'll give you a fair price.'

She choked an acrid laugh, looked fiercely at him. 'She might have been like a mum to you, but you didn't know Peg very well, did you?'

'What makes you say that?'

'Nothing . . . ' she muttered and turned her face aside. The seconds ticked by. 'You'd better let me out,' she said. 'Me dad'll go for you. He'll be looking for me. I should've been indoors by now.' It was the truth; but she realised she didn't care any more about George Payne's bullying. Whatever her father said, she was leaving home.

'Why d'you say that about Peg?' Jake ignored the threat and beckoned once more for whatever it was she had to sell.

'Because she didn't only fence stuff . . . she was an abortionist,' Rebecca burst out.

'What?' he scoffed, and dropped his outstretched hand back to his side. 'Who told you that rubbish?'

'My aunt. She didn't know Peg had died.' Rebecca sighed in defeat. 'She told me about this place. She was going to accompany me here next week. I didn't want to wait; besides, I'd sooner do this by myself. So I did.'

Jake's expression didn't change; he remained quite still and staring at her while the colour drained from his face.

He thought he was clever, so did other people. They told him all the time he had a wise head on his shoulders. He'd been dense as well as naive about this, he savagely mocked himself. He'd clued up now though and had quickly joined the dots between agitated women turning up when it was dark, to Peg taking their valuables and banishing him and Herbie to the outhouse while she dealt with them alone.

Jake used the back bedroom rather than Peg's bigger one at the front of the house. The medical instruments he'd seen in her chest of drawers he'd believed had been kept as a sentimental reminder of her nursing days. Out of respect and affection for her, everything remained as she'd left it. He still did love and respect her. But he was glad she wasn't here right now.

'You didn't know, did you?' Rebecca said sadly. She could tell she'd shocked him. Not just about Peg. About her too.

'If you're knocked up you'll need money,' he said, harsh and businesslike. He turned away from her and tapped the table. 'Put it down there.'

'I'll go elsewhere ...'

'You damn well won't.' He kicked the chair into place under the table. 'Your father doesn't know, does he? Maybe he does.' He arrowed a look at her. 'Has he thrown you out?'

'It's none of your business.'

'It is my fucking business. You've come to me. Who is he?'

'None of your business.'

'He won't marry you, will he?'

She swallowed the lump in her throat. He wasn't pretending to be angry now but she wasn't afraid of him. She knew she could leave. She had a clear path to the door behind since he'd moved in front of her. But there was no reason to run; there was no secret to hide and it was too late to deflect shrewd looks. She approached the table and sat down.

'All right ... what will you give me for that then?' She'd taken the brooch from her pocket and placed it on the table. If she went elsewhere, somebody might recognise her and tell her parents what she'd been doing. She trusted Jake. He wouldn't grass on her and he'd no liking for her father.

Jake sat down opposite and drew the brooch towards him. He'd played with that as a child, when his mother left it out on her dressing table. Before he lost her love completely, Violet Harding would wobble the delicate gold herself to make him laugh watching the jewels dance.

'S'pose you want me to tell you where I got it,' she said to draw his mesmerised gaze from the brooch.

He grimaced almost amused denial. 'I know where you

got it. How d'you manage to steal it? Was she wearing it at the time?'

Sensing he suddenly knew more than she did, she pushed back her chair in readiness to jump up. 'I didn't steal it. I told you I don't thieve any more. It was given to me. By him. So I'd get rid of the baby and never tell what he'd done to me.' She snatched up the jewellery and was half standing when pulled back into the seat by a hand that had whipped across the table.

'Explain that,' said Jake, deadly quiet.

Rebecca yanked herself free and had reached the door before he said, 'That brooch belongs to the woman who adopted me. I'd know it anywhere. Did Ian Winters give it to you?'

Rebecca blanched and slowly turned to face him. She moistened her lips. 'No, his son did.'

'Rebecca!' Molly shouted and began to dash up the stairs to her daughter's bedroom. She was halfway up when George leaned over the banisters.

'What's going on?'

Molly stopped and gasped. 'Where's Rebecca?'

'I thought she was with you.' He had a whisky in his hand and swigged from the glass as he descended the treads. 'If she's not home, where is she then?'

Molly returned to the hallway to escape him looming over her, breathing alcoholic fumes. He'd been drinking more than normal lately. Her guts felt tied in knots by panic, more painful than when pangs of a grumbling appendix afflicted her. She wanted some answers from George but daren't alert him to the trouble Rebecca was in. He was more volatile when drunk. He'd knock his daughter black and blue and her too. She was the girl's mother, he'd roar, and should have taught her how to behave herself.

'Rebecca's not been herself since you took her to the headquarters when I was at the doctor's.' Molly crossed her arms over her chest to subdue her rapid breathing. 'What went on that evening? You never really said.'

'I did tell you.' He gave her a sullen look as he joined her in the hallway. 'She practised on the typewriter. If she's slipped out with friends without asking permission, she'll get a hiding.'

'No, she won't.' Molly turned her back to conceal her agitation. 'You said you had chops for dinner. Where did you go to eat?' She'd interrogated Rebecca over this but had been fobbed off. Molly suspected George had threatened her to keep quiet.

'Oh, all right, if you must know Ian Winters invited us to his house.' He appeared annoyed to be explaining himself. 'Winters said his wife was away, so I reckoned it was safe to go. I knew you'd cut up rough so didn't tell you.' The whisky had flushed colour across his cheekbones and his temper was deepening it. 'If Violet was going to sue over the business with Rupert Harding she'd have done it by now. She don't even remember you, I reckon.' He pointed a finger while continuing to amble to and fro. 'So, I don't want to hear no more about it from you. I'm carrying on as normal and seeing people I want to see.'

'Ian Winters,' Molly whispered, covering her mouth as nausea rose in her throat.

'What's wrong?' George was concerned by her pallor and approached her. 'It was only a quick dinner, love. We weren't there more than an hour and a half. I swear Violet was out and Winters didn't drop no hints about her first husband into the conversation. Rebecca seemed happy enough and enjoyed her dinner.' He gestured wildly. 'Then all of a sudden she wanted to leave. Little cow didn't have no manners. Winter's son was back from university and tried to keep her amused while we talked business over a Scotch . . . '

Molly lashed out, knocking the glass from his hand to smash on the floor. 'You bloody stupid fool,' she cried in anguish and started backing towards the door.

George was too stupefied to retaliate straight away. Then he set off after her, yanking her back by the hair before she had the door fully open. 'What's wrong with you?' he snarled and slapped her face. 'Where d'you think yer going?'

'To find her,' Molly said and used all her might to shove him away from her. She watched him stumble, hoped he'd fall. At that moment she hated him more than she would have thought possible. 'And I don't need you,' she said coldly before rushing on her way.

'Were you really adopted?'

Jake nodded.

'Did you ever know your real mum?'

He shook his head. 'Was only a baby.'

'How old were you?' she asked in a voice hushed by sympathy.

'Not sure . . . less than a year, I think, when they took me in. I started off in an orphanage. My dad used to speak about it when we were little, but she didn't. He died when I was seven . . . too young to take enough notice. Wish I had now.'

Rebecca had heard him disguising his emotions beneath a grunted laugh. She stretched a hand to touch his fist, resting on the table.

He looked at her hand, curled over a blood blister where he'd caught himself with a hammer. He wound his fingers into hers.

'Where did you come from originally, Jake?'

'The East End of London ... somewhere like this, maybe.' He glanced around. 'Only know I was from a poor family that couldn't afford to keep me during the war.'

'Would you like to know more?'

He nodded. Lately he had been thinking he'd like to find his real anchor; which street, which room had housed him for a short while before he'd been dumped in Mayfair. He'd never belonged there. Even when his father had been alive he'd been restless for change.

'I expect my father was killed on the Western Front. My mother might've had older children to care for and me arriving was the last straw.'

'You might have real brothers and sisters then ... better than him ... ' She tailed off into silence.

'Tell me what happened, Rebecca.'

She avoided his eyes and withdrew her hand from his. 'I'm not sure about where I come from.'

'What d'you mean?'

'I heard my parents arguing. It's all they ever do lately, and that'll only get worse now after this ... ' She quickly resumed. 'They were talking about my mum's affair with another man. I didn't hear much and I couldn't ask ... they'd go mad. But I know Mum was quite racy in her day. A good-time girl, I heard my aunt say about her.' Rebecca gave a half-smile. 'My mum's very pretty.'

'So are you,' said Jake. 'Will you have the baby then have it adopted?'

'Can't ... Dad can't know I'm pregnant; he'd kill me.'

They stared at one another but the brooch resting midway between them had become a barrier to another touch. It had focused their eyes. 'How did you get this?'

She shook her head. 'Can't tell you ...'

'Did he rape you?'

The silence lengthened.

'I'll help you sort this out, Rebecca, but you have to tell me, or I can't.'

'Don't know ... maybe he did ... or maybe it was my fault ...' she said. 'I liked him at first, you see. He seemed familiar ... as though I knew him. He seemed like you ... I know it's daft.'

'No ... it's not. We grew up together.'

'Is he really your brother?' Rebecca blinked back tears, thinking nothing could be worse than hearing he was.

'Yes ... but we're not blood. We once shared the same name and parents. That finished when I was sent away.'

'What happened to split you up?'

'Doesn't matter. Tell me what went on between you and Toby.' He waited. 'Please ...'

'We were bored listening to them talk politics after dinner so his father said why not go in the other room to play cards. There was a brandy decanter and we both took a swig. We were laughing and he just kissed me. I didn't mind too much. He seemed nice ... funny. We played poker. He kept winning and said we should try strip poker. I told him I wasn't taking my clothes off.' She halted, breathless from pouring it out so fast. 'I thought he was joking ... being funny again.' She resumed slowly. 'We sat on the

279

sofa ... I can't believe he really did it with them right in the next room ...' She covered her face with her hands. 'I could have shouted but I knew my dad would kill him ... and he reminded me of you.'

Jake got up and moved around the table. He crouched down by her side and took her hands, hesitantly as though believing she might throw him off. She didn't, and when he drew her out of the chair she allowed him to hold her in his arms while she wept.

The sudden clatter of the bell was so unexpected and so loud that they jerked apart, Rebecca with a sharp inhalation and Jake with a low curse. A muted commotion could be heard and he hurried to pull open the door, and give volume to a woman's hysterical voice.

'Oh, no,' Rebecca groaned, massaging her forehead. 'It's my mum. My aunt must've told her after all. I have to go.' She gave him a warning look. 'Don't follow, whatever you do. If my dad's with her and sees you, he'll think ...' She shook her head. 'Won't matter what I say. He won't listen. He'll kill you.'

'Don't care,' said Jake. Illogical from his anger and distress he tried to storm outside.

'No ...' Rebecca grabbed him back, put her arms about him in a controlling embrace until she felt him become still. 'Give me the brooch.' She held out a hand. 'They'll know I've been paid off with it; I expect my aunt's told them everything.' Rebecca didn't dwell on Queenie's betrayal; she was more concerned with imagining how her father would deal with this. The people he crawled to were the worst sort of degenerates, but George Payne wasn't naive. He probably knew exactly what they were like. He might not cut ties with them for his daughter's sake but decide to cover up her abuse to keep in with them. He might find somebody less powerful ... more decent ... to blame. 'If I haven't got the brooch my dad'll come in and smash the place up looking for it. You have to give it to me,' she pleaded. 'I don't want you getting hurt because of me.'

'Tell them you sold it to Peg's replacement.' Jake went to a drawer in the dresser and took out a cash box. He turned the key and withdrew a fistful of notes, counting them as he strode back to her. 'Here ... eighty quid. It's all I've got lying around. The brooch is worth more but they won't know that if they've not seen it.' He thrust the cash at her. 'Take it.'

The noise outside increased as Molly shrieked her daughter's name and the gate was rocked against its hinges. The light shining out from next door's drawn-back curtains had put a strip of yellow on the concrete path.

'I must go ... somebody might call the coppers with the commotion she's making,' said Rebecca. They gazed at one another, unwilling to part with so much still unsaid, but knowing they had to.

'Send her away ... tell her you're with a friend,' he said in his desperation to keep her with him.

'Can't, Jake ... but thanks for this.' She moved the hand that grasped the money. A small fortune for her but he'd seemed quite easy with it. She took a swift pace away then came back to brush her lips on his cheek before hastening towards the gate.

He remembered her kissing him like that when she'd stolen from him. On that occasion he'd only lost his money and trust to her.

He closed the door and stood with his back to it, listening, but the shouting had stopped; there was only the hiss of the gas mantles and the sound of his torment growling in his throat.

Chapter Twenty-Five

'Didn't think you was coming,' said Johnny as he ushered Jake inside.

'Sorry ... got held up.' Jake rubbed a diffident finger beneath his nose. 'Congratulations to you both.'

'You're here now, that's the main thing,' said Dora, giving the late arrival's stubbly cheek a welcoming kiss. She pushed a glass of bubbly into his hand.

Jake hadn't shaved or had more than a brief wash before dashing out on remembering where he was supposed to be. His conscience had overruled a temptation to stay away and dwell on the muddle of emotions driving him mad. He felt a fraud though, smiling and toasting the newlyweds' happiness when he wasn't really listening to anything being said. His mind was jammed with something awful and fantastical. Yet, it wasn't so difficult to comprehend how this collision of families had come about. Jake had known for some time that Rebecca's father was friendly with the man who would be his stepfather had destiny's wheel spun differently. He was glad it hadn't and he'd ended up in the Barnardo's home. His constant wish to have lived his life with Toby had vanished.

'Come and meet some of my family,' said Johnny, steering Jake by the arm towards a woman with auburn hair and smiling green eyes. She looked older than Johnny and had an air of calm that failed to soothe Jake. 'This is me big sister, Clover, and her husband Neil.' Johnny turned and said proudly, 'This is my boss, Clo, the one I've been telling you about. Like to introduce you to Jake Harding.'

Jake politely held out a hand. He was smiling over clenched teeth. What was happening now? Was her father beating her? He wanted to race to find out. But that would make matters worse. She'd told him to stay away. He calmed himself with the thought that the eighty pounds might distract George Payne, for a while at least.

Clover took his hand then kissed his cheek without knowing why she was being over friendly with a young man she was meeting for the first time. He smelled familiar, though, and she told him so.

Jake forced his attention to the woman dressed in green velvet, looking quizzically at him. 'Oh ... that ...' He rubbed his chin. 'It's sandalwood soap. Treat meself to it sometimes,' he said.

'So do I ... sometimes,' said Neil. He'd taken to this young man who had similar green eyes to his wife.

'Here ... have a proper drink, Jake.' Johnny had returned, upending a brown bottle into a tankard. He thrust the glass into Jake's hand. 'You work too hard, y'know.' Johnny had noticed the strain on his face. 'Everything all right?'

''Course ... cheers, and hope you'll both be very happy.' Jake put down the sparkling wine to take a swig of beer.

'Johnny tells me you're looking for a carpenter,' said Neil and received an admonishing elbow in the ribs from his wife.

283

'What?' Neil said, all innocence. 'The man needs a carpenter. I'm a carpenter.'

'Not tonight at Johnny's wedding reception, you're not,' said Clover.

'I do actually need a carpenter ...' Jake said. 'There's a big job lined up for the New Year.'

'Just so happens I might be at a loose end in January.'

'Johnny knows where I am, so come over ...'

'Have a dance with the new Mrs Cooper?' Dora interrupted, holding her arms out to Jake. 'Come on ...' she urged when he looked awkward. 'Bet you never thought when you was little that you'd be dancing with your mum's housemaid one day, did you?' She chuckled.

'Go on ...' Johnny said. 'Be a pal 'n' give me toes a rest.'

'You're the one with two left feet,' his bride fired back, giggling as she led Jake away. They joined a crush of couples, swaying to the music emerging from the gramophone in the corner of the room.

'Who's that?' Annie had come to stand beside Clover. 'He's a bit of a dish.'

'Don't let Tony hear you say that.' Clover nodded to her sister's boyfriend who was helping distribute drinks. Tony was an under-butler in a neighbouring establishment to the one in which Annie worked. They had both managed to get time off from their respective employers to attend this special occasion. Clover knew what her younger sister meant though about Jake Harding: he was a well-built, handsome man.

'Oh, Tony's got nothing to worry about,' said Annie dreamily. 'He's the one for me.'

'Think I've heard that before ...' Clover rolled her eyes and went to open the window and let some fresh air into the stuffy room.

'We're going to make a move in a moment,' said Nettie, who was cradling her youngest daughter against her shoulder. Leonora was sound asleep despite the noise, but the eldest girl was fretfully pulling on her father's hand and rubbing her eyes. 'We've had such a lovely time but Jenny's out on her feet, poor love.'

'Not stopping to see the bride and groom cut the cake?' asked Mrs Spooner; she'd baked a wedding cake for the couple in lieu of buying a present.

'We'll hang about for that,' said Archie with a smirk.

'Don't say I blame you,' said Clover. 'It looks delicious.' Lately, Archie seemed nicer to be around and she hoped it was a permanent change, for everybody's sake.

'Did I hear somebody say cake?' Herbie had bowled in from the backyard where he'd been taking a breath of fresh air, in between smoking and canoodling with Maria.

'You've got ears like a bat, son,' said Mr Spooner, more in envy than jest. His own hearing had suffered from the shelling during his wartime service.

The ceremonial cutting of the cake was accompanied by loud cheering, then slices were distributed by the Spooners with fresh cups of tea. Dora and Clover tucked in, while the men went in search of something stronger to wash it down. 'This tastes as good as it looks,' said Clover, licking sticky marzipan off her thumb.

'Very kind of them, it was,' said Dora. 'Barely know them myself although Johnny speaks highly of Mr Spooner.' She paused. 'Biggest thanks go to you and Neil.' Dora sounded humble as she looked at plates of sausage rolls, fairy cakes and sandwiches, plus bowls of jelly and trifle that stretched from one end of a trestle table to the other.

'You're welcome, Dora. I enjoyed doing it and Annie got

time off so she could come over to help. She's turned into a good cook. All the small cakes and the trifle are her work. Anyway, that's what family's for: pitching in together.'

'It's not only this wedding breakfast I have to thank you for.' Dora put down her plate. 'It's everything. I know Johnny listens to you. If you'd gone against me, things might've turned out differently. Especially after what happened with him . . . ' She didn't name Archie or look at him but they both knew who she meant. 'I still feel ashamed.'

'Johnny loves you. All I want is for him to be happy.' Clover rubbed Dora's arm. 'I know we've not always seen eye to eye but that's in the past. You make my brother happy, and that's good enough for me.' She sipped her tea. 'Actually, I should thank you for being gracious and inviting my best friend. Nettie would have wondered why she'd been left out when all her family knew Johnny from when he was little.' Clover passed a glance over the congregation. 'You couldn't have done a better job of putting him in his place. He knows neither of you give a hoot about him or you wouldn't have had him here today.' Clover turned to embrace her new sister-in-law. 'Welcome to the family, Dora. And by the way, you look lovely in that outfit.'

'Found it in Petticoat Lane market,' said Dora, smoothing her hands over the nipped-in waist of her powder blue costume. 'Second-hand stall, and only paid a guinea, but it's got Bond Street on the label.'

'Must've cost ten times that new,' said Clover, running a hand over the fine wool crepe of Dora's sleeve.

While they finished eating their cake, Clover watched the group of men talking together. The youngest of them looked distracted, as he had when he'd arrived. Jake discreetly moved his cuff to check his watch as though he had to be elsewhere. 'I overheard you talking to Jake about his past. I didn't realise you'd known him for so long, Dora.'

'Oh, known him fer ages, from the time I was thirteen and got a job in service. A few years later we lost touch when he was sent away from home. I left that place in Mayfair not long afterwards.'

'Johnny mentioned to me that he'd had a bad start in life.' Clover hadn't enquired further then but she was interested to know more now she'd met him.

'He's certainly managed to pull himself around after what happened to him.' Dora sounded full of admiration. 'My employers didn't have any kids and adopted him and his brother when they were babes in arms.' Dora paused, feeling awkward bringing that up with a childless woman.

Clover smiled her understanding and prompted, 'Go on ... what happened to Jake?'

'Well, Mr Harding was nice enough, but I never took to his wife.' Dora wrinkled her nose. 'Cold fish, was Violet, and after her husband was killed, she seemed even worse.' Dora shook her head. 'Terrible to-do that was so it's not surprising the woman went a bit crackers.' Her eyes became round as she related the tragedy. 'When Jake was about seven his father was stabbed and robbed in the street and they never caught the person who did it, either.'

'How awful ... ' Clover was shocked and glanced at Jake. 'Those poor boys.'

'It was awful all right, especially for Jake.' Dora nodded in emphasis. 'Shortly after the fellow was laid to rest ... about the time his will was read actually, Jake's mother said she couldn't cope with bringing up two sons alone. Jake was sent to a Barnardo's home while the younger lad, Toby, re-mained with her.' Dora paused. 'I was about sixteen when all of this happened. I was always clued up about money though and remember wondering if her dead husband had left her with debts. Even so I felt angry about the way Jake was treated.'

'Does he see his brother?'

'He doesn't seem to want to speak about it.' Dora shrugged and sipped her tea. 'The cook had been with the Hardings for years and remembered the babies being brought home during the war. Both blond and bonny, she told me, and that they looked alike although they weren't believed to be blood kin. Apparently, Mrs Harding wasn't keen on adopting war orphans in the first place. That was down to her husband, and I suppose once he'd gone she thought she'd done enough.' Dora grimaced her disgust.

'War orphans . . . ' Clover repeated softly.

'Mmm,' said Dora. 'And not from similar stock to them who'd fallen on hard times, either. Jake and Toby had been abandoned in the East End and started off being looked after by nuns in a convent before being moved to an orphanage. Mr Harding was a decent sort. It was something he would've done: given slum kids a chance in life, whereas she was more concerned with keeping up appearances, if you know what I mean—'

'What're you two nattering about?' Johnny interrupted before giving his bride a boozy smacker. He rested his chin on her blonde head with its wide dark parting where her natural brown hair had grown out. 'Shame Dad didn't turn up,' he said wistfully.

'Not sure I agree with you on that,' said Annie who'd refilled her glass with bubbly then come to join in the gossip. 'He always puts a dampener on things when he's around.' She pulled a face. 'It's a shame Nan and Granddad couldn't make it, though.' Bill and Lucy Lewis had been invited but, as Johnny and Dora were off tomorrow to spend a week's honeymoon with them in their house on the Essex coast, the couple had said they'd come later in the year rather than make a flying visit.

'It would've been nice to see everybody today, but we've had a lovely time despite absent friends.' Clover put an arm about her brother, knowing he was hurt by his father's indifference to his big day.

She continued to look at the young man who had eyes like hers ... eyes she'd inherited from her mother.

Sensing he was under observation, Jake looked over his shoulder and gave her a hesitant smile. Clover smiled back, then turned away, not wanting to make him feel uncomfortable by staring. But as the bride and groom went to wave off their guests, Clover brooded on Dora's story of his early life. She also thought about what Johnny had told her over a month ago; it had seemed insignificant at the time. His young boss had turned eighteen at the end of October and they'd gone to the pub for a boozy celebration.

She was being ridiculous, she told herself. Lots of orphans started life in convents during 1916 and had autumn birthdays. Soldiers who'd fathered children in the early part of that year, and had perished in Somme mud, had left widows unable to cope. Many had little choice but to give away their new-born infants. She was obsessed with babies because she had a secret of her own she daren't yet speak about. It had brought back memories of Gabriel, the brother she'd known for only a few hours and had prayed would fight to stay alive. Rarely a day went by when she didn't think of him.

Even her beloved Neil didn't know she was late this

month. And she wouldn't tell him yet. Not while there was still a possibility that her dream would trickle away. She couldn't bear to see him have his hopes raised again only to be dashed. So she'd wait, a little while longer in case the nagging pains came to uncross her fingers and see her weeping alone.

'What's up, love?' Neil sat down on a chair and pulled his solemn wife to perch on his lap. 'It's not Fletcher, is it?'

'No ... he's been on his best behaviour with everybody,' she said, slipping an arm around his neck.

'Something's on your mind.' Neil put down his half-finished beer and gave her his full attention.

'I know I'm being daft ... ' She gazed intently at him. 'But do you think Johnny's boss looks like me?' She glanced at Jake, who was taking his leave. He'd turned in their direction and raised a hand in farewell that she acknowledged.

'What?' Neil's chuckle faded away and he swung his head to watch Jake Harding disappear into the night. 'He has green eyes like yours.' Astonished enlightenment glimmered at the back of Neil's eyes. 'Tell me what you're thinking, Clover.'

'I'm not sure I should in case you think me mad. Maybe I am.' She shook her head and stood up. 'I'll keep my thoughts to myself for now; I need to go and see somebody first before saying a word.' She urged him to his feet and kissed him lightly on the lips. 'Now ... this clearing up won't do itself, you know.' She started stacking empty plates and offered him the one with a solitary ham sandwich. 'Eat up; it's starting to curl.'

In fact, Sidney Cooper had been on his way to Silvertown to attend his son's wedding reception.

The prospect of a free feed, rather than of seeing his family, had urged him to dress up in his best clothes and cross Blackfriars Bridge on his journey into the furthest reaches of the East End. He'd alighted from the bus in Whitechapel close to an old haunt of his from way back when. He'd been intending to have a livening drink and a catch-up with some old pals in the Blind Beggar to prepare him for the rest of the evening pretending to be happy for his son.

All of that was forgotten though; on passing Rook Lane a moment ago he'd spotted Molly Deane, dragging her daughter along by the hand. Molly lived in Lambeth and he wouldn't expect to see her in the East End at this time of the evening, looking distressed.

Setting up something permanent with Molly was more important to him than a pint with old pals or jelly and cake for supper. She looked to be in need of a helping hand and might appreciate seeing him. He put on a spurt to catch up with them. He removed his hat to slick down his hair, happy he was looking his best.

'Hey ... wait up, Molly ...' he called, haring into the High Street. He sauntered up as she slowed down and swung about.

'Everything all right?' he asked, looking from mother to daughter. Even in the dark he could see they'd both been crying. The girl was still hiccupping lightly and trying to control herself. A weak smile appeared on Molly's face, reassuring him that she was pleased to see him.

'Oh ... yeah ... we'll be all right, Sid. Can't stop now, though.' If circumstances had been different Molly would have welcomed this meeting. Sidney looked rather suave this evening. She was ready to take that first step with him. But she knew George was after her and possibly not far behind.

After pushing him over at home, she'd managed to gain a head start on him by running to the end of the road and jumping on a bus. Through its upstairs back window she'd seen he was following behind in the Humber. Luckily, the vehicles had become separated in traffic crossing the bridge. Molly had dashed down the stairs and got off. She'd hidden until sure she'd given him the slip before continuing on her journey to Rook Lane. George knew she was somewhere in the East End, though, and would be searching for her.

'Are you off home?' Sidney gave the girl a smile but received little response.

'Sorry, we're in a rush.' Molly put a protective arm about Rebecca. 'I'll catch up with you another time, Sid.' She was darting scouting looks about and urging her daughter to move along. 'We're catching the Tube back to Lambeth.'

An underground journey to Queenie's place would be the safest way to avoid George who'd be prowling the neighbouring streets. Molly intended hiding out with his aunt until she'd seen a solicitor about forcing George out of her house. The property was in her name and she'd never given in to George's chivvying to make him an equal partner. Queenie was on her side in this because of her fondness for her niece. The woman had told her to get the law involved to evict George if he got violent. Molly could stand up for herself. But he'd bully the life out of Rebecca and both women knew it.

Sidney patted her back in farewell, disappointed not to have discovered the nature of the trouble. Reading between the lines, and from a hint of a bruise sprouting on Molly's cheek, it was obvious all was not well at home and she was ready for change. Sidney was impatient to take George Payne's place. 'Maybe I'll see you soon, then,' he called as the women headed off.

Molly hadn't heard his parting words; they were drowned out by the blast of a car horn.

'Get going, Sid.' Molly spun about and yelled a warning, pointing at the approaching Humber.

Sidney needed no second telling. He'd recognised the scowling face behind the windscreen of the car screeching to a halt at the kerb. He'd take George Payne on, but on his own terms and on home ground. Not here. Sidney put his head down and strode away. Once around the corner, he stopped and from a vantage point watched the scene unfold.

Molly and her daughter were dashing towards the Tube station and George was slamming his car door to lope after them.

Sidney hesitated no more than a few seconds before following. The women had already disappeared down the steps into the underground station but George remained in his sights. A knot of people were blocking the entrance and George's progress. He pushed through them and Sidney, now close behind, pulled his hat brim low in case he was spotted.

The men emerged onto the platform fifteen yards apart and in time to see a train pulling off with Molly and her daughter on it. George used a fist to thump on the moving carriage, drawing stares from those who'd disembarked and were heading for the exit.

George bared his teeth and roared his frustration. With the departing train's draught standing his dark hair on end, he appeared a ferocious sight. Then he swung around and

293

noticed Sidney and his snarl transformed into a devilish grin. He pointed a finger.

The gesture needed no explanation. Sidney walked quickly along the platform towards the stairs, trying to catch up with the commuters leaving the station, to hide in among them. He sent darting looks over his shoulder and saw George was gaining ground on him. Sidney gave up on nonchalance and broke into a run. He could hear pounding footsteps behind.

'Yeah ... I know it's you,' bawled George. 'You've been messing around with my wife, ain't yer?'

Sidney was taking the stairs two at a time but his legs were tiring and his lungs burning. Even the sound of heavy breathing close behind couldn't lend him the energy needed to seek safety in a crowd. The others had disappeared into the starry night glimpsed at the top of the stairway. He was on his own with the madman behind. He knew he couldn't escape so anchored himself against the handrail and raised a leg to ward off his assailant. George was close enough now to throw a punch towards his guts and confident enough to laugh at him while doing so. Sidney lashed out with a foot and the sole of his boot caught George in the hip. Off balance, he teetered for a moment on the edge of a step, arms flapping and eyes bulging as he tried to grab the handrail for support. Sidney speedily repositioned himself and kicked again, his lips flat on his teeth in a triumphant leer. With a grunt, George toppled backwards down the flight of steps, bouncing and rolling to the bottom.

Sidney was outside and dashing across the road when the sound of a woman's scream was heard and he knew George had been found.

Chapter Twenty-Six

'What in damnation do you think you're doing barging in like this?'

'Come to return something,' said Jake and proceeded steadily towards Ian Winters. The man was lounging against the wall, whisky in hand, having emerged from the drawing room at the alert of the housekeeper's raised voice. A glow of light escaping from the half-open doors accentuated his haughty expression and glossed his oily hair.

Jake hoped he'd not got the servant into trouble. When she'd answered his knock he'd walked straight in, aware permission wouldn't be granted.

'Where's Toby?'

'Get out, or I'll throw you out.' Ian straightened up so he matched Jake's height. He felt unsettled by the younger man's confidence.

'No, you won't,' said Jake. 'Where's your stepson?'

'What's the matter?' Violet appeared on the threshold to see for herself as Jake drew level with the double doors. They were barely a yard apart and she froze, trying but failing to speak to the son she'd banished, now an imposing and rather intimidating sight.

'Hello, Mother,' said Jake dispassionately.

'You shouldn't be here,' she finally whispered.

'I agree . . . and I have to thank you for sending me somewhere better than this place.' His contemptuous glance flitted over silk walls and marble floors. 'But that's not the reason I've come.'

'What are you doing here?' This enquiry came over the banisters and sounded welcoming.

'Wanted to see you.' Jake turned towards the stairs.

Toby ran down, chuckling gleefully. Ignoring his parents, he stretched to slap an arm about his taller brother's shoulders, urging him into a room Jake remembered had been their father's study. It now housed a brace of card tables and several small sofas positioned on an ivory rug.

'I hoped you'd turn up again.' Toby closed the door. 'Why didn't you come back sooner? Been dying to see you.' He paused, sensing an atmosphere that had little to do with the hostile couple outside. 'I would've come looking for you, Jake, but didn't know where to start.'

'Why aren't you at university?'

'Got sent down . . . sort of expelled,' he explained with a wink. 'Didn't sit well with you know who . . . ' He jerked a nod at the door. 'Fancy a drink?' He poured two large brandies from the decanter and offered one to Jake.

Jake took the crystal glass and put it down on the green baize of a gaming table.

'I want you to leave.' Violet had burst into the room while Ian Winters peered across her shoulder at the two strapping young men. His stepson might not be as tall and athletic-looking as his older brother but he had a temper that needed little provocation to inflame it.

'I want *you* to leave us alone.' Toby moved aggressively

towards his parents. He pushed his mother outside and closed the door in her face. 'Bitch ... ' he muttered. 'She should never have got rid of you.' Toby knew he wasn't wanted now either. Ever since she had a brat in the cot and another in the oven, he wasn't her poppet any more. He told himself he didn't give a damn. He'd take the apartment they were planning on renting for him, and the job in the City he'd been offered by one of his stepfather's cronies. And he'd make them give him an allowance, too. Now his big brother was here, everything would be all right, in any case.

'Let's go out to a club in the West End.' Toby swallowed what remained in his glass and looked Jake over. He was envious of his stature and how old he appeared. His brother could pass for twenty-one without question.

'No ... not going anywhere. I only came to return something to you.'

Toby shot back Jake's untouched brandy. An alcoholic flush crept into his cheeks. 'Brought me another present, have you?' A quizzical look tilted his lips but the half-smile had gone the moment he saw what it was. 'Where in damnation did you get that?' He barked an astonished laugh as he gazed at the brooch glittering on his brother's palm.

'I fence stuff ... it was brought to me.'

'Really?' Toby sounded awed. 'You're a bloody crook?' He punched the air. 'Bloody marvellous.'

'It isn't.' Jake studied his brother, wishing he could feel sorry for him, and looking for that hint of himself that had always been there. It barely existed any more. Toby was so changed in the time that had passed since they'd last spoken that he hardly felt an attachment to him. He'd already been slipping away Jake realised, on that Christmas Eve when they stood outside in the snow. Toby's looks had deteriorated since: he had the beginnings of jowls and a paunch from overindulgence strained the buttons on his shirt. It was clear he despised his stepfather but Toby was already halfway to being him.

'A girl brought this to me,' said Jake, holding up the brooch. 'She said you gave it to her.'

'I did. The baggage had the sauce to ambush me outside and ask for money,' Toby sneered. 'She accused me of impregnating her.'

'And had you?'

'God knows ... possibly.' Toby gestured airily on his way back to the decanter. 'With a slut like that ... could've been anybody's sprog. Seemed easier to pay her off though.' He wagged a finger. 'In some respects, Winters is an all right sort, y'know. He brought her here, with her father ... proper lowlife on the make is George Payne. But people like that have their uses.' He crashed the decanter against the glass and poured. 'I imagine my stepfather thought I needed a shag to calm me down. Probably thought I'd never done it before and it was time I did.' Toby snorted into his drink. 'What he don't know is ... I got kicked out after another chap and I made a night of it with a girl in the village. She weren't as good-looking as Payne's daughter though ...'

Jake hit him full in the face, sending him back on his heels towards the sofa where he collapsed and watched, bewildered, as blood began dripping from his chin onto his white shirt. But he'd managed to hang onto his drink and took a gulp. 'Why d'you do that?' he whined.

Jake walked towards him and dropped the brooch onto his lap. 'You'd better give that back.'

Toby picked up the jewel and swung it drunkenly between thumb and forefinger. 'Keep it, if you want ...' When

Jake didn't reclaim it Toby tossed the brooch onto the rug. 'Sell it then, you're a fence. We'll go halves.' He emptied the glass and licked his lips. 'I covered my tracks. Told 'em I saw the day girl steal it. She's been up in court. So it's yours if you want it. No comebacks.'

Jake swooped on the brooch twinkling on the brandy-spattered Aubusson, and headed for the door.

'What's she to you then, this little scrubber?' Toby called.

'A friend.'

'Well, don't bother asking them about it. They won't make me marry her ... ' he hissed in an undertone.

'She wouldn't have you,' said Jake and went out.

He knew they'd been listening through the door but he didn't stop; he gave Violet back her brooch on passing, barely glancing at her.

'Just can't find quality to work for these days, eh?' he said to the drop-jawed housekeeper. And stepped outside into crisp night air.

Johnny and Dora were packing a suitcase to go on honeymoon when they received a visitor.

'What's up?' Johnny asked as his boss walked in. 'Oh, no. You ain't persuading me to do a shift. Not today ... '

'Not here for that.'

'Cuppa tea?' offered Dora, folding petticoats.

'No, thanks. Can't stop.' Jake smiled. 'Come to wish you a nice trip.'

'Thanks ... ' Johnny grinned, pairing up his socks and stuffing them into a corner.

'Here ... didn't buy you a present, so have a drink on me when you get there.' Jake passed a couple of banknotes to Johnny.

'There was no need for that, but thanks very much,' said Dora. He might fool Johnny but she knew there was more to it than good wishes and holiday money. She watched the men shake hands then Johnny pocketed the cash.

'Anything up, love?' Dora asked Jake while her husband squashed down the lid on the suitcase, oblivious to an un-spoken question in the air.

'Not really ... well, I thought you might know the name of George Payne's fence, that's all.'

Dora and Johnny exchanged a glance. They had banned one another from speaking about that troublemaker after he'd turned up in the middle of the night, hoping to get into bed with Dora.

'Why d'you want to know about Big Queenie?' Johnny planted his hands on his hips, looking baffled.

'No particular reason.'

'Ain't thinking of going back into that game, are you?' Johnny sounded interested.

'Nope. She's Payne's aunt, right?'

'Yeah, that's who Big Queenie is.'

'Do you want her address, Jake?' Dora was already open-ing a drawer to find a pencil and paper.

'Thanks,' said Jake and shuffled his feet while Dora wrote and Johnny continued frowning at him.

'Well, won't hold you up. Bring us back a stick o' rock.' Jake winked at them and slipped out of the door with the paper in his pocket.

Johnny turned to Dora. 'What was that all about?'

'A girl,' said Dora and shook her head at him for being obtuse.

Johnny might not have noticed the chemistry between Rebecca and Jake in the Bricklayer's Arms, but she had.

She'd also read the look in Rebecca's eyes on the day Jake's name had cropped up in conversation. Dora had bumped into Rebecca at her great-aunt's and when walking home together they'd had quite a heart-to-heart. Jake had got to know the girl well enough to discover she was close to her aunt and the woman could be a go-between.

All the action had taken place years ago now.

Jake and Rebecca hadn't forgotten one another, though, any more than she'd got over Johnny when they'd been apart. Slow-burn love affairs sometimes worked out to be the best sort in the end. She gazed at her husband, rubbed his cheek to bring him out of his trance.

'Come on, shake a leg, or we'll be late catching the train.'

'Where you off to then? Going on yer 'olidays?'

Sidney Cooper twisted around and cursed beneath his breath. He'd hoped to slip away from London unseen. Now he thought about it, though, it would be as well to provide a plausible excuse for disappearing rather than allowing people to speculate.

'Not as such,' he told his elderly neighbour who was taking in his milk off the step. He put down his suitcase and locked the front door. 'Missing me kids, y'see. Shouldn't have left them behind. So . . . I'm done with old Blighty. I'm back to France fer good.'

The neighbour frowned. 'Thought Johnny was yer kid and some others over in Silvertown.'

Sidney swallowed his irritation at that place being mentioned. He didn't want reminders of East London. He wanted to get away in case the coppers came knocking, investigating George Payne's death. He knew Payne was dead, too. He'd gone back there the following morning for a scout about. He'd bought a newspaper from the kiosk by the station's entrance. The vendor had sucked his teeth and told him to watch his step as a fellow had broken his neck, falling down those stairs. Smelled of drink apparently, he'd said, and as yet nobody had come forward to identify the poor blighter.

It had been good news for Sidney, but his relief wasn't complete and he was taking no chances. In time, George's next of kin would be tracked down and questioned about what they knew of his last movements. Molly might mention that she'd been in the vicinity of Whitechapel underground station that night, as had been a certain Sidney Cooper. In her own defence she might add that Sidney had witnessed George acting aggressively, causing her and her daughter to run off and jump on the Tube.

'Who's that lot in Silvertown then, Sid?' His neighbour insisted on having an explanation.

Sidney resisted the urge to tell him to mind his own business. He didn't want to arouse suspicion by appearing rattled. 'Oh, they're me first wife's kids. All grown up and past needing their dad. Me French kids ... well they're younger and still me favourites.' He gave the fellow a wink. ''Course, I don't tell the other lot that.' He offered his hand in farewell. 'S'long then. Look after yerself.' With that, he picked up his case and set off in the direction of Waterloo, whistling through his teeth.

'You're too late, love, if you're after him.'

Molly gave the old-timer hobbling towards her with the aid of a walking stick a measured stare. 'Why's that then?' she clipped, deciding against telling him he was being overfamiliar.

'Sid's gawn ...' Having reached his front door, the fellow put down his bag of groceries and pushed his key into the lock. 'Went first thing this morning, back to France to be with his family.' The woman's astonishment was audible, making him snigger. 'Sounds like you didn't know he had French kids any more'n I did.' He shook his head. 'Wasn't easy to read, that one, was he? Crafty bugger, I reckon.' Still chuckling, he went inside and closed the door.

With a sigh of disappointment, Molly gathered her coat around her and hurried away down the road.

A brewery colleague of Sidney's had given her this address, and had told her Sidney hadn't shown up for his shift the previous evening. Molly had come to tell him he could move in with her just as soon as George was off the scene for good. Having seen this run-down street, she'd reckoned Sidney Cooper would have jumped at the chance to move to the better side of Lambeth.

She'd changed her tune now she knew about his French family. After his close shave with George the other night, Sidney might have decided against getting involved with her. He might have had enough of being brushed off and think Molly Deane wasn't worth the trouble of a fight when he had another hearth to settle at. It was a shame she'd not had a chance to persuade him to stay as she reckoned George might not have put up much of a battle after all.

After returning to Queenie's and staying the night, Molly had left Rebecca there the following morning and plucked up the courage to go home to have things out with George. It had been obvious from the untouched bed that he'd not returned there either. She'd wondered if he had a bit on the side. It wouldn't be the first time he'd cheated on her or disappeared for a few nights. On the evening they'd

303

clashed badly over Rupert's wife being at the restaurant, he'd stormed out of the house. The following morning she'd smelled Jicky perfume on him. She'd guessed he'd been hanging around with Dora Knox again. Normally, she'd have felt jealous enough to make a scene. This time Molly hadn't given a damn who he slept with. She'd already known she was finished with him and ousting him would be easier if he had somewhere else to go.

She decided to return sporadically over the week to catch him at home and confront him. In the meantime, and before father and daughter came face to face, it was vital Rebecca was helped out of the mess she was in.

In that respect, Molly had a lead. She wished Rebecca had sought her advice rather than Queenie's about an abortionist. Unlike Peg Tiller, the woman Molly had visited over the years to make sure no more children arrived was still in business in Poplar. Molly had gone there last week after realising her grumbling appendix was actually something else entirely.

Chapter Twenty-Seven

'Have you finished packing? The taxicab is outside.'

Violet didn't receive a reply from her son; he remained standing with his back to her, alternately flinging his clothes into a trunk and swigging from a hip flask.

'You shouldn't drink so much. It is barely noon. Hurry ... close the lid ... your stepfather is growing impatient,' she said. They'd both heard Toby's name being barked from the hallway. 'Leave the rest; we can send it on for you with the removal people.' She touched her son's arm to gain attention, but he savagely flung her off.

'This is for your own good, Toby, to avoid the unpleasantness of any more enquiries into the theft,' Violet said.

'I told you who stole it but you don't believe me. You'd rather believe a halfwit girl.' He gestured contempt. 'The matter was over and done with. She'd been in court yet you've dragged it up again.'

'She didn't steal it, you did! Stop lying!' Violet sighed in frustration. In truth, she would have left things as they were to avoid a scandal. But the hullabaloo between the brothers, and the brooch's return, had been witnessed by their housekeeper. The woman had been fond of the fourteen-year-old daily help. 'If you wanted money urgently why didn't you say? Why deal with strangers rather than with us?' She sounded exasperated by his stupidity.

Toby snorted his scorn that such a question needed to be asked. 'Strangers don't grill me over why I want spending money. I'm eighteen soon and don't have to account to you for everything I do.' He was glad his parents were still in the dark about some of it. They'd assumed he'd stolen the brooch to pawn it. But sooner or later they would hit on Rebecca Payne's involvement in his crime. Or more likely he'd get hit. It wouldn't be the sort of punishment Jake had meted out. Her father would annihilate him. Toby was glad he was leaving home today. He hoped his smug stepfather would get a drubbing instead from George Payne.

'How did *he* get the brooch to return it?'

'D'you mean Jake?' Toby jibed. 'You can use his name, y'know, Mother.' He looked pleased and proud when announcing, 'My brother fences stolen goods; he's into that sort of thing: dealing in jewellery.'

Violet looked taken aback. And so did her husband, who'd stomped up the stairs to investigate the delay and had heard what was said. They exchanged a glance.

'We've had a bloody crook in the house?' trumpeted Ian Winters.

'Well, you can't accuse Jake of lifting it, can you, when he brought the damned thing back.' Toby put his hip flask into a coat pocket then swung a look between them. 'Well, nice knowing you but I'm off. Send my things on to my apartment will you. And make sure my allowance is paid into my account or I'll come back for it. You won't want that, Mother dear, will you?' He hesitated on the threshold of his bedroom. 'Maybe I'll bring Jake with me and really give you a fright.' He smirked with hateful amusement.

'We heard you two talking about a girl. Who is she?' Violet called as he strode along the landing towards the stairs. It had been hard to make out the facts when eavesdropping through the closed study door with her husband nagging in her other ear. She waited for Toby's explanation, but he didn't even acknowledge the question. 'Tell me who she is.' Violet pursued him down to the hallway, clinging to the banister with one hand and supporting her swollen belly with the other. Toby marched out of the house and climbed into the cab. She watched from the top step as it pulled away without him once glancing her way.

'Good riddance . . .' said Ian, joining her by the open doorway. He drew her back inside and pushed the door shut.

'Do you think there's somebody he likes? Did he give her my brooch as a gift?' Violet still couldn't believe the boy she'd once adored would change so much and treat her like this.

Ian gestured his scepticism to that and issued a warning. 'Mind what you say.' The nursemaid had come out of the front parlour leading their toddler son by the hand. 'Let's hear no more of it,' he growled in an undertone. 'Toby's gone and the daily help's been compensated for the wrongful arrest. She believes a simple mistake was made. It'll all blow over. Money has a way of making grievances disappear.' He watched his wife hurrying towards their child to fuss over him. Ian moseyed towards his study, brooding on somebody else requiring a handout to keep things sweet.

The common denominator in all of it was George Payne's daughter. Ian could stab a guess at what had gone on between the brothers. Both boys knew her, in the biblical sense he guessed, and a rivalry over her had arisen. Toby had given her the brooch to avoid a paternity suit, would be another guess. That might have been the end of it if his damnable brother hadn't interfered. If she didn't get rid of the baby, a visit from her father would be in the offing. Rather than have George Payne come here and blackmail him about marriages or bank drafts, it would be prudent to bump into him elsewhere to nip things in the bud.

He wished he'd not brought George and his daughter back here but at least he'd kept their visit from Violet. The staff had been in disarray that day with the cook down with flu and the housekeeper travelling to Wales for a funeral. If the household had been running smoothly he wouldn't have risked it. An agency replacement had been hired and had prepared them a meal. There'd been no regular staff present to enlighten Violet to unscheduled guests while she'd been out of town visiting her sick sister. She'd never know unless the Paynes told her themselves.

Violet was also thinking of that family. She wanted a divorce. After her second baby was born she intended to leave Ian. He was seeing women again and drinking too much. She blamed him for introducing Toby to whisky when trying to find common ground with the stepson he struggled to like. But he wasn't the only consideration in her decision to leave London; the two East End boys she'd never really wanted had brought the trouble she'd envisaged. Rupert had never seen what was in store for them. But she had known blood would out. She didn't want her real children to be sullied by a connection to slum dwellers' spawn. Toby's decline had started at adolescence. Once mingling with older boys at Rugby School, he became crueller and debauched. They'd had complaints from the University

Dean about his behaviour before he was expelled for carousing in the village. It was ironic that the stepfather and stepson with no blood tie and little liking for one another should be similar characters.

To leave them both behind, Violet needed to secure her own financial independence. She'd every intention to start on that tomorrow.

'Might I have a word with you?' The absence of a reply prompted Violet to add, 'I'll only take a few minutes of your time. It's in your interest to be obliging if you want to avoid arrest.'

'Are you threatening me?'

'Yes. And I think we both know why.'

Molly had received an unpleasant shock when opening the door but had controlled herself and invited the woman inside rather than risk a scene taking place on the step. She jerked her head, indicating the parlour just along the hallway.

Once they were inside the room, she went to the decanter and poured herself a stiff drink, re-stoppering the bottle when her guest declined a morning tipple with a grimace of distaste. 'I didn't think you recognised me that night.' Molly began fiddling with her hair to cover the fading bruise on her cheek. She didn't want her visitor smirking over that.

She wasn't quite as jittery as she'd been on the summer evening they'd dined in Soho with Mosley and she'd fled in a panic, although with everything else that was going on, this showdown was ill-timed.

'Oh, I knew you, Molly Deane . . . how could I miss those cheap clothes and dropped aitches.'

Molly smiled acidly but her confidence was building that

309

she had enough of a case to win this most belated of battles. 'You're inconveniencing me but ... ' Molly gave a careless shrug. 'As you've saved me a trip to the West End to call on you, I'll hear you out.'

Violet pricked up her ears. 'Oh? And why would you wish to see me?'

'Age before beauty. You go first, Mrs Winters.' Molly put a hand against the mantelpiece and sipped her drink.

'I want this house and the money stolen from my husband,' declared Violet, simmering from the insult. She glanced about at furnishings that were rather tasteful. As was the tan-coloured wool crepe dress her nemesis was wearing that showed off her voluptuous figure and rich brown hair. But she refused to be impressed by any of it, and kept her top lip curled. 'If you don't willingly give back what is rightfully mine you'll appear in court and be sent to prison. I've already spoken to lawyers about taking steps to recover the assets you embezzled ... '

'Bet you have. But I'll stop you there, and save you wasting any more of your breath.' Molly swallowed what remained of her drink, smacked her lips and returned the glass to the mantelshelf. 'Your son raped my daughter and tried to pay her off with a brooch when she told him he'd made her pregnant.' Molly watched the woman's face turn white.

'You're lying!' croaked Violet.

'I only wish I were,' said Molly. 'Now, your late husband believed himself to be my daughter's father and signed documents to that effect. We both know he wasn't; but that's immaterial to how the world will view this revolting news about Rupert Harding's son and my daughter.'

'You're lying.' The accusation was delivered with more strength this time.

'We've been through that. And about this, I'm really not. Toby Harding ... Winters ... whatever you want to call him, raped my daughter. I'll admit that at first I thought your husband was responsible. But Rebecca has told me what went on when she was invited to your house and her father's back was turned. She also explained how she came into possession of a brooch set with diamonds rubies and sapphires. Unusual tremblant design.' Molly was grateful to Queenie for having described the piece to her. 'I know you were out and were unaware of what went on ... '

'You're lying ... '

'Fer Gawd's sake, give it a rest,' said Molly. 'I'm not lying, ask your husband about the night George and Rebecca had dinner with him after a meeting at Party headquarters.'

Violet felt frozen with alarm and hatred for Ian. He must have had an inkling of the troubles they were facing. Everything fitted, especially Toby's lechery, which had got him expelled. 'Whatever the truth of it, it doesn't alter the fact that you swindled me.' Desperation harshened Violet's tone as she saw her carefully planned future slipping away.

'Yes, I did; but I'll never admit to it outside this room because I've been punished for it through my daughter,' said Molly. 'You and yours have had your own back on me and mine. I reckon we're quits, Violet. But if you want to take it further, go ahead. And so will I.'

Molly stared at the woman she'd once envied and now pitied. Violet Harding hadn't lived a perfect life any more than she had. Her son was a rapist; her second husband a leering braggart from what Molly remembered of him at the dinner table.

'If you want a fight; I'll give you one. Your accusations won't stand a chance against mine. Frauds are ten a penny.

Salacious headlines are what people remember. Adopted son rapes his sister.' She glanced at the woman's protruding belly. 'You'd better hope that one in there isn't a girl. The welfare might take your baby away, for her own good.'

'You wouldn't dare spread such despicable lies.'

'Try me.' They stared at one another until Violet took a few unsteady steps backwards then turned towards the door. 'See yourself out,' said Molly and her shoulders slumped in relief at her mean victory.

She waited until the street door was banged shut then moved an edge of curtain, watching the other woman hurrying away. She poured herself another drink and downed it in one. Within a minute, her thoughts were back with the matter that had been troubling her before Violet Winters' arrival.

Rebecca was with her aunt; Molly had come home hoping to find George. But there was still no sign of him having been here. She was starting to feel uneasy about his long absence. If he had another woman, he would have been back by now for a change of clothes and his shaving things.

Tomorrow, she intended to retrace her steps on the last time she'd seen him. If she had no joy discovering something in East London, her next ports of call would be local hospitals. After that the police station ... although it went against the grain to bring in the coppers.

For now though, her daughter remained her priority. With a final look around the room, and a check that the gas was off ... although she knew it was as she'd not turned it on ... she set off back to Queenie's to collect her daughter.

Chapter Twenty-Eight

She'd never been back here but Clover could remember everything about the day she came, pushing the pram over sticky, droning grass. The smell of cider was always enough to bring this place to mind but there were no windfalls scenting the air and luring a swarm of insects to a feast.

The baby had been born in the autumn; today it was winter and the apple trees were bare.

She had been sixteen when given the daunting task of spiriting away her half-brother before her father discovered the proof of his wife's infidelity. Urgently, she'd propelled the pram away from their house, her mother's safety at the forefront of her mind. Sidney Cooper would have taken his revenge with his fists for something as bad as that.

Clover had been light-headed with fear, not on her own account, but for the baby concealed beneath a blanket at her toddler sister's feet. He'd been so minute that she'd marvelled at him being alive. In fact, at first she and her mother and grandmother had believed him a stillborn to be secretly laid to rest. She alone had heard his first murmurs and the shock had forced her to a halt many times on the journey to check if she'd made a mistake. But he was still breathing right up until the moment she left him for the nuns to find.

She clattered the bell of the convent and waited, staring down at the step that eighteen years ago had held a blanket-wrapped bundle. She had concealed herself in the trees to watch for the second the baby was scooped up by a nun and carried inside. Relief had shaken her body then and the memory of it put a phantom shiver along her spine. She'd never felt content that she'd done as much as she could for him. Now, she had renewed reason to try to remedy that and finish what she'd started.

A young novice opened the door on creaking hinges. It wasn't the woman she'd hoped to see.

'I've come to speak to Sister Louise if that's all right.'

'Oh, you mean the Reverend Mother. Is she expecting you?'

'I'm afraid not.' Clover relaxed, thankful that a name from long ago was still known.

The hinges squeaked again as the door was fully opened. 'Well, let's see if she's about. We've just finished Matins and she might be in her office.'

The stone flags echoed to the sound of their footsteps as they walked side by side along a corridor then stopped before an arched door.

'Come in . . .' was called in answer to the rap on black oak.

'Oh . . . forgot to ask your name,' whispered the novice with an apologetic look, and a hand hovering over the door handle.

'It's Clover . . . Clover Cooper,' she said, her mind still immersed in the past.

As they entered, a small bespectacled woman levered herself up using the edge of the desk.

'Mrs Cooper to see you, Reverend Mother.' The nun withdrew and closed the door as the visitor was beckoned to approach.

'It's nice to see you again. What a long time ago that was,' said Reverend Mother, removing her glasses. 'I wondered if I'd ever find out what happened to you and yours.'

'You remember me?' Clover sounded pleased and surprised. But then she'd recognised this woman in return. Despite the furrows on her brow and at the corners of her eyes, she radiated the same warmth and serenity as she had as a white-robed novice during the war.

'I do remember you,' said the Reverend Mother. 'We talked on the night of the factory explosion, about your boy.' She shook her head. 'A dreadful time; it seemed like the end of the world. But we've all carried on, haven't we? We're all still here.'

Clover smiled wistfully. 'He wasn't my boy actually, and I must own up to not correcting your assumption that he was. He was my mother's child,' said Clover. 'All the people concerned are gone now so there's nobody to hurt.' She paused. 'Other than one person, and I'm praying that if he has survived, he'll welcome hearing the truth about his start in life and his birth family.' There was a catch of emotion in her words and she cleared her throat with a cough. 'And I'm Mrs Ryan these days; have been for quite a long while.'

'And have you children, Mrs Ryan?'

'Not yet ... ' Clover's hoarseness was back.

'Soon though ... I expect ... ' said the Reverend Mother and indicated her visitor should take a seat. 'Nice as it is to have you come to see me, I think something specific has brought you back after all this time.'

Clover acknowledged the woman's acuity with a smile.

315

'My half-brother would be eighteen now so I realise I might be hoping in vain ... but have you any records of what happened to him after he left here?' Clover paused. 'You told me he had been put in a council orphanage, although he remained frail from being very premature. Did he remain in London, and was he adopted by well-to-do people?' Clover noticed a spark of something akin to disappointment in the Reverend Mother's eyes.

'I think I might have met him recently, you see,' Clover quickly explained. 'Quite by chance I think our paths have crossed. Of course, I could never say a word to him without better proof.'

'I see ...' the Reverend Mother steepled her fingers and gazed over them in some excitement. 'How wonderful that would be for you both.' She gazed ceiling-ward. 'Well, let me see; he *was* adopted by people in London; that I do recall. I had a special interest in him and another child who arrived in the early summer of the following year. That child was taken to the same orphanage. They were two peas in a pod, and as your tiny little one was still catching up on his weight, the boys were almost the same size ... could have been twins.' She brought her eyes back to meet Clover's. 'Were they both your kin? I did wonder at the likeness.'

'I think I know the baby you mean. He would be related to my half-brother, not to me.'

'Ahh ...' said the Reverend Mother and rolled her eyes. 'Complicated.'

'Indeed,' said Clover ruefully.

'I put in a request for the two boys to be kept together, if possible. They formed a sweet attachment, the older would soothe the younger when they were put in the same cot. I had a special interest in them and would go to the orphanage to watch them progress. A few months after the younger child was taken there, they were adopted. And I was delighted to know they'd stayed together.' She paused. 'I didn't see them again after that.' Having concluded her reminiscence the Reverend Mother pushed herself to her feet with an ooh of pain. 'Arthritis,' she explained. 'From kneeling on cold floors. Now, if you have time to wait, Mrs Ryan, I'll see what I can find in the archives. I believe I wrote to ask how my boys had fared in their adoption and I did receive a reply though names and exact locations escape my memory now.' She sounded intrigued, and keen to help solve a mystery. 'Archives are kept in the cellar. I hope you can wait while I rummage around.'

'I'll stay for as long as I need to. Thank you.'

The woman limping around the desk received a spontaneous hug. 'Don't be too sad if it's not the news you're hoping for, will you,' the Reverend Mother said, gently disengaging herself.

'No ... no I won't ... ' Clover turned and watched as the door closed on the person holding her dreams in her hands. And Henrietta Fletcher's dreams, too, maybe.

Nettie had intended to hide her pregnancy and give birth secretly at a refuge. Keeping out of sight of neighbours in the final months hadn't been hard but hiding the truth from her mother had been impossible. A distraught Mrs Randall had smuggled her daughter's illegitimate baby here after he was born at home. Another tragedy for the woman to bear, to add to the deaths of her husband and son weighing on her.

Clover would be overjoyed to have news of Gabriel. Nettie might take a different view of her own seventeen-year-old heartache and guilt being resurrected. Her husband believed their first child had never drawn breath, and Archie Fletcher wouldn't take kindly to discovering he'd been deceived.

If the Reverend Mother returned empty-handed then nothing would need to be done: things for everybody would continue as they were. But if her prayers had been answered then speaking privately to Nettie would be essential.

The need to close old wounds had brought Clover here, but at the back of her mind lay the knowledge that the tangled web of lies she was unpicking could reopen them as well.

Chapter Twenty-Nine

'Don't think I know you.'

Queenie peeked round the edge of her door at the stranger. She was open for business, but being extra cautious, in case her nephew leaped out, accusing her of interfering in his domestic woes. She wouldn't put it past George to use a decoy to hoodwink her before forcing his way inside. Not that he'd have any luck finding Molly and Rebecca right now, even if he had got wind of them lodging with her. They were out, but due back by this evening.

'Who told you about me then?' Queenie barked suspiciously and cocked her head to get a better look at the bottle-green van parked at the kerb. It had a builder's ladder on the top. She didn't recognise that from round here either.

'Johnny and Dora Cooper.'

'Johnny *and* Dora Cooper.' Queenie relaxed her grip on the door. Johnny hated George so she felt on safer ground already. 'Dragged him down the aisle at last, did she?'

'Not quite. They got hitched at the council offices,' said Jake.

Queenie opened the door and crossed her arms. 'You're friends with Johnny 'n' Dora then. So what?' She noticed he

319

wasn't carrying a holdall. 'What've you got for me? Ain't just yer crooked smile I'm interested in, son.' She pinched his cheek. 'I'm too long in the tooth to be taken in by a pretty face.'

'More a case of what you've got for me,' said Jake, removing her teasing hand.

'Is that right?' Queenie smiled. He was a charmer, no doubt about it. Confident but not cocksure. 'Better come in then,' she said.

'Don't offer people no tea or nuthin' until I know 'em better.' She explained her house rules as they entered the parlour. 'But you can sit down, if you want.'

He did, then stood up again. 'Get straight to it, if that's all right. I think you knew Peg Tiller.'

Queenie's suspicions were back in double measure. 'So what if I did?' she rasped.

'You sent your niece to see her because you didn't know she'd died.'

'What the . . .' Queenie started to propel him towards the door by the elbow, thinking that van couldn't have been his after all. It was a ruse to trick her. Oh, they were cunning buggers. 'You're a plain clothes copper, aren't you? Well you can sling yer 'ook and don't come back without a warrant.' She knew, as did most people, that backstreet abortionists operated illegally. Somebody must have grassed them up for trying to solicit Peg's help, had been Queenie's first concern. Her second was that her cellar was crammed with stolen merchandise.

Jake shrugged her off and gestured his surrender. 'Not Old Bill, honest; I was a friend of Peg's. I took over her business as a fence.'

'*You're* the fellow who give Rebecca the eighty quid fer the brooch?' Queenie squinted in disbelief.

'I am.'

'Well, if you've discovered it's paste, you won't get your money back.'

'It's not paste.'

'It was worth more then.' Quick as a flash Queenie held out a hand.

'Yeah, I know,' sighed Jake, ignoring her beckoning fingers. He cut to the chase. 'What did Rebecca say about me?'

'Not much . . . ' Queenie sensed an undercurrent as though he really wanted to ask where Rebecca was. The girl hadn't wanted to talk when she'd arrived here that evening, either to her mother or to Queenie. He'd given her cash then turned her out, was the extent of her dealings with Peg's replacement that she'd admitted to. Further questions were fielded by her insisting she was tired and needed to go upstairs to bed.

'You sure you're not the fellow causing ructions?' Queenie widened her eyes on him. 'You know what ructions I mean, don't you?'

'I do and I'm not here to cause trouble. I know Rebecca likes you and trusts you. You want to help her and so do I. I like her very much. If you tell me where she lives I'll go and speak to her and her parents.'

'To say what?'

'Don't know yet.' He sighed and gestured his hopelessness. 'Just go and see what can be done, I suppose. I don't want her father hitting her.'

Queenie stared at him, thinking he seemed the genuine article and she was as cynical as they came. 'I could tell you where they live but you won't find Rebecca or her mother there. Might not find her father there either as he seems to have gone on the missing list. Which is probably news you'll be glad to hear.'

'Where is Rebecca then?'

'Right now? Trying to get herself out of the trouble she's in.'

'She's having an abortion today?' He paced in agitation, shoving a hand through his hair. 'Where's she gone?'

'What's bothering you most; your conscience or your heart?'

'Don't know . . .' said Jake with hoarse honesty and he stood still, frowning into middle distance.

Queenie crossed her arms. 'Don't know much, do you?' She approached and patted his arm. 'Not to worry, son, cos I reckon it'll all come to you when you get there,' she said and pulled out a pencil and notebook from the box of tricks in her apron pocket.

Since Johnny had proclaimed his driving skill sufficient to take the van out alone Jake drove everywhere. Today, when he really needed a vehicle to get him around quickly, a traffic jam had held him up before he reached Bermondsey. In a panic, he'd parked the van up, jumped out and continued on foot. By the time he reached Poplar High Street, he'd been running for twenty-five minutes. When he loped into Cotton Lane, clumsy with exhaustion, he almost knocked down a woman chatting on her doorstep with a neighbour.

'Oi, you,' she bawled, jutting her chin in a belligerent manner.

'Sorry . . . sorry . . .' he called over his shoulder, then swung about to gesture apology while travelling backwards. 'D'you know where number thirty-four is?' He stopped to fold over at the middle to catch his breath.

'Yeah, I do,' she said. 'It's over there . . .' She pointed across the lane to a house that looked sprucer than the rest.

Jake found his second wind and charged towards it to bang on the door then push at it. He was about to barge it open when a woman appeared balancing a toddler on a hip.

'Are you the abortionist?' he panted.

'No, I bleedin' ain't,' she said, narked, and used her thumb to gesture up the stairs.

Jake bounded up them and burst into the room at the top of the flight. He saw a woman jump to her feet from a chair. She looked like an older version of Rebecca. Her face was white and strained.

'What's going on? Who are you?'

'Where's Rebecca?' He didn't wait for a reply but strode to another door that was closed, with silence behind it.

'You can't go in there ... ' Molly, still in shock from this disturbance, belatedly sprang into action.

'Rebecca?' he said hoarsely and stepped closer.

'Who's this?' The abortionist glared at the girl lying on the scrubbed pine table, with her skirt about her waist. Getting no immediate reply, she stomped threateningly towards the wild young man, chest rising and falling in frantic rhythm.

'It's Jake,' said Rebecca who'd turned her pale frightened face to look at him. Her smile seemed quizzical, as though she believed he were an apparition. But she slowly adjusted her skirt to cover her naked pelvis.

'You coming with me?' He dodged the harridan and came right up to the table to take Rebecca's hand and gaze down into her huge brown eyes.

She nodded and closed her eyelids against tears slipping from beneath them.

'You ain't getting yer money back,' said the woman, clattering together her unused instruments.

Jake scooped Rebecca off the table and carried her outside then down the stairs with her mother rushing after them.

'Rebecca,' Molly shrieked. 'What do you think you're bloody well doing?'

'I'm going with him, Mum. I want to. You can't stop me.'

'But who is he? Don't you even tell me who he is?'

Rebecca gazed at Jake's profile. 'She wants to know who you are. So do I.'

'I'm Jake Harding ... your fiancé.'

'Is that true?' she asked, resting her head on his shoulder as they emerged into the street through a gaggle of women snooping on proceedings.

'It is if you say you'll marry me.' He looked at her through a blur of tears. 'Will you? I've got you a ring. It's emeralds and diamonds and belonged to Peg. She was like my mum and so I'd like you to have it.'

'I will marry you and I'd love to have Peg's ring ... thank you.'

The woman Jake had nearly knocked flying started to clap, setting the rest off. Although they hadn't all heard what was said, they guessed it was good news being as the girl who'd gone into the abortionists had come out looking happy rather than white-faced and blubbing.

At the end of the street, Jake stood Rebecca on her feet and kissed her softly on the lips. 'I love you.'

'I love you,' she said and gave him a fierce hug. 'Where are we going now?'

'Well, I've got some work to do to pay for a wedding.' He brought her against his side, moulding their bodies together as they walked on. 'As for you ... reckon you'd better speak to your mother.' He jerked a backwards nod at Molly; they could hear her footsteps pattering close behind.

'I will. Will you wait?'

''Course.' Jake got out his cigarettes and contemplated the horizon while he smoked. He told himself he was acting daft. His emotions were getting the better of him. He was just a silly, sentimental fool.

Rebecca came back and said, 'Mum's going back to Aunt Queenie's to see if me dad's been there yet. He's disappeared, you see, and she's worried something's happened to him. I told her I don't care if it has 'cos he's a rotten bully. I said I'm going with you and we're engaged. You do want me to come with you, don't you, Jake?'

''Course I do.' He put his arm around her shoulders. 'What d'you think's happened to him?'

'Don't know. After I left the brooch with you that night, he chased us into the underground station. We managed to escape but he'd already hit Mum and she said he'd threatened to hit me too.'

'Well, he won't. I promise you that,' said Jake. He kissed her brow, and to cheer her up, said, 'Any good with a saw, Rebecca?'

'What?' she giggled.

'Johnny Cooper's off on his honeymoon and I'm short-staffed.' He dropped the half-smoked cigarette and trod on it as they strolled to the corner.

'No, I can't use a saw.' She punched his arm for teasing her.

'Have to start you off on a paintbrush then,' he said, swinging her up in his arms again. He walked on with his head tilted back.

'What can you see up there in the sky?'

She let her head fall back against his arm and contemplated the grey heavens. To her they looked as glorious as those on a summer's day. 'Clouds. And lots of them.'

'Can you see a motorcycle and sidecar?' He slipped a hand free of her, almost dropping her while pointing to a cliff of stormy crags soaring up from the horizon.

'Don't think so.' She squealed, hanging onto his neck.

'I can,' he said and started to laugh.

Epilogue

January 1935

The room was crowded with people; they weren't all strangers, he'd met most of them before but some he didn't know well. Which made it all the more peculiar that they were looking at him intensely, but with barely-there smiles and expressions that were hard to read.

The atmosphere was equally odd; thick and throbbing with anticipation, it had warmly cloaked him as he entered the house where Johnny had had his wedding reception. Jake had no idea why he'd been invited here this afternoon. Johnny had given nothing away when dashing in and out of Rook Lane. He had seemed to want to avoid being questioned.

'Have I done something wrong?' Jake asked, rubbing the bridge of his nose as a half a dozen pairs of eyes continued to watch him.

'No ... you certainly haven't ... '

He'd expected Johnny and Dora to lead the welcome as they were good friends; instead, Johnny's sister had spoken.

Clover's soft-as-velvet voice echoed in his mind as she pulled him towards a chair.

'Thank you for coming, Jake. Won't you sit down? Where's Rebecca?'

'She's gone to Lambeth to help her mum with the funeral arrangements.' He perched on the settee, wishing Rebecca was with him for support on this odd occasion.

A collective sound of sympathy rolled around the room at the mention of the deceased. Everybody knew about George Payne's accident at Whitechapel underground station. Only Jake knew that he'd fallen down those stairs during an angry pursuit of his wife and daughter.

A visit by Molly Deane to Leman Street police station had revealed that a man matching her common-law husband's description had been involved in a tragic incident. The body had been identified and if the widow didn't appear as upset as might have been expected, nothing was said. George Payne's reputation as an Elephant Boy had travelled into the East End, and the yellowing bruise on the woman's cheek told its own story.

'Is Rebecca keeping well?' asked Clover.

'She is, thanks,' said Jake. 'A bit queasy in the mornings though.'

'Ah ...' said Clover with a private smile. She'd also felt a bit queasy that morning, but that wasn't solely due to her growing baby. Her whole body had been alive with excitement and trepidation from the moment she'd left the convent a week ago. She had told Neil what had gone on. But nobody else. She had wanted Johnny to return from his honeymoon – extended by a few days – before she broke the momentous news about their half-brother. As for her friend Nettie, she had been content to hear that her son was settled with a good family but she wanted things to stay as they were. Archie wouldn't understand why she'd lied to him she'd said. Clover had agreed to never speak of it again. She had returned her thoughts to her predicament. She had weighed up whether to speak to Jake alone first, but Johnny knew him better than she did. They were real friends and Annie shouldn't be left out of the first celebrations either. Neither should the woman who had nurtured him at the beginning when his fragility seemed insurmountable. Sister Louise – as she would always think of her – was seated in an armchair.

Jake glanced at the nun with a shy smile. She also had a secret in her shining eyes, and a look of pride.

'This is the Reverend Mother from the Sisters of Mercy Convent.' Clover was aching to put him at his ease. She wanted to get to the part where she could hug him, pour out the love that had been imprisoned inside her. She skimmed a look over the assembly, reading her nervousness mirrored in every face. Even Sister Louise looked ready to burst. Johnny and Dora, Annie, Neil – her family were all here. Bar one. Their father was missing ... but unmissed. Johnny had discovered that Sidney Cooper had returned to France. Not one of them was sad about that, in fact it were as though their mother had had a hand in clearing the path for her lost child to return unhindered to those who loved and wanted him.

'The Reverend Mother has something to tell you about your early life ... and so have I,' said Clover, struggling to keep her tears from mangling her words.

'My early life?' Jake repeated eagerly. His agile brain leaped ahead. 'Is this something to do with my adoption?' Rebecca had encouraged him to find out more about his roots if he could. She wanted their baby – and he was theirs – Jake had told her, to them and to everybody else – to grow up with extended family if at all possible. 'Was I born at the Sisters of Mercy convent?'

'Not quite, my dear, but you spent some months with me and those were months I shall always cherish.' Sister Louise looked to Clover to take up the story. It was hers to tell. The blond boy with the green eyes wouldn't be here now but for his sister's bravery.

'You were born here, Jake,' said Clover to the sound of Annie and Dora's quiet snuffling. 'In this house.' She extended her hand to him and without hesitation he took it and allowed her to lead him from the room.

'In here, on this bed, our mum gave birth to you. I'm your half-sister and so is Annie, and Johnny is your brother.'

Jake licked his lips and shook his head. 'No . . . is it true?' he pleaded, grasping his skull in his hands.

'Yes . . . it certainly is. We're your family. Are you pleased?' she asked, her green eyes roving over features that she might have seen reflected back at her from a mirror. She'd known from the first moment she'd met him, smelled his skin.

'You're my real family?'

She watched the joy in his face and her tension flowed out with her laugh. 'We are, Jake. Welcome home.'

Author Note

Elephant and Castle gang

The Elephant and Castle gang, or 'Elephant Boys' as they were known, operated from early Victorian times into the first half of the twentieth century. Its members were violent criminals who would rob, and run illicit gambling rackets, or any other lucrative scheme they hit upon. Their female counterparts were known as the 'Forty Thieves' or 'Forty Elephants'. Based around Lambeth in south-east London, the women were equally rough and ruthless, and would shoplift prolifically from top stores. They also ventured further afield to smaller towns when their faces became too well known in the West End. They wore especially designed coats with huge inner pockets and voluminous bloomers to hide their 'shopping'. The stolen merchandise would be passed quickly through a network of 'fences' (crooks who receive and sell stolen goods) to outwit any police hot on the thieves' trail.

The gang was in operation during the inter-war years but its influence began to wane as London slums were cleared and prosperity improved. Store security was better too, increasing the risk of being caught. By the 1950s, the notorious 'Forty Elephants' shoplifting gang had closed up shop.

Exclusive Sneak Peek

Keep reading for an exclusive early peek from the next book in the series ...

Chapter One

June 1 1940, Northern France

Given a choice he would rather have died in England. But he'd left it too late to pick a side.

Had they set off for Calais yesterday they might have stood a chance at making it. But his children wouldn't leave. They had thought he was overreacting. Nothing like that was about to happen. The Allies were strong and would protect them. Victory was imminent. It would all be over soon, Papa, they'd reassured him.

The problem with the young was they'd not been there the first time round. He had, and had heard it all before: enlist and it'll all be over by Christmas, they'd been told. Crafty buggers never said which Christmas.

Luc and Elise were no longer small enough to be carted off whether they liked it or not. They were young adults and knew their own minds. Sidney Cooper had never hesitated in saving his own skin in the past. For the first time in his life, he'd behaved as a good father would and stayed by them, for whatever use he proved to be.

At almost sixty years old, he was paying for four decades

of debauchery, and was tired and weak in body and mind. But he had a gun and if necessary he'd use it. And that was that.

He could hear them getting closer and his guts leapt and dived and gurgled in protest. Twenty-five-year-old memories flocked in his head: carrion shadows ... shrill whistles ... dawn sprints towards an enemy trench, never knowing if a second of life remained to him.

The inside of his mouth had dried out and he took a swig of beer. He'd immersed himself in the French custom of wine-drinking but had already been a drunk before settling in France. His wives had tried to tame him for his own good: his first had been fifteen when they met in London's East End. Nine months and a shotgun wedding later they'd been parents. When Iris passed away during those war years, he'd been serving on the Western Front. Newly widowed, he'd abandoned London and his children and moved in with his French mistress. They'd never married but had lived together as though they were husband and wife. Sophie Bouchard had been buried in the village churchyard seven years ago, dead of pneumonia. He'd made an attempt at rearing their two children but found the business too trying. His son and daughter had been despatched to their maternal grandmother and he'd bolted back over the Channel. Being so much older, the English kids were less of a bother.

He'd come back to suit himself rather than his French family, but since being reunited with Luc and Elise a sense of duty, and his mortality, had been making itself known. Too many women and too much alcohol had pulled apart his health and he had no time left to put things right. He'd been a bad father to all six of his children, but his regrets were with the youngest two.

He drained the glass of beer, wiped his mouth on the back of an unsteady hand, and listened.

The noise was the same: boots beating time, heavy equipment creaking. A tank division, possibly. No horses this time. The stamp and snort accompanying the rattle of the gun carriages and mess wagons had been everywhere in 1914. Snatches of soldiers' chanting drifted to him – bawdy songs no doubt, but he didn't understand much German. French was a different matter. He was fluent, having lived here on and off for more than a quarter of a century. His daughter would giggle at his accent mangling the words. They spoke mainly in English though, and it made him smile to hear his French girl twanging like a Cockney sparrer. His beautiful little Elise, the image of her mother: hair almost black and eyes as grey as the slate on the roof above. He'd wasted precious time they could have spent together.

As though his thoughts had conjured her up, she hurtled in through the back door, startling him out of his brooding and almost giving him a heart attack to finish him off. He would have happily gone that way.

'Papa, you were right. Tanks are coming. The Nazis are everywhere in the village and Luc is still in the fields ...' she panted out and rushed against his side to cling to him.

'Hush now, and listen to me.' He stroked curls with the gloss of a raven's wing off her flushed cheeks. 'They might pass us by. But if somebody has told them an Englishman lives here they will stop. You must be prepared if I'm arrested.'

'No ...' she interrupted, swinging her head wildly away from his comfort.

'Hush,' he said, cupping her face to still her agitated movements. He gazed intently at her. 'They might not take me, but if they do you must go and find your brother. You must both stay with your grandmother and never come back here until I do.'

'Nobody will betray you. They wouldn't be so mean. The Nazis will think you're French, Papa. You are French now,' she said and stamped in a rage of fear.

'Yes, they might think that,' he soothed her. To comfort himself he touched the weight of the pistol hanging inside his trousers. A cord tied around his waist held it suspended between his thighs. The Luger was loaded with two bullets and had been relieved from the corpse of a dead German officer. A souvenir from the Great War. A poor description if ever there was one.

Elise ground her forehead against the rough cloth of her father's shirt. 'I'm sorry, Papa, you were right. We should have left for the coast earlier in the week.' A spark of hope and determination lit her eyes. 'There is still time. We could go out the back way and hide in the fields. Then pick up Luc on the way. Grandma too if she will come. There are lots of refugees already on the road.' She started pulling her father towards the door that gave access into the poppy-headed meadows.

For a second, Sidney was tempted, fired by her youthful optimism that everything could come right. But it was too late to outrun misfortune as he had in the past. 'No, love, it would be worse to be caught fleeing. Don't fret. I was wrong, it wouldn't have been wise to leave last night. The roads are dangerous, crowded with the retreating troops and their tanks. It is safer for you here.' His seventeen-year-old daughter's beauty would attract the attention of soldiers of any flag. Her brother would try to protect her and put himself in jeopardy. At nineteen, tall and well built, Luc would be a target. He'd be rounded up as forced labour or sent to an internment camp. At least these flint walls provided some protection.

'If they stop and come in, we'll play it by ear. Let me do the talking ... they might not have much French, these Boches.' He led her to a chair hoping she couldn't feel his hands quivering. 'Sit down and do your knitting. Act naturally.'

Her upturned gaze was pitilessly direct and glistening with unshed tears. Acting naturally was impossible.

'If they take you away, will you come back here after you've answered their questions or stay with us at Grandma's?' She gnawed on her thumbnail while they waited in an agony of tension. The atmosphere rocked with the sound of marching and Elise's jaw ached from clenching her teeth. 'They will see you aren't a threat and let you go, won't they?' Her whispers became quieter as the noise grew deafening.

'I'll return here ...'

'Why mustn't we come back here then, Papa?' She began to rise, but he guided her back into her seat with an untouching hand.

'Just don't,' Sidney said softly. 'When I'm sure it's over I'll fetch you from your grandmother's.'

He couldn't tell her that she mustn't be alone ... that she might end up like her mother. Sophie hadn't wanted to catch a German officer's eye in 1915 or be passed around his friends until she ended up diseased. Her distraught parents hadn't intervened when their only child started working in a brothel. It had been too late to undo a scandal and inviting attention from the men involved wouldn't have been wise for Resistance fighters.

When Sidney met her at the brothel, she had said she was clean again, so he needn't worry. She'd said he was a gentleman in comparison to some of the other men she'd dealt with. It was the first time Sidney Cooper had received such praise. Women might tell him he was handsome but quite soon after followed it up by complaining he was a selfish pig. He couldn't deny treating most of them badly. Sophie had rarely nagged him and it had made her special. She'd told him her parents had been shunned by neighbours who believed Sophie Bouchard was a collaborator, as well as a whore.

The invaders were back, jogging memories, and it terrified and enraged Sidney in equal part that his children might become the victims of decades' old grudges. Women were always at risk during war and soon he wouldn't be able to protect his daughter from a similar fate.

'I should go and get Luc. He'll look after us.' Elise couldn't sit still. She jumped up and went to the open back doorway to search the horizon for her brother. Luc worked on a neighbouring farm. By now he would know about the enemy's advance driving back the Allies. Everybody would know. Surely Luc would come home.

'Sit down, Elise. Say nothing about your brother to them. They might search for him and take him too.' Sidney's voice could hardly be heard over the din outside. Their eyes clashed as several sets of footsteps became distinct from the rest.

'Will Luc know to hide?' Elise hoped her brother would stay away now rather than rush home to them.

'He's no fool.' Sidney's hissed reassurance was drowned out by a hammering on the cottage door.

It was burst open before Sidney could reach it. A German

officer strode in and behind him came two armed soldiers. His arrogant blue gaze flashed from the man with greying hair to the girl with defiance shining in her eyes.

A quiet ensued and Sidney noticed his daughter was drawing the most attention. 'What do you want, monsieur? We have little food or anything else to give you ...'

'Are you the English man?'

Sidney felt as tense as a coiled spring. He'd not fooled the bastard. He'd spoken in French but the German had answered in English. Sidney sent his daughter a warning look. Elise reacted by barging in front of him.

'Of course he isn't English.' She gestured away the absurdity. 'My father's as French as I am.' She spoke her own language but again the young officer smiled and answered in English.

'You understand English Mam'selle.' He looked her up and down in a way that made her stomach squirm. 'Who taught you?'

'A schoolteacher. Who taught you?'

'My schoolteacher.' He removed his cap revealing a neat head of blonde hair. 'So ... as we are such good students, we will talk in English so everybody understands. My apologies, I should introduce myself. Hauptmann Konrad Stein at your service.' He extended a hand to her. She ignored it. With apparent reluctance he turned his attention to Sidney. 'Come with us please, Mr Cooper.'

'No!' Elise launched herself forward as though to push Stein away.

Sidney yanked her back before she could touch him. 'You remember what I told you?' he murmured hoarsely.

She nodded but refused to let go of his hands.

Sidney raised her hands to his lips, rubbed his cheek

341

against their soft backs. 'Don't worry, I'll see you again soon, dear. And I love you, Elise.' He took his coat from the peg and shrugged into it.

She tried to follow but the soldiers blocked her way as her father went out with the officer. She watched from the open doorway, and listened to the officer shouting at his men in German.

Her father didn't look back. Stein looked at her over the car roof before getting in the vehicle. Elise stared at him through a blur of tears that magnified the furious loathing in her eyes.

'Papa! She cried as the car drove off. The brigade marched by watching her, not singing anymore. She withdrew inside and leaned back against the door, sobbing.

She knew now why her father had told her to go from here. Some of them might come back looking for her next time.

The Hauptman didn't make much conversation as the vehicle bumped over the rutted road. They'd make him talk though, Sidney knew that, and they wouldn't accept he didn't know anything even though he really didn't.

'You are English?' Stein sounded bored and surveyed the blooming hedgerows close enough in places to skim the car windows as they passed.

'Yes, from London.'

'Your daughter is also from London?'

'No, she's French. Her mother was French.'

'Your wife is dead?'

'She died years ago.'

'Your daughter is all alone . . . ' He smiled to himself. 'You will want to help us quickly then to return home to her. Pretty girls shouldn't be left alone.'

'I've nothing to tell you.'

'We will see. You were here the last time. I think you were a Tommy who fell for a Mam'selle.'

'I was. Now I'm too old for all of that.' He chuckled. 'I'm so old I need to pee all the time. I need to go now.' No lies so far.

'What?' The younger man swung him a glance of distaste.

'Got a bit of a problem with the old waterworks.' He rolled his eyes at his groin. 'If you don't stop the car, I'll wee on the seat and your nice uniform will suffer.' He gazed at the grey thigh close to him and a highly polished boot. He'd enjoy pissing on that.

Stein gestured his disbelief but shot forward to clap the driver on the shoulder. He scrambled out before the vehicle had come to a complete stop fearing he might be a laughing stock and soon stink of piss. He strode around to open the door and let his prisoner out, his teeth grinding on an easily identifiable German oath.

'Don't need no toilet paper, thanks,' said Sidney and suffered a cuff for his insolence and having his coat pockets searched. He hopped from foot to foot to show it was an emergency. The Hauptman gave him a shove, sending him away. With a smirk Sidney walked to the shrubbery at the side of the road. He stepped modestly in amongst the trees, fiddling with his trouser buttons.

Half an hour had passed, he judged, time for Elise to be a fair distance away from the cottage. There was nothing else he could do to help his children than this. But he wished there was another way ... turn back the clock and do things differently, be a better person ... a better father. He had killed before and not just during the war. Death didn't bother him, it was the dying ...

343

He wasn't a spy; he was a coward. They would assume he was an English spy though and he'd suffer for it. He slid his hand inside his trousers and pulled out the gun and his cock. Two bullets. It would be a shame to waste one of them. He began wetting the undergrowth in front of him as a drift of tobacco smoke reached him. He would have liked a final cigarette himself. He took a proper grip on the gun and let his leg get wet as he turned.

The first bullet hit Stein and spun him around. Sidney felt a burst of elation that he could still do it. The second entered his mouth before the driver had got his door fully open.

Chapter Two

'Your father's gone?' Mathilde Bouchard swung a horrified look between her grandchildren. Her son-in-law had abandoned these two in the past when things got difficult, but this time a more sinister reason than his selfishness was to blame for his absence.

'They took Papa away. He said we must come here and stay with you until they let him go.'

'He was right to do so,' said Mathilde and hastily ushered them inside, closing the door against prying eyes.

When Elise reached the farm, Luc had been stowing the tractor in the barn having heard the noise of the approaching army. He'd jumped down the moment he saw her and listened in dismay to her report of their father's arrest. His boss had been herding his poultry into the barns to keep it out of sight of scavenging soldiers. Luc had told him he'd no time to help with the chickens and they'd set off immediately for their grandmother's village north of Lille. The settlement comprised a cluster of whitewashed cottages on a narrow lane. At its eastern end it widened into a square around which sat a church, a forge and a bakery.

To avoid the troops they'd used shortcuts over the fields

and along narrow paths denied to the hordes. Scouting parties would soon be infiltrating the countryside though and they'd be stopped and interrogated.

'Why didn't you come and get me sooner, Elise?' Luc continued pacing to and fro, squinting at his sister. After the heat and glare of the June sun, the atmosphere inside seemed cool and shady.

'Papa forbade me and there was no time anyway. What shall we do?'

'I'm doing what I should've done before. I'm joining the Army,' declared Luc. 'At least, what's left of it.'

'If they've taken your father, you should both keep your heads down here for a few days and see what happens,' their grandmother cautioned. 'Be quiet and stay inside until he comes for you. Did anybody see you arrive?'

'The lane was quiet, nobody was about,' said Luc.

'Good, they're all still at the market, I suspect.' A weekly market in the neighbouring village drew most of the house-wives away for the mornings. They'd be hurrying back now though to batten down the hatches at home. 'Nobody must know you're here with me,' said Mathilde. 'Why did you not heed your father and go to England?'

'It's my fault ... I didn't believe Papa when he said it would be bad for us.' Elise covered her guilty face with her hands.

'I wanted to stay put as well.' Luc embraced his dis-traught sister. 'Why has this happened to France, anyway? This isn't our fight. So much for Maginot and his line,' he spat in disgust. 'It's all mad ... '

'War is mad. It always starts with some man's insanity.' Mathilde whirled an angry finger by her temple. 'Here, drink this.' She poured hot coffee from a metal pot and handed them a cup each. Before they'd tasted it, a sound of strident conversation outside prompted Mathilde to shoo her grandchildren into the bedroom. She put a finger to her lips just as the door received a bang and a neighbour called to Mathilde to open up.

From their place behind the half closed door, they sipped coffee and listened intently to their grandmother being told about a calamity. The market had been alive with talk of a German officer having been shot by a local man. The advancing troops had halted not far away to deal with the incident. It was rumoured the assailant was English and had also been shot. Was it Mathilde's son-in-law? Where was Sidney Cooper? The woman demanded to know. And what about reprisals?

Luc stifled his sister's gasp of anguish with his hand. Quickly, he put an arm around her to comfort her and to prevent her bursting into the parlour. He'd learnt from his grandmother's behaviour that not even longstanding acquaintances could be trusted.

Mathilde denied knowing anything and got rid of the elderly widow, before spying on her through the narrow casement as she rejoined the others outside. At intervals the little group turned around to stare at the cottage.

'Is she talking about Papa?' Elise whispered, coming out of the bedroom.

'I think so,' Mathilde answered with a sigh. 'Do you know if your father had a gun?'

Elise shook her head in despair as Luc said, 'When I was a kid, he showed me a German revolver from the Great War but I didn't think he still had it. I've not seen it in ages.' He gave his sister a little shake to liven her up. 'Could he have taken something like that with him, Elise?'

347

'I don't know, maybe it was in his pocket. He took his coat from the peg.'

'If your father is responsible, you two aren't safe,' Mathilde interrupted. 'You mustn't go back to work, Elise. You will be easily found there.' Hastily, she got from the larder half a loaf and a wedge of cheese, wrapping it in a cloth. 'The town will be crawling with Boches.'

'Madam Laurent closed the shop as soon as the first soldiers arrived. She locked up and pulled down the shutters.' The couturier where Elise worked sold gowns of fine silk and lace. Madam Laurent had told her that during the last occupation some soldiers – both Allies and enemy – had acted like swine when drunk. They stole her lovely clothes to give to their women back home. 'Somebody betrayed Papa. The Hauptman knew his name was Cooper. Who could have told him that?'

'When people are frightened they think only of themselves. It was the same last time.' Mathilde pointed to the window through which the neighbours' rapid voices penetrated. 'She was widowed during the Great War. Your grandfather survived the fighting but never recovered from what went on. He knew he wouldn't make old bones. And so did I. Some people contain their bitterness, others spread it around.' She approached her grandchildren and raised her hands to cup their faces. 'You two must think only of yourselves and travel to England somehow. You must shelter with your father's family in London. We cannot be sure of his fate. But I know if he is able to, he will somehow find his way there to be with you.' She went to a drawer and found a tin, pulling out some folded banknotes. She halved the amount, holding out cash in both hands. 'Here ... you will need this until you find work.'

She pressed the notes into their hands when they seemed reluctant to take her savings. 'If it's too risky to travel to Calais, go south and hide amongst the refugees heading away from the fighting. Speak only French and keep to yourselves. Trust nobody.'

The voices outside became louder and Luc strode to peep through the window. Helmeted heads and grey torsos were all that was visible of the infantry approaching through the long meadow grass. The neighbours had spotted them and were dispersing indoors in a panic.

'A patrol's coming this way.' Luc swung back. 'It might be a coincidence.'

'It might,' said Mathilde. 'They scavenge for milk, bread, anything they can lay their hands on.' She glanced at her white-faced grandchildren. 'You two must go quickly. They won't bother with an old woman. I'll find them some beer and send them on their way.' She gazed at her strapping grandson; they would find work for him. And Elise, too, would draw their interest. Mathilde pulled open the drawer again and withdrew a notebook. She tore out a page. 'Your father gave me this address after your mother passed away, so I could let his English family know if he was about to meet his maker. Even back then I think he knew he'd get there before I did.' She thrust the paper at Elise. 'Guard it. Sidney told me these Coopers are good people.' Her son-in-law had been a liar as well as all the rest. She'd believed him on that though. His other children had never visited him and Mathilde found that quite understandable. 'Good luck. God bless and keep you safe.' She gave Luc the wrapped food to put in his pocket.

'Come, hurry ... ' Luc caught his sister's arm before briefly letting go to hug his grandmother in farewell. Elise also embraced Mathilde and kissed her wrinkled forehead. She was returned a swift kiss then pushed away.

'Be brave, both of you.' Mathilde warded off her granddaughter's grasping hands. 'Go! There's no time to waste. I love you both. We'll see each other soon. God speed my dears.' The last was addressed to the door swaying on its hinges. She swiftly closed it without giving in to her yearning for a last look at them. She sank into a chair and put a thin hand to her forehead where her granddaughter's warm kiss lingered. She had calmed herself by the time she heard them in the lane. She got up and peeked out of the window at a trio of soldiers working the water pump. They were jovially filling their bottles and their tin helmets then pouring water over their sweaty faces. Mathilde turned away and shook a fist at the ceiling. 'Why?' She cried in despair. 'Only twenty years . . .why this again already?'

No guttural voices had demanded they halt as they raced along the banks of the stream. It was the shortest route to the woodland that would give them protection on their journey north. Finally they reached the oaks and plunged thankfully beneath a cool green canopy of leaves, hurdling undergrowth and zigzagging between trees. Luc led the way and at intervals stopped to encourage his sister as brambles tore at her legs and arms and her harsh breathing penetrated his own gasps.

Working on the farm had built his strength but Elise was slender and shop work hadn't prepared her for this. He slowed down the second he glimpsed the road up ahead and within a minute Elise had caught him up. Luc turned and put his finger to his lips. Between pants she nodded in understanding. Close by everything seemed still and quiet;

in the distance though was the rumble of the German army and the intermittent crack of rifle fire as Allied troops skirmished with their pursuers.

They picked their way onwards until a few ancient trunks were all that lay between them and open space.

Luc grasped her arm and turned to look at her. 'We're still in front of them but need to keep going.'

'Will you come to England with me?' Elise read her answer in his solemn gaze. Her black hair was wild about her shoulders and she gathered up a thick hank and wound the ribbon more securely around it. Her eyes darted here and there as the gunfire got louder and startled crows from the trees to flap and caw overhead.

'I'm staying to fight, Elise. We must all fight or we'll never get rid of the bastards.' He touched her face, pink from exertion and scratched from a thorn. 'I'll stay with you until we reach the coast. Don't be frightened, I'll look after you.' He crept forward to the road, signalling for her to stay put. Having looked around to get his bearings, he darted back.

'We're about five kilometres from Lille.'

Although they'd travelled a good distance north from their grandmother's house, they were still far from the sea; there'd be no scent of brine to hearten them until late tomorrow.

A twig cracked somewhere close by. They ducked down in unison and strained to listen for another sound. There was nothing but the rustle of small creatures and the creak of timber.

Heavy running footsteps made them quickly conceal themselves behind a tree. Elise sent her brother an optimistic look. Luc had also heard somebody declaring himself 'bleeding knackered' in a London accent similar to their father's. He prevented his sister breaking cover nevertheless.

'English!' insisted Elise. She was keen to speak to the soldiers and find out everything they could about what was happening.

'Careful, it could be a trap!' Luc refused to let go of her arm.

'Good advice . . . ' drawled a voice from behind. 'So who are you two?'

Luc jerked around and immediately put up his hands on seeing a man in khaki battledress pointing a rifle at him.

'Who are you?' Elise boldly took a step towards him.

'I asked first.' He gave her a half-smile.

'Luc and Elise Bouchard,' Luc hastily said, sending his sister a warning glance to mind her tongue. This Tommy with two stripes on his uniform sleeve could be a god-send . . . or a danger.

'Who are *you*?' Elise insisted. 'Are there more of you?'

'Three of us; Middlesex Infantry.'

'Is that it?' she sounded disappointed.

'The others might be about somewhere. With Jerry too close for comfort and taking pot shots, we got separated.' He studied them. They looked French with their dark hair and continental complexions. But that didn't make them friends yet. 'You speak good English.'

'Our father's English,' said Elise. 'He was taken by the Germans only a few hours ago.'

Luc frowned a warning at her not to say too much; he took up the conversation. 'We're not sure why they want him or what's happened to him. We've scarpered in case they come back looking for us.'

Elise was a daddy's girl but Luc saw his father for what he was: a parasite and a drunk. He'd hated him at times for disappearing then swanning back to pick up where he'd left

352

off as though it was his right to treat them as he did. If his father had found the gumption to shoot a German it would be out of character; a memory for his son to cherish.

'Your father's a British agent?' The Tommy lowered his rifle a fraction, looking dubious.

'No, of course not!' Elise butted in. 'He's a civilian. He's lived in France for years ... decades.'

The soldier's gun lowered further. In the last village they'd passed through, locals had been talking of a foreigner who'd shot a Nazi. They were raising a glass to the dead Englishman. 'Where are you heading then?' He didn't want to be the bringer of bad news especially as it might be the wrong man.

'To the coast for safe passage to England,' Elise said.

'Good luck with that.'

'What's that supposed to mean?' she asked sharply.

'There's a crowd in front of you wanting to get to England, miss. Most of them British army and they're royally ... browned off.' He remembered his manners at the last minute.

'I'll join your lot. I intend to stay in France and fight,' Luc declared.

'You'll be on your own then, mate. We're retreating to Dunkirk beach hoping to get picked up and ferried back. Trouble is Hitler ain't about to let us off the hook just like that.' He looked at Elise. 'If I was you, miss, I'd take your brother's route. Stay in France. Head the opposite way together or you'll end up right in the thick of it.' He paused. 'Maybe your father's safely home by now.'

'You're all giving up and going back to England?' Elise sounded disgusted.

'A lot of your French army's hoping to come along with us ...' A whistle from the road drew the soldier's eyes away from them. 'That's my lads. Best of luck then. Reckon we're all going to need it.' He gripped Luc's arm in farewell. 'Look after your sister.'

'She's in danger here.' Luc dashed in front of the corporal to halt him. 'Germans don't know me, but have seen Elise. Some can identify her. If our father has killed one of their officers ... ' He couldn't speak his worst fear about reprisals his family would suffer. 'Would you take her to Dunkirk ... get her on a boat?' Luc pulled his sister towards the Tommy. 'We've family in London, you see. She'll be fine over there.'

'You said you'd stay with me,' Elise cried. 'You're only going back to be with Yvonne.'

'I'm not,' he said but blushed at the mention of his boss's daughter. 'I have to stay and fight. There'll be Resistance groups somewhere if the army's finished.'

'I'll stay as well then,' said Elise. 'We'll chance it together. This soldier's right; Papa might have been released. The shooting might be nothing to do with him.'

'You've heard about that trouble then?'

Luc nodded and was eager for more details. 'What do you know about it?'

'A Hauptman got shot, the assassin got shot ... that's all, nothing more specific.'

Luc saw his sister wince and cover her mouth with a hand. He recalled she'd said a Hauptman had taken their father away. How much proof did they need? He knew this was bad but put an arm around her and encouraged, 'Nothing specific, see, Elise. The place is littered with Hauptmans and assassins now this has all blown up. I'm joining the Resistance and that's it.' He'd fight in his father's memory, to honour Sidney Cooper. 'Do you know any people?' he asked the soldier.

'Wouldn't tell you if I did. Don't know you.'

Elise dried her eyes with her knuckles, thinking the Tommy had said something very sensible.

'Woss goin' on, Corp? They're gonna be up our arses in a moment if we don't get going.' A short skinny private had loped into the trees, rifle leading the way. He gawped at the strangers, his eyes swivelling from the tall youth to admire the petite girl.

'French refugees, just asking questions. You 'n' Wilmot get going, and keep your eyes peeled, Evans. I'll catch you up in a sec.' He turned to Elise. 'I can't stop you tagging along if you want to. You'll be more of a target with British troops though and my advice would be to turn around. At Dunkirk you'll take your chance along with the rest of us.' He gazed at her, thinking she was far too young and pretty to be stuck with a crowd of angry and frustrated servicemen. Nobody wanted this humiliation: fleeing with their tails between their legs like whipped curs. 'If you say you're a nurse or something like that you might get put to the front of the queue.' He shrugged that he couldn't make any promises then started jogging after his comrade. 'Good luck,' he called back.

Luc hugged his sister then pushed her away. 'Go on. He seems an alright sort. It's your only chance of getting to England. You must take it.' He tilted up her chin so she'd see the urgency in his eyes. 'Once you get to the coast, you might find a French fishing boat; the skipper might take you over to Kent. Papa told us about the hop fields there, didn't he. He would go hop picking with his mum and dad when he was a little kid. Yalding, that was the place. I bet you'd like it there, love.'

Elise knew her brother was trying to buck her up to keep

her mind off the unfolding disaster. 'Come with me then Luc,' she pleaded.

The English soldier was many yards away and almost out of the trees when a whistling sound sent him hurtling back, yelling at them to get down. He flattened Elise beneath him on the scratchy ground. The exploding shell sliced the crown off a tree close to the road and it toppled sideways with a groan. He jumped up and pulled her with him into the clearing, shouting at Luc, 'Get into the open or you'll risk getting brained.'

Ears ringing and hearts hammering, Luc and Elise pelted for the fields and waded into the paltry camouflage of thigh-high barley that slowed them down. The soldier's comrades were now far in the distance.

After a few minutes of driving themselves deeper into the crop, Luc came to a stop and turned to his exhausted sister, straggling behind. 'I'll make a detour back to Lille, then on from there.' He embraced her, kissing her forehead. 'Keep safe. And remember what Grandma said, don't trust anybody.'

'What about him?' Elise jerked a nod at their guide several yards ahead.

'He's one of us; he's helped us so far. You have to trust him, Elise. Who else is there?' Luc backed away. 'Love you. Good luck.'

'Don't go ...' she pleaded.

Tears sprang to his eyes but he shook his head and continued to back away from her. The moment she came after him he turned and made a push towards a field of tall grass that would provide cover on his journey south, back towards Lille.

Elise stood and watched him with silent sobs heaving

her chest. He was a good distance away when a crack of rifle fire startled her into darting looks around. She whipped her head back to see her brother's dark figure had disappeared.

'You can't help him.' The corporal gripped her arm. He'd stopped and come back for her. 'We have to keep going.' He dragged her on, then when she fought him silently and savagely he pulled her down into the barley with him and gripped her face in his hand. 'You want to end up like your father and your brother, do you?'

'Luc might be alive. They both might be.' She tried to shove him off, weeping hysterically.

'He might. Or he might be dead. Or he might have taken a dive to protect himself. Your brother's no fool.'

'I'll go and see.' Elise pulled back and he unexpectedly let her go. She tumbled onto her posterior, her skirt rucked up about her thighs, but righted herself quickly and faced him on her hands and knees, looking ready to spring at him.

'If he's alright, he doesn't need you. If he's dead, he doesn't need you. If he's wounded, he'll be seen to. He's French, in civvies. This lot on our tail's got more to do than bother with civilians roaming the countryside.'

'They bothered with my father, didn't they?' she said fiercely.

'I know and I'm sorry.' He shook his head in defeat. 'Your brother hoped you'd get to England. It's up to you though. Come with me or go after him but I can't wait. I'm not carrying you either. You need to keep going or I'll leave you.'

'I don't need you to carry me.'

'Good.' His lips twitched at her spirited indignation. 'I don't know what's safest for you either way, miss. But if they recognise you as the Englishman's daughter, waiting for them to catch up with you ain't the wisest choice.' He rose to a half crouch and started off again.

Elise scrambled to her feet and gazed at the place where she'd last seen her brother. She said a prayer for him and for her father and as she followed the corporal, she said one for herself.

Acknowledgements

My thanks to the Piatkus Editorial team for their support and encouragement for my Women's War series of novels. And to Brian McDonald for his book: *Gangs of London*.